Perish

Murder in Wicker Park

a novel by

Tom Steele

LLUMINA ☆ STARS

This book is a work of fiction. Names, characters, locales, businesses, and institutions are either the product of the author's imagination or are used fictitiously. Any resemblance to actual persons, living or dead, is entirely coincidental.

ISBN: 978-1-93362-636-9

Printed in the United States of America by Llumina Stars

Library of Congress Control Number: 2008908050

For Linda

Introduction

With a population of 2,896,016, Chicago is the third largest city in the United States. It is a city composed of sixty-two distinct neighborhoods. Wicker Park is one of Chicago's neighborhoods, and is a part of the city's West Town community, an area populated by 87,000 people.

The region that makes up Wicker Park was incorporated into the City of Chicago in 1837. The neighborhood derives its name from a four-acre parcel of land that was donated to the city in 1870 by Charles Gustavus Wicker, a real estate developer who stipulated the donated land should be used as a public park.

Wicker Park became a fashionable upper class neighborhood in 1885 when wealthy families moved to the western edge of the city and constructed large stone mansions there. The huge Victorian homes still surround the park, and are monuments to the fear that possessed 19th century builders after thousands of wooden homes were devoured in the Great Chicago Fire of 1871.

In the summer of 2001, a larger-than-life size bronze statue of Charles Wicker was erected in the public park. Since then, there has been controversy over who should receive credit for the donated acres of land, but the imposing presence of the bronze statue gives popular credit to Charles.

Wicker Park has always been a draw for a mix of ethnic groups who add distinct flavor to its attractiveness. Throughout its history, the neighborhood has seen growth, decline, and revitalization; the most recent changes in the area brought rebirth, gentrification, cultural development, commercial growth, and a large number of young people.

North Damen Avenue, North Milwaukee Avenue, and West Division Street border the heart of Wicker Park. The neighborhood is filled with vitality that is the natural outcome of an area swarming with the movement of 7,387 people per square mile; every night, adventurous crowds of people intermingle in its restaurants, clubs, shopping centers, art galleries, and theaters.

Wicker Park is known for its unique eclectic nature; however, murder in Wicker Park is not distinguishable from any other neighborhood in the city. Instead, it is a reflection of Chicago metropolitan crime statistics. Each year, fourteen people are murdered in the Wicker Park/West Town community area, but only once has a person been murdered in front of the statue of Charles Wicker. This is the story of that murder.

Chapter One — Murder in the Park

A frenzy of 9-1-1 calls caused four Chicago police cars to descend upon the west side of Wicker Park, blocking traffic on Damen Avenue and sending vehicular traffic on a detour around the park via Wicker Park Avenue and Schiller Street. Two hundred curious gawkers formed a semicircle around the seven-foot tall bronze figure of Charles Wicker, each person maneuvering to get view of the bloody body that was lying at the foot of the statue. Flashing emergency lights swirled and bounced off the spectators' faces, as eight policemen began to tape off the crime scene, pushing the crowd further back into the park.

"Come on folks," a police officer barked out. "Give us some room here."

A screeching siren announced the arrival of another emergency car. The new vehicle was from the medical examiner's office. The car pulled over the curb and drove directly into the park, where two men got out and walked toward the body. It took very little time for them to assess the condition of the victim.

"He's gone," the senior medical officer said to one of the police officers. "Looks like a frontal shot to the chest with a small caliber weapon. We'll take him in, but there's no hurry."

"We've got a call into homicide and tech support," the police officer replied. "There should be a couple of detectives here shortly."

Moments later, two homicide detectives arrived and began examining the crime scene.

"There's no wallet, but we did find a driver's license and a credit card in the victim's right front pocket," Officer Ochoa said while handing the license to one of the detectives. "His name's Robert Bradford."

Ochoa turned his head and pointed southeast toward Schiller Street.

"He lives right over there in that house with the red doors."

"Okay," Detective Findley replied. "Ask around to see if anyone saw any of this."

"I've already asked some preliminary questions. So far, the only one who saw anything is old man Wicker," Ochoa said as he pointed toward the statue of Charles Wicker. "Most of this crowd was over at the basketball courts. There's a married couple here somewhere…Officer Pawlack's with them. They claim they saw something and shouted for help. Then this swarm of people came running. There must have been over forty 9-1-1 calls. Everybody and his brother have cell phones."

"Yeah," Findley agreed. "Everybody's talking, but no one sees anything or hears anything. Was there any money on the victim?"

"He had about one hundred bucks in cash on him. If robbery was the motive, the shooter got scared off before completing the job."

"Detective!" Officer Pawlack hollered. "Got something for you over here."

Detective Findley moved toward Police Officer Pawlack. Pawlack was standing in front of the yellow crime scene tape that had been stretched across a portion of the park to hold the crowd back.

"What've you got?" Findley asked.

"These are the people who came up on the victim first. They say they saw a man running away from the area right before they realized what was wrong."

"All right…let 'em through so I can talk to 'em," the detective responded.

A man and a woman, middle-aged and married, ducked under the yellow tape and made their way to Detective Findley. Findley sized the couple up as responsible citizens wanting to help the police make the world safe. He was right.

"Detective, my name's Bob Barrett."

Barrett reached out to shake Findley's hand and turned his head to stare in the direction of the murder victim. Confronted with the scene in front of him, Bob Barrett was forced to stop talking for a moment.

"I've never seen anything like this," he said, shaking his head in dismay.

Barrett purposefully turned away from the grisly view and focused his attention on the detective.

"This is my wife, Francis," he said. "We live on the other side of the park, over on Wicker Park Avenue."

Barrett slowly shook his head back and forth again.

"This is horrible…a thing like this happening in the middle of the park. It can get real rowdy over here, but this…"

Detective Findley took out a small notebook and began jotting information in it.

"What did you see, folks?" he asked.

"Well, first we heard a shot," Francis Barrett replied, "Or something that sounded like a shot. Then we saw a man running away from the statue area. I saw him first because I thought I'd heard someone yelling by the statue. I turned to look and saw this young man sprinting that way."

Francis Barrett lifted her right arm and pointed south toward the intersection of Damen and Schiller.

"He was sprinting," her husband said. "Running as fast as he possibly could. He ran into the intersection, crossed Damen, and ran west on Schiller. He was running like someone was running after him…that's when we walked over to the statue and found that man lying face down on the ground. We immediately called out for help."

The detective looked at Francis.

"Ma'am, you said you thought you heard someone yelling around the statue area. Did you hear what was being said?"

A puzzled look appeared on Mrs. Barrett's face. She wrinkled her brow while she pondered the question.

"I'm sorry detective," she said. "I'm really not sure what was being said. It could have been a person's name...Perry or Berry, or maybe a foreign sounding name...or two names. I'm really not sure."

"Was this before or after you heard the gunshot?"

"It was right before we heard the gunshot," Mrs. Barrett said.

"How about the man that was running away...did you get a good look at him?"

"He was tall," Bob said. "I think he was Hispanic."

"Where were you standing?" the detective asked.

"We were right over there...right by the edge of the pavilion. We always take a walk around the park late in the evening."

Detective Findley turned his head, looking back and forth between the pavilion and the statue, guessing at the distance between the murder victim and the building. He judged it to be approximately twenty yards.

"Think you could see well enough to determine his race?" he asked. "I mean...maybe during the day, but at night?"

"We think we've seen him here before," Francis answered. "During the day."

"You think the man you saw running is someone you know?"

"No, no." Francis replied. "We don't know the man. He just looked like a young man we've seen in the park before. That's why we think he's Hispanic."

"This man...the one you've seen in the park...what does he look like?"

"Detective, we're not sure the man running away is the same man we see here," Bob Barrett said.

"But it might be?" the detective said.

"We couldn't say that. There are a lot of young people in this park...and a lot of them are Hispanic. It wouldn't be fair to link the man we saw running away with someone else."

"Look folks, it would help if we could get an idea about what the man running away looked like...just a composite sketch. You don't have to identify the man running away with the guy you see in the park, but if we can get some kind of idea...well, that would help."

"Like we said," Bob began. "The man was Hispanic. He was tall with long, bushy black hair...and he was fast. I mean he even looked like a runner...real lean and long-legged...kind of wiry, too. You know...well built, but not bulging muscular."

"And the guy you see in the park…he looks like that?"

"Yes," Francis answered. "But, he's a nice young man. We see him over there on the other side of the park playing with a little boy on the swing sets. I'm sure it's not the same person."

"When do you see this young man?" the detective asked.

"Always around four o'clock," Francis answered. "Not everyday though, but always with the same little boy."

"Bradford's little boy," Bob Barrett chimed in.

"Robert Bradford?" the detective asked.

"Yes, Robert. Do you know him?"

"Are you friends of Robert Bradford?" Findley asked.

"Acquaintances," Bob replied. "Just casual acquaintances. The Bradford's live over there in the house with red doors. Mrs. Bradford runs a bookstore on North Damen and Division."

The detective looked toward the house with the red doors; he sighed, and then turned to face the Barrett's.

"I have bad news for you," he said. "The man who was killed is Robert Bradford."

Francis Barrett let out an audible gasp and then covered her mouth with her right hand.

"Oh dear," she mumbled.

Bob Barrett stared in disbelief toward the technical support officers who were hovering over Robert Bradford's body.

"We'll want to know more about the young man you've seen in the park," Detective Findley said.

Chapter Two — The Babysitter

While Mike Findley continued to ask questions of Bob and Francis Barrett, his partner, Detective Rice Battin, left the crime scene and walked to the Bradford residence. On the way there, Rice noted an array of information that could become important in the investigation of the Wicker Park homicide - distances, structures, parked automobiles, street lighting, fences, shrubbery, trees, picture windows, porches - all of these things could be valuable in solving the crime.

From the appearance of the Bradford home, Detective Battin concluded the family was well off. He was impressed with the neatness of the lawn, the careful attention that had been paid to the overall maintenance of the home, and the size of the house. He walked through a gate, up the steep front door steps, and rang an antique doorbell. A teenage girl partially opened the door and apprehensively peered out. A heavy chain lock was stretched tightly between the door and the metal door jam.

"Hello," the teenager said.

Detective Battin reached into his sport jacket, pulled out his wallet, and displayed his Chicago police badge.

"Good evening," he said. "My name's Detective Rice Battin."

The girl stared at the wallet, and then looked beyond the detective, her eyes intently focusing on the flashing police lights that danced and swirled on the west side of Wicker Park. To get a better view, she pushed her body up by standing on her toes.

"Is something wrong in the park?" she asked.

"I need to ask you some questions," Battin said. "May I come in?"

"I'm the babysitter," the girl said. "The Bradfords aren't home right now."

The detective held his wallet up higher, and moved it closer to the girl's face.

"May I come in?" he said again.

The door closed briefly, Battin could hear the sounds of the chain being unlatched, and then the door opened fully.

"Do you need a warrant or something?" the girl asked. "I don't want to get into any trouble with the Bradfords."

Battin smiled warmly, trying to allay the girl's fears.

"I just need to ask you a few questions. We can talk right here if you like."

"Okay. I really don't want to wake Robbie up. Robbie's the Bradford's little boy. He's asleep upstairs."

"I promise you I won't disturb him. Can you tell me your name please?"

"Paige," the girl answered.

"And may I know your last name?"

"Paige Bonner. I live over there on Wicker Park Avenue," the girl said pointing in the direction of a number of old Victorian style homes that lined the street east of the park.

"And where are the Bradfords this evening?"

"Mrs. Bradford is at her bookstore. I expect Mr. Bradford to be home any minute now. He's a professor at UC. He called me and said he was having car trouble, and that he would be late getting home. Mrs. Bradford didn't think she would get home until after ten. Are they all right?"

"We just need to talk to them. Can you stay here a little longer with their son?"

"Sure...if that's all right with the Bradfords," the babysitter replied. "Do you want me to call Mrs. Bradford? I have her store number."

"No. Give me the bookstore name and address. We'll go over there and talk with her."

"What about Mr. Bradford? What should I tell him when he gets here?"

"We'll take care of all of that for you," the detective answered. "I'm going to have a police officer come over here and watch the house until Mrs. Bradford comes home. We'll go over to the bookstore and bring her here in about an hour. Okay?"

"Sure," the babysitter replied as she looked apprehensively toward the park.

"Paige!" a voice suddenly called out from the sidewalk in front of the Bradford home.

Detective Battin turned to watch a man hurrying toward the Bradford's front porch.

"That's my dad," Paige said.

"Paige, what's going on here?" the man asked.

Battin held his wallet up and flashed his police badge.

"Mr. Bonner, I'm Police Detective Battin."

The man looked at the badge, and then glanced toward his daughter.

"Are you all right, Paige?" he asked.

"Yeah, Dad...the policeman just been asking me some questions."

"Is everything all right here?" the man asked Battin.

"There's been some trouble over in the park," Battin replied. "I've asked your daughter to stay here with the Bradford's son while we go and talk with Mrs. Bradford. It would be a good idea if you stayed, too."

Mr. Bonner made a half turn and looked toward the park.

"I saw all the lights," he said. "I came here to check on my daughter."

"I'm fine, Dad," Paige repeated.

Mr. Bonner turned back to face the detective.

"Are the Bradfords all right?" he asked.

"We just need to talk to Mrs. Bradford," Battin said. "I'm going to have a police officer come here until we can bring Mrs. Bradford home. If you'll stay with your daughter, that would be helpful."

Sadness appeared on Mr. Bonner's face. He turned again and looked toward the flashing police lights. His relationship with Diane Bradford was casual, but he felt a deep sorrow for her. He was certain Detective Battin would soon be telling her something no person wanted to hear.

"Sure, anything to help," he said.

Chapter Three — Diane Bradford

Detectives Findley and Battin left the park and arrived at Diane Bradford's bookstore at 9:30 p.m. The store had been closed for thirty minutes and, with the exception of Mrs. Bradford, all of the store workers had gone home. Diane was thumbing through a stack of papers when Detective Battin rapped three times on the store's large plate glass window with one hand while pressing his identification up against the glass with his other hand. Mrs. Bradford looked up and saw the police badge. She immediately dropped her papers on the customer service shelf and headed toward the front of the store. The detectives watched her pull a key chain out of her pocket, twist open the lock with a key, and open the door for them.

"How can I help you gentlemen?" she asked, as the two men entered her establishment.

"Are you Diane Bradford," Findley asked.

A worried look appeared on Diane's face. Her eyes darted back and forth from one detective's face to the other.

"Yes, I am," she said.

Findley's eyes roamed around the bookstore in search of a proper place to talk.

"Mrs. Bradford," he said. "It might be better if we all sat down."

He pointed to a small table that had four chairs surrounding it.

"Is it all right if we sit there?"

"Yes. Please gentlemen, come in and have a seat. Can I get you anything?" Diane asked.

"No thank you. We just need to talk with you," Detective Findley said.

Diane Bradford moved quickly toward the table, followed by the two detectives. An uncomfortable feeling churned in her stomach. She sat down and felt a clammy sensation washing over her body, engulfing her in a cold dread.

"Is there something wrong?" she asked.

"Mrs. Bradford, we have bad news for you."

Diane Bradford wet her lips and folded her hands together on the table. She began to prepare herself for the pain she knew the detectives would be delivering into her life.

"We believe your husband is dead," Detective Findley said softly. "We're sorry."

Diane's face dropped. She wrung her hands together slowly, staring at them as she squeezed her fingers tightly together. Her body quivered, and then she looked up into detective Findley's face.

"What about Robbie?" she asked.

"Your son is fine. He's home with the babysitter," Detective Battin replied. "The babysitter's father is with her, and your son is asleep."

Detective Battin watched Diane squeeze her hands together again. Her fingers turned red and tears spilled down her cheeks.

"You said you believe Robert is dead. Can you be mistaken?"

Mike Findley reached into his sport jacket and pulled out a Polaroid photo that had been taken at the crime scene. He showed the photo to Diane Bradford.

"Is this your husband?" he asked.

Diane looked at the picture, closed her eyes, and turned her face away from the grisly image. Her body shuddered.

"How?" she said in a gasping tone.

"He was found in the park. He was shot," Findley answered.

"Robert? Robert shot? No. Who would do that?"

"We don't know," Battin said. "Do you have any idea?"

"No one would kill Robert," she answered. "People get robbed. Do you think someone tried to rob him?"

"We're not sure, Mrs. Bradford," Findley said. "Can you tell us if you have another babysitter for Robbie…besides the one who is with him now?"

"No…just Paige. You've talked with Paige, right?" Diane said in a panicky tone. "You said Paige is with Robbie. Isn't that true?"

"Yes," the detective answered. "But it's not Paige we're talking about. Do you have a male baby sitter…one who plays with Robbie in the park?"

"Javier! How do you know about Javier?" Diane asked.

"What is Javier's last name?" Battin interjected.

"Morales…Javier Morales. But why would you ask about Javier?"

"This may mean nothing," Findley said. "A man was seen running away from the area where your husband was shot. A witness told us that the man looked like Javier Morales."

Diane's body shook and she began to cry.

Detective Battin left the table, walked twenty feet away, and made a call on his cell phone.

"Find a residency for a Hispanic male by the name of Javier Morales and have a squad car pick him up for questioning in the murder of Robert Bradford," Battin said into his phone.

Detective Findley gently touched Diane's arm.

"Mrs. Bradford," he said. "You need to go home to your son. We have an escort for you."

Diane stood up slowly. At first she seemed stunned and disoriented, but she quickly regained her composure. She held her head up, wiped her face with her hand, and looked at the detectives.

"Javier Morales would never do such a thing," she said.

"I'm sure you're right," Findley replied. "This is just a lead we have, but we have to follow up on it. We will need to talk with you further after you have had some time. Again, we are sorry for your loss. Is there anything you need tonight?"

"No. You are right. I need to go home and be with Robbie. Does Paige know what has happened?"

"The officer who escorts you home will tell her," Battin replied. "You take care of your son. We will make sure Paige and her father get home all right. Is there anyone we can call for you right now?"

Diane looked down at the floor of the bookstore and thought of Elena Markova. She found it strange that the Russian woman from Vologda would be the first name to pop into her head at such a moment.

"No," she said.

Chapter Four — The Cook County Morgue

Mike Findley and Rice Battin left the police station in their unmarked squad car, heading south on Damen Avenue toward the Robert Stein Forensic Institute, more commonly known as the Cook County Morgue. It was 6 a.m. and they had an appointment to view the autopsy of Robert Bradford.

"This is your first visit to the morgue, right?" Findley said to Rice.

"Yeah," Rice replied. "I admit I'm a little squeamish. I've seen plenty of dead bodies, but this is different."

"You mean viewing the autopsy?"

"Yeah," Rice replied. "Aren't we leaving a little early? I thought the autopsy was scheduled for seven,"

"It is, but I want to give you a quick tour of the facilities. I think that will be helpful for you."

"How will that help?" Rice asked.

"It's a personal thing, but I think a cop has to adopt several philosophies when he becomes a homicide detective," Findley said. "The philosophies help you get through it all. I think they help us solve crimes."

"I don't get it. What do you mean?" Rice asked.

"I'll explain…but this is my own personal belief. You can use it or throw it out…doesn't matter to me."

"I'd like to hear it," Rice said. "You're highly respected in the department and everyone says you're a success. I'm lucky to be working with you…I know that."

"Okay then, here it goes. I think it's important to find out as much as we can about the victim…both before and after the homicide. I think it helps to understand death and the processes we all go through when we die, and I think it helps a homicide cop if has a holistic approach to death."

"What'd you mean by holistic approach to death?"

"I mean you need to look at others who have died and were admitted to the morgue along with Mr. Bradford. You need to look at the business of death. That's why I'm offering you the tour. Robert Bradford will be our focal point this morning, but I think it would be good if you see the journey he took through the morgue before we watch the autopsy. The morgue is a ghoulish place, but it is a sobering experience, too. And I think you need to meet some of the people who work there. It's a tough, tough job."

Rice turned onto West Harrison Street, drove one block west, and turned into the morgue parking lot. Although he was generally talkative, Detective Rice Battin became quiet as he contemplated what Findley had said.

The two detectives climbed out of their car and walked toward the building.

"Most people enter the morgue from the front doors on the west side of the building," Findley said. "I'm going to take you in through the entrance where the bodies are admitted."

Mike Findley made his way to a set of double sliding glass doors that had a security camera mounted above them. He rapped twice on the glass and waved at the camera. The doors slid open.

"Hey Kevin," Findley said as the two detectives entered the building.

"Hey Mike," a man in a green scrub uniform answered.

"Kevin, I want you to meet my new partner. This is Detective Rice Battin. Rice this is Kevin...he's going to give us the tour."

The two men shook hands and traded short pleasantries.

"So, you've never been here?" Kevin said to Rice.

"No, this is my first time."

"Then let's start with admittance," Kevin said pointing to a reception counter. "When we get a body, we register it here. If we have an ID, we note that. But whether we have an ID or not, we assign a registration number to the corpse and toe-tag the body."

Kevin moved to the counter, picked up a clipboard, and showed it to Rice.

"This is list of all of the bodies we've had come in since midnight. The guy you're interested in would be on an earlier sheet."

Rice looked at the clipboard and counted nine names on it. Eight of the names were male, seven of which were labeled John Doe.

"Lot of indigents," he said.

"Yeah, this is an indigent place," Kevin replied smiling. "But, if they do have IDs and personal effects, we bag them here and store their belongings in those lockers behind the desk."

Then Kevin turned and pointed toward a large single door that resembled the type of door one would see on a walk-in freezer.

"After the body's been registered, we wheel it into the cooler. I'll show you."

Kevin walked toward the door and opened it wide.

"Let's go," Findley said.

The three men walked into the cooler. Rice followed behind the other two. A blanket of cold air engulfed them, as they stepped inside the room. Rice took a breath to adjust to the cold. His nostrils filled with a pungent, sickening smell. It was not the smell of the death. It was the smell of death being stored. The smell overrode his other senses. He closed his eyes and tried to take shallow breaths. He cleared his throat, shook his head slightly, and then began to visually examine the cooler. It was a cavernous room filled with dead bodies, each neatly placed on long metal shelves. The shelves were stacked six high and rose up over fifteen feet from the floor. All of the bodies were laid out on their backs. Rice's eyes fixed on the face of a corpse that was closet to him. Although the dead man's face was gruesome, Rice found it difficult to turn his gaze away. The body was that of a small man. Rice quickly assessed the man's age to be in his early fifties. His body was frozen in time, and he was dressed in casual clothing. His face was mesmerizing. His skin color was grayish and his hair was long, blonde and unruly. His eyes were closed, but his mouth projected an eternal death smile, as if he were greeting the three men, welcoming them to the room that was filled with his dead companions.

Kevin walked deeper into the cooler, motioning for the two detectives to follow him and breaking the frightening grip the dead man's stare had on Detective Battin.

The three men strolled among the racks of dead bodies.

"How many bodies are in here?" Rice asked.

"I'd have to check the figure to be entirely accurate, but I know there's over seven hundred here today."

Everywhere Rice looked, he saw death sprawled out in macabre positions; body after body uniquely dressed in the last set of clothing they had donned on the day of their death.

Rice looked up high, and stared at a corpse on one of the top racks.

"Why is that guy dressed in a formal suit?" he asked.

"His relatives brought the suit by one day and told us a funeral director would be picking him up for burial. No one showed up, and we haven't heard from anyone since."

"Stood up," Mike Findley commented.

"Yeah, I guess you could say that," Kevin said with a smile. "If no one claims a body, then we bury them in a pauper's grave in one of those pine boxes."

Kevin pointed to sidewall where three pine boxes were stacked, one on top of the other.

"The guy you're looking for is over here," he said.

Kevin led the two men to a steel gurney. The gurney was placed in front of two closed double doors, each door had a large glass insulated window and, when Rice looked through one of the windows, he saw the doors led out to an operating room. Robert Bradford's body lay on top of the gurney, still dressed in the clothing he was wearing when he was murdered in Wicker Park. Rice had seen the body at the crime scene, but Bradford looked different now. Rice was struck by the difference between a fresh kill and the chilled body that lay before him. Maybe it was the chill of the cooler or the smell of the room. Maybe it was Bradford's single dead body being surrounded by hundreds of other dead bodies. Rice could not nail down what the difference was, but there was a difference.

Findley was right, Rice thought, this part of Bradford's journey to the grave is as important as the up-coming investigation of his life will be. It matters to know what happens to a victim once the body is admitted to the morgue; the whole journey though life matters.

Suddenly the double doors opened and a medical examiner dressed in operating garb entered the cooler.

"Ah, Detective Findley," the medical examiner said. "Good morning to you."

"Morning doctor," Findley replied.

"So you are going to be with us this morning?" the M.E. asked.

"Yes, me and my new partner will be observing. I'd like you to meet Detective Rice Battin. Rice, this is Dr. Barb Kesh. Dr. Kesh is the pathologist for the autopsy."

"Good to meet you, detective," the doctor said, nodding in Rice's direction. "Kevin, let's wheel Mr. Bradford out and get started."

Rice was happy to leave the cooler and enter into the brightly lit and warmer operating room. He walked to the center of the room and inhaled deeply. The taste and the stench from the odor in the cooler stayed on the roof of his mouth and in his nostrils. He watched as assistants to the doctor positioned the gurney under a bright light.

"Here," Findley said. "Put on this surgical mask and these plastic gloves."

Rice slipped the mask over his face and pulled the gloves on. He watched as the doctor examined the body and spoke into a small lapel microphone, recording her procedures and discoveries on tape.

"This is a white male, believed to be forty-one years of age, and alleged to be one Robert Bradford," she said. "There is a large amount of dried blood on the front of his shirt. The bloodstain is approximately seventeen centimeters wide and thirteen centimeters long. There is a hole in the shirt that looks to have been made by a round from a small caliber pistol."

As the doctor registered her verbal notes, a photographer began taking pictures of the corpse and an autopsy technician hung x-rays of the deceased up on a lighted panel.

"It looks like a foreign object is lodged behind the right atrium, possibly penetrating the superior vena cava," the technician observed as he looked at the x-ray.

Findley leaned over and whispered to Battin.

"Dr. Kesh will examine the clothing for powder burns, measure the hole in the shirt, and then strip the body. We'll get a full report from her later, but this morning the doctor will be able to give us a cause and manner report on how Bradford died. After she digs the bullet out of him and examines it, she'll give it to the evidence technician, and he'll get the bullet to us so we can maintain a chain of custody on it."

The autopsy technician and the evidence technician stripped the body of all clothing and placed the clothing in plastic bags. The doctor proceeded to autopsy the body in an efficient and quick manner. She was an expert in dissecting the dead and determining the cause of death.

"The body has an entrance wound that is five centimeters below the suprastural notch. We are turning the body over to examine the victim's back."

The assistants rolled the body on its side, and then pulled on the right arm and leg, flipping the body over completely. The photographer snapped four pictures of the Robert Bradford's back.

"There is no exit wound," the doctor continued. "There are several small contusions on the shoulders and upper back, probably a result of a fall after the shooting."

The doctor ran her fingers through Robert Bradford's hair, pulling the hair away so she could examine the back of his skull.

"There is a large contusion on the lower mastoid."

After further examination, the assistants turned the body onto its back, and the doctor used three different syringes to draw liquid samples from the body, collecting fluid from the eyes, urine from the bladder, and blood from the leg.

"I am making an incision across the chest," the autopsy technician said into his lapel microphone.

Using a large, portable electric device the technician opened Robert Bradford's body by cutting horizontally across the chest and vertically down to the lower abdomen.

"I will now extract the breastplate from the corpse," he said.

The technician picked up a large tool that reminded Rice of an electric pruning shear, and began cutting away at the sternum, the clavicle, and the ribs. When he finished, he pulled up on the breastplate and removed it from the body.

While the breastplate was being placed on a table, Mike Findley's gaze caught the eyes of the evidence technician, who was standing to the left side of the gurney on which Bradford's body was being autopsied. The technician was wearing a surgical mask, but his eyes could be seen clearly, and he was using his eyes to draw Findley's attention to Rice Battin.

Findley turned and looked at his partner; Battin's face was pale, his eyelids were fluttering, and his body was swaying slightly. Findley placed the palm of his right hand on the small of Battin's back and gripped tightly onto his left shoulder.

"Hold on, guy," he said.

Mike Findley walked his partner out of the autopsy room and into the hallway. He pulled his own mask off, and then lifted off Rice's mask.

"Breath in," Findley said. "You'll be all right. I'm going to walk with you to the restroom. We'll wash up there, and then we'll head back to the precinct. You've seen enough of the morgue.

• • •

Professor Robert Bradford was forty-one years old when his life was taken away by a shot fired in Wicker Park, but the circumstances that caused his death did not take forty-one years to transpire. Instead, those events occurred over the four-month period of time that immediately preceded his murder.

Chapter Five — Brae Larson's Nightmare

Seated on a modern black leather couch, Brae Larson's voice trembled slightly as she began to share her deepest secret with her roommate and friend, Ann Yin.

"The dream is recurring. It is always the same in detail," she said slowly.

"How often does it happen?" Ann asked.

Brae's lips quivered. Her voice became halting. She turned her face away from Ann and looked out the window of their apartment. A soft darkness prevailed in their living room, the only illumination generated by a distant quarter moon and a sliver of light that meekly protruded through Ann's all but closed bedroom door.

"Too often," she replied. "At least three times a month."

Brae reached for Ann's hand. Throughout their college years the two women had become close, and Ann had come to respect Brae's open way of revealing her emotional needs. Ann moved closer to Brae, hoping to provide her with more support.

"It is always the same," Brae continued.

She paused and looked at her fingers, intertwined with Ann's. Her roommate's fingers were small and thin; she wore a jade ring on her thumb that belonged to her grandmother. The dark green jade stone was ancient and had been mined in the Chinese province of Xinjiang where Ann's family had lived before coming to America. Brae had felt close to Ann from the moment they met as freshmen at the University of Chicago; Brae was there to major in literature and Ann's major was biology.

Now, for the first time in Brae's life, she was about to share her haunting nightmare with a friend. She had been through a number of professional counseling services in attempts to understand the nightmare that had plagued her for over 10 years, but none of the services had satisfactorily explain the dream or alleviated her fears.

It was difficult for Brae to talk about her nightmare, but she wanted to let Ann know how debilitating the dream had become. She needed to unload her burden and she longed to share her anxieties with Ann, hoping the close camaraderie they had developed over the years might be a key to easing her pain.

"When the dream begins, I am in large old house. For some reason, I know the house is supposed to be my home, but I have never been in such a house, and there is no comfort in being there. Instead, the house surrounds me with dread. I want out, but I cannot leave."

Ann saw Brae's chest move with heaving, deep breathes; she felt Brae's hand grasping tightly onto her hand.

"It is as if I were suspended or trapped," she said. "I am held by some force to stand at the top of a flight of stairs. I try to look around, but I can only look down at the steps. I know I am supposed to walk down the stairs, but I am terrified of making the journey. When I do move, the staircase narrows and takes on a life of its own. The stairs draw me downward. I move slowly and I feel my skin becoming clammy and cold with each step. I am frightened, but compelled to continue. I know I cannot turn around and escape. I am encompassed by the dark nature of the stairs."

"Do you recognize the staircase?" Ann asked. "Are you sure it is not some place you have been before?"

"No. I never lived in an old house," Brae replied. "And, I've only seen a staircase like it in creepy movies. I know the staircase is leading to a basement of some kind, but it is not a place that I know."

"What happens when you reach the bottom of the stairs?"

Brae's voice became softer. She spoke as if she were talking to herself. A trance-like expression appeared on her face.

"I hear noises…someone calling to me. It's a girl's voice, but I do not see her. When I reach the bottom of the stairs, the entrance to the basement becomes totally black. I am afraid. I want to turn around and run back up the steps, but I feel pressure…the force again…pushing at my back. The force wants me to move into the darkness, but I hold back. I refuse to move. I push back with all of my strength. Somehow I know that if I enter that dark room I will be thrust into a horrendous vortex that sucks me deeper into the darkness. It would be like entering my own grave."

"Take your time, Hon," Ann said. "You said you hear voices…do you mean more than one person?"

"Yes. The girl's voice calls out to me. I think she is crying for help, and I can make out her calling my name. I think she is desperate for me to enter the room, but most of her words are muffled."

"What about the other voices?"

"There is just one other voice. It is a man's voice. He is hurting the girl. I can tell that from their voices. I think the girl wants to come to me for safety. I know the man is holding her, hurting her in some way. She wants my help, but I am afraid to enter the room."

"Brae," Ann said. "Have you ever been hurt by a man…maybe when you were a little girl?"

"Suppressed memory, huh?" Brae replied. "No. It's not that. All of the counselors have taken that road. One of the counselors even hypnotized me."

"Oh God, really? Did that work?"

"Nothing has worked," Brae responded. "I think you're my last hope. I'm sorry to be so dramatic. It's just that it all seems to be coming to a head, and I am afraid."

"What do you mean?"

"Ann, you are my closet friend. You know I am a strong person. I'm doing well in college. I plan to get my master's. But, I've fought this dream for ten years…it's wearing me down."

Brae stood up and walked to their apartment window. She looked for a brief moment at the prominent slice of moon that dominated the night sky, and then she turned to face Ann. She wrapped her arms around her chest and unconsciously massaged her upper arms.

"I'm afraid, Ann. It's strange, but I am afraid of *not* entering that basement. I need to know what is there. I need for this nightmare to stop. I need to confront that darkness and those voices. The nightmare isn't just a dream any more. Lately, I have been finding myself thinking about it during the day. It interrupts my concentration. It stays with me…stalking me…demanding that I act…demanding that I enter the room."

Ann got up from the couch, moved toward Brae, and looked into her friend's eyes; she saw utter despair. She felt helpless, uncertain of what to do to help Brae and fearful of offering the wrong advice.

"The nightmare is not knowing," Brae continued. "The nightmare is that assiduous pause at the bottom of the stairs and the terror in that girl's voice."

"Brae," Ann said slowly. "What about your older sister? Could it be her voice you are hearing?"

Brae's eyes filled with moisture and tears streamed down her face. Her mind reeled back in time. She felt the air being sucked out of her lungs. Her knees became weak. She turned back to the window, her hands falling on the windowsill and her mind swirling with memories of her sister's death. Inhaling deeply, she straightened her back, trying to recover her composure.

"This is all such bullshit," she said loudly.

Ann rushed to Brae and held her. Brae's head collapsed on Ann's shoulders. Brae cried openly while embracing her roommate.

"Why the fuck is this happening to me?" she sobbed. "I'm the person who can handle anything. Why can't I handle this? If I can't enter that room…if I can't confront this…"

Brae's body shook in Ann's embrace, and Ann became frightened by Brae's alarm.

"Brae…Brae," Ann said. "I don't know what to tell you. This is more than I expected. I'm not complaining, but I just didn't expect this. It all seems so surreal. Brae…can't you just drop it? Can't you just get it out of your mind and think of something else? Do what I do…think about some guy or a concert or …something else."

Brae began to compose herself. She loved her roommate, but she knew Ann's approach to life was flighty, and she knew Ann would have difficulty relating to the problem Brae had described to her.

"People always tell me to just let it go," Brae replied. "It doesn't work that way. A strong feeling of hopelessness and fear engulfs me at times. I would rather have a physical ailment...something I could under-stand...something that I could see healing. This feeling is eating away at me, consuming my energy and my ability to think. Somehow I have to expunge it...I have to take it out of my subconscious so I can deal with it."

"Okay Brae, you want my advice, right? You love poetry. Write about the dream. Have paper by your bed and write about it immediately when you wake up. Maybe that will help you to understand it."

Ann grabbed onto Brae's wrist and squeezed it, hoping to bring her friend back out of the despair that gripped her.

"Has this helped? Has it helped telling me about it?" she asked.

Brae smiled at Ann. Gradually an awareness was creeping into her mind. She came to realize the more she confided in Ann, the more she would have to deal with this problem alone; there would be no outside help for her.

"I don't know yet," she replied. "I think I feel better. Crying always helps, and you holding me helps, too."

Brae pulled slowly away from Ann.

"Listen, Ann...here's the thing. I just think I can handle this better if someone who cares about me knows. I don't want to make this a regular oc-currence. I just wanted to share some of my anxiety with you. I think that will help. I'm not knocking the counselors, but talking with them is not the same. I'm a case file for them...I understand that. I just want someone who really cares about me to know."

"Have you ever told your mom any of this?"

"I've tried. But for some reason, I can't talk about it with her. I can't even start talking to her about it. When I try, it's like there is a barrier stopping me. She doesn't even know about the dream. She knows I've seen a counselor, but I just tell her its anxiety."

"I don't think I've been much help, Brae. I'm better at picking which movie we should see or where to find a deal on a purse. But I'll always be here for you if you need to just talk or cry. I promise you that," Ann said.

Brae smiled at Ann, and decided to lie to her.

"I know you will," she said. "It has helped...talking with you as been helpful."

A moment of uncomfortable silence hung in the room. Brae was first to speak, moving away from the subject of her personal problem.

"Ann," Brae said. "I think I will head over to library and do some re-search. You want to come along? It's open until midnight."

"Well...the thing is...I'm supposed to meet this guy...research, too," Ann replied with a laugh. "Maybe an all-nighter."

Brae laughed and took a light punch at Ann's arm.

"Typical," she said. "I head out to study and you're going to do some guy. We make quite a pair."

Ann smiled and winked at Brae.

"Get a guy, Brae," she said. "That's my advice."

"Maybe I'll find one at the library," Brae replied with a laugh.

Chapter Six — Kallie Larson

Brae took the elevator down to the first floor of her apartment building. The apartment she and Ann were renting was on East 57th Street and Drexel and was conveniently located within walking distance of the university. She exited the building, heading north toward the Regenstein Library. When she saw the library lit up with floodlights and looming in front of her, she decided to take a longer walk before committing herself to two full hours of research. She walked past the library and headed for the green space of the Quadrangle.

Finding a bench that was away from everyone, she sat down and assessed her conversation with Ann. The botanical beauty of the quad was exposed by a string of decorative lampposts that filled the grounds with soft lighting and made the campus look like a large impressionist painting.

Ann…she is the closest friend I have, Brae thought. I don't have many friends. I know people do like me, but I just don't bond well with any one person.

Brae looked up into the night sky and thought of the confession she had just made to her friend. She couldn't tell if talking with Ann had helped or not. A passage from *Song of Myself* drifted into her head: *You are also asking me questions and I hear you. I answer that I cannot answer.*

I doubt Ann will ever have real answers for me, Brae sighed. Damn! Why did she have to bring up my sister's death?

Brae's mind began to fill with tragic images from the past. Her thoughts became flooded with memories of her older sister's death. Brae was only eleven years old when her sister, Kallie, was killed while driving home from school.

• • •

"Brae," her mother had called out gently to her over ten years ago.

Brae looked up from playing with a doll and saw a terribly distraught look on her mother's face.

"Brae darling, come here," her mother repeated. "Mommy has something to tell you."

Brae's mother stretched out her arm and took Brae's smaller hand in hers, leading Brae to her older sister's room. She sat down on Kallie's bed, pulled Brae up onto her lap, and kissed her hair. Brae felt her mother's loving arms wrapped around her, and then she felt her mother's body shake with sobbing convulsions.

"Mommy what's wrong?" Brae asked. "What's wrong Mommy?"

Brae's mother regained her composure. Her mind focused on Brae's well being. She positioned Brae in her lap so she could look into her eyes.

"Brae, my darling Brae," she began. "There has been a car accident. Your sister has been hurt."

Brae's mother felt her daughter's body shudder, and she saw Brae's eyes widen in fear.

"Where is she?" Brae asked.

"Oh Brae," her mother cried out. "Our Kallie's in heaven."

Mother and child collapsed in each other's arms and sobbed openly.

• • •

The following week was a blur for Brae. Family and friends moved in and out of her house, bringing messages of sympathy, food, and offers to do whatever had to be done. Brae's mother was constantly by her side, comforting her, and helping her through the mourning process. They stood together holding hands at the visitation, the funeral, and the grave ceremony. They slept together and held each other until sleep gave them temporary respite from their grief. Brae's mother always took time to answer any question Brae had and to explain the ceremonies of death to her.

Two days after Kallie's burial, Brae's mother sat her down at the dining room table, telling Brae that she had something important to give to her.

"Brae, you know your sister was interested in famous books," the mother began.

"Kallie told me she was going to study literature," Brae's sweet voice replied.

"That's right. She was going to study literature and philosophy at college. She started reading famous books in high school. I bought her this book."

Brae's mother held up a copy of a book entitled, *Henry David Thoreau-Walden and Civil Disobedience*. Brae smiled in recognition of her sister's book.

"I saw Kallie reading that book," she said. "She read some of it to me, but I don't understand it."

"Someday you will," Brae's mother said. "A month ago, I saw your sister reading this book, and she told me she wanted you to have it when she was done. So I'm giving it to you as a gift from her. You don't have to read it now, but you can keep it until you're older…keep it in your room. Okay, Hon?"

Brae smiled and took the book to her room. She liked the idea of having a part of Kallie with her. She closed the door to her room and sat down on her bed, holding the book in her small hands, and then pressing it close to her lips, kissing it and thinking of her sister. The cover of the book was dark blue leather with gold leaf lettering. Brae thought the book looked like a Bible, and she handled it with reverence. She opened the book carefully, finding joy in looking at words her sister had read. When she had thumbed through three-quarters of the book, she paused to examine a single piece of paper that was folded in half and wedged between two pages. Brae pulled the paper out of the book, unfolded it, and saw her sister's handwriting. Two words were neatly written on the paper: *Don't tell!*

Brae's hand shook as she placed the paper back into the book. She stood up and moved slowly, walking toward the writing desk in her room. She placed the book on a small ledge at the top of the desk and turned to walk away.

Still sitting at the dining room table just outside of Brae's room, her mother heard the heavy thud of an object falling onto the floor. She rushed to Brae's room and found her daughter lying unconscious three feet away from the desk.

• • •

Brae's eyes misted over as she sat on the quad bench and recalled her past. She remembered being rushed to a local hospital, her mother panic stricken at the thought of losing another child. A series of medical diagnoses were performed on her, but nothing was found that could explain her collapse into unconsciousness.

Don't tell! The two words haunted her as much as the dream.

Sailing slowly across the star studded sky, a small solitary cloud pressed at the edge of the moon, pushing the lunar light behind a gossamer shield and casting an ominous shadow over Brae's chosen place of reflection.

"Don't tell," she whispered to herself. Goose bumps hurried up and down her arms, causing her to shiver in the temporary eclipse of the moon.

"Don't tell." The words seeped slowly from her lips again.

Looking straight ahead, Brae's hand reached automatically inside the large dark tan handbag she always carried with her. Her fingers found what her mind was searching for. She pulled the weathered copy of *Walden and Civil Disobedience* from her purse and held it on her lap, staring at it as she had done for ten years. She turned to page four hundred and twenty-nine and found the piece of paper her sister had left in the book. She unfolded the paper and looked at the words.

Don't tell what? She wondered.

Blood rushed to her head. She knew the words and her nightmare were elaborately woven together in some inexplicable way. She had tried to guess at their meaning, but always feared being wrong in her assessment.

"Guessing…it's not fair to Kallie," she said to herself as she gazed at the paper. "It's not fair to me or her…*knowing*…that's what's important. Some-how, I have to know."

Chapter Seven — A Classroom Discussion

Does the duality of magical realism inherently force Anglo-American literary critics to over estimate the impact of "fantasy" found in the writing style? Are Western critics able to comprehend the "fantasy" found in diverse Third World cultures and to delineate its impact on the author's writing?

The question was written with a blue erasable marker and scrawled three feet across a white board that stretched for six feet in the front of a second floor classroom in Eckhart Hall. The question had been posted on Friday as an assignment for Dr. Robert Bradford's upper level class in New Literary Genres in the 20th Century. The fifteen students in the class had been given five days to reflect upon the question and to write a rough draft five-page paper that would be the basis for future classroom discussion.

It was Wednesday morning, and Dr. Bradford was about to begin class. Everyone on campus knew a severe but fair penalty would be imposed on any student absent from, or unprepared for, the professor's class. All fifteen students were present and had their rough draft papers with them.

"Ladies and gentlemen…excluding the time college students devote to debauchery on Friday and Saturday nights, and your Sunday recovering needs, you have still had ample time to delve into the question at hand. Who will be first to add clarity to our search for understanding in the genre of Magical Realism?"

Although no lecture was occurring, fifteen twenty-year-old students directed their eyes downward and pressed their pens on notebooks they had diligently placed on top of their desks, doodling away in the hope of finding refuge from Professor Bradford's search for a volunteer.

"Mr. Blaine," the professor called out. "Why don't you start our discussion?"

Justin Blaine was a favorite student of Professor Bradford's. He was a senior at the University of Chicago and a serious scholar.

Relieved that a spokesperson had been chosen for them, the other fourteen students looked up from their notebooks, slouched back in their desks, and waited to hear what Justin had to say.

Classroom discussions in Professor Bradford's class were a true give-and-take adventure and, although no student wanted to begin the verbal academic quest, all of the students admired Professor's Bradford's extraordinary ability to inspire them and to pull information from their minds through the use of his own Socratic techniques.

"I think I agree that the term magical realism resulted from a post-colonial analysis of non-western literature…that analysis lacks a full understanding of the internal cultural struggles, which were the inspirational force for the genre," Justin began.

Professor Bradford walked slowly among the students, weaving his way around the desks that made up the seating pattern in the classroom. He paused beside Justin and thumped his knuckles down on the student's desktop.

"So," Professor Bradford intervened. "You think the genre has been mis-labeled by Western literary critics who, due to their own cultural bias, cannot understand it. Is that correct?"

"Yes," Justin replied while slowly nodding his head. "Yes, I do."

Professor Bradford continued his walk, directing his attention toward a young woman who sat in the middle of the classroom. He stood beside her and pressed his fingertips down on the top of her desk.

"Ms. Schmidt," he said. "What say you? Do you agree with Mr. Blaine? Can you add insight into our discussion today?"

Angie Schmidt was dressed in cut-off jean shorts, a light gray t-shirt, and flip-flops. It was 10:00 in the morning, a time of day considered to be very early by most college students. Angie shook her tousled brown shoulder length hair, trying to expunge the remnants of sleep from her mind and her eyes. She placed her hands on top of her head, shaking her brain into action with a firm quick massage.

"I do agree," she answered. "I think the duality of magical realism was created out of a lack of understanding by Western critics. Further, I believe that the reference to fantasy is misplaced and could be akin to representing Catholic communion as a mystical ceremony surrounded by spectacular flights of fantasy…the changing of wine to blood, the cleansing of the soul, the presence of a god-like figure, the bread becoming a broken body, etc, etc. What's the difference between our "fantasies" and the so-called fantasies of the non-western cultures?"

Professor Bradford's facial expression turned more reflective. He looked out through the classroom windows, staring southward toward the campus quad.

"So," Professor Bradford continued, "you see more realism in the genre than magic?"

"I do," Angie replied.

"Could it then be that all literary expression is misunderstood," Professor Bradford said slowly. "Could our own cherished classics be mislabeled if the world was turned upside down and the powers that be were made to be the victims of colonial exploitation?"

"I know so," Koffi Assitou's baritone voice boomed out from the east side of the classroom.

Koffi Assitou was a foreign student from Togo. He possessed a brilliant mind and had become an astute observer of the America's propensity to impose its own visions of reality upon other cultures.

Professor Bradford quickened his pace and almost hurried across the room toward Koffi.

"Ah," he exclaimed, as he moved eastward toward Koffi. "We now hear from an objective third party...a man who straddles two cultures and struggles to understand both."

Koffi's face broke into a broad smile. He admired Professor Bradford and recognized the professor was engaging in humor to make a point. He knew Professor Bradford wanted to hear more from him, and he knew the professor respected his point of view.

"Tell us, Mr. Assitou. Tell us what the East thinks of the West."

"Oooh maaan," Koffi replied jokingly. "In the East, we try not to think of you at all."

The room exploded with laughter and Professor Bradford laughed along with his students, using the energy created by Koffi's observation to continue with the discussion and pressing Koffi for more. He pointed to the question hanging in front of the class on the white board.

"When you examined this question, Mr. Assitou, to what conclusions did you arrive?"

"Obvious conclusions," Koffi said. "Conclusions that might only be drawn from a man who does, as you say, straddle. And yet, I admire Angie's observation, too. In Togo, many follow the belief of animism, and I know such a belief is shrouded in mystery for westerners, but it is very real for us, and it is as legitimate as Catholic communion."

"Is magical realism a misnomer?" the professor interjected, asking the question to the entire class.

"Perhaps, not so much a misnomer," Justin said. "Perhaps, it is a term that should be universally applied to any writing that combines the fantasies of its own culture with realism."

"Hmmm. That is an interesting thought," Professor Bradford commented. "Where does that thought take us as it relates to the question on the board?"

"It provides opportunity," Justin said. "It provides the opportunity to recognize the universal impact of the supernatural...to understand its impact on events, and to incorporate it more fully into all writings."

Professor Bradford's classroom stroll had now taken him back in front of the class. He paused beside the teacher's desk that occupied the center of the room. He sat down on the edge of the desk, his facial expression revealing his deep interest in the way in which the discussion was progressing.

"I like these thoughts," he announced to the class. "Yes...I do like these thoughts."

"Professor Bradford," Angie called out. "Could a unique Western magical realism be created...perhaps something woven in poetic form? Something akin to ancient Greek literature...something that analyzes the direction this culture has taken, poeticizes the fantasy within it, and makes it real?"

"Perhaps," Professor Bradford answered. "Perhaps. Of course, now we have to ask ourselves what is realism, don't we? Perhaps both terms need to be redefined in some universal manner. Complicated. Very complicated. And, certainly a theme for further examination."

The professor walked briskly to the white board and stood off to the side of the area where the discussion question was written. He pointed to the question while looking at the students.

"But, what must be woven now is the polished paper you will all complete based upon your rough draft, our discussion, and the question before you," the professor said. "This has been a very good discussion. I am hopeful that the ideas expressed today will give you direction in how to proceed with your rough draft."

Professor Bradford moved behind a lectern that stood next to the teacher's desk. He placed his hands on each side of it, wrapped his fingers tightly around the thin flat wood, and looked out at the class.

"You will find the requirements for the paper on the class web page," he said. "Of course, I will always be available to discuss any of your concerns or to listen to any new ideas you have. Office hours are 2 p.m. to 3:30 p.m. Monday and Wednesday. The paper is due one week from today," he added with a smile.

Chapter Eight — Robert Bradford's Past

After dismissing class, Professor Bradford picked up his briefcase, looked at the writing assignment on the board one more time, and then headed out into the hallway. Robert had a noon appointment with the dean of his department, and there was almost an hour to kill before that obligation. He decided against going to his office, opting instead to take a stroll on campus.

"Professor Bradford," Amisha Patel called out, as the professor made his way down the hall.

Robert turned around to watch Amisha walking rapidly toward him with a bright smile on her face.

"Good morning, Amisha," Robert said. "What can I do for you?"

"I wanted to know if you will be the professor for the Indian literature class next fall. I really enjoy your 20th century lit class and I want to take another class of yours."

"Why thank you," Robert replied. "The schedule is not official yet, but I can tell you I will be the instructor for the class."

Amisha smiled again.

"Then I will be signing up for it," she said. "I like the discussion in your classes. We all like it. It's so much better than an hour of notes."

"You are kind, Amisha. I enjoy it, too. I learn from listening to all of you, and I like the free exchange of ideas. I'm hopeful everyone is learning while we discuss. Do you have any questions concerning the writing assignment?"

"Not right now," Amisha replied. "I may later. I do have a good start on it, and our discussion gave me a new perspective. My country is a very mystical land. I think I will include some Indian writings in my paper."

Professor Bradford listened to Amisha, but began slowly walking down the hall.

"I do not mean to rush you, Amisha, but I have an appointment. Do you mind if we walk and talk?"

"That's okay, professor," Amisha said. "Actually, I have to be going, too…in the opposite direction. Thanks for the information."

"Have a good day," Robert said, as Amisha turned and headed away from him.

Amisha is a very pretty girl, Robert thought. She's bright, too. She probably knows more about Indian literature than I do. But knowing about something and teaching about something…those are two different levels of competency.

• • •

Robert hurried down the stairway and made his way out of Eckhart Hall. It was beautiful outside, sunny and warm.

We spend too much time indoors, he thought. I always like being outside better than being inside.

Once outside, he decided to walk south through the quad. He strolled along the circular sidewalk, heading for Harper Library. His intention was to go in the library and look at some poetry books, hoping to find some inspiration from them. Robert arrived at the library in only a few minutes and paused outside, looking up at the impressive old English Gothic building. He visually examined the two magnificent one hundred and thirty-five foot towers that rose up like giant bookends attached to the north and south ends of the library. He stared at the towers and reflected on the men who built them.

I'll bet that was exciting work, he thought. There must be quite a view from up there. What an achievement! Those were real men.

While admiring the building and daydreaming about the men who built it, Robert decided against going in the library. It's too nice to be inside a library, he concluded.

Instead, he sat down on a bench, looking north toward the quad. A smattering of people, mostly students, scurried along the sidewalks. A lot of people are probably eating lunch right now, he correctly surmised. It's good to have time and space to myself. As he looked far across the quad, Robert began to rehash his life at the university.

• • •

Robert Bradford was a university brat. He had literally grown up inside the world of the University of Chicago. Robert turned his head in the direction of Stuart Hall, mentally looking beyond it and thinking of the Laboratory School complex that existed two blocks east. It was at the complex that Robert's academic career was molded. Robert's entire pre-college training, indeed the plan that would chart his life, had been mapped out in the complex's pre-kindergarten through high school buildings.

"Very few young men in the world are as fortunate as you," Robert's mother, Adela, would often say. "Being a part of the University of Chicago's Laboratory School is an auspicious opportunity for a young man."

Robert never quite agreed with her.

It was true that Robert was bright; his I.Q. scores attested to that, and his academic record at the Lab Schools reflected his intelligence and his scholarly ability. After graduating from the University of Chicago High School, he went on to receive a bachelor's degree, a master's degree, and his doctorate from the university. Robert Bradford had always had the ability to be an acclaimed scholar. What he lacked was will and enthusiasm. However, what Robert lacked in will, his mother made up for in her obsession to see him become accomplished in the areas where she wanted him to succeed. Robert had ability; his mother had drive.

• • •

Adela Bradford was an acclaimed scholar. Her degree and the honors she accrued were in the field of business. While Robert was acquiring his scholastic credentials, she was an associate professor in the university's Graduate School of Business.

Robert's family was matriarchal; Adela Bradford planned Robert's educational path from the day he entered the world. Robert's father, Jonathan Bradford, was an attorney and was often away from home, a situation that seemed to please Jonathan. Adela also found she was happier when her husband was away. Five years into their marriage, the Bradfords reached an agreement; they would stay married and apart.

It was Robert's grandfather who became a surrogate, albeit distant, father for him. Grandpa Ostermann was a skilled carpenter. When Robert visited him, the two of them would always build or repair something with grandpa's tools. Young Robert enjoyed working with his hands. He enjoyed seeing his work develop into a tangible presence. He liked solving problems by repairing or creating objects out of wood. At his grandpa's house, he discovered he liked physical labor over mental exertion. And, at his grandfather's house, Robert discovered Karl Marx.

Robert's grandfather, Franz Detlef Ostermann, was born in Tier, Germany, the birthplace of Karl Marx. All of his life, Granpa Ostermann had made a living by working with his hands. Franz was not a Marxist, but in Tier, he had attended lectures on Karl Marx's book, *The Poverty of Philosophy*, and he came to believe that the value of any object should be determined by the labor needed to create the object. Franz was not a scholar or a philosopher, but he was adamant and vocal in his support for the workingman. Franz's German background made him suspicious of the people in society who claimed to be elite. Twice in his lifetime, he had seen Germany and Europe torn apart by the very people who claimed to be experts in one thing or another.

"Robert," Grandpa Ostermann would say. "I want you to become educated, but keep your roots. My name is Franz Detlef Ostermann. Do you know what those words mean?"

"No grandpa," Robert replied, as he watched his grandfather measure a piece of wood.

Grandpa Ostermann put his measuring tape down on the board he was about to cut and straightened his back.

"Franz Detlef Ostermann…free worker from the east," Franz replied. "I am a free man who works with his hands. I build. I create. I work with other men who have built this country, and who keep it running. We are the backbone of society. You have brains, but we are the true backbone. Don't forget us like the others have."

"Who grandpa?" Robert asked. "Who has forgotten you?"

"Politicians, intellectuals, capitalists, bosses…people who think ideas are more important than workers…people who use workers to make their own lives better…people who send us off to die in the wars they create…people who have forgotten what it's like to work hard and to suffer. Learn Robert…become educated, but do not forget us."

When Robert would mention the conversations to his mother, she would always make light of Grandpa Ostermann's ways.

"Your grandfather is old. He grew up in Germany," she would say. "Everything is different now. Grandpa lived through some difficult times and he has some strange ideas in his head, Robert."

"But mother, I do like working with my hands. I think I would like to be a carpenter," Robert replied.

Adela Bradford looked sternly at her son. Robert immediately cast his eyes downward.

"Robert. You are a freshman at Chicago University High School. You are majoring in liberal arts with an emphasis in literature. You are a brilliant boy. Someday you will be a full professor at the University of Chicago."

Adela reached for Robert's chin and pulled his face upward so she could look into his eyes.

"Haven't we talked about this before?"

"Yes," Robert replied.

"A boy with your intellect cannot waste such a talent on manual labor. You forget what Grandpa Ostermann says and pay attention to your mother and your teachers."

• • •

At one time in his life, Robert used to smile when he thought of his grandfather. Now, he frowned, disappointed that he did not follow Franz Ostermann's advice.

Robert sighed, rose up from the bench he was sitting on, turned his back on the library, and reluctantly headed for his meeting with Dean Allen Hall.

Chapter Nine — Dean Allen Hall

Robert Bradford sat in an overstuffed leather chair in the outer office of the University's Division of Humanities in Walker Hall. His right leg was crossed over his left knee, his fingers were intertwined, and his hands rested in his lap. It was spring and he was dressed in casual khaki slacks, loafers, a light blue shirt, and his favorite subdued yellow tie. He unlocked his hands and spread the fingers of his left hand out in a fan-like fashion. He stared intently at his hand, rotating it back and forth, examining first the palm of his hand, then the back of his hand, and finally his extended fingers. A sneer of disappointment appeared on his lips as he looked at the hand that had made him an Associate Professor of Poetry.

"Professor Bradford. Dean Hall will see you now," a secretary called out.

Robert rose quickly from the chair, straightened his back, and headed toward two large, dark cherry doors that were the entrance to the dean's private office. He thumped the secretary's desktop with his knuckles as he glided past her.

"Thank you, Janet," he said.

Janet looked up briefly from the small stack of papers that sat in front of her. She turned her head to the side, taking time to admire Robert's trim physique.

"Say hello to Diane for me," Janet said while scribbling her initials on the top sheet of paper.

"Will do."

Robert paused momentarily before the doors, breathed in deeply, twisted a doorknob to his right, and entered the dean's office.

"Robert!" Allen Hall exclaimed from behind his huge desk.

Hall stood up, stretched his right arm across the desktop, and greeted Robert with a smile and a firm handshake.

"Good to see you, Robert. Please take a seat. I just need a moment to finish reading this last paragraph."

Robert sat down in a chair that was in front of the dean's desk and offset to the dean's left-hand side.

"Fabulous stuff, this," Dean Hall said as his eyes poured over the manuscript he held in his hands. "The author is that young prof we hired to replace Millie."

Dean Hall laid the manuscript down on his desk and swept his hands above it in a manner that resembled a ceremonial blessing.

"It's writing like this that maintains our tradition of excellence," he said.

An expression of deep satisfaction appeared on the dean's face. He patted the manuscript with his right hand, picked it up carefully with both hands, and gently laid it down on the right hand side of his desk. Folding his hands together on the top of his desk, Dean Hall leaned forward toward Robert.

"So how have you been, Robert?"

"I'm fine, Allen."

"And Diane? How is she? She still owns that little literary shop on Damen, right?"

"Yes. Literature is Diane's passion," Robert answered.

"Well, she married the right man then," Dean Hall said smiling. "Your knowledge of poetry and your writings…well, you two must have wonderful conversations at home."

"We both take our work seriously," Robert replied.

Dean Hall moved back in his chair. He grabbed a pen that was sitting on his desk and held it between both of his hands. He bent down on both ends of the pen, causing the center of the pen to arch slightly.

"How are your current writings coming?" he asked.

"Very well," Robert responded. "I think I told you I have been working on a series of poems."

"Yes, we talked about your work. I think it was in December…something about framing your work in the paradox of the union of opposites…maybe in a literary mode similar to Gabriel."

"Yes…something such as that. Using that genre of fusion between realism and fantasy by examining the universal impact of the supernatural…comparisons of animism and our own unique religious beliefs…the awakening of the sub consciousness and the inner self…an examination of Western magical realism woven in poetic form. But, of course, I would rely upon my own writing style."

"Absolutely! That's good, Robert. That's very good. I don't want you to think I'm pressuring you, but we haven't seen any of your poetry for quite some time. I like your ideas, Robert…and, don't get me wrong, but I'm wondering…just thinking out loud here…maybe more emphasis on writing poetry itself and less emphasis on critical analysis. Something more…"

"Something more marketable?" Robert asked.

"Well, yes…a broader reading public," Allen replied. "Books are expensive to publish. The cost has gone through the roof."

Robert smiled, momentarily dropped his head, and stared at his hands again. His right hand passed over the top of his left hand in a caressing manner. He lifted his head and looked at Dean Hall.

"I am working on it," he said. "I expect to finish my writings by the end of this summer and to incorporate them into a book of poetry and literary analysis. I think you will like what I have done."

"That's great, Robert," Dean Hall said. "It's just what I wanted to hear. We want more of your poetry. Your poetry is quite unique. It's the reason we wanted you here. To be honest, I have never been a big fan of Magical Realism...too much supernatural for me. But an analysis of that genre by using your own poetic images...well that would be great...might be a real market out there for that type of book. It should be heavy on the poetry, though. My wife has a book of your poetry. She loves it. And, I approve of the direction you are taking. It's in sync with the seminars you have been instructing"

"Thank you," Robert replied. "I think you will both be pleased with what I am doing."

Dean Hall patted the manuscript lying on his desk. He stared at Robert with a look of satisfaction on his face.

"So...the end of this summer, you say. That should be about right. It's a little under the wire, though. But I was very impressed with your last publication of poetry. Let's see, that was four years ago wasn't it?"

"Yes," Robert replied. "That was some of my best work."

"It was a good seller, too. Keep in mind, we always get better, Robert. Around here, we always get better. I'm not here to pressure you, but I know you will get better, too."

"I appreciate your confidence in me, and your understanding," Robert said. "I think you know Diane and I have had some personal difficulties."

"Of course, Robert," the dean replied. "I want you to know we all understand. Your father-in-law's death...tragic...and then your mother-in-law! We all understand how difficult these last two years have been for you and Diane. And my gosh...your own sweet mother. How is her health?"

"Mother's having a very difficult time," Robert replied.

"You know, I just sent her a card yesterday," Allen said. "We are family here at UC. We are all praying for her recovery."

"Thank you. I know she will appreciate it."

"I know she will, too. But, it's time to move on, Robert...time to grow and to publish. That's what your mother would want. You're a real part of this institution, Robert...you've spent your whole life here...elementary lab school, graduate of our middle and high school programs. You know what we need from you! Say Robert...how are you classes going?"

"Terrific!" Robert indicated with a noticeable spark of enthusiasm.

"I think we have a batch of fine students this year," Dean Hall commented. "You always get high marks from our student surveys. The students love your teaching."

"I enjoy them. I love teaching."

A smile appeared on Robert's face as he thought of the recent discussion generated in his class.

"We had an excellent discussion today. We were addressing the impact of the dualism that exists in Magical Realism…"

"That is great, Robert," Dean Hall interrupted. "Really that's great. I know I will see glowing remarks from your students when we begin your bi-annual review. As I said, the students love you…they enjoy your style of teaching. Great job there. That part of your review is always tops."

Dean Allen Hall rose up from behind his desk.

"I wish I had more time to talk with you," he said. "I'm always interested in how our students are doing. But right now, I'm in the middle of reading this young profs submission. I have a meeting scheduled with him later this afternoon, and I want to be prepared. Writing such as this has to be encouraged."

Dean Hall walked around his desk, moving toward Robert.

"We will talk more, Robert…when you have something to submit to me," he said shaking the professor's hand, as Robert rose up from his chair.

Then placing his arm around Robert's shoulder, the dean walked with Robert to the office door.

"This institution thrives on teaching and publications, Robert. I know you are aware of that. I'm looking forward to seeing what you will give us."

Chapter Ten — Adela Bradford

R obert was happy to leave Allen Hall's office. His meeting with the dean had ended earlier than he expected, leaving him with time on his hands. He decided to use the extra time by paying a visit to his mother. His mother, Adela, had been hospitalized two weeks ago and was being cared for at the Bernard A. Mitchell Hospital, an adult care facility of the University of Chicago's Medical Center.

Robert drove the short distance to the Medical Center, parking his car in the self-park garage just west of the hospital complex. He would have preferred to walk to the Medical Center, but his time was limited. He had reservations to play racquetball at 1:00 o'clock and, in order to keep the appointment, he would not be able to spend much time with his mother; he was glad of that.

One year ago, Robert's mother had become seriously ill. She had been a dominant force in Robert's life, but now that light was fading. She did not have long left in the world, and Robert approached that reality with mixed feelings. He loved his mother, but he had never been able to stand up to her; he felt her presence in every decision he made. Knowing he would have to explain himself to her, he always acted in a manner that satisfied her long-term goals for him, often making decisions at the expense of his own wishes.

Adela Bradford was sitting up in bed reading a letter when her son entered her hospital room.

"Hi Mum," Robert greeted. "How are you today?"

His mother looked tired and worn. She lowered the letter away from her face, slowly allowing her hand to drop down on the bed sheet. Her arm and hand looked transparent. Her face was pale.

"Robert," she said. "This is a letter from Dean Allen Hall wishing me well and good health. Isn't that nice?"

Robert moved close to his mother's bed and bent over to kiss the top of her head.

"Everyone at the U is thinking about you, Mum," he said. "They're all praying for you."

"Humph," Adela snorted softly. "There are no prayers that will do my health any good."

"Perhaps they're praying for your soul, Mum," Robert said with a smile.

Adela tossed a stern glance toward her son.

"Do you pray for my soul?" she asked.

"Mum, you know I am an atheist. My prayers won't do you any good."

"Don't remind me of that," Robert's mother said. "Anyway, an atheist can pray, too. God listens to all of us. He will forgive you for your doubts, Robert. I know He will. I pray for that everyday."

Adela looked down at her letter.

"Dean Hall says that he is very proud of you. He says he can't wait to read your up-coming publications. How are those coming?"

"Fine, Mother," Robert replied.

"Can I see some of them?"

"No one gets to see any of them until I have finished. You know that's how I work. That's the way I have been doing it since day one."

"I never agreed with that system of yours," Adela snapped. "I could have been a real help on your last publication. I may not be a poet, but I know how your mind works. I know you. I know what you think. You used to let me help you."

"Mother," Robert said. "The last time you helped me with an assignment was when I was a freshmen in high school."

"And you got an excellent grade on that paper," Robert's mother recalled. "Keep in mind Robert, these publications you are working on, they're very important…important to your career here at the university."

"I know, Mother."

"And, the publication is important to your image as associate professor of literature. I am proud of what you have accomplished at the university. It took a lot of hard work for you to get where you are, but we did it. There were times when you might have strayed, but we stuck to our plans. You have become an integral part of university life. I'm proud of you, and I want your career here to always improve. You're a shining star, Robert. We both are. People admire what we have accomplished. My career is over, but you…you will continue for both of us. You'll become a full professor."

Robert stood silently.

"Don't slouch, Robert. And, take that grumpy look off your face," his mother said. "I'm just reminding you how much people like your poetry."

Robert shuffled his stance and straightened his back.

"Mum, you're a stitch," he said. "But I didn't come here to talk about my publications. I came to see you and find out how you feel today."

"Lousy, Robert. I feel lousy. I don't like being here, and I am too young to be hospitalized."

"You know there's nothing we can do about this. You need around the clock attention. This is the best place for you."

"I know, Robert. I just don't want to be here. But I am trapped."

Adela sighed in recognition of her situation. She lifted her arm up and pointed to a small closet across the room.

"Robert," she said. "Go over to the closet and bring me the brown grocery bag that is on the top shelf."

"What's in it?" Robert asked.

"Just get it and bring it here," his mother said, waving her hand up and down in the direction of the closet.

Robert dutifully did his mother's bidding, bringing the bag to her bedside.

"It's heavy," he said.

"Put it on that small table and look inside of it."

Robert obeyed.

"It's a bottle of wine," he said with a surprised tone.

"A bottle of wine and two wine glasses," his mother corrected. "I've had a glass of wine everyday of my life since I was twelve years old and I am not about to stop. Take the bottle out and pour us each a glass."

Again, Robert complied with his mother's instructions. He handed one glass of wine to his mother and took the other for himself.

"To your health, Mother," Robert said as he started to lift his glass to his lips.

"Robert! Hold the wine glass by the stem. You'll smudge the crystal if you don't."

"Of course, Mother," Robert said. "Sorry. I'll try to do better."

Adela raised her eyebrows in recognition of her son's sarcasm. She took two small sips of wine and then a thoughtful look appeared on her face.

"Robert," she asked. "When I am gone, what will you do with our home in Hyde Park?"

"Mother, I haven't given that a thought. It is your house. Maybe, you will be able to go back to it someday."

"I won't be going back there," his mother said.

Robert took a gulp of wine, purposefully moving his fingers up the sides of the wine glass, and remained silent.

"I'm dying, Robert. We both know that. Everyone knows that. I will die in this bed. There is no escaping that. I know what is going to happen to me and when it will happen. It will happen soon, so you had better be prepared. You need to think about the house."

"I have a home, Mother," Robert said.

"Diane's home you mean. Her mother's home to be precise."

Robert sat his empty wine glass down on the bedside table and looked directly at his mother.

"We've gone through this numerous times, Mum. I live in Wicker Park and that is where Diane wants to stay. I want it, too."

Adela Bradford sat her wine glass down on the table, folded her arms, and frowned.

"And what will happen to our house in Hyde Park? I suspect you will sell it before my body is cold and in the ground," she said.

Robert moved backward toward a chair that was near the hospital bed. He sank down and sat with a gloomy look on his face.

"Mother, do we have to talk about this now?"

Adela Bradford sighed heavily.

"No. You can talk about it with Diane after I have passed on. She's the one who will decide the fate of our house."

Robert rose up out of his chair.

"Damn it, Mother!" Robert exclaimed. "The Hyde Park house is in my name. I'll decide what to do with it, but I will not be living in Hyde Park. I live in Wicker Park. Why can't you accept that?"

"The university family is in Hyde Park," Adela snapped back. "Don't you see that? I'm only trying to help you with your career. I'm only thinking of you."

Silence gripped the room.

Robert walked to a window and peered outside. Then he turned and faced his mother.

"Let's not argue, okay?" he said.

Adela sighed loudly again.

"I'm tired, Robert," she replied. "I need a nap."

Robert walked to his mother, bent over the bed, and kissed her head again.

"You get some rest, Mum. I'll be back to see you on Friday. Do you want me to wash out the wine glasses and put everything back in the closet?"

"No. The nurse knows about it. I suspect Dr. Yuskis does, too. He lets it be my little secret. Now go and let me rest."

Robert walked toward the door of the hospital room, but paused when he heard his mother call out to him.

"Robert! We'll talk more about the house on Friday," she said.

Robert left the room and walked rapidly down the hallway, wanting to put distance between himself and his mother.

Chapter Eleven — Racquetball

Robert pulled out of the hospital parking garage, drove north on Maryland Avenue, then east on 56th Street, heading for the Ratner Athletic Center. He parked his car in the Ellis Avenue parking garage, grabbed his sport bag out of the back seat, and made his way to the Center.

On Wednesdays Robert had a standing racquetball date with Bob Wachtel. He and Bob had been playing racquetball for five years, and Robert had developed an admiration for his court opponent. Bob was the head maintenance man for the athletic center. Wachtel was lacking in a formal education, but he was a master-of-all-trades. Robert was looking forward to playing an aggressive game against Bob, hoping to put to rest some of the demons that had arisen to afflict him.

I've given my whole life to the university, Robert thought, as he walked into the sports center. I've seen a lot of people come and go here, and a lot of them were deans. Allen's my third dean, but it doesn't seem like they ever change…publish, always publish. Every one of them knows what's best for the university. None of them could teach or knows anything about teaching. Damn! I'm an excellent teacher, but there is no credit for that. Publish! It's always about publishing. Well hell, he thought sighing to himself, I'm pumped with adrenalin, and my kill shot should be fast today. I'll just keep imagining the ball is a college dean.

Since the time Robert left his academic studies and began to teach, he had developed a new appreciation for the Bob Wachtel's of the world. Robert knew it was the Wachtel's of the world who kept everything working so that eggheads like him could delve into literary questions. Throughout time, the people whose names appear in history books accomplished their notable deeds by standing on the backs of men like BobWachtel.

"Hey professor," Bob hailed when Robert entered the athletic center's locker room. "Ready to take a beating?"

Bob was six years younger than Robert, but the two men were in excellent shape. Their racquetball games were always what both men wanted, highly competitive and exhausting.

Robert walked directly to a bench in the locker room and sat down in front of a row of beige gym lockers.

"All I have been doing today is sitting on my ass and thinking…thinking about beating you," he replied. "Plus, I have a chip on my shoulder. You won't be able to stand up after I get done with you."

Bob walked to a locker he had commandeered when he first began working for the university. He spun the combination dial around rapidly, pulled down on the padlock, and pushed the lock away from the locker handle.

"Chip huh? You must've stopped by the admin building before you got here. How's the dean?" he said.

Robert stopped pulling his gym clothing from his locker and looked toward Bob.

"Is it that obvious?"

"In my job I work underground a lot, but I'm not off the planet," Bob said. "Half of the complaints I hear are directed toward his office. What's he bugging you about?"

As they talked, both men began changing from their street clothes to the sports gear that would make them racquetball court gladiators. Pulling on the lace of his tennis shoe, Robert turned his head and looked at Bob.

"You know, Bob, I envy your subterranean existence," he said. "Sometimes I wish I could do my job without a spotlight shining on me."

As they prepared themselves for their up-coming game, the men paid particular interest to the tension they placed on their tennis shoe laces and on the strap of their racquetball glove. The shoes and the glove had to become one with the player. Soon they would become combatants, each taking advantage of the slightest mistake the other man made, and poorly fitted clothing could cause mistakes to happen.

"You're a great teacher, Robert. I talk with a lot of the students. They always say how much they enjoy your classes. They say you're a genius. What could be a better spotlight than that?"

Robert's relationship with Bob was unique. The two men never saw each other except on Wednesdays. Their common bond was the need they both had to play racquetball aggressively. Other then racquetball, and an occasionally beer, they had no other social interaction. Robert's view of Bob was Marxian, a view that had come to dominate his philosophy of human relationships. In fact, Robert believed Bob ran the university with as much authority as the people who sat in the Administration Building. Robert respected Bob's proletarian status and his utilitarian abilities. Overtime, Wachtel had become a sounding board for Robert, a confidant who lived apart from the university's world of academia. Wachtel lived below Robert's world and was free to move about and observe its operations without being bound by the obligations the institution placed on the instructional staff. Although he worked below the university, Wachtel possessed a unique overview of the entire institution. He was a shadowy figure whom Robert had come to trust.

"Ah yes, teaching. One would think that should be the essence of being a professor," Robert replied as he held his racquet in both hands and examined the tautness of its strings.

Bob leaned back against a locker and examined the strings of his own racquet.

"Oh, oh," he responded. "It must be time to publish. God, I am glad I just work here and don't have to be involved in the bullshit they make you guys run through."

Robert laughed, happy to hear Bob's observation.

"If you think publishing is bullshit, you ought to attend one of our quarterly faculty meetings."

"I would rather you gave me a quarterly beating with that racquet," Bob said smiling.

Robert laughed again, and then a serious look appeared on his face.

"But really Bob," he said. "Publishing isn't part of the bullshit, but the pressure to publish is, and the direction in which they push me is. Christ, I'm going to wind up writing some kind of interpretive minutiae instead of writing poetry...some analytical bullshit that will end up being a pissing contest between me and my fellow academicians. There are dozens of different ways to interpret someone's writings, and I'm going to have to pretend that my analysis is the most enlightened way and the most important way. Then I will have to defend my interpretation against an array of critics who will pretend their interpretations matter more than mine. And then, I will have to pretend I give a rat's ass which interpretation matters. God, I wish I could just come up with some poetic verse and screw the interpretation crap!"

Robert slammed the door to his locker shut.

"Damn!" he exclaimed as the door banged closed.

"I feel for you, professor," Bob said. "We don't get much of that bullshit here. Either the boiler works or it don't...it's all practical. And, there's no one coming down here to argue with me over how things work. I decide what is wrong and how to fix it."

"Well, in my discipline," Robert replied, "the pressure to publish stifles creativity...it has for me."

Tired of talking about his frustrations, Robert stepped over the locker room bench and started walking to get out of the locker room.

"What court are we on?" he asked

"I reserved court nine," Bob said. "I don't think anyone signed up for it, so it should be open right now."

The two men left the locker room and headed for the racquetball courts. Bob tapped twice on the door with his racquet to insure no one was on the court, and then entered, followed by Robert. Robert sat a small can of new racquetballs down in the back, left corner of the court.

"So you're having a little mental writing block, huh Professor? I've read some of your poems. I'm no expert, but I like them. You can do it again."

"Thanks, Bob. I do like writing poetry," he replied. "I guess I am having a mental block, but it'll pass. Just takes time. Beating you today should help."

Bob threw a racquetball up in the air and hit the ball toward the front wall of the court.

Robert responded to the warm-up shot by striking the ball dead center with his racquet and sending it hurtling back to the front wall.

Robert's return shot bounced off of the front wall and fell midway onto the court floor. Bob quickly stepped to his left, waited for the ball to bounce six inches off the floor, and hit the ball toward the front wall. The ball slammed into the front wall two inches above the court floor and died, a perfect kill shot.

Throughout their game, Robert was to be a frustrated witness to many more similar shots from Bob. The two men always played for an hour with the best two out of three games deciding the winner. Five years ago when they had first begun playing, Robert won frequently. But over the last two years, the number of his victories had declined. Bob was now the better player and, although he never said anything to him, Robert was aggravated by the way things had changed.

• • •

Sitting in the locker room after having showered, the two men were in the process of returning to their work-a-day clothing. Their normal after the game banter was decidedly quiet. Bob looked over at Robert and saw him examining his left hand.

"You okay, professor," Bob asked. "Is your hand all right?"

"It's fine," Robert replied. "I think I almost had you in that third game."

"Our games are always close," Bob replied. "You're just in a slump. Hell, you used to beat me regularly. You'll bounce back. Are you sure your hand is all right?"

"Yes, it's fine. I think I always beat you at first because I'm a lefty. That threw your game off, but you've adjusted to it now. I just have to find some new way of getting the edge on you. I need to be more creative in my approach to our game."

"Well, you taught me how to play this game with precision, professor," Bob commented. "Like I said before…you're a great teacher."

Robert cupped his left hand in his right hand and stared at it.

"You're right about that," he agreed. "Do you have time for a beer, Bob?"

"Not today, professor," Bob replied. "But if you stop for one, drink another one for me, okay?"

"I just may do that," Robert said.

Chapter Twelve — Elena Markova

A heavy Chicago rain caused stranded pedestrians to crowd under window awnings and pushed large numbers of them inside as they sought refuge from the sudden downpour.

One of the refugees was Elena Markova; who held a purse over her head and hurried purposefully in her flight from the rain. She ran an extra ten yards in order to find safe haven in the Damen Literary Bookstore, a store she had often passed on her way home from work. Now, the inclement weather provided her with an excuse to enter the establishment and address her curiosity concerning the types of books that would be found there.

"Oh you poor thing," a woman exclaimed while Elena stood just inside the store entrance, her spring jacket and her long dark hair dripping wet from the rain.

"This rain? It is nothing," Elena replied with a sneer. "In Vologda, rain pounds down twice as hard as this."

Undeterred by the sarcasm, the woman moved toward Elena with a fist full of large soft paper towels she had grabbed from behind a cash register counter.

"Let me take your jacket," the woman said while holding the paper towels out toward Elena.

Elena peeled off her jacket and extended it away from her body.

"Is this your bookstore?" she asked.

The woman smiled and took Elena's jacket, hanging it over a chair that was pushed under a small reading table.

"Yes it is," she said. "I have been here for over ten years. My name is Diane Bradford. You are from Russia, correct?" Diane queried.

"Vologda, Russia," Elena replied, looking past the storeowner and scanning the hundreds of books that packed the store's shelves.

"Do you have anything by Russian authors here?"

"We do. I was just about to have some tea," Diane said, pointing at a table that had a steaming cup of tea set on it. "Why don't you join me, and we can talk about the books you are looking for."

"You are kind," Elena said, while moving slowly toward the table.

Elena sat down and watched Diane pour another of cup of tea from a service cart that held a permanent position alongside the east wall of the store and was readily accessible to the store's customers.

"Do you have sugar lumps? I take my tea with two sugar lumps," Elena said in a slightly commanding tone of voice.

"I will bring you two," Diane cheerfully replied.

"Not many Americans drink hot tea," Elena said, her eyes still searching the décor of the store. "You Americans drink everything with ice. Hot tea is better for you."

"I agree," Diane answered as she sat down at the table. "Now, what are you looking for in Russian literature?"

Elena dropped the two cubes of sugar into her teacup and stirred the mixture with a spoon. She looked up at Diane with haughty scholarly expression. "Have you ever heard of the Russia poet, Anna Akhmatova?" Elena asked.

"Yes I have. We have a copy of *Rosary* in English. Is that something that would interest you?"

"Perhaps," Elena said. "I have never read her work in English…that may be interesting. But, I am more interested in the works she wrote during Stalin's reign. I have never seen any of those books, and I am always looking for them."

Elena's tone had softened. She was impressed with Diane's awareness of Russian literature, thankful for the tea, and thankful for a place to hide from the rain.

"Hmmmm," Diane exclaimed. "I know we have a book on suppressed Russian poetry that deals with the Stalinist Era. I am sure some of Akhmatova's works are in the book.

"I have been hoping to find *Requiem*. Do you know of it?

"I am sorry I do not," Diane said. "I know her as a poet and an advocate of women's rights. What is the theme of *Requiem*?"

"It is good you know of our female poets," Elena complimented. "I am impressed with your knowledge of our country. *Requiem* is a series of poems about oppression under Stalin. It was banned under his regime."

"Tell me more about it," Diane asked. "I had understood many of the writings banned during the Stalinist era were released in the 1950s."

"Not *Requiem*," Elena replied. "I do not know why the ban continued, but I think it was because her poems expressed too much individuality. I have heard it can be purchased in Russia today, but I have never seen the book"

"May I ask how long you have been in America?" Diane said.

The hard stream of rain that had brought Elena into the bookstore turned into a steady but mild downpour. Elena looked through the storefront window at the rain.

"I have been in Chicago for nine months," she said. "I work as a waitress at the Piazza Navona restaurant. Do you know this place?"

"Yes," Diane answered.

"In Vologda, I had a good job. In Vologda, I was a professional. In America, I am a professional waitress," Elena said with a laugh. "I do not like being a waitress, but it is work and it pays my expenses."

Diane could detect grief in Elena's comment. She guessed Elena was a proud woman living a difficult life.

"Elena, may I offer you some cookies? I keep a box of Dutch cookies behind the counter. This is my break time and I normally have two cookies with my tea. Will you join me?"

"You are very kind," Elena replied. "I would like a cookie."

Diane left the table to get the box of cookies. She returned quickly, placing the opened box on the table in front of Elena.

"Thank you," Elena said as she took three cookies from the box and put them on a napkin.

"Do you live near here?" Diane asked.

"Not far from here. I live close to the Ukrainian Village. Anna Ahkmatova was from the Ukraine. Did you know that?"

"I only know she wrote in St. Petersburg," Diane replied.

Elena took a bite of one of the cookies. She was pleased that she was able to tell things to Diane about Russia, things that Diane did not know.

"Do you really own this store or is it your husband's?" Elena asked, pointing to the wedding band on Diane's finger.

"The store is mine," Diane said. "My husband is an associate professor at the University of Chicago."

"Hmmm. He is intelligentsia and you are bourgeois. America!" Elena exclaimed while holding her teacup up as a toast to Diane.

Diane clicked her teacup against Elena's and laughed softly.

"Not quite," she said. "This bookstore was owned by my father, Artem Prutko. My grandparents emigrated here from the Ukraine in the 30s"

"Ahhhhhh a Ukrainian family," Elena exclaimed.

"Yes, my grandfather was a wealthy aristocrat who fled the Soviet Union. Here, in Chicago, he owned many stores, and my father inherited them all. My father died two years ago, and I have been running this bookstore ever since. I worked here when I was a little girl and while I attended college."

"You inherited your father's wealth...now you are wealthy. What does your husband think of this?"

It was not Diane's nature to talk about her personal life, but somehow, she felt engaged by this Russian woman's brashness and she found herself wanting to discuss life with her.

"The male ego...it can be fragile," Diane replied. "You have a husband?" Diane asked pointing at a band on Elena's finger.

"Sasha," Elena answered. "Sasha is in Vologda."

"What does Sasha think of you being here?"

"Sasha did not want me to leave, but I send money home. It helps."

"Strange," Diane commented.

"What is strange?"

"The world," Diane replied. "We are similar, yet very different."

"Our husbands you mean?" Elena said.

"Yes. Things have changed for men in the world, and women, too. I think we have adjusted to the change, but I don't think men have."

Elena smiled in agreement.

"Perhaps it is more difficult for men," she suggested. "Everyone expects them to be successful...they expect it. Maybe, it is harder for them to fail. I don't know the answers. I know what happens to them in Russia when they fail."

"What happens in Russia?" Diane asked.

"Vodka!" Elena said laughing.

Gaining her composure, Elena looked at Diane.

"Tell me, what happens to men in America?" she asked.

"Hmmm...I'm not sure," Diane replied.

"What is your husband's name?"

"Robert," Diane answered. "He is a good man...although, I think he is going through a change. Or maybe, I have changed. It is a complicated situation."

Elena saw moisture in Diane's eyes.

"I am sorry," Diane said. "I should not have said that about my husband. I don't know why I did."

Elena smiled and took a small bite from one of her cookies.

"Life," she sighed. "Life is complicated."

The rain stopped and Diane could tell that Elena was thinking of leaving. She finished her tea, wrapped the two cookies she had not eaten in her napkin, and stood up.

"I should go now," she said. "Thank you for being so kind."

"Elena, I want to invite you to come to my bookstore whenever you can. I find it easy to talk with you."

Elena reached for her jacket, shoved her arms through the sleeves, pulled the jacket over her shoulders, and then slid the two wrapped cookies into a pocket of the jacket.

"I would enjoy doing so," she replied. "It is not easy being a foreigner in a strange land. I would like to be able to drink tea and talk with a woman who knows about complications."

Chapter Thirteen — The Wicker Park Home

West Schiller Street is the southern border of Chicago's Wicker Park. The houses that line the south side of the street were built twenty years after the Great Chicago Fire, and their massive stone nature is a reflection of the lessons learned when the fire spread rapidly due to the city's overuse of wooden buildings. Visitors to the Wicker Park area are visually struck by the 19th century architectural designs of the homes — many of them erected with no more than five feet of separation between each home due to the urban demand for scarce land.

One of the most unique houses on Schiller Street is a substantial three-story structure that boasts five decorative Roman Tuscan columns, a towering turret, and large plate glass windows that allow the owners to look out onto the park. The house is the home of Diane and Robert Bradford and their seven-year-old boy, Robbie.

The Bradford home is surrounded with an array of beautiful plants, all of them landscaped in a manner that is pleasing to Diane's taste but is a slight irritation for Robert.

• • •

"Di," Robert said in an exasperated tone, "If you put those two hostas there, we will have absolutely no front lawn. I might as well keep the mower in the back yard forever."

Diane looked up from her gardening in an attempt to provide Robert with the prevailing amount of courtesy he should receive by virtue of being her spouse. She saw a look of discontent registering on his face as he looked around the small thirty by twenty foot space that comprised their front yard.

The yard was crowded. A six step, five-foot tall by four-foot wide concrete stairway led to the Bradford's front door. A four-foot wide brick path led from the stairway to the public sidewalk that extended east and west along the residential side of West Schiller Street. Black metal fencing ran parallel to the sidewalk and enclosed the yard. A seven-foot tall gate provided an entranceway through the fencing. Three metal bars fashioned into an arch curved over the gateway, and the sculptured face of a small child was welded onto the bars. The child's face looked down on anyone who entered the yard from the sidewalk.

Robert stood on the brick path, holding his briefcase in his left hand. He was dressed in casual brown slacks and a short-sleeved blue shirt. He had just returned from the university campus.

"It would be nice if there was enough space so that Robbie could play in his own front yard," Robert continued to complain.

Dressed in outdoor work clothing, Diane stood up and threw a belated greeting toward Robert.

"Welcome home to you," she said with a touch of sarcasm in her voice. "Haven't we had this conversation before?"

Diane pulled a gardening glove from her right hand, placed her hand on Robert's shoulder, and gave him an obligatory peck on the cheek.

"Robbie is very happy to play in the park, and I think of this space as my garden area," she said. "Bad day at work?"

Robert sighed and returned Diane's kiss with a peck that skimmed quickly off her cheek.

"My classes are fine," he replied. "It's Allen Hall," he grumbled. "I don't remember him publishing anything of worth recently. The man has some nerve to pressure me."

"Well, you're home now. Come inside. We'll have a glass of wine and talk."

Robert followed Diane up the six steps that led to their front door. They passed through the doorway and into a large sitting room that was tastefully decorated in a classical décor. A large Persian rug covered most of the old wooden floor. A scrolled iron wine rack with three glass shelves sat against the east wall. Five bottles of wine were stored in it.

"Sit down, Robert," Diane said. "I'll pour the wine. Red or white?"

"Red," Robert answered.

Robert sat and watched as Diane prepared two crystal glasses of wine, filling them three-quarters full from a bottle of Smoking Loon Pinot Noir. He looked around the room and another expression of discontent registered on his face.

Classical motif, he thought. No wonder I can't get inspired. The damn interior of this house is depressing. A little splash of color would do wonders. Her house, though...her house and her front yard.

"So, tell me about Dean Allen Hall," Diane said while handing Robert a wine glass with the initial 'A' elegantly engraved on the side. "Did you see him today?"

The initial on the glass stood for Artem Prutko, Diane's Ukrainian father. The house the Bradfords lived in on Schiller Street was the home in which Diane had grown up; it had been bequeathed to her after the death of her father two years ago.

"We had a small conversation," Robert answered with a frown. "He said to say hello to you."

"Allen may be an ass at times, but he is always polite," Diane said.

Diane moved away from Robert and sat down in an antique chair across from him, holding her glass and allowing the wine time to breath.

"Did Allen say anything about your bi-annual review?" she asked.

"He didn't have to," Robert answered, while taking time to sniff his wine. "Every day that goes by without me published accelerates the inevitability of that day. Damn! I teach. Isn't that enough? Ask any student on campus who are the top ten professors and my name will always be on that list."

"I agree," Diane responded as she sipped her wine. "But Robert, what's happened with you? Creativity was also a high mark for you."

Robert took a gulp of wine, purposefully moved his fingers up to the sides of the wine glass, and remained silent.

"Are you working on something?" Diane prodded.

"Yes. Yesssss," Robert replied. "I have some ideas and some sketches in my head. I'll come through."

Diane smiled, but doubted Robert's words. She looked at him sitting back in his chair. His head was bent back and rested against the top of the chair's backrest; his fingers played with the wine glass in an absent-minded fashion, and his eyes scanned the high ceiling of the room.

"Di," he said after finishing his wine with another gulp. "This room needs color. Maybe, a modern art deco motif would work in here...take away some of the dreariness...provide inspiration."

"Are you blaming your doldrums on the interior design of our house?" Diane asked.

"No," Robert sighed audibly. "You've done a great job with the house. I was just thinking out loud."

Diane watched as Robert left his chair and refilled his empty wine glass.

"I've maintained the elegance of this house in a manner that is a tribute to my father, my mother, and my grandfather." she replied.

Robert stood next to the wine rack. He swished down another half a glass of wine and then filled his glass again.

"Oh yes...Artem and Olena...they would be proud. I know that. If they had their wishes they would have been buried in the back yard. Only there isn't enough room back there to accommodate the enormous tombstones they had to have," Robert said.

Diane's facial expression turned sour. She stared at Robert, loathing the disrespect he had directed toward her parents.

"Did you stop and have a drink on your way home?" she asked.

"I had a beer with Michael."

"Michael and *a* beer," Diane said. "Michael hasn't had just *a* beer since he was twelve."

"We had a pitcher, okay? What's wrong with me having a pitcher of beer with Michael?"

Diane tried to compose her anger but lashed out at Robert instead.

"I like Michael. He's a little eccentric, but I like him. What I don't like is the comment you made about my parents," she said in a huff. "At least my parents wished me well in every endeavor I pursed, and they never planned my future for me."

Robert went back to his chair, sat down, and momentarily sulked over the one-upmanship of Diane's retort. Eventually, a look of contrition appeared on his face and his demeanor became boyish.

"I apologize," he said. "You're right. I was rude. I went to the hospital today."

"You saw Adela? How is she?"

"She's...Mum, and she's not well," Robert said.

Diane's anger turned to sympathy.

"Can she go home?"

"No, and I don't think she wants to. I think she is afraid she would die if she went home. Her parents died in that house. She's better off at the Medical Center."

"Has she heard from your father?"

"I don't have a father," Robert replied.

"Does he know how ill she is?"

Robert remained quiet, and Diane decided not to pursue the topic of his father.

"What did you and your mother talk about?"

"She asked me about her house in Hyde Park again," Robert replied. "She wants us to move there when she dies."

Now Diane remained quiet.

"I told her we will stay here," Robert said.

The housing issue was not a subject Diane wanted to broach.

"What else did your mother say?" she asked.

"She got a card from Allen. She was reading it when I got there."

"That was nice of Allen."

"It was typical Allen," Robert said. "He's prodding Mum to get her to prod me. Getting me to publish, that's what he's all about."

Robert's voice took on a dejected tone.

"Maybe, I've lost my creativity. Maybe, I just don't place as much importance on publishing as I should," he said. "Maybe, I never had the creativity needed for my position. I don't know."

"I know it's difficult, Robert. Your field is difficult. I'm sure Allen wants you to crank out a series of poems like you did before. It can't be easy to be expected to be creative."

"Believe me, it's not. I need some sense of inspiration, but right now I just can't come up with anything."

"Perhaps, you need to get away," Diane suggested. "Perhaps, travel."

For Robert the conversation had turned in a direction he did not want to go. For reasons yet unknown to him, he could not discuss his dilemma with his wife. He knew he had to ferret out his problems without confiding in Diane because, in the back of his mind, he wondered if she was part of the problem.

"Get away, huh? Maybe," he replied. "What's for supper?"

"Lamb and eggplant lasagna," Diane replied. "It'll be about forty-five minutes."

"Well...it's good one of us is still creative," Robert said laughing. "It sounds delicious. Right now, I'm going to go change and work out on the elliptical machine."

Robert walked across the room and kissed the top of Diane's head.

"See you at supper," he said as he walked out of the room and headed for the staircase.

Diane remained seated. She continued to sip her wine and think about Robert, wondering when things had changed between them.

Maybe, it is the house, she speculated. Perhaps, that is when things changed. Or maybe, it was the birth of Robbie. Right now, Robert is not the same man I married. I love him but somehow he is less...less than what I imagined he would be.

The thought of Robert being less was painful for Diane to contemplate.

Do I have a right to expect him to be something he's not ...something he doesn't want to be? Maybe, it's a phase he is going through...it could be just a phase for both of us, she thought.

She looked around the room, visually examining the décor that had been a part of her life since her childhood. She thought about her parents and their relationship with each other.

Strange, Diane thought. I've become my father in this house. I am the head of the house and the major breadwinner. When did all that happen?

Chapter Fourteen — Javier Morales and Elena Markova

A crowd of early lunch patrons began to file into the Piazza Navona Restaurant on West Division Street. The beautiful sunny day broadcast assurance that a large number of customers would be vying to be seated outside at one of the restaurant's fifteen wrought iron tables. Deep maroon colored umbrella tops loomed above each table. The maroon umbrellas matched the awnings that hung over the restaurant's large open windows, the colors creating a splash of brilliance to the otherwise mundane sidewalk. Large pots with lush greenery were strategically placed in the outside eating area, adding appeal for the hordes of pedestrians who were fleeing their work-a-day world in search of an acceptable place to take their break.

Elena Markova was filling in for an absent maitre 'd. She stood behind a four-foot high reception stand that was positioned on the restaurant's outside patio. Tall and willowy, Elena was dressed in black pants, a black waistcoat, a white blouse, and black heels. Her long dark hair swished around her slender neck as she handed out menus, marked seating assignments on a laminated table diagram, and took the names of the parties who waited to discover where they would be placed. She was professional in her manner and seemed unmoved by questions, greetings, or the frequent wisecracks that some of the restaurant patrons threw her way. Most often, a look of boredom or disdain dominated her facial expression. The coldness of her nature was accentuated by her heavy Russian accent.

Elena was in America on a work permit and she was unhappy with her current employment. All of her adult life, she had been a complainer and, even though the Chicago area offered her much better accommodations then she had ever had in her hometown of Vologda, she still found reasons to continue her objections concerning her lot in life. She had been working at the Piazza Navona Restaurant for six months and her three major complaints were the low minimum wage she was paid, the hours she had to work, and Javier Morales.

Javier Morales was West Division Street's Antonio Banderas, except Javier was younger, better looking, accessible, and an illegal immigrant. Javier had worked at the restaurant two months longer than Elena. Both of them were struggling with loneliness and with all of the difficulties that are inherent in being an immigrant.

Although she was seven years older than him, Javier took an immediate interest in the beautiful Russian woman. He worked with her, made small talk with her, and observed her. But he waited two weeks before he engaged her in any meaningful conversation.

• • •

"Lena, do you like poetry?" Javier had asked her one evening in January after they both finished their work shift.

Elena was seated at a bench outside of the restaurant, waiting for the CTA bus that would take her away from the drudgery of the restaurant. Chicago was bound up in a seasonal chill and Elena was wrapped in a winter coat.

"Some," she snapped in reply. "I enjoy Russian poetry. Do you read poems?"

Elena Markova was a woman who felt compelled to be demonstratively aloof, believing her coldness presented an aura of authority and control.

Javier sat down next to her, admiring Elena, and finding pleasure in letting his gaze roam freely over the sharp features of her face. He engaged her in conversation, but his focus settled on the glistening wisps of hair that fell softly over her ear and cascaded down her long neck.

"I listen." Javier said. "I write things".

Elena stared away from Javier, not wanting to make eye contact with him, but finding his interest in poetry and his desire to write intriguing.

"If you write, you are a poet," she said.

"No," Javier quickly responded. "I only write what I see here."

Javier Morales was a poor and humble worker. Although he had little formal education, he was moved to read and write by his sense of the injustices that existed in the world. He used poetic verse to explain the suffering and the beauty of his own world, capturing those contrasts in images formed through his own unique style of writing. Javier did not considered himself a poet, but he was wrong and, in time, the world would realize his genius. Once discovered, his poetry would be a bridge that spoke to human suffering, providing insight and relief to people from all walks of life.

"You write about your life as an immigrant? You write about how difficult it is?" Elena asked.

"Si," Javier replied.

"Then you are a poet," Elena concluded. "Suffering is the origin for all great Russian poetry."

Javier nodded in agreement.

"Many people suffer in the world and want escape from this suffering," he added. "Poetry does this for me."

"How do you suffer?" Elena asked, turning her face toward Javier and finding herself captivated by his dark, handsome features.

"Look around us," Javier replied pointing to the restaurant. "Is there pleasure in working here? Is there acceptance in America for the poor? Maybe, it is different for you… a pretty Caucasian woman, but for me…I am not a man here."

Elena could see a fiery spirit reflected in Javier's eyes. His words expressed deep frustration, yet the tone of his voice was defiant. She admired his willingness to be vulnerable in front of her, and she admired how his entire presence expressed courage in the face of such hopelessness. For the first time since she met him, she became aware of how physically powerful he was. His shoulders were broad, his arms were lean and muscular, and his chest expanded with rage as he talked about his new life in America.

Elena could feel the protective shield she had built around herself cracking as she listened to Javier talk. She felt her mood soften and her heart warm. Javier was a lonely man and she was a lonely woman.

Knowing it was a mistake, Elena invited Javier to her apartment for supper.

Chapter Fifteen — Javier Leaves Home

Javier Morales had been raised in the Mexican state of Guerrero. American awareness of Javier's home state would be tied to images of Acapulco and the luxurious Mexican Riviera. But Javier's life in Mexico was a reflection of the saying that Mexico is a country of great contrast in which the inequities are embarrassing; the embarrassment in Guerrero is that fifty-seven per cent of its population lives in poverty.

The Morales are mestizos, and their history of poverty is as old as European colonialism. Javier was born in a small mountainous village located between Acapulco and Iguala. Over two million people in Guerrero live outside of the resort areas in abject conditions. Javier lived in a small hut with four other siblings; their home had a dirt floor, no running water, and inadequate drainage. Javier's formal education was sporadic and poor in quality. He spent a good deal of his youth working in the cornfields with his father, who also engaged in wood working to help eek out an existence for his family. Javier's father was a skilled wood carver whose creations of Mexican peasants were coveted in the Iguala market place.

Even though he was extremely poor, Javier considered himself to be lucky. His parents were kind and loving, and he loved his two sisters and his two brothers. Javier was the oldest of the Morales children. He doted on his younger siblings and was particularly fond of his youngest brother, Roberto.

Although Javier's days and nights were filled with work and family, loneliness began to encroach upon his world when he turned fifteen. From then on, he was a man in search of something that could not be found in his mountain village. Javier's mother knew he was an extraordinary boy. When he was little, she read poetry to him, which created a yearning in Javier's heart. What Javier desired was the opportunity to write poetry and to be recognized for his creativity; what he needed was to be in an environment that provided him with books and time to write.

"Our Javier needs to leave this place," his mother said one day to her husband.

Her husband was seated on their rickety wooden front porch, slowly whittling his two hundredth plus Mexican peasant. He stopped carving and looked around the harsh landscape they called home, a landscape that had beat him and had prematurely withered him into an old man.

"Where would he go? We have always been here," he said. "And, who would help me with the crops?"

Javier's mother had expected opposition from her husband on her request, but she knew her husband to be a good man who had also seen something special in their oldest son.

"I will help you with the crops and we have four other children to help. You have a talent. You are an excellent wood carver. If you did not live here, you could make your living carving. Give your son a chance to make a living elsewhere."

"America?" the father guessed.

"America," the mother replied. "Javier is special. He deserves more than this."

From that day on, Javier's parents sacrificed beyond the subsistent lifestyle they had always known. Half of the tourist money they received for the woodcarvings was socked away in order to pay the costs for Javier to make his way to America. However, there was never any thought of having Javier immigrate through legal channels; there was no hope of that happening. Instead, the money would be used to pay for Javier's long journey from southern Mexico to El Guamuchil, where Javier would learn more about crossing the border.

Javier initially objected when his parents presented him with the idea of going to America. He wanted to go, but he did not want to leave.

"Javier," his mother said. "In America, you can get a job and send money back to us. We will use the money to help your brothers and your sisters. They will be able to go to school, and to have things we cannot afford."

Javier's heart sank when he listened to his mother's words. He would do anything for the benefit of his brothers and sisters, even leave them.

It was decided. Javier was approaching nineteen years of age when his parents began the process of sending him to America, an ordeal that would take almost a year to complete.

Chapter Sixteen — Javier's Journey

Javier's aunt and uncle lived in the small village of El Guamuchil, 900 miles north of Iguala. The inhabitants of El Guamuchil had become a part of the upward economic mobility that some Mexican citizens were experiencing due to tourism. Many of the people who lived in El Guamuchil worked in the hotel industries of La Cruz and Sayulita.

Javier made his way to El Guamuchil by bus, hitch hiking, walking, and depending upon the generous nature of Mexican peasants. He stayed in El Guamuchil for five months, working as a bus boy in order to continue his journey north. It was in El Guamchil that Javier first witnessed the injustice of the world. In El Guamuchil, Javier became aware of the uneven distribution of wealth that exists among people.

Javier's uncle introduced him to people who knew first hand about being illegal immigrants. Some of them had made the journey north more than once and had been turned back by the U.S. Border Patrol. Others had been successful in crossing over to the U.S., had worked in the U.S., been discovered as an illegal, and were sent back to Mexico. He listened to stories told by those who had gone to America and filed away in his mind the information he needed to make his journey successful.

Javier also directed his time in El Guamuchil toward his desire to become educated. While working in La Cruz, Javier was able to purchase a book of poetry. He had borrowed books before, but this book, *Liberty Under Oath* by Octavio Paz Lozano, was the first book he owned. The book became his most prized possession. He read the poems in the book over and over again and fell in love with the idea of liberty. In El Guamuchil, he came to believe that education and writing poetry would make him a free man.

Leaving El Guamuchil was very difficult for Javier. He had visited his aunt before when he was ten years old, stayed for one month, and then returned to his home in Iguala. But now Javier knew his leaving would take him further away from his family, and he knew the next leg of his journey would be filled with strangers and danger.

From El Guamuchil, Javier traveled north, heading for the border town of Ambos Nogales. Ambos Nogales is an international community made up of Heroica Nogales, Mexico and Nogales, Arizona. A highway running through the town marks the border between Mexico and the United States, and divides the city into north and south.

Annually, the U.S. Border Patrol apprehends 1,137,282 Mexicans who are trying to enter the United States illegally. Forty-three percent of those who are apprehended and turned back are caught along the Arizona-Mexico border.

Javier knew if he were going to cross successfully, he would have to avoid the populated area of Ambos Nogales and walk across the border, using the wastelands of the Sonora Desert as his entryway.

Javier was cautious about crossing the border. He had heard many stories about immigrants who were caught by the Border Patrol and sent back. He made up his mind he would not be caught. He decided to stay and work in Heroica Nogales for a month before attempting to make the crossing. He would wait, earn more money, and learn more about the dangers of the crossing before he headed north to the United States.

It was in Heroica Nogales that Javier met Jose Ortiz, a fellow immigrant who was also making plans to cross the border illegally. Jose was an impatient young man who believed nothing could stop him from going to America. He was fleet of foot, a braggart, and sure of himself.

"Come with me," he said when he first met Javier. "I know the desert and I am strong. I can cross the Sonora in two days."

"Jose," Javier replied. "We should take our time. We need to listen and learn. We need money and proper supplies. I do not want to get caught by the Border Patrol and sent back. When I leave, I am going as far north as I can and get lost in a big city where I cannot be found by the authorities."

Jose was impressed with Javier's plan. In reality, Jose was a frightened young man who hid his fears behind a show of false bravado.

"Amigo," Jose replied. "We will go together, si?"

Javier liked the idea of having a partner for his journey and he admired the brashness of Jose.

"We will travel together, Jose," he agreed. "We will go to Altar to find our way to America."

"Altar?" Jose replied. "Altar is south of here. Why not cross the border here? All we would have to do is walk across and not come back."

"There are too many guards here," Javier said. "Many Mexicans are caught and turned back here. We need to go to Altar and then to El Sasabe where there is room to evade the border guards. In Altar we can get the supplies we need for our journey."

• • •

When they had saved enough money, Javier and Jose took a bus to Altar. In Alter, they joined 1500 other Mexicans who were shopping for the supplies they needed to make the trip northward across the desert and into the United States.

"The Red Cross has a small hospital here," Javier told Jose. "We will go there first and get a check-up."

"What do they check us for?" Jose asked.

"They check to make sure we are able to withstand the walk through the desert. They will give us maps and anti-inflammation pills. They will talk to us about the conditions we can expect in the desert."

"I am not afraid of the desert," Jose declared.

"You should be," Javier replied. "We need to respect the power of the desert, Jose. We need to know what to expect there. We will go to the Super el Coyote store where we will buy other supplies that will protect us during our journey. Others may fail in their journey north, but we will not."

Chapter Seventeen — Javier and Jose Cross the Border

From Altar, Javier and Jose paid nine dollars each for a three-hour ride to the Mexican border town of Sasabe. In Sasabe they paid three dollars to spend the day sleeping in a crowded, dirty adobe home, waiting for evening to fall so they could join hundreds of others who would climb over a small fence, step onto American soil, and scurry into the desert to begin their trek northward. The darkness of the night would provide them with protection from the Border Patrol and from the 120-degree heat of the desert sun. They would walk for fourteen to sixteen hours at a time, hoping to get to the town of Three Points, Arizona on highway 86 in less than three days.

• • •

The desert crossing is cruel; hundreds of illegal immigrants lose their lives to the harsh conditions of the desert while attempting to evade border patrols, vigilante groups, and gangs that prey on their misfortunate. Javier and Jose approached the desert obstacle with eight other men who had joined together to increase their possibility of success. All of the men were young and inexperienced in illegal activities. They were ambitious men, afraid, and hoping for a better life for themselves and the families they were leaving behind. When they began their walk northward, each man carried two gallons of water, one in each hand, and they had a pack strapped on their backs, stuffed with supplies. It was not long before they ran into their first major obstacle: torrential rainfall that turned the desert ground into slippery mud, slowed their pace, disrupted their vision, and soaked their clothing.

"I did not expect this," Jose complained as he and Javier huddled near a large cactus.

"Open my back pack," Javier yelled loudly above the noise of the rainfall. "Pull my poncho from it."

The two men spread the poncho over their heads and squatted down, trying to protect themselves from the downpour. Rain and wind whipped around them, drenching them to the bone. When the rain stopped, the group moved on, shivering in the dark desert coldness. They walked until mid-morning and then stopped to build a refuge from the sun by stretching their ponchos between tall cactus plants. Clothes were stripped off and hung out to dry while the men slept on the stony desert ground that had been baked dry by the sun.

In the early evening when they awoke, Javier found his right hand swollen; a bite made by some desert creature caused his fingers to throb with pain. He studied his hand, took two anti-inflammatory pills, and pulled his clothing back on in preparation for their second walk north. He picked up one of the gallon jugs of water with his left hand, but found he was unable to hold onto the other jug with his injured right hand. Frustrated, he consolidated as much of the water as he could into one jug and left the other jug behind.

"Javier," Jose called out after two hours of walking. "Stop for a moment."

Javier stopped and waited for Jose.

"My boots are hurting my feet," Jose said.

Jose pulled off his left boot and sock and asked Javier to examine his foot.

"You have blisters, Jose. You should have bought your boots in Nogales and worn them for a week like I told you," Javier exclaimed in an exasperated tone. "The desert is no place for new boots."

Javier pulled a first aid kit from his pack and worked on soothing and covering Jose's blisters. He had Jose put fresh socks on his feet and they paused to rest for ten minutes, allowing the others to walk ahead of them.

"We will catch up," Javier yelled to the other men as he poured Jose a cup of water.

"I am sorry, mi amigo," Jose lamented. "You go ahead. I will catch up later."

"I am not leaving," Javier said. "We will cross this desert together, Jose."

• • •

As it turned out, Jose's misfortune saved him and Javier from being apprehended by the Border Patrol.

"Jose," Javier whispered, flapping his free hand in a downward motion and ducking down behind a small sand dune. "Get down, Jose."

Jose ducked down, loosened his pack from his back, and low crawled to Javier's position. Together they watched the Border Patrol giving water to their fellow migrants and writing down each of their names. The six other men were rounded up into a van and hauled away, where they would be placed in a detention area until they could be taken back to Mexico. Javier and Jose stayed hidden, frozen in place, waiting for the border guards to leave.

"We are alone now," Javier declared. "We will have to make it through the desert by ourselves. Do you think you can do it, Jose?"

"Si", Jose answered. "Things will get better for us."

But Jose's blisters became worse and the two men had to stop frequently. Javier never complained and always dressed Jose's foot with compassion and understanding.

"Our journey will take longer, but we will be okay," Javier always said.

"Mi amigo…I owe you my life," Jose declared.

It never rained again, but now their clothes were soaked from perspiration. Their legs, their backs, and their arms ached with pain. At the end of the third day of walking, they had run low on water and food supplies. They were in despair until Javier heard a welcoming sound.

"Do you hear that noise," Javier said to Jose.

"I hear it," Jose replied. "What is it?"

"It is flags flapping in the wind. The flags are meant for us to hear. Remember the Coyote we talked with in Sasabe? He said there are humanitarian groups who place water and maps near utility poles to help us, and they tie flags to the poles. I'm sure that is a flag flapping in the wind. Stay here, Jose, and I will look."

Jose allowed his weary body to fall back on the hard ground as Javier left to investigate the sound. He looked up into the star studded evening sky and prayed for their journey to end.

• • •

It took Javier and Jose four days to cross the Sonora Desert and reach the city of Three Points Arizona. From Three Points, they headed north.

"We will go to Chicago," Javier told Jose. "It is a large city with many immigrants. We can find work there and hide from the authorities."

Jose and Javier made the remainder of their northbound voyage by bus. In a week, they were both working as waiters at the Piazza Navona Restaurant in Wicker Park.

Chapter Eighteen — Javier and Elena

Supper at Elena's consisted of two bottles of wine and some take-home risotto that was left over from the restaurant. The two newly arrived immigrants sat on a nine by six foot oriental rug in the living room of Elena's second story flat, drinking glass after glass of red wine while Elena listened to Javier's fiery poetic discourse. Three lit candles provided the only light, filling the room with a romantic glow.

Elena quickly discovered that Javier's life mirrored hers. The common bonds the two shared as strangers in a new land were accentuated by similar experiences they had both endured in their native cultures. Immigrating had not created loneliness in Javier; instead, he had carried his unique brand of loneliness to America from Mexico, just as Elena had done on her journey from Vologda to Chicago. In America, away from family and friends, a new loneliness set in for both of them.

The red wine, Javier's passionate poetry, and his commanding presence raced through Elena's mind, completely whisking away her cold façade. His dark eyes darted around the living room as he spoke fervently of his life. Elena listened intently to him, hearing him tell his story in phrases that captured her own anguish. His eyes were mystical and spell binding. His words were a torrent of emotions, spilling over her and drawing her to him. She felt bound to sooth his troubled spirit, and she longed for release from the emptiness that gnawed at her own soul.

She moved closer to him, interrupting the tirade he was directing against restaurant managers, the INS, the Mexican government, and the aristocrats of the world. Elena ran her fingers through Javier's long black hair and pressed her lips to his ear.

"Javier," she whispered softly. "Stop, Javier. Stop talking. Look at me. Look into my eyes."

A look of need appeared on Javier's face. He stared directly at Elena, his gaze becoming fixed on her eyes. He felt his troubles melt away. Elena's eyes captivated him, drawing him away from his fiery poetic world and providing him with a sanctuary that was being created by her presence. The beauty he recognized in Elena on the first day he met her now engulfed him. The muse from his workplace, who had filled his nights with poetic inspiration and desire, was touching him and was within his grasp. His mind swirled. His body shuddered. His hand shook as he reached to touch her. He touched her face with trembling fingers, softly examining her beauty.

"Shhhh, Javier," Elena said quietly. "Shhhh."

He continued to shake with anticipation as he touched Elena's lips. She kissed his hand and he felt his heart beating rapidly when she bit him, nibbling tenderly on his fingers. He tried to speak. He tried to be poetic, but found himself lost in her presence.

"Elena," he whispered.

Elena pressed her fingers against his lips.

"Shhhh, Javier," she said again. "Bring your poetry to me. Share your passion for life with me."

Elena pushed Javier back against a small couch that occupied the west wall of her flat. She straddled his body with her long legs and pressed her lips to his. She felt his desire rising beneath her. His right hand cupped the back of her head and he pulled her mouth fully over his. Her body began to rise and fall, pounding down on him. Javier moved in sync with her. His large hands grabbed at her small waist and pulled her down onto him as he arched his back and pushed his body between her legs.

Filled with desire, Elena hurriedly unbuttoned Javier's long-sleeve, white shirt, pulled it from his body, and threw it on the couch. She watched as he slowly unbuttoned her blouse. He took pleasure in each opportunity to expose more of her flesh. She saw wonder in his eyes as his fingers unsnapped her bra and pulled it away, exposing her breasts. Javier's fingers touched lightly on her nipples and a look of deep concentration appeared on his face as he fondled her. She heard him swallow hard and she saw his chest heaving up and down while he cupped her warm breasts in his hands. His gaze roamed over her upper torso, and then became fixed on her eyes. Elena's long hair cascaded down over her bare shoulders, spilling onto her breasts. She leaned forward, allowing her hair to fall down onto his body while she tenderly kissed his forehead.

"Javier," she said quietly. "Come with me to my bedroom."

Elena moved to get up from Javier's body, but found herself being lifted off her feet. With grace and strength, Javier swept her up, his tall frame standing high above the couch while he cradled Elena in his arms. He paused to lift her higher, bringing her mouth to his and kissing her fully. Cuddling her against his broad chest, he walked quickly to Elena's bedroom and laid her down on the bed. He bent over her, pulling her slacks and panties off, and allowing them to tumble down onto the bedroom floor. He stood up again and looked at her. The beauty of her naked body was illuminated by a small amount of outdoor lighting that filtered in through the window blinds. Javier envied the light's ability to completely caress her.

Elena stared back at Javier. His shaggy black hair hung down, just touching the top of his broad shoulders. His chest and his stomach were tight. His hands moved to unbuckle his belt. He never stopped staring at her as he pulled at his belt and the snap on his pants. He seemed to be a man who was both content with where he was, but in a hurry to move forward. She knew he would have been happy to just look at her, and she knew he needed to make love to her.

Javier pulled off his pants and stood naked at the foot of Elena's bed. He stroked himself with his right hand as he continued to stare at her. Elena reached between her legs with her right hand. Her eyes closed, her shoulders pressed down on the mattress, and her back arched as she felt her wetness. She caressed herself momentarily, and then watched Javier climb slowly onto the bed, straddling her naked body with his. His face dropped down to hers and they devoured each other's lips. She felt the warmness of his naked flesh pressing against her and surrounding her. She wrapped her arms and her legs around him as he entered her, engulfing her in passionate pleasure.

Elena slept very little that night. Javier was continually at her side, pressing against her, touching her, looking at her, and kissing her. He constantly demanded more from her, always wanting her, and constantly willing to give himself to her.

• • •

In the early morning, Elena awoke and stared at her bedroom ceiling. She lifted her head up from the mattress and saw Javier next to her. Her bed had been destroyed, the covers and sheets were askew, and the pillows were lying on the floor. Javier was asleep.

She let her head fall down onto the mattress while her thoughts turned to her home in Vologda, Russia.

Chapter Nineteen — Vologda

When asked why she had left Russia to work in America, Elena Markova always gave an answer that focused upon financial need. But finance was not the primary reason for her leaving Vologda and coming to Chicago.

Vologda is 286 miles north and east of Moscow; it is the administrative center for the Russian Semi-Autonomous Province of Vologda. The city boasts a population of 300,000 people who are annually subjected to its northern climate of low temperatures and frequent precipitation, elements that constantly test the ability of its citizenry to remain cheerful.

In addition to the weather, other adverse factors also assault those who live in Vologda. Difficulties that abound in the Russian national condition are mirrored in Vologda; its annual gross domestic product is only one-fourth of America's; its citizens are underemployed; its economic future is tenuous, and the Russian life span is fifteen years less than the life span in the West. For Elena Markova, the forces that caused her to leave Russia were rooted in those statistics, but there were other reasons causing her to leave, too.

Elena lived in Vologda with her husband, Sasha, in a small apartment that was once part of the public housing system provided by the Soviet Union. When the Soviet Union fell, the new Russian government transferred ownership of the public housing quarters from the state to the individuals who inhabited them. But private ownership of the apartments is nothing to boast about; the rooms in the apartments are tiny; the plumbing is old and inadequate; the heating system operates sporadically, and there is no air conditioning.

While married to Sasha, Elena had traveled to America without her husband on six trips that dealt with educational exchanges. During her visits, she had come to prefer the American standard of living, and she enjoyed the times she had spent away from home. Each time Elena returned home from her travels, she found it more difficult to readjust to the lifestyle of Vologda.

By the time she decided to go and work in America, Elena had been married to her husband for five years. Sasha was a hardworking man and he was devoted to Elena. But, like all Russians, he was caught up in the aftermath of a system of "reforms" called perestroika and glasnost. The economic and political reforms that swept across Russia left Sasha and millions of other Russian males free to be improvised, while providing more opportunities for females to earn a minimum wage. The reforms resulted in further emasculation of the Russian male and additional nourishment for a rift that already existed between Elena and Sasha, a rift that was an outgrowth of Elena's natural state of being.

Elena worked in the Vologda Regional Library and, when she was twenty-four years old, she read *Civilization and Its Discontent* by Sigmund Freud. The book had been banned by the Soviet Union, but became available to the Russian people when the totalitarian government collapsed. Freud's explanation of the inherent conflict that exists between individual freedom and the need for civilization to restrain freedom was a poignant awakening for her.

In every culture, there are numbers of people who are discontented and restless because they do not fit into any of society's molds. Elena was just such a person; she existed outside of accepted behavioral patterns. Yet, anyone observing her would not be able to detect her discontent. She hid the restlessness that filled her being from family, friends, and associates. She had tried to conceal her dissatisfaction from her husband, but their closeness left her no place to hide. For Sasha, Elena's discontent was manifested in comments she made and in the two romantic affairs she had during their marriage.

• • •

"Sasha," Elena confessed one day, "I have been untrue to you. There is a man who has become my lover."

Sasha Markova was not surprised to hear his wife's declaration of guilt. In fact, he suspected that she was seeing another man. He responded to her confession with silence.

"Do you hate me, Sasha?" she asked.

"No," he replied.

"Do you want me to leave?"

"No," he replied again.

Elena's guilt was a heavy burden, and her admission to the affair caused her to become emotionally drained. She wanted Sasha to condemn her, to be upset with her, and to punish her for what she had done. His calm forgiving manner confused her.

"What do you want me to do?" she asked of him.

Sasha looked directly at Elena. She was seated at a small kitchen table in their second floor flat. Her head was cast down, her eyes were fixed on a lone blue plate that was positioned in the center of the table, and her hands were folded together on the tabletop. Sasha put his right hand under her chin, lifted her head up, and stared into her tearful eyes.

"I want you to always be with me. I want you to always come back to me," he said.

Sasha got up from the table, bent down and kissed the top of Elena's head. He walked to the living room and pulled at the foldout couch. The couch sprung to life and was transformed into a bed.

"Lena," he said. "Come and sleep with me."

Elena walked into the small living room and stood across from Sasha on the opposite side of the bed. Tears ran down her face as she watched him begin to undress. Without saying a word, she slowly pulled off her clothing and let each article of her dress fall down on the floor. Soon, both husband and wife stood exposed to the other's careful gaze.

Silently they crawled into bed. Sasha lay down on his back and Elena straddled his body, kneeling over him while he looked at her naked beauty. She reached down and positioned his hard desire between her legs. She felt his swollen lust press against her wetness; she pushed down with her hips and let his yearning fill her completely. Sasha's body arched, his hands grabbed onto Elena's waist. He pulled her down on him while he pushed and pushed against her. Elena rode her husband hard, staying with him and letting him know she loved him.

After making love, they fell asleep in each other's arms. But Elena and Sasha discovered that she was incapable of loving just one man. Society's obsession with monogamy was a mold in which Elena would never fit.

During the time she was with Sasha in Vologda, there was one other Russian lover. Elena did not acquire lovers out of a need for sex or adventure. She acquired them because she was adrift. She was always searching for an anchor, but was never able to moor herself in one place. Elena Markova would always be restless. She was the discontented element in Freud's equation, and it was her lot in life to never be happy. She came to accept that.

When she was twenty-six, Elena decided it would be better to be unhappy in America, and she became part of a national movement by Russian women who immigrate to the West.

Now, in her Chicago apartment at four in the morning, she found herself lying in bed with Javier Morales, an illegal Mexican immigrant. She sighed loudly, thinking of what she had allowed to happen.

This is not why I left Vologda. This is not what I came to America for, she decided.

Chapter Twenty — Javier Meets Robbie

After making love with Elena four times, Javier cuddled along side of her, holding her body close to him and finding pleasure in the smell of her presence. At three-thirty in the morning, Javier drifted off to sleep. When he awoke, he looked to his right at the digital clock that sat on a small table next to Elena's bed.

5:50 a.m.

He rolled back, kissed Elena's shoulder, and then kissed her face.

"Lena," he said. "I must go."

Elena rolled away from him onto her side. She curled up into a fetal position and pulled a sheet over her.

"Javier," she said in a quiet voice. "I need to sleep."

Elena's eyes closed and her breathing was shallow.

Javier kissed her shoulder one more time.

"Sleep my love," he whispered.

Javier climbed out of Elena's bed, dressed, and let himself out of her apartment. He decided to walk the twelve blocks home from Elena's flat on Erie Street.

It was very early, the air was cold, and a dark sky was just beginning to yield to sunlight. Damen Avenue was free of the large number of people who would soon be swarming over its sidewalks, making their way to work.

For the first time in many months Javier was happy. His body was filled with energy and a smile dominated his face as he walked briskly north toward his apartment. His mind raced with images of the night he had just spent with Elena. Each time they had finished making love, she would drift off to sleep and he would spend time touching her back, gently kissing her soft skin, and watching the light from the street glisten in her hair.

Javier Morales' being was filled with exuberance, but his happiness would be fleeting. At six in the morning, on a winter Chicago day, what Javier did not know was that Elena had merely spent all night having sex with him; for her, loving Javier was not an option. Unaware of the disparity in their feelings, Javier's day would be defined by happiness and hope.

• • •

Javier crossed Division Street, turned west on Crystal, and stood in front of the three-story building where he shared an apartment with Jose Ortiz. He paused and thought about walking five more blocks to Wicker Park, the energy in his body still in need of release. He knew Jose would be fast asleep. Running his fingers through his long hair and smiling broadly at the morning sun, he resolved to stay outside where the memories of holding Elena and the winter morning air made him feel alive and free.

In route to Wicker Park, Javier stopped at a 7-11 Store, bought a bottle of orange juice, and then entered the park on its western side. A covey of four homeless people sat at a stationary concrete picnic table. Each person was heavily dressed in layers of old clothing, and their scant worldly wealth was gathered around them in large black plastic bags. They watched Javier approach the territory they had laid claim to, and they whispered lowly amongst themselves about this early morning intruder.

"Hola," Javier said, smiling and tipping his bottle of juice in their direction. Javier was disappointed with the minimal response he received from the early morning picnic group, but he continued walking with long hurried strides. He headed toward the playground equipment at the northeastern section of the park. He planned to act out his exhilaration by soaring back and forth on the swings like a child.

The sun rose full in the morning sky and flooded the park with light as Javier opened the steel gate that granted him access to the playground. He was surprised to see two people inside the gated playground area, and the two people were surprised to see him.

• • •

Diane Bradford and her seven-year-old son, Robbie, had just arrived at the playground. Diane was fulfilling a promise she had made to her son. The Wicker Park playground was Robbie's backyard. Two weeks ago, he had expressed an aspiration to see the playground and to play on the equipment at sunrise.

"Mommy," Robbie had asked on one of their visits to the playground, "do people play here at night?"

Robbie was an inquisitive young boy, and Diane Bradford always encouraged his desire to discover. She had found the playground area to be a wonderful place for him to explore and to learn.

"No, Robbie," she had replied. "The playground area closes at sunset."

"Why?" Robbie asked.

"I think for safety reasons. Closing it protects all of the equipment and keeps little boys like my Robbie from getting hurt in the dark."

"Oh," Robbie replied in thoughtful observance of his mother's explanation.

"Why do you ask, Robbie?"

"Well…we always come to the park after you get home from work. I want to know what the park is like at another time. Maybe in the dark, we would be the only ones here."

"Would you like that, Robbie? Would you like to come here when we are the only ones?"

"Yes," Robbie replied. "But during the day so I don't get hurt."

"How about sunrise," Diane suggested. "Do you think you could wake up early and come to the park with me and see the sun rise over the playground? We would be the only ones here."

"Let's do that, mommy," Robbie said excitedly. "Will we do it tomorrow?"

Diane laughed, loving her little boy's enthusiasm.

"We will have to wait, Robbie," she said. "It will have to be a Saturday morning when your father is home from the university and you do not have to go to school. We will do it in two weeks," she promised. "But sunrise is very early, so you will have to go to bed earlier on that Friday night so I can wake you up. We will get here just as the sun rises. We can eat our breakfast here on one of the park's benches."

Robbie smiled at the thought of their up-coming adventure.

• • •

Now, the adventure was being realized, but Javier had become an intruder in Robbie's wish to have the playground all to himself. Robbie noticed Javier before his mother did. He tugged on his mother's winter coat.

"Mommy," he said, "There's a man here."

Diane Bradford turned and saw Javier standing twenty feet away. He had paused in his entrance to the playground, surprised by the presence of Diane and Robbie.

"Good morning," she said with a genuine smile of welcome. "We're here to greet the sun and play on the swings. Will you be joining us?"

Diane's words and demeanor exuded sincerity; her warmness reflected the state of Javier's romantic heart. He smiled broadly, walked closer to Diane, and bowed gracefully in front of her and Robbie.

"If I may," he said winking at Robbie.

He spoke slowly and with a thick accent, but his words bore the clarity and precision he had learned to express from working at the Piazza Navona.

"Your son?" he asked of Diane while continuing to smile at Robbie.

"Yes," Diane responded. "This is Robbie Bradford, my son and a second grade student at Sabin Elementary School."

Robbie lowered his gaze to the ground, embarrassed by the attention he was receiving.

"Robbie," Diane continued, "Shake hands with the gentleman."

Javier extended his long arm toward Robbie as the little boy raised his arm up to comply with his mother's instructions. Javier's large hand swallowed up Robbie's little hand. He pumped their arms up and down two times and gave a friendly greeting to the boy.

"Please to meet you, Robbie Bradford," he said. "I am Javier Morales. I have a little brother, Roberto Morales, in Mexico. He also is seven and he likes swings, too."

Robbie's eyes lit up, and he smiled at Javier. He knew immediately that Javier was a friend.

"Does he go to school?" Robbie asked.

"Yes," Javier replied. "Your school is nicer than his, but he goes. May I swing with you?"

Javier looked at Diane for approval of his idea and found her facial expression receptive.

"Do you want to swing with our new friend, Robbie?" she asked.

Robbie nodded, moved next to Javier, took his hand again, and led Javier to the swings.

Chapter Twenty-One — Javier and Diane Talk

D iane sat on a park bench bundled up in warm winter clothing, reading the book she had brought with her, and dutifully taking time to watch Robbie play with Javier. In her early morning encounter with Javier, she had detected a sensitivity that caused her to feel comfortable about letting him play with her son. She read sparingly, devoting most of her time to observing the glee on Robbie's face as Javier pushed him in the swings and chased him through the jungle gym. She watched Javier, too. His movements were filled with boundless energy as he laughed and pursued Robbie. He was a man connecting with a boy, becoming a boy himself, and sharing joy with Robbie. She was glad the world had been kind enough to introduce Javier to Robbie and to her.

"Javier. Robbie," Diane called out after the two had played for twenty minutes. "Come here."

Robbie stopped playing and looked reluctantly toward his mother, not wanting to stop playing the monster chase game he had invented.

"Robbie," Javier said. "Do what your mother tells you."

Javier took Robbie's hand in his and walked with him to the park bench. Diane reached down into a small bag that was sitting beside the bench and pulled out a thermos and two cups.

"Javier," she said as the two approached her. "I brought mango juice and muffins with me. Robbie wanted to play in the park and eat breakfast here. Will you join us, please?"

Diane saw Robbie's face light up at the idea of sharing breakfast with his new friend.

"It would not be right, Mrs. Bradford," Javier replied. "You have only two cups, and I'm a stranger."

Diane pointed to Robbie's saddened expression and watched Javier look at Robbie's face.

"I can use the top of the thermos for a third cup, and we don't think of you as a stranger," she said. "Do we Robbie?"

Robbie squeezed Javier's hand.

"Please, Javier," he said.

"Gracias," Javier said to Diane.

"Robbie," Diane asked. "Do you know what *gracias* means?"

"Thank you," Robbie answered.

"And what do you say?" Diane asked.

"Recepion," Robbie said. "Welcome."

Javier smiled at Robbie, bent down on one knee, and looked directly into Robbie's face.

"Gracias, mi pequeno hermano," he said. "Thank you, my little brother."

"Take the bag and the thermos to the park table," Diane said holding the bag and the thermos up toward them. Javier took the bag and Robbie held the thermos in both of his arms as the two new friends walked together toward a park table.

Diane remained seated and watched Robbie walk away, struggling with his awkward load. She saw Javier take the thermos from her son so that Robbie could run full steam toward the table. She watched the two new friends set the table with juice, cups, napkins, and muffins.

"Come on, Mom," Robbie called out when they had finished. "We fixed breakfast for you."

Diane quickly joined her "two boys" at the park table, sitting next to Robbie and across from Javier. For the first time, she noticed how handsome Javier was.

"Do you live near here?" Diane asked Javier.

"Not far. Crystal Street is where I live."

Diane pointed in the direction of her own home.

"Do you see the home with the red double doors," she said. "That is where Robbie and I live."

Javier looked at Robbie and smiled.

"This park belongs to you my little brother," he said. "It is your front yard."

Robbie laughed, tore a chuck of muffin off with his fingers, and plucked it in his mouth. Then he put both hands on top of his head and made a silly face.

"Robbie," Diane said. "Use your manners at the table."

Javier laughed at the face Robbie made and thought of his own family.

"My little brother, Roberto, makes the same face," he said.

"Are you here in America alone, Javier?" Diane asked.

A noticeable caution descended over Javier. He seemed uneasy.

Diane reached across the table and touched Javier's hand.

"Javier," she said. "It is none of my business where your family is or why you are here. We are just happy to meet you and to enjoy your company."

Javier looked into Diane's eyes. He could tell her words were honest and sincere, but he knew it would be wise to always remain anonymous in any relationship he had with an American. He smiled at Robbie.

"I am happy, too…happy to meet both of you," he said. "Thank you for sharing your breakfast and for playing with me. My little brother, I must go now."

"Will we see you again, Javier?" Diane asked.

"Do you have to go?" Robbie quietly asked.

Javier reached across the table and rubbed Robbie's head.

"I do have to go my little brother," he said. "Maybe, we will play again. Do you come here a lot?"

"We do," Diane answered. "And we always come to this place. I know Robbie would like to play with you again, wouldn't you Robbie?"

Robbie's head was hanging down from disappointment.

"Yes," he said in a squeaky sad voice.

Javier looked at his sad friend and felt remorseful. He turned his head and smiled at Diane.

"Mrs. Bradford," he said. "I do walk through the park on Monday and Thursday afternoons. I go to work late on those two days. I would like to see Robbie again."

Robbie lifted his face up and smiled at Javier. His eyes sparkled with happiness. Javier smiled back at Robbie.

"Would you like to play again?" Javier said.

"Si," Robbie said laughing.

But the biggest smile at the table was that of Diane Bradford. She knew Javier was a ray of sunshine in Robbie's life. It pleased her that Javier cared for her little boy and wanted to see Robbie again.

"What time would you be here," she asked.

"Ahhh…Si…we have to work this out. Not this early," he said laughing.

"We are here around 3:30 in the afternoon," Diane said. "Is that a good time for you?"

"Perfecto," Javier answered while flashing a smile. "That is the time I come here. I will be happy to see you both again, but I must leave now. Thank you for letting me share the park with you."

Chapter Twenty-Two — Javier and Jose

J t was a short walk from Wicker Park to Javier's flat. Javier arrived home at 8:00 a.m. The exuberant feeling he had experienced from being with Elena and Robbie had finally worn off, and he felt fatigued. He was surprised to find Jose awake and forging for breakfast in their kitchen.

"Como estas, mi amigo," Jose greeted as Javier attempted to quietly enter his upstairs flat.

"Estoy excelente," Javier replied.

"Debes estar cansado."

"Ingles, Jose. English. Acordamos hablar en ingles. Speak English," Javier said.

"Como se dice?"

"Debes estar cansado…you must be tired," Javier instructed. "Why do you say that to me?

Jose looked at Javier with a puzzled expression. "Como se dice?" he asked again.

"Por que dices eso," Javier repeated slowly gesturing with his hands. "Why do you say that? Repeat it in Ingles, Jose."

"Why do you say that?' Jose repeated smiling. "Huh…como se dice," he continued, pointing in the direction of Javier's bedroom. "Tu cama…no sleep?"

"Si," I have not slept in my bed," Javier replied looking away from Jose and smiling to himself. Javier pulled a chair out from under the small table that dominated the southwest corner of their kitchen, and dropped his body down hard onto the seat.

"Por favor. Coffee," he said.

"Ah, Ingles," Jose chided. "Coffee please…English, mi amigo."

Jose brought two cups of coffee to the table and sat with Javier.

"Late night?" he asked with a smirk on his face.

"Estoy muy bien," Javier shrugged and took a sip of coffee.

"Sure you are fine," Jose said. "I can see you are fine. Como se dice, donde has estado?"

"Where have you been," Javier said slowly. Donde has estado…where have you been. Say it in English, Jose."

"Where have you been, mi amigo," Jose said clicking his coffee cup against Javier's.

"Secreto," Javier replied in a tired voice.

"Secreto," Jose repeated. "No secrets here," he said slowly. "We are brothers."

"Jose, mi amigo," Javier began. "This must be secreto between you and me. Entiendes?"

"Si, I understand."

"I was with Elena,"

"Elena? La Rusa?"

"Si. I was with Elena," Javier confirmed.

"Como se dice...felicitaciones," Jose asked.

"Congratulations," Javier replied.

"Congratulations. Elena es muy bonita," Jose exclaimed. "Were you there all night?" Jose asked. "Debes estar muy cansano!" he said, leaning back in his chair and laughing.

"Amigo, we made love. Amor, Jose. Amor."

A sober look appeared on Jose's face. He could tell his friend was serious.

"Amor, Javier? Felicitaciones, mi amigo," Jose said. "Como se dice...estoy feliz para ti?"

"Estoy feliz para ti...I am happy for you." Javier translated. "Gracias mi amigo."

"Javier," Jose asked, "You sure...amor? Elena...mujer fria...como se dice?

"Si. Mujer fria," Javier repeated. "Elena is a cold woman...at work...mujer fria. But she is lonely and very warm at home, Jose. Caliente...warm."

"Caliente all night?" Jose asked with a smirk.

"Warm all night," Javier said with a distant look on his face. "Warm all night."

"Eres un hombre afortunado, mi amigo," Jose replied. "Afortunado."

A contemplative look appeared on the faces of both men. Jose envied Javier's good fortune and longed for such fortune for himself. Javier's mind spun back to the night before, remembering Elena's embraces and reveling in thoughts of her softness and the smell of her hair.

"Afortunado," he said softly.

Javier's fingers slipped off of his coffee cup, his eyes closed, and his head bobbed downward.

Jose smiled again as he watched his friend doze off in the kitchen chair. He reached forward and nudged his sleepy friend.

"Javier, mi amigo," Jose said. "You need sleep."

Javier woke and looked at Jose with heavy eyelids.

"Jose. Elena and me...secreto," Javier reminded.

Javier rose up from his chair and walked sluggishly toward his bedroom. He paused at the bedroom door and turned to face Jose again.

"Secreto, Jose. Secreto." He repeated.

"Secreto, Javier," Jose assured him.

Chapter Twenty-Three — Elena's Promotion

At the Piazza Navona Restaurant, individuals more prominent than Javier or Jose also admired Elena Markova's beauty. The restaurant manager, Jimmy Conti, was known for hiring pretty women, and he considered Elena to be one of his best employment choices. Jimmy was flirtatious with all of the women he hired, but ineffectual in completing the numerous passes he made. Although the women employees universally regarded Jimmy as an ass, he never gave up in his attempts at conquest. In his effort to gain Elena's favor, he resorted to job promotion; Elena had only worked at the restaurant for three months when she was promoted to maitre d.

"Babe," Jimmy called out to Elena one day.

Elena was standing next to the restaurant's bar, sipping on tea, and talking with the bartender, Patrick. Jimmy moved his hand toward Elena and rested it on her hip. Elena scowled in disgust at his all too familiar need to touch her. She wanted to move away from him, but as usual, Jimmy had chosen his approach well; he had cornered her into a place from which there was no way to escape his adolescent behavior.

"I think your talents are being wasted on waiting tables," Jimmy said as his hand rubbed against Elena's backside. "I'm thinking about putting you out where all the customers can appreciate your beauty. What'd you think of that?"

Elena squirmed away from Jimmy's touch, only to have him move closer to her. She pushed a bar stool away from the bar, and maneuvered behind it, using the stool as a protective buffer zone.

"What job?" she asked.

"Maitre 'd," Jimmy responded. "You'll be out there greeting all of the customers. A classy woman like you should be out front. This is a promotion, Babe. It's me promoting you to a better job…more money, too. You want to make more money, don't you?"

"Yes, thank you," Elena replied."

"Hey, you can always show me your appreciation later," Jimmy said smiling.

Patrick extended his hand toward Elena, purposefully butting in to assist her.

"Congratulations, Elena," he said. "You should go and tell your co-workers the good news."

Elena used the opportunity to flee from Jimmy, who vigilantly watched her rapid departure.

"She's a good looking woman," Jimmy commented to Patrick. "Wonder if she puts out? You heard anything, Pat?"

"I don't spend my time gossiping," Pat replied. "Elena's a hard worker. I know that."

"Yeah sure," Jimmy said. "She seems to keep to herself, but I've seen her talking with Javier. Can't be anything there, though. Javier's good looking but he's just another poor immigrant."

"Javier is a good worker, too," Pat commented.

"Yeah, he's okay. The strong, silent type…kinda moody."

"Javier is sensitive. He's a good man. He writes poetry."

"Javier? A poet?" Jimmy said. "Maybe, that's what she sees in him."

"Who?"

"Elena," Jimmy replied. "I told you, I've seen them talking a couple of times."

Pat knew Jimmy was right; he had seen Elena and Javier talking, too. But no one knew how upset Elena had become over the time the two were sharing as lovers. Their relationship was a whirlwind affair that caught Javier up in an emotional and destructive swirl. Initially, Elena thought about ending their relationship, but was drawn to Javier by the sexual energy and the exhaustive pleasure that came with the times they spent in bed. She was alone in America and she had found Javier to always be a gentleman. She viewed his company as exciting, but she did not want to be seen with him in public. She avoided talking to him at work. The time they did spend together was always at Elena's flat, where they would drink wine and Elena would listen to Javier's poetry and to his observations concerning the world. Sometimes they would talk about their past lives.

• • •

"Lena," Javier said one evening. "Will Sasha ever come to America?"

"Nyet," Lena replied. "We have an understanding. Sasha will not leave Russia and I will not go back."

Javier lay stretched out on Elena's sofa with his head resting in her lap. Elena's fingers played with his thick black hair and massaged his scalp. Javier was dressed only in black trousers. They had consumed a bottle of wine and were enjoying their second bottle.

"What about your marriage?" Javier asked.

Elena sighed noticeably. She did not want to talk about Sasha; yet, she wanted Javier to know she would always be attached to her husband.

"Sasha and me…we have always had an understanding. Sasha loves me, but I do not love him in that way. Once I did…now I do not."

"Will you leave Sasha?"

"I belong to Sasha," Elena answered. "I will always belong to Sasha."

Elena's fingers moved down to Javier's broad chest. She caressed him and watched his eyes close as her fingers moved down his body.

"Elena, I don't understand," Javier sighed.

"We don't need words," Elena replied, as her fingers slipped into Javier's trousers.

• • •

Javier and Elena were of a different mindset and Javier would never understand Elena. Early in her life, Elena's experiences had moved her toward the need to be in control in bed. For her, sex was to be used to obtain pleasure, while managing the actions of her partner. She allowed Javier to have sex with her, but she did not want to share affection with him.

Elena's need to be in control and her clinical approach to sex were unrealized by Javier. For him, the times he spent with Elena in her flat were extraordinary. He reveled in Elena's beauty and her appreciation of his poems. Time was his enemy while he visited her; it ticked away, rapidly moving toward the moment when he would have to leave. He used the time he spent with her to look into her eyes, to touch her arms, to smell her hair, to kiss the back of her neck, and to put his arms around her body. He used the time to make love to her, and the time he spent with her caused him to fall in love with Elena.

Chapter Twenty-Four — Wachtel Helps Robert

"Hello, Bob. This is Robert Bradford," the professor said into his cell phone. "I'm calling to confirm your help this afternoon. Are we still on?"

"Yep. No problem," Bob replied. "I'll pick you up at 4:30 on South University Avenue."

"That's great. See you then," Robert said. "Thanks again for doing this."

Robert Bradford had put off checking the pilot light on his home furnace for a month. Chicago Utilities Company turned off the gas to the Bradford home one month ago in order to install a new meter. The Bradford's furnace was hidden behind a removable four by eight foot sheet of decorative paneling in the basement of their home. Removing the paneling required more effort than the utility company worker was willing to commit to, so the worker left a note stating that if the pilot light was electric, it would turn on automatically but, if the pilot light was not electric, the Bradfords should notify the company or get some else to light the pilot by hand.

Robert Bradford's dilemma was that he could not remember if the pilot light was electric or had to be lit by hand. When he talked about the situation with Wachtel, Bob had volunteered to examine the Bradford's furnace. It was agreed that Bob and Robert would ride out to the professor's Wicker Park residence together in Bob's pickup truck, and Robert would leave his car parked overnight on campus. Robert would use the 'L' to return to the campus on the following morning.

At 4:30, Robert saw Bob's truck pull off of 58th Street and head up University Avenue. He waved at the truck, Bob pulled over to the curb, and Robert got in the vehicle.

"Hey professor," Bob called out as Robert settled into the front passenger seat and set his briefcase down on the floor between his legs.

"Hello, Bob. I really appreciate this. You know I want to take you out for supper tonight as pay back for this favor."

"Well you're in luck because I'm a cheap date," Bob replied while pulling out onto the street.

"There are a lot of great places to eat in Wicker Park," Robert commented. "Just let me know what you want to eat."

Robert looked out the open window of the truck's passenger door. He watched the Calvert House and the Quadrangle Club slip by as Bob's truck picked up speed, heading north away from the campus toward 55th Street.

"There's a deli in Wicker Park that I always go to when I'm in the neighborhood," Bob said. "Have you ever eaten at Lucia's Deli on North Avenue?"

"I have. It's only a few blocks from our house...the deli's part of Lucia's Ristorante, right?"

"That's it," Bob said. "I like their pizza. A pizza and a couple of beers...I'm cheap."

As the two men talked, Robert realized that he had not ridden in a pickup truck in over twenty-five years. For a brief moment he imagined Bob and he were workingmen on their way to a job; somehow that thought and sitting in the cab of Bob's pickup gave him a sense of comfort.

"You know what, Bob? I don't know much about you," he said. "We play racquetball and we've had a couple of beers together, but I don't even know where you live. Do you live near the campus?"

"Nope. I live west of the city. I bought a small house there and renovated it. I'm what you would call utilitarian. I don't own much and I don't want much. I'm a simple man, professor."

"You're not married. Are you a happy man?"

"Happy? Yes. I'd say I'm happy. I like my job. I like running the campus from down under, so to speak. I like fixing things and making them run right. And, I like being in the shadows, away from prying eyes and bosses."

"I admire you," Robert said chuckling.

"Little tired of intellectualville?" Bob asked.

"Maybe. I'm not sure. I know I like the concept of working with things that are concrete...making things run, as you said. There must be a lot of satisfaction in that. My grandfather was a carpenter. I used to help him around his shop when I was a boy. I loved working with him...but all of that slipped away years ago."

"You took a different path, huh?"

"Let's just say the matriarchal side of my family won out in that argument, and I was encouraged to be a college professor. Although I want you to know, I can handle taking the wall off for this project...that's no problem. It's turning on the gas to the furnace and the pilot light that concerns me. I don't like messing around with gas. And it will be nice to have two people handling that four by eight paneling...it's awkward to do it just by myself."

"Well, if it means anything, I admire your intelligence," Bob said. "Sometimes I think I would like to be in one of those ivory towers, looking out over the campus and teaching."

"I suspect everyone looks for greener pastures."

"Not everyone," Bob said. "I don't mean to be rude, but some of your esteemed colleagues think they have a monopoly on green. Some of them have some real big heads."

Robert laughed in agreement.

"You're right there. Hubris is alive and well among many of the teaching staff," he said.

"Hubris…that's Greek for a big head, right?"

"Right," Robert confirmed.

● ● ●

The drive to Wicker Park took forty minutes and, once they arrived, Robert directed Bob to a parking place in front of his home.

"I'm impressed," Bob said as he looked at the Bradford home. "I've seen these old homes, but I've never been in one. Yours is beautiful."

"Technically, it's not mine," Robert said. "The house was owned by my in-laws and left to my wife when they passed away. It's the reason we live in Wicker Park rather than Hyde Park."

"Well it's too splendid for my taste, but it is beautiful," Bob repeated.

"Let's go on in. I'll show you around the house. Diane has it decorated in a classical Ukrainian motif. It's not my preferred taste, but her parents were Ukrainian. I'm afraid my wife and son aren't at home. I would like my wife to meet you, but she and Robbie are at a school function right now, and then they are going over to a friend's house."

The two men entered the metal arched gateway, made their way up the steps to the Bradford's front door, and entered the house.

"Wow!" Bob exclaimed when he walked into the large downstairs living room area. "It is classical, that's for sure."

Looking around the living room made Robert glad he had recently purchased a condo near the university campus. Not only was the condo convenient for those times when he had to stay late on campus, but the condo was *his*. He liked being able to decorate it and to think of it as his own. He did not like the way their home was decorated. He wondered what a man like Bob thought of the way Diane had covered every room in an old world classical pattern.

"Does your 'wow' mean you like the way the house is decorated," he asked of Bob.

"Professor…it's not for me to like or dislike. It's a private matter between you and your wife. Like I told you, I'm utilitarian."

Bob turned and looked at Robert.

"But…I'm guessing you are not a big fan of classical Ukrainian," Bob said smiling.

Robert lightly patted Bob on his back.

"Good guess," Robert replied. "The motif of this house is another victory for the matriarchal side of the family. Come on, let me show you around."

The two men took a brief tour of the downstairs. Each room they entered was filled with old world Ukrainian treasures. Robert pointed out the uniqueness of rugs, lamps, bowls, tables, and chairs. Bob politely listened, but looked on with limited interest at the decorations. Instead, he seemed more interested in the high ceilings, the wood floors, and the wide panel moldings.

Robert could tell the tour was being wasted on Bob, and once again, he found another reason to admire his racquetball partner.

"I have an idea," Robert said. "Let's cut the tour short, head down to the basement, and take a look at that furnace…and the foundation of this huge home."

Bob smiled and laughed lightly.

"Am I that obvious?" he asked.

"Well, I know a little bit of Ukrainian décor can go a long way for some," Robert said. "The door to the basement is in the kitchen. Follow me."

• • •

It took thirty minutes for Robert and Bob to complete their work in the basement. Bob took another fifteen minutes to look at the foundation and admire the wide wooden support beams.

"They don't build them like this anymore," he said.

"It's a sturdy old house," Robert said. "But it cost a lot to have any maintenance done on it. Without Diane's inheritance, we couldn't afford to live here. I certainly would have never purchased a house like this…the heating and cooling bills are tremendous."

"You ever think of moving?"

"I do, but not my wife. She loves this house."

Robert stood with his hands on his hips. He slowly turned his head from left to right, his eyes sweeping across the large basement area.

"Diane loves this house. I tolerate it," he said with a sigh.

"Well, it is a beautiful house," Bob commented.

"Yeah, it is," Robert replied. "Let's go eat some pizza?"

Chapter Twenty-Five — A Staff Meeting

T here are forty-eight professors and associate professors that teach in the Department of English Language and Literature at the University of Chicago. Dean Allen Hall chairs the department and requires the entire staff to attend two annual meetings. The two meetings are held in the Quadrangle Administration Building in a small auditorium normally used for public presentations. The room provides seating for one hundred people and is equipped with a small-elevated stage.

The spring staff meeting is dedicated to the accomplishments of the department, to an open discussion directed at analyzing the department's curriculum, and to a presentation concerning future goals of the department. Robert Bradford always considered the spring meeting to be an exercise in administrative bullshit; he was never alone in that summation.

"Robert," Michael Sheridan said, giving a slight knowing nod in Professor Bradford's direction as the two men entered the auditorium and headed down the east aisle in search of seating.

"Michael," Robert replied. "Are we prepared for this?"

"I always look forward to our spring meeting," Michael said sarcastically. "I don't know how I would get through the year if I were not presented with the opportunity to have our illustrious dean rehash the departmental accomplishments."

The two men moved to take seats center left of the stage. They chose seating that would allow them to be as far away from the stage as possible, but would still be within an acceptable range so as not to be seen as distancing themselves from the up-coming activities.

"Don't forget," Robert said, "we'll be doing curriculum review, too."

"Christ," Michael groaned. "One thing about life, Robert…there is no limit to, and no escaping from…bullshit."

Robert sat down next to Michael and looked around the auditorium, watching it fill up with his colleagues.

"Right," he replied in agreement, "and this auditorium is about to swim in it."

Robert saw Dean Allen Hall enter onto the stage accompanied by a group of departmental advisors.

"Enter the purveyors of bullshit," he added as he nudged Michael's arm with his elbow.

"God help us," Michael moaned.

The meeting would last two hours, one hour beyond human endurance and need. Robert and Michael sat silently through the ordeal, knowing that any comment they might make would only prolong their torment.

Dean Hall's presentation centered upon the need to publish. He made several tributes to those in the audience who had recently issued publications of merit. The recipients of the tributes beamed with gratitude as they acknowledged their own scholarly achievements by reciting passages from their works.

"Scholarly masturbation," Michael commented quietly while one of their colleagues lectured the audience from the stage on his findings. "Hopefully, he will ejaculate soon and we can move on."

Robert sat up in his seat, placed his hand over his mouth, and rubbed his chin, imitating a gesture that seemed to suggest interest in the topic. In reality, he was only trying to keep from laughing out loud.

The most annoying part of the meeting was devoted to a discussion concerning future goals. Both Robert and Michael were in agreement that over eighty percent of the faculty was made up of hard working and academically productive professors. But "others" would dominate this part of the meeting, and they would be verbose in expressing their opinions.

"In order to improve our adjunct recruitment program, I am proposing that we include a mini-teaching experience, a mission statement writing project, and a sample essay grading assignment for each applicant," Hall announced.

"Perhaps we could form a committee to interview all of the applicants and to observe the mini-teaching session," one of the professors said.

Michael Sheridan squirmed in his seat as the meeting proceeded. Sheridan taught poetry at the university. He was Irish, an inspired poet, and a drunk.

"I really need a drink," he said to Robert. "Or, just shoot me now."

"Hold on big guy," Robert advised. "The worst is yet to come. You should've had that drink before you came here."

"I did," Michael said. "But the numbing effect is wearing off. It's getting so I can actually hear these people talking."

"So are you going to volunteer for the committee?" Robert asked smiling.

"Fuck the committee," Michael replied. "I really need a drink. Do you think any one would notice if I slipped out of here and never came back?"

"Wait fifteen minutes and I'll go with you," Robert replied. "Better yet, wait ten minutes, I'll leave and then have you paged."

"Damn you're good," Michael said. "It's a deal."

The meeting droned on. With their plan in place, Michael and Robert found the proceedings to be less painful. Robert slipped out of the auditorium without notice. He immediately went to a reception station in the front of the building and asked a student runner to fetch Michael. It was not long before Michael came walking toward Robert with a big grin on his face.

"I think I owe you," he said. "I'll buy the first and second rounds. Where do you want to go?"

"Let's head over to Woodlawn and go to Hunters," Robert suggested. "I'm a little hungry. Hunters has great hamburgers and students don't normally hang out there."

"That's fine," Michael replied. "Hunters it is."

"Have you ever been there?" Robert asked.

"Do they serve alcohol?"

"Of course, it's a bar," Robert said.

"Then I've probably been there."

The two men headed east on 58th Street, cutting across the quad and rapidly putting distance between themselves and the Administration Building.

"Have you ever thought about giving up drinking, Michael? Maybe, you drink too much," Robert said as they turned north on Woodlawn Avenue.

"Have you ever thought about giving up on screwing?" Michael countered.

"No," Robert replied.

"Well, writing poetry, drinking and screwing are the three things that I do best, and I have never thought about quitting any of them. What about you?"

"Right now I am batting two out of three," Robert replied. "And I am not so sure that everyone would agree with that."

"We'll talk," Michael said while opening the door to Hunters and letting his friend pass into the establishment.

Chapter Twenty-Six — Tavern Talk

"Hey Michael," the bartender called out as the two men entered Hunters. "Hi, Dave," Michael answered. "Good to see you. Could you get a waitress to bring us two hamburgers, some fries, and a pitcher of Millers? Everything on the burgers. We'll be over in the corner stall."

"Sure thing, Mike," Dave replied. "We'll get the beer over right away and I'll put the burgers on the grill."

"Thanks, Dave."

Robert smiled at Michael as the two men slid into their respective seats of a corner booth.

"I should have known," Robert said, shaking his head back and forth. "I should have known."

"Man does not live by academics alone, Robert."

A good looking twenty-something waitress brought Michael and Robert a pitcher of beer and two glasses. She was wearing jeans and a tight knit blouse. Her hair flowed over her shoulders and her face sparkled with a warm greeting.

"Hi Mike," she said smiling. "I'll bring you a bottle of ketchup with your fries."

"Thanks, Sherri," Michael said.

Robert shook his head again.

"Excuse me for thinking that I may have been in a bar in which the employees don't know you," he said.

Michael watched the waitress walk away and then poured beer from the pitcher into the two glasses. He looked at Robert, winked, and smiled.

"More to life than academics," he repeated.

Holding his glass up, Michael gestured to Robert letting him know that he was about to make a toast.

"Here's to the two smartest professors in the university's literature department," he toasted. "That meeting is probably still going on, but we had the good sense to tunnel out and escape."

"And here's to the reason I am here…Dean Allen Hall," Robert added. "If it were not for him, I might have stayed."

The two men clicked their glasses together and each man downed his entire glass of beer in one fell swoop of bravado. Robert reached for the pitcher and filled the glasses up again. He took a small sip of beer from his second glass, set the glass down, and looked at Michael.

"Fuck," he said quietly.

"Bad times, Robert?" Michael asked.

"Bad times," Robert replied.

"Want to talk about it? Or shall we just get drunk?"

"Maybe a little of both," Robert suggested.

"How's your writing coming?"

"Well, that's going right to the point," Robert sighed. "And, further to the point, my writing is not going at all. I'm in a slump, or maybe I just don't care anymore. I don't know."

The waitress brought two plastic baskets to the table and placed them in front of the men. Each basket contained a large hamburger wrapped in a sesame-seed bun and adorned with lettuce, tomato, pickle, cheese, and mustard. A greasy order of French fries pushed up against the hamburgers, filling up half of the baskets. While the men checked out their meal, the waitress pulled a bottle of ketchup out of a pocket in the small apron she was wearing and set the bottle down in the middle of the table. She rested her right hand on Michael's shoulder and pointed to the beer pitcher. The pitcher was now one-quarter full of beer.

"Want another pitcher?" she asked as her fingers massaged Michael's shoulder.

"That would be great, Sherri," Michael responded.

The waitress turned and headed off to fetch another pitcher. Robert watched her walk toward the bar. His eyes meandered up and down the backside of her body, coming to rest on her slender waist and her firm buttocks. Her body was proportional and Robert found it enjoyable to contemplate the possibilities of engaging in pleasure with her. Soon, he turned his attention back to Michael.

"Any history there?" he asked.

Michael took another sip of his beer.

"More like a current affair," he answered. "Sherri is a beautiful woman. We are enjoying each other's company."

"Is she a student?"

"She takes some courses part-time," Michael answered. "Business courses. I never see her on campus. We met here. She keeps me from being bored." Michael turned his head, taking a quick look at Sherri. "I really don't know what I do for her...I think she feels safe with me."

"Safe?"

"Yeah...as opposed to having to deal with those dumb-ass young men who only appreciate themselves."

Robert sat quietly reflecting on Michael's relationship with Sherri and watching her carrying another pitcher of beer to their table. Michael's comment about boredom resounded in Robert's head as he watched her approach.

"There you are, Babe," she said as she sat the pitcher down. "You let me know if you need anything else."

It was 11:30 and the beginnings of a lunch crowd began to enter the bar. Sherri turned away from the two men and walked over to greet the new customers.

"Maybe, I am bored," Robert said out loud, not meaning for the words to be heard.

"Maybe," Michael answered while spraying ketchup onto his fries. "Trouble at home, too?"

"I don't know," Robert said. "Well…yes I do. Trouble writing. Trouble at home. Fucking trouble. I wonder what the fuck happened to our lives, Michael?"

Michael took a huge bite of his hamburger and looked at Robert with a quizzical expression on his face while chewing away at the food in his mouth. He swallowed the tasty chunk of beef and washed it down with a gulp of beer.

"What do you mean?" he asked.

"Hey…we were both wonder boys at this institution. We both graduated from their in-house lab schools and we both got our doctorates here. We were supposed to be models of academia. Instead we're skipping out of meetings to drink beer and eat hamburgers."

"Wonder boys, huh," Michael replied. "Well, that was our parents' expectation…your mother's expectation…my father's dream."

"My mother," Robert said quietly, staring reflectively at his beer glass. "I wonder what Adela Bradford thinks of my inability to write? I know it would break her heart if the university found me less than stellar."

"Does she know?" Michael asked.

"I don't know. I know our dean sent her a get-well card with some reference to his looking forward to reading my publications. Maybe, I'm paranoid, but I think that gesture had nothing to do with her getting well and everything to do with nudging me forward. Dean, mother, wife…it's a lot of pressure."

"Whoa, Robert," Michael replied. "You've got this all wrong. You're still letting other people define success for you. If attending that bullshit meeting and being interested in Dean Hall's observations are success, then count me out. I'm tired of allowing other people to define my life for me. Christ, all Hall is interested in is his own promotion. If he isn't kissing the president's ass, he's kissing the ass of one of the trustees…the UC family…that's all he every talks about. UC isn't family for him; it's a stepladder he is using to climb to what he perceives to be the top. And, the only reason he wants to be at the top is because his ego is so big there's no room for him down here with us peons…all he will do at the top is piss on us. As for your mother, ask yourself this, when do you ever get to be in charge of your own life?"

A look of exasperation appeared on Robert's face. He picked up his hamburger and took an unenthusiastic bite, chewing slowly and thinking about what Michael had just said.

"Look, Robert," Michael said. "You enjoy teaching, right? And, I know the students enjoy you. You're a great teacher. What is so awful about that?"

"Retention and promotion. Publish or perish," Robert said quietly. "You know the game. We have to fill our website up with accomplishments. By the way, your staff website sucks."

"Fuck a website," Michael said. "Those fucking websites are all self-aggrandizements. God I hate them…especially the ones filled with personal philosophies and fucking mundane observations that are suppose to pass for deep insights. You know what those websites are like? They're like those Christmas cards people send out listing every fucking thing they did all year long."

Robert agreed with Michael about the websites, but did not want to pursue the topic any further, preferring instead to center on his current troubles.

"But publication… that's what the university wants. And, it is for sure what Dean Hall wants."

Michael reached for a French fry, bit it in half, and then swirled the remaining half into the puddle of ketchup that rested at the bottom of his plastic basket.

"Hall's putting pressure on you to produce, huh?"

"Yeah. And I'm fending him off with lies about what I have in the works," Robert said. "The truth is, I've got bubkes in the works. I sit and try to write, but…nothing…just doodles and start-ups that go nowhere."

Michael sat up, breaking away from interest in food and leaning against the back of the booth. He took another sip of beer and looked directly at Robert.

"You know what your problem is, Robert?" he asked.

"Tell me oh wise sage," Robert said sarcastically. But then his voice became serious. "Actually, I would love to hear your take on it."

Robert sighed, and then frowned. A look of contrition appeared on his face.

"I mean that Michael," he said. "I want to know what you think."

Undeterred by the initial sarcasm, Michael placed his elbows on the table and folded his hands together.

"This is it," Michael said. "You've discovered that much of the world is bullshit and is often run by jerks. My guess is that seventy percent of the people in leadership roles are idiots. They pursue those roles because they like being in charge, not because they want to solve problems or help people…they never really do solve problems…they just reconfigure the problems so they can continue to have something to manage and people to boss around."

Robert squared his shoulders, pushing his body against the booth's backrest. He smiled slightly and shook his head.

"Now what the hell am I suppose to do with that insight?" he asked.

"You have to out bullshit the bullshitters, Robert. That's the thing. It's a game. The websites and the publishing are the way they keep track of the score. You have to play the game, but you have to know it's a game. It's all just a game. Pay homage to their asshole rules, but do what you want. Enjoy teaching, Robert, and bullshit the rest."

"How does that help me write?"

"I don't know," Michael answered. "But maybe knowing will help. Robert, you told me before that you've changed since we walked down that aisle of doctoral grandeur. You have this Marxian approach to the world...something you only toyed with before. You've changed. You're not the same fair-haired wonder boy this institution and your mother created. I can see it. It's tearing you up inside and it's made you lonely. You're different, Robert. We're both different. We see the world differently and it hurts. Hell, why do you think I drink so much and fuck Sherri?"

Robert could see anguish in his friend's face.

"You okay, Mike?" he asked.

"Yeah, I'm okay, but I'm not much help for you. Your situation is very different than mine...you're a married man with a child, a wife, and a dying mother...a mother you don't want to disappoint. I know there's more pressure on you to produce and to be...what's the word I'm looking for?"

"Stable?"

"Yeah, stable. Thank God I don't have to be that. Sorry, Robert...I'm not much help for you."

"You're wrong about that, Mike. You're the only person who does understand."

Mike smiled at Robert and lifted his glass up.

"Let's drink a toast," he said.

Robert lifted his glass and smiled back, knowing what Mike was about to do.

"Here's to your mother and my dad. We made them proud...God rest my father's soul, and God grant peace and understanding to your mother."

Robert ceremoniously clicked his glass against Mike's.

"We made 'em proud," he said. "So far, we've made them proud."

Chapter Twenty-Seven — Elena's Confession

"Elena!" Diane Bradford cried out as Elena Markova entered Diane's bookstore.

Diane moved quickly across the store to hug Elena.

"It is good to see you," she said. "I was hoping you would come today and join me for tea."

Elena smiled and hugged Diane. It had become a weekly habit of Elena's to visit Diane at teatime and talk with her.

"You are always such a good host, I thought I would return the favor," she said. "I have Russian tea cookies for our tea break. Can we have tea now?"

Elena reached into a cloth shopping bag she was carrying and pulled out a small plate that was covered with aluminum foil.

The initial coldness that Elena brought into the bookstore had been worn away by Diane's kindness and the two women had developed a genuine friendship. The tea and the cookies they shared became conduits that allowed them to talk openly about their lives.

"Certainly. I would love that. Come," Diane said. "Bring the plate over to the table. I'll get the cups and tea and join you."

Elena unwrapped the plate, exposing half a dozen butter cookies that had been rolled into quarter-sized balls and were sprinkled with powdered sugar. Diane quickly joined her with a teapot and two teacups.

"The recipe for these cookies has been handed down in my family for years," Elena said.

"The cookies look delicious," Diane replied. "I told you my parents were from the Ukraine. My mother made cookies that looked similar to these. I am anxious to try one."

"Please take one," Elena said. "I am sure your mother's cookies were delicious, but there is no better tea cookie in the world than a Russian tea cookie."

Diane and Elena sat down at the table and Diane picked up one of the appealing cookies.

"I brought you a plate with sugar cubes on it," Diane said. "I know you always like two lumps in your tea."

"You are a wonderful host," Elena exclaimed. "Please taste my cookies."

Diane bit into one of the cookies and found them sweet and buttery.

"Yummm, they are delicious," she said smiling at Elena. "It is very nice of you to bring them with you."

"I enjoyed our last tea time," Elena said. "It is good for women to talk and drink tea."

"And eat cookies," Diane added while popping the remainder of her cookie into her mouth.

"Oh Elena, I almost forgot! I have a gift for you," she said.

Diane hurriedly left the table, picked up a paper bag at the sales counter, returned to her chair, and handed Elena the bag.

"I found some poetry written by Anna Akhmatova," Diane said. "Her works are difficult to find, but I want you to have the book as a gift."

A surprised expression appeared on Elena's face. The expression quickly turned to one of complete gratitude as she pulled the hardbound book of Russian poetry out of the bag. Holding the book up with her left hand and pressing her right hand against her chest, Elena expressed her appreciation for the generosity of her new friend.

"Diane!" she gasped. "This is very kind of you. Very kind! You are a true friend."

Tears appeared in Elena's eyes; she reached for a napkin and wiped away the tears.

"This is a precious gift," she said.

Diane was touched by the sincerity of Elena's reaction; her eyes became misty. She knew literature was a precious gift and she felt a kindred spirit with Elena's emotional reaction.

"It is my pleasure to give this to you," she said. "Your enjoyment will be my enjoyment."

Diane partially lifted herself up from her chair and kissed Elena on her cheek. Elena reached out with her free hand, gently touching Diane's face. The two women smiled at each other.

"I will look forward to reading these poems," Elena said as she carefully slid the book back into the bag and sat the bag down on the table.

"We have exchanged gifts, now we can talk," she said. "How is your family?'

"Let's start with you," Diane commented. "How are things at work? And how is Sasha?"

Elena dropped two cubes of sugar into her teacup. Hot vapors of steam floated up from the cup as she stirred her tea with a spoon.

"Work is work," she began. "I am a maitre d now, and I like it much better than being a waitress, but I pay a price for it."

"What price?"

"The manager is…how to you say…a wolf?"

"Oh," Diane said. "Do you know, Elena, there are laws here in America protecting you from sexual harassment?"

Elena tested her tea by taking a small sip. The tea was too hot to drink.

"Yes, I know. But he is more of a sheep in wolf's clothing," she said laughing. "I know how to handle him. It is another man I have some difficulty with."

Elena purposefully paused and took a cookie, waiting to see what Diane's reaction would be to her confession.

Diane hesitated for a moment and then replied.

"Do you want to talk about him?" she asked. "I do not want to pry into your life, Elena, but if you need someone to talk with, I will listen."

"I would like to talk with you," Elena said. "I am confused about this man."

"Tell me as much as you want, or as little as you need to," Diane said.

"I am happy to hear you say this. I do not want to talk about the man. I want to talk about my feelings for him. I am a private person and I want to be respectful of him and of me. Do you understand, my friend?"

"Yes I do, Elena," Diane replied. "I am a private person, too. I dislike gossip very much. I will not tell anyone what we say here."

Elena touched Diane's hand.

"You are a true friend," she said.

Elena took a bite of cookie and another sip of tea. She smiled at Diane.

"This man…he is my lover," she said.

"Ah," Diane said softly.

"Are you surprised?" Elena asked. "Have you ever had a lover outside of your marriage?"

"No," Diane replied. "But Elena, I want you to know I will not judge you because of your lover."

"You do not think I am a bad person for this?"

"I do not know, Elena. I don't cast stones. Do you know what that means?"

"Please tell me."

"It is a biblical saying. Christ said, 'Let those among you who are without sin cast the first stone.' He meant we should not condemn others, but should be aware of our own sins. Do you know that part of the Bible?"

"I was not brought up with a religious training, but I have heard of that saying. You are a good person, Diane."

"I am not a traditional person," Diane said. "My ideas concerning life and morality are different from most. I believe in forgiveness. May I ask you something?"

"Please do."

"When you say that this man is your lover, do you mean that you love him? Or do you mean you go to bed with him?"

"At first, I tried not to love him, but he is so passionate. I do have a love for him, and we do go to bed often. He is…how would I say this? He makes love to me many times…he is very healthy," Elena said smiling.

Diane smiled back and laughed.

"Healthy? Healthy and energetic?" she asked.

"Yes! That's the word…energetic. He is very, very energetic," Elena replied laughing.

"Do you miss Sasha?" Diane asked. "I am not judging you, but I wonder if you miss your husband?'

"I will always love Sasha. He is a good man and he loves me. I know this, but Diane…I am a lonely woman. I will always be lonely. Do you understand?"

"I think I do," Diane answered. "There is loneliness in my world, too. But this other man…he does not take away your loneliness?"

"No. He adds to it," Elena said sadly. "His love is temporary."

"Does he love you?"

"He loves me very much. He is consumed with love for me."

Diane took a sip of her tea, sat her teacup down, and stared toward Elena.

"Consumed," she said repeating Elena's word. "Then this man is dangerous. He will break your heart."

"Yes," Elena replied. "He will break my heart."

"What will you do?"

"I have to break his heart first."

Diane reached for a cookie, but put it back down on the plate. A sad look appeared on her face. Sitting in her bookstore, surrounded by books filled with drama, she was aware that a profound drama was being played out before her very eyes. She became overwhelmed by the complexity of life. Her eyes misted over as she looked at Elena.

"Elena," she said, her voice trembling. "I am sorry for you, and for him."

"You are kind," Elena replied. "Isn't it ironic how life plays out? My lover…we…we are so good together when we are alone, but there would be no happiness for us in this world."

"Happiness can be difficult to find, and difficult to keep," Diane said.

"Are you happy?" Elena asked.

"I thought I was. I am not sure now."

Both women remained quiet for a moment as they thought about their lives. Elena broke the reflective mood first by reaching for her tea.

"We are lucky to have each other," she said. "And, we are lucky to have tea!"

Diane reached for her teacup and raised it up in recognition of Elena's informal toast.

"Yes," she said smiling. "Yes, we are lucky to be friends."

Chapter Twenty-Eight — Brae and Robert

It was seven forty-five in the evening when Robert Bradford left Eckhart Hall. Trudging down the stairway from his second story office, he thought about having a drink before he would decide what to do with the rest of his evening. He had already called home and told his wife he would be staying over night in the condo. He was hopeful being alone would give him time and inspiration to write. So far, his hopes had not been realized. He had just entered the quad when he heard Brae Larson call out to him.

"Professor Bradford," Brae hailed.

Brae had been at the Reg Library and had decided to take a break from her studies by enjoying a walk around the quad. Professor Bradford stopped walking and turned to say hello to her.

"Good evening Brae. I hope you are heading to the library," the professor said with a slight smile on his face.

Brae had been a student in Professor Bradford's class during her junior year of school. She enjoyed his class and was impressed with his knowledge of literature. She had called out to him in a natural reaction to his presence, but now she felt nervous as he stood in front of her.

"I am," Brae blurted out while setting her backpack down on the sidewalk. "I mean, I will. I'm taking a break right now…but I've been there already. I'm working on a lit paper."

"It's a beautiful evening," Professor Bradford noted. "A person can study too much. We all need some down time."

"What are you doing?" Brae asked. "Did you have a class tonight?"

Robert watched Brae fidgeting in front of him and found her nervous energy attractive.

"No, Brae. I had some work to do. I've been in my office, but now I'm out for a break."

"Oh," Brae said.

A small pause occurred in their conversation. Both Brae and Professor Bradford felt a slice of awkward tension slide between them.

"What will you do for your break?" the professor asked.

Brae pointed toward the center of the quad. It was twilight and the beauty of the university surrounded them.

"I was going to walk on the quad."

"I was going to have a glass of wine," the professor answered. "Would you like to join me?"

"Really?" Brae responded. "I mean…do you mean that?"

"If you're of age, I do," the professor laughed.

"Actually, I just turned twenty-two," Brae said. "When I was five, I had some medical problems. I entered school a full year behind the kids my age. I've always been older than my classmates."

Brae stopped explaining and smiled, realizing she was telling the professor more than he needed or wanted to know.

"Where were you thinking of going?" she added in a bubbly tone of voice.

"Well how about we take my car and head toward the city. I know an Italian restaurant that has a great outdoor patio. Is that all right? Would you like to get away from the campus for a couple of hours?"

"I would love that, Professor Bradford," Brae replied. "Can I go dressed like this?"

Brae was dressed in a short jean skirt, an open white blouse, a green t-shirt, and flip-flops.

"You look fine," the professor said. "It's always casual dress there. Let me take your backpack. My car is over on Ellis Street."

Professor Bradford reached down and picked up Brae's backpack.

"You don't have to do that," Brae said.

"Nonsense," the professor said smiling. "All literature professors take extensive courses in chivalry. What kind of a gentleman would you take me for if I did not help you with your things?"

Brae smiled to herself but felt a sense of confusion and awkwardness; she was unaccustomed to such male graciousness.

"Thank you for being so kind," she said

Brae turned and followed along side of Professor Bradford as he headed for his car. She felt good about him carrying her backpack and, for the first time in years, she felt good about being with a man.

"Have you gotten a good start on your paper?" the professor asked as they strolled through the quad.

"I've got some good ideas and a good thesis statement," Brae answered.

They turned north on Ellis Street and walked only a short distance when the professor punched the door lock release button on his car keys. The headlights on a black Ford Fusion lit up, the auto locks clicked open, and Professor Bradford moved swiftly ahead of Brae to open the door for her. Brae felt special as she slid onto the passenger seat.

"Thank you," she said smiling.

What a gentlemen, Brae thought while she waited for Professor Bradford to walk around the car and enter the driver's side.

Professor Bradford dropped Brae's backpack onto the back seat of his car, and then slid into the driver's seat.

"We're all set, right?" he said.

"I'm all set," Brae replied. "But I can't believe I'm going to have a drink with you. I'm glad, but I can't believe it."

"Why?" Professor Bradford asked.

"I mean, I never would have guessed this would be a part of my evening." Brae said.

"If it helps, I would not have guessed either," the professor replied. "But I am glad you agreed to come. One should not drink wine alone...you do like wine, don't you?"

"Oh yes," Brae replied. "I'm partial to red wine. Is that okay?"

"Red wine it will be," the professor said.

• • •

It only took fifteen minutes to reach the restaurant. Professor Bradford requested an outside patio table from the maitre d, and the two were promptly seated.

"I'm going to order a bottle of wine for us," Professor Bradford said, as he examined the wine list. "Is that all right?"

"That's fine," Brae said.

Brae looked up at the night sky and then scanned the outdoor patio. The floor was decorative laid brick; there was a four-foot high stucco concrete wall surrounding them on three sides, and a sidewall of the restaurant building completed the enclosure. Ivy crawled up the walls, and a thick layer of an ivy-leaf plant formed a two-foot wide strip along the ground between the walls and the brick floor. Only one other couple shared the outdoor facilities with them, and that couple was seated three tables away.

Brae looked across the wrought iron table at Professor Bradford and watched him searching the wine list. She guessed his age to be in the early forties. She had always found his appearance to be appealing. She knew he was married, but she decided not to think about that. A romantic feeling engulfed her as she watched him order the wine.

"Have you ever been here, Brae?" the professor asked.

"No, I haven't she replied. "Do you come here often Professor Bradford?"

"Brae, would you mind calling me Robert? I feel uncomfortable being called Professor Bradford while we are here drinking wine."

Brae smiled. Her dark eyes flashed in the patio lights.

"Robert," she said. "Yes, I can call you Robert. Thank you for telling me. I would rather call you Robert. I like that name."

A waiter brought them two wine glasses and poured the wine for Robert to taste.

"Let the young lady do the honors," Robert said to the waiter. "I am sure I can trust her judgment."

Brae was flattered by the request. She was not a wine connoisseur, though she knew what she liked, and she was certain she could handle the task Robert had just assigned to her. She swirled the wine around in her glass, smelled the wine's bouquet, and savored its taste as she let a small sample of it swish inside of her mouth.

Robert watched Brae examine the wine. His eyes studied her facial features and he found her beautiful.

"This is wonderful, Robert," she announced.

"I agree," Robert replied.

"But you haven't tasted it," Brae said.

"I meant the company."

The waiter filled each wine glass three-quarters full and left the two alone.

"What shall we drink to?" Brae asked.

"Let's drink to this evening," Robert suggested. "I am happy to be with you, Brae. I fear my evening could have been very boring."

"I will drink to that," Brae agreed. "I know my evening would have been boring, too."

The two clicked their glasses together, and looked into each other's eyes as they took a long sip of wine.

There was no boredom for Brae and Robert as they sat drinking wine. They talked, laughed, and enjoyed each other's company. Words and ideas flowed between them as readily as the wine they were consuming. Brae reached out and innocently touched Robert's hand three times during their conversation. The softness of her fingers and the compliments she showered upon him concerning his intellect did not go unnoticed. She made him feel special.

Reaching for Brae's hand, Robert intertwined the fingers of his right hand with hers. Brae welcomed his touch. He held her hand and lifted the wine bottle up with his other hand.

"Brae," he said. "We have finished the wine. I would like to order another bottle and continue our conversation, but I am driving. Allow me to make a suggestion. I have a condo close to campus. I bought it as an investment and use it when I have to stay over. I am going to stay over tonight. Would you join me for another bottle of wine at my place?"

"I would," Brae answered smiling "Let me use the bathroom, and then let's head back."

"We'll both do that," Robert said.

Brae made her way to the ladies room. She felt a little dizzy and attributed her dizziness to the wine and the evening she was sharing with Robert. After using the toilet facilities, she stared into the mirror, examining her inner self. She knew what the right thing to do was, but she decided to do something else. She walked out of the bathroom and rejoined Robert.

Chapter Twenty-Nine — Robert's Condo

Robert's condo was on the second floor of a building located four blocks away from the university campus. Upon their arrival, Robert parked his car in a slot designated for him. As he and Brae walked to his condo, they continued to talk, walking closer to each other than they had previously and occasionally bumping into each other. They took an elevator to the second floor and strolled down the hallway in a merry mood, their arms around each other's waist. Brae leaned lightly against Robert while he turned the key that opened his entranceway door.

"Let me get the lights," Robert said.

"No," Brae replied.

Reaching for Robert's hand, Brae gently pulled him to her. Robert wrapped his arms around Brae, pulling her closer. They kissed tenderly. Brae heard Robert sigh and felt him squeeze her tightly in his arms. He moved his mouth to the left side of her face.

"Brae," he whispered in her ear.

He nibbled at her ear and took pleasure in the softness and the smell of her hair. Brae felt him becoming aroused. She pushed her hips forward to meet his desire. Their bodies gyrated in sync as they held onto each other in the darkness of Robert's condo.

"Brae," Robert whispered again. "Come with me to my bedroom."

Brae pulled back from Robert. She reached up and caressed his face with her fingers. She stared into his eyes.

"Do you have candles here?" she asked softly.

"Yes," Robert replied.

He kissed her forehead, turned, and walked into the kitchen area. Brae heard a drawer open and the sound of a match being struck. Soon she saw a soft glow from the candlelight dancing up and down the walls of the condo. She leaned back against the entrance door and watched as Robert walked toward her with a candle in each hand. He held out one of the candles for her to take, took her other hand in his, and slowly guided her through the kitchen and into his bedroom.

A large queen size bed dominated the bedroom.

"Brae," Robert said. "Put your candle on the nightstand next to the bed."

Brae moved to position her candle on the nightstand while Robert placed his candle on top of a set of dresser drawers. The candles illuminated the room with a faint radiance.

Brae and Robert met at the foot of the bed. They reached out, held hands, and stood looking at each other.

"You know I am married?" Robert asked as he stared into Brae's eyes.

"Yes," Brae replied. "Right now, I don't care."

Robert moved his hands to Brae's shoulders.

"You should know," he said. "I'm looking for an escape. I have trouble in my life and I just want to share pleasure with someone. I want to get away from everything. Tonight I want to hold you and make love with you."

"You should know," Brae replied. "I'm a little drunk, but I know what I'm doing. I want to be here and, right now, I want to be with you. I can't promise how I will feel later, but I can tell you I won't look back. I won't make demands on you. You can trust me, Robert."

Robert and Brae knew this was as good as they could expect from each other. They knew what they were about to do was dangerous. In a way, they both felt as though they had already been intimate through the topics they had shared at the restaurant. They had achieved a special bonding through their conversations; they were philosophically in tune with one another and now they wanted to share affection and physical pleasure. They wanted to stop being alone.

No more words were required. Robert began to undress Brae. He took his time, undressing her slowly to admire her beauty. Brae allowed him to undress her. She enjoyed the pleasurable look on his face as he examined her with his eyes and his fingers and his lips. He scattered her clothing about the floor as he undressed her. Each time he revealed a portion of her body, he touched her and kissed her in the area he had uncovered.

When she was completely naked, he backed away from her and visually scanned her body. Brae kept her eyes focused on Robert's face. She remained quiet while he looked at her.

"Please turn around, Brae," Robert said calmly. "I want to look at your backside."

Brae moved slowly, turning her body around so that her back faced Robert. She took a deep breath and stood still. She felt Robert's fingers touching her bare shoulders. His touch was light and his fingers glided over her soft skin. He moved forward and began kissing her neck and her shoulders, using his lips to taste her. He was in no hurry; there was no uncontrollable rush of passion, and Brae liked that. His fingers slid down her back. He paused at the small of her back, taking time to trace the curvature of her spine; then he ran his fingers over her buttocks. She could feel his hands quivering. She knew it was his desire for her that caused him to tremble.

"Stay as you are, Brae," Robert said. "I am going to undress."

Brae looked out through the blinds of the bedroom window. She moved her hands up and caressed her breasts. She closed her eyes, listened to the sounds of Robert undressing, and hoped that Robert would make love to her all night long. The anticipation of what they would do caused her body to shiver. She wanted escape, too. She was tired of her emotional burden. She wanted to forget the world and she wanted to share pleasure with Robert.

Brae's head moved backwards as she felt the naked embrace of Robert's body pressing against her skin. His hands moved around her body, joining Brae in caressing her breasts. He bit tenderly at her neck. He was rock hard as he slowly slid his swollen desire up and down against her buttocks. Brae moaned at the feel of his touch.

"Brae," Robert said softly into her ear. "Lay down on the bed."

Robert watched as Brae climbed onto the bed and crawled toward the headboard. Her movements were graceful and cat-like. She turned over when she reached the pillows, laying down on the mattress, fully stretched out and totally naked. Robert took time to look at her again. He saw that she was looking at him. He reached for her foot and played with her toes as he absorbed the wonder of her. Then he bent down, tenderly kissed her foot, climbed onto the bed, and began moving up her body, kissing and touching her.

Brae shuddered with excitement. She loved Robert's tenderness, and she loved the time he took to kiss and taste her. Her back arched; she moaned over and over again, softly whispering his name. Brae spread her legs to welcome Robert's exploration. His upper body fell between her legs. She reached for him, put her hands on his head, and helped to guide his impassioned advance.

Brae and Robert gave and received pleasure from each other. Afterwards, the lateness of the evening and the wine they had consumed caused them to easily drift off to sleep.

It was a joy for Robert to sleep with Brae. He felt good about having her with him. She was escape. She was simplicity. She was untarnished beauty. Michael was right; Robert's perception of the world had changed and he felt alone. Being with Brae seemed to take all of that away.

Chapter Thirty — Ann Questions Brae

After leaving Robert, Brae returned to her apartment at eight o'clock the next morning. Her roommate was awake and had just taken a shower. Ann was standing in their small kitchen area, pouring a glass of orange juice into a coffee cup that she used for a multitude of drinks. A large light blue bathroom towel was wrapped around her petite oriental body.

"Out late last night?" Ann asked smiling at Brae.

"This is a first," Brae said as she smiled back. "Imagine me getting in later than you."

"Do I know the guy?"

"No," Brae said. "And he's not a guy, he's a man…a gentleman."

"Whoa…a man and a gentleman? What does that mean? You mean he's older?"

"I mean he's not one of your adolescent, immature, self-absorbed boys."

Ann sat her cup down on the kitchen counter and focused her attention on Brae.

"Brae, there's something you need to know. No matter how old they are, males are all self-absorbed. They don't stop being self-absorbed until their testosterone level reads two quarts low. Want some juice?"

Brae laughed in agreement and moved to get a small glass from the cupboard.

"Sure, I'll have some juice," she said setting the glass down next to Ann's cup.

Ann filled the glass with juice while Brae fired back a response to her observation.

"That may be true," she said. "But all the guys you date have testosterone levels that are two quarts over full."

"Okay. Okay. Are we done taking swings at each other?" Ann asked. "Let's agree on something. I won't judge your 'gentleman' and you leave my 'boys' alone. Agreed?"

"Agreed," Brae replied.

Ann sat down on one of the kitchen stools, placing her elbows up on the counter and looking at Brae.

"Is there anything you want to tell me about your night?" she said.

Brae sat down on another stool and swiveled around to look at Ann.

"I will tell you this, I feel very good right now. A little apprehensive about some things, but overall I feel very good. Somewhat confused, too."

"You look good," Ann said. "I mean you look…well…you know."

"Like I just got laid?" Brae laughed.

"Yeah," Ann said joining Brae in laughing. "It's been a long time for you, right?"

"It's been a year."

"Worth the wait?"

"Yeah, it was worth the wait."

A far away look appeared on Brae's face.

"So your gentleman was good in bed, huh?"

"Very good. And I was good, too. It takes two you know."

"And is this more than just sex?"

Brae hesitated in her response.

"Yes. It's more than sex," she said. "We've talked about this before, Ann. You know I'm no good at just sex. There has to be something more. I can't do the *just sex thing*."

Ann took a long drink from her cup and shook her damp hair.

"Define 'more' for me," she asked.

"Well…we connected before going to bed. We connected philosophically. Our minds met. We shared our beliefs and we communicated. I could tell he wanted to know about me and I wanted to know about him."

"Hmmm. That does sound good. Where did this connection take place? I thought you went to the library last night. Or was that just a story you told me?"

"I went to the library last night," Brae answered. "That's where I met him."

"In the library? Is he a grad student?"

"No and no," Brae replied. "I met him while I was taking a break from studying. And we connected while drinking some wine at a restaurant."

Brae stood up, kicked off her flip-flops, and leaned against the kitchen counter. She covered her face with her hands and sighed loudly.

"When was the last time I blew off a class?" she rhetorically asked.

"This year?" Ann asked. "I don't think you ever have."

"I'm going to ditch my classes this morning."

"I see…he was good then," she said.

"Yeah. But it's not just the sex. Don't get me wrong…that was very good. It's the whole package, the whole thing. It's a little exhausting for me to comprehend."

"Do you want to talk more about it?" Ann asked.

"Not right now," Brae replied. "I'm just not sure where all of this is going. Right now, I just know it's going and I'm going with it. I want to go with it. I *need* to go with it. Can you understand that, Ann?"

Ann looked at Brae, and shook her damp hair again.

"How many guys…boys…have I been with this year?" Ann asked.

Brae sighed again, and looked at Ann.

"I really don't track your guys," she answered. "Let's just say the answer is more than two."

"Okay," Ann laughed. "We'll say more than two. My point is, you have never judged me, Brae. Not out loud anyway. The truth is, I don't know what I'm doing. Maybe, I'm looking for what you found…philosophical compatibility. I don't know. I know I act carefree about guys, but I'm not."

Brae looked at Ann and saw a tear flowing down her face.

"You okay?" she asked.

Ann wiped her eyes and smiled.

"I'm upset with myself," she said. "And I'm envious of what you just said. I don't know anything about your 'man', but I admire the connection you've made. I wake up in the morning wondering why I'm with some guy…except for Mike…and he cheated on me. I guess my point is…I do understand and I hope you don't get hurt."

"I'll get hurt," Brae replied. "And, he'll get hurt, too. That's a given."

"A given? Why? Is he a lot older?"

"He's older than he should be," Brae said. "There's no future for us. I know that."

"Then why are you dating him?"

"It's like I said," Brae replied. "It's what I want to do now. I'm tired, Ann. Tired of doing what everyone wants me to do…tired of being afraid of my dream…tired of sleeping alone…tired of playing games with the boys who hit on me. I just want to share something special with someone, and I don't want to share that someone with anyone else. I liked being alone with him. I like him being anonymous. I like being anonymous with him. Do you get it?"

"I know you are a private person, Brae. And I know that you are a quiet rebel. I've always respected that in you. Me…I blab everything I know to people, and someone always fucks me over about something I said to them…yeah, I get it."

Ann scooted off her kitchen stool, picked up a comb that was lying on the counter top, and starting combing her long black hair.

"I do get it," she said. "You're tired of being judged. I am, too."

"I just want to make my own mistakes," Brae said. "And, you're right. I don't want to be judged by others…I want to handle it all myself without the 'holier than thou' types hovering around and pointing fingers."

"You'll never escape them," Ann said laughing.

"Then I want to learn how to ignore them."

"What about him…this gentleman of yours?"

"What about him?"

"What does he think? Does he want to be anonymous, too?"

Brae remained quiet.

"Ann…I know you mean well…and I know we will talk more. But right now, I need to be private. There is a lot I don't know. Give me some time, okay?"

"You got it, Babe," Ann said. "You get some sleep. I'm going to get ready for class."

Ann moved toward her bedroom, leaving Brae leaning against the counter top. She walked into her bedroom, but then immediately reappeared in the kitchen.

"This really *is* a first," she said smiling. "Me going to class and you sleeping in."

Chapter Thirty-One — Javier, Jose and Brae

Twice a week Brae Larson volunteered to help immigrants learn English skills. She found the work interesting and believed she learned more through the process than the immigrants did. The University of Chicago, along with several local businesses, sponsored the literacy program. College students were shuffled around the Chicago area from one location to another in order to staff the program. Brae's spring/early summer location was a rented storefront in Wicker Park. Every Tuesday and Thursday morning she would ride the 'L' green line from the university, transfer to the blue line to reach the Damen stop, and then walk three blocks to a storefront classroom where she assisted newly arrived Spanish-speaking immigrants. One of her best students was Javier Morales.

"Javier," Brae said one Thursday morning, "your writing has improved remarkably. Do you practice at home?"

"Yes Miss Brae," Javier replied.

"Javier writes poetry," Jose said. "Someday he will be famous."

Javier shot a stern look toward Jose.

"Jose," he said. "My writing is not real poetry."

Javier turned toward Brae.

"It is a hobby for me," he said. "I like to write."

"That's wonderful, Javier. I would like to read your poetry. Do you have some writings with you today?"

A look of embarrassment appeared on Javier's face.

"I keep my writings in a briefcase where I live, but I have one in my notebook."

"May I read your poem?" Brae asked.

"Miss Brae," Javier said. "I am trying to write poetry in English. It is hard for me but I am learning. My poetry is not good but I want to get better. Would you look at my poem to correct my English?"

Brae smiled at Javier.

"I would love to do that, Javier."

Javier sat his notebook down on the table that Brae used as a makeshift desk. His notebook was neat and well organized; he turned to the back of it, unsnapped the three rings that held the paper secure, and pulled out an eight by eleven piece of writing paper on which he had written a short poem.

"This is not good," he said as he handed the paper to Brae. "I wrote it when I arrived in America. I ask you to wait and read it after we have gone."

Brae took the paper and placed it on the tabletop. She looked up at Javier.

"I'm sure it is good, Javier. Poetry is self-expression. You are very good at expressing yourself. I will read it when I get back to my apartment. I will tell you what I think of it next Tuesday. Is that okay?"

"Yes," Javier replied. "If it is not good, you will tell me so?"

"I will tell you what I think of your poetry, Javier. But remember poetry is very personal; what I like may not be liked by others. Do you understand?"

"Gracias, Miss Brae. I understand."

Brae rose up from behind the table, placed Javier's poem on top of a stack of papers, and stuffed all the papers into her tote bag.

"Miss Brae," Javier said. "May I ask about your bag?"

Brae held her tote bag up, displaying it in full view to Javier.

"What is your question?" she said.

"The person on the bag…it is Che Guevara?"

Brae smiled at Javier.

"Yes," she replied. "He is a hero of mine. Do you know about him?"

"Si," Javier said. "I did not know Americans liked Che."

"Most Americans don't like him. Many Americans do not know anything about him."

"Why do you like him?"

"I like him for the same reasons that I give up my time to teach here," Brae said.

"You get no pay for being here?" Jose asked.

"No," Brae answered. "I do it to help."

Javier and Jose looked at each other and smiled.

"Gracias, Miss Brae," Jose said.

Brae threw her backpack over her shoulder, grabbed onto the handles of her tote bag, and headed toward the door. Jose rushed to the door, opening it for his teacher.

"Thank you, Jose," Brae said. "You and Javier are good students. Enjoy your weekend and keep practicing your English."

When she left, Javier walked over to Jose.

"Miss Brae is a good person, Jose," he said.

"Si," Jose replied.

• • •

The train ride back to the UC campus took 35 minutes. It was mid-morning and the train was not crowded. Brae took over a double seat by throwing her tote bag and her backpack on the seat next to her.

As the train pulled away from Wicker Park, she thought about what things she needed to do when she got home. She planned on stopping at a small grocery store on her way home, so she began making a mental list of the items she needed to purchase, wishing that she had made a grocery list before she had left her apartment. She was certain she would forget to get all of the items she and Ann needed. Looking out the train window, Brae decided to stop concentrating on the grocery list. She decided to play her shopping trip by ear; she would walk the aisles of the store and grab what looked right.

As the train rumbled down the tracks, Brae looked at her tote bag and noted that she would need to correct the student papers tonight. She wanted to put them behind her so she could focus on her college work over the weekend. She stared at the bag and remembered Javier's poem. Reaching into the bag, she pulled his paper out, settled back against the train seat, flipped the paper over, and read the poem.

A bitter Chicago wind slaps and stings the faces
of those who venture outdoors.
Bundled pedestrians trudge off to work, bracing against the winter chill.
Frosty metal steps clack under the weight of multiple footsteps.
Masses of people stand like frozen human statues on cold wooden platforms,
anxiously awaiting the appearance of a train.
A clear blue morning sky surrounds the city,
blanketing it in crisp, Arctic air.
Each day, I move among anonymous crowds…pushed and resented.

Brae reread the poem and smiled to herself. Javier writes well, she thought. She read the poem again, deciding that she liked the images Javier had created.

The following Tuesday, Brae asked Javier to stay after class so they could discuss his poem.

"Si," Javier answered. "Jose, wait for me at the Sultan's Market. We will eat lunch there, mi amigo."

"Bueno," Jose said. "But do not take long, I am hambriento."

Javier took a chair to Brae's table. He sat down, nervously watching her pull his poem out of her tote bag. He was eager to find out what his teacher thought of his writing. He placed his elbows on the table, rested his chin on his folded hands, and looked at Brae.

"My poetry has not been read by anyone," he said.

"No one?" Brae answered in surprise.

"One person," Javier said correcting himself. "I write poems to her."

"Oh," Brae replied. "She is a lucky woman. I liked your poem. Does she like them?"

"Si. But it is easy to write poems to her. She is beautiful."

Brae smiled at Javier and saw him blush.

"Tell me about this poem," she said. "I love the imagery. I want to know more about the thoughts you were expressing."

A confused look appeared on Javier's face.

"I want to know why you wrote the poem, Javier," Brae explained. "Do the words tell us about you?"

"Ah…Si. Si," Javier answered.

"Can you tell me what the words mean?"

Javier seemed reluctant to answer. He hesitated and was apologetic in his reply.

"Miss Brae," Javier replied. "You are a good person. You help Jose and me learn English. I do not want to be disrespectful to you. We are immigrants, and life is hard for us here."

Brae smiled at Javier. A look of compassion swept across her face.

"Javier, I understand," she said. "I know your life is hard. Your poetry has to be about your suffering. Suffering often leads to creative writing. Have you ever heard that?"

"Si," Javier replied. "There is a poet from my country, Octavio Paz Lozano, who wrote about oppression, suffering, and liberty during the revolutionary times in Mexico. I have read his poetry. And I know Russian poets have also suffered."

"That is true, Javier."

"Tell me, Miss Brae…do American poets suffer?"

"Much of our poetry is about suffering," Brae answered.

"How do Americans suffer?" Javier asked.

"There is suffering in all societies, Javier."

"I do not understand this. Where is the suffering for Americans?"

Brae found she was backed into a corner. She smiled and laughed slightly, realizing Javier was more astute than she had thought.

"You are wise, Javier," she said. "American poetry about suffering comes from those who are…well…oppressed or disadvantaged."

Javier sat back in his chair with a look of understanding on his face.

"Poor people," he said softly.

"Yes," Brae answered. "Minorities and the poor."

"Jose and me."

Brae felt embarrassed.

"Yes," she said.

Javier looked away from the table and down at the floor. His facial expression was grave.

"The poem is about suffering," he said. "It is not a good poem, but it comes from suffering."

Brae turned Javier's paper around and pointed at the poem.

"Tell me about each stanza," she said. "Help me to understand…what do the first two lines mean?"

"It is the wind from the North…a harsh wind that blows upon us," Javier said.

"Do you mean America?"

"Si, America. We fight the wind when we come here. We fight the wind when we work here. Always it is unpleasant."

"What are the steps?"

"We work here. We try to do well…to make things better for our families and ourselves. I don't know how to say…"

Javier struggled for the words that would explain his frustration.

"You try to move up, to improve, and to get a better job," Brae said. "Is that what you mean?"

"Si," Javier replied. "So many of us trying to move up. We wait for a chance to make things better. We are frozen in time…frozen in poor jobs. We do the jobs others will not take. We do work Americans need done, but we are resented for being here. This is the meaning of the poem. It is my first poem. I know it is not written well."

Brae placed both of her elbows on the table, resting her chin on her folded hands. She looked down at Javier's poem, reflecting upon what he had just said.

"So much suffering in so few words," she said softly to herself.

Her eyes darted up at Javier. He saw sadness in her eyes and he knew something in her life was causing her to suffer.

"Are you all right, Miss Brae?" he asked.

Brae dropped her hands down on the table. She sat back in her chair.

"You are a poet, Javier," she said. "You are the voice of people suffering."

"Then there is much for me to write about," Javier replied. "Many people suffer."

Chapter Thirty-Three — Elena Leaves Chicago

Diane Bradford was having a good day at the bookstore. Everything was going well – sales were above average, customers milled happily about the bookshelves, a shipment of books she had ordered arrived on time, and she had been able to take a well-deserved lunch break. But Diane's carefree day came to an end late in the afternoon when Emily, a woman who worked at the bookstore, called Diane to the phone.

"I think it is for you," Emily said as she handed Diane the phone. "I can't quite understand the woman."

The phone call was from Elena Markova. Elena's voice sounded desperate.

"My friend," Elena said. "I need to talk with you. Could we talk today?"

"Of course, Elena," Diane said. "Are you all right?"

"I need to talk with you," Elena repeated. "I will be fine, but I want to talk with you somewhere away from your bookstore. Can you get away?"

"Yes, can we meet later in the day?" Diane asked.

The two friends agreed to meet at the Pontiac Café on Damen Avenue at 6:00 o'clock.

• • •

Diane arrived at the restaurant first and acquired a small table on the huge outdoor patio. Elena arrived three minutes later, saw Diane waving to her, and walked over to join her. Diane greeted Elena with a warm hug.

"How are you?" she said.

Elena returned Diane's hug.

"I am fine," she said. "I am sorry I was so upset on the phone."

"Please sit with me, Elena. I ordered us a snack and glasses of wine. I hope that is all right with you."

Elena looked at the table, noticed the wine glasses for the first time, and then sat down next to Diane.

"Diane, you are such a good friend," she replied. "I will miss you."

"Miss me! Are you going away?"

"I will be leaving tomorrow afternoon. I'm going back to Vologda. Back to Sasha."

Diane sank back in her chair and looked at Elena.

"I will be sad to see you leave. I have enjoyed talking with you and sharing stories with you."

"I am sad about leaving, too. I like America. I wanted to become your good friend, but I must go."

A waitress brought a small plate of nachos garnished with beef, lettuce, tomatoes, cheese, guacamole, and sour cream.

"This is a lovely treat," Elena said. "I am hungry."

"Elena, is there anything I can do to help you stay here? Do you want to stay?"

"No," Elena said. "I must go. I have told no one about my leaving. I haven't even told the people at work."

"What about your pay?"

"Tomorrow is payday. I will collect my money and leave a note for the manager. He is a pig. I do not mind leaving him without notice."

Elena took a sip of wine and tore a large nacho chip away from the stack piled on the plate. She pushed half of the heavily laden chip in her mouth while holding a napkin under her chin.

"These are delicious," she said.

"Why are you going? Is something wrong at home?" Diane asked.

"No. There is nothing wrong at home."

Diane could tell that Elena wanted to confide in her but was reluctant to begin.

"Elena, if you want to talk to me about this, I will listen."

Elena took another sip of wine. A tear ran down her cheek as she sat silently looking down at the table.

"I do miss Sasha," she said. "I have made a big mistake, and I feel bad about it."

"What mistake?" Diane asked.

"My lover."

Tears streamed down Elena's face.

"Has he hurt you?"

"No. He is a good man. I enjoy being with him very much. I have fallen in love with him"

"Have you told him you are leaving?"

"I cannot. I must leave without him knowing."

Diane took a sip of wine. Elena stared away from Diane with a distant look on her face. Diane could see the pain that was racking Elena's body and soul. The pain was carved into her face and reflected in her eyes.

Diane reached for Elena's hand, squeezing it for comfort. Elena grasped Diane's hand tightly. The pain Elena felt resounded throughout her body, manifesting itself in continual waves of anxiety. Diane felt a tremble in Elena's grasp.

"I feel badly for you," she said to Elena. "I know your life has been hard, much harder than mine."

Elena smiled slightly, trying to regain her composure.

"Tell me about your life," she said. "Always we talk about me. Today we will talk about you."

"No, Elena," Diane replied. "It would not be fair. We are here to help you."

"Diane, it would help me to hear about you. It would help me to forget."

Elena took another sip of wine.

"Tell me about your husband. Do you like him?" she said.

Diane laughed.

"I have been married to him for twelve years…almost thirteen," she said.

"That only means you liked him before," Elena replied laughing. "Do you like him now?"

Diane looked at her glass; it was nearly empty. She thought of Robert and decided she would like to talk with someone about him.

"Let's get a bottle of wine," she suggested.

"Ah, you need courage," Elena said, laughing again.

Elena reached for another nacho chip, pushed the chip deep into the guacamole, and shoved the chip into her mouth.

"You see," she said. "Already I have forgotten about my problem. My appetite is back. I think it is easier to drink wine and eat these chips than to think about men."

Diane flagged a waitress over to the table and ordered a bottle of wine. She reached for the nachos and sampled one of the chips.

"I do need courage, Elena," she said. "I have never talked with anyone about Robert. At least, I have not done so for many years. The wine will help."

Elena could see her friend needed to talk.

"I'm not making fun," she said. "I want to be your friend. I want to help you."

"I know you do."

The waitress brought a bottle of wine, opened it, and attempted to go through the pouring and tasting process.

"Thank you," Diane said. "We will pour our own wine."

Elena watched the waitress leave and laughed as Diane poured the wine.

"She seemed upset," Elena said.

"I'll give her a good tip," Diane replied. "Besides, I have been tasting wine at restaurants for over twenty years and I have never sent a bottle back. And, if we are going to talk, I don't want her hovering around us."

Diane filled both glasses, and took a deep drink from hers.

Elena was surprised by Diane's action and by her comments. She took a deep swallow of her drink, too.

"I have never seen you like this," she said. "You are a different woman."

"Elena, I am a practical woman who loves literature. Do you know what that makes me?"

Elena looked befuddled.

"It makes me an anomaly. Do you know that word?"

"No," Elena replied.

"It means that I am inconsistent. It means that I can be compassionate some of the times and cold and business-like other times. My compassionate side comes from reading literature; my cold side comes from…well, from running the bookstore, and from my parents."

Elena smiled and sat up straight in her chair.

"I am an anomaly, too!" she announced proudly. "At work I am cold and professional, but with my lover I am open and warm. When I go out into the world, I become very rigid and I am not friendly. But when I come to your store to talk with you, I am friendly and I talk a lot. We are both anomaly."

Diane laughed gleefully at Elena's use of the word, and then enjoyed another sip of wine. Her face took on a philosophical expression.

"Who really ever knows a person?" Diane asked seriously. "All we can do is try."

"Is your husband an anomaly?" Elena asked.

Diane laughed.

"He is more of an enigma."

"Enigma I know," Elena replied. "Russia is a riddle, wrapped in a mystery, inside of an enigma. Winston Churchill said that. I never knew what it meant until I married my Sasha."

Diane raised her glass.

"Here's to two anomalies that married two enigmas," she said.

Both women smiled, shook their heads, and took drinks of their wine. Elena cupped her wine glass in her hands and looked at Diane.

"Tell me about your Robert," she said.

"Life is not easy, Elena. Robert is not the same man I married…or maybe, he is not the man I thought I married. We are having some difficult times."

"Do you talk?"

"We argue. We always make up…not in bed, but in a courteous and respectful way."

"Oh," Elena said.

"I envy the passion you have with your lover. I understand it is not right. Again, I do not condemn you for it. I just understand how difficult it must be for you when you compare him to Sasha. I know how alone you must feel. I feel alone, too."

Now Elena reached for Diane's hand and squeezed it.

"I wonder which is worse," she said. "The loneliness or the guilt?"

"I don't know the answer to that," Diane replied. "I know I put Robert on a pedestal. He was my academic knight in shining armor. I loved talking with him about literature and I loved reading his poetry."

"Your Robert writes poetry?"

"Yes. He is published. I have a book of his poetry in my bookstore. It is not a best seller…in fact it does not sell at all, but it is hard to be a famous poet. It is easier to write about murder and goblins."

"My lover is a poet," Elena said proudly. "Not a Russian poet, but a very good poet."

"Is he published? Would I know him?"

"No…nyet, nyet…he writes poems to me. Maybe, someday he will be published. I will never know," Elena said sadly.

Elena pushed the sparsely touched plate of nachos aside.

"What do you think has happened to your husband? Has he changed or have you changed?" she said.

"Time. Time erodes all things," Diane said in despair. "I should not say that. I know lots of people who have only gotten happier in their marriages. But time does change everything. I think the trick is to always communicate. For some reason, Robert and I quit doing that. He has gone one way, and I have gone another. And he…well, he has a lot of pressure in his life right now."

"What pressure?"

"Elena, I am very successful because of my parents and because of my work ethic. My store does very well, and I have wealth given to me by my parents. I never took anything for granted though. I have always worked hard. I know I am part of an old world aristocracy. I think Robert resents that. I don't know why, but I know it has come between us. You would think having money would be a good thing, but I don't know how to share it with him. The wealth is obstacle for both of us."

"That is the pressure?"

"No. The pressure is at his work. As an associate professor it is expected that he publish scholarly articles and books. He is having trouble doing that. He thinks he has lost his creativity. And Robert…well, Robert's mother always wanted him to be a full professor at the University of Chicago. I think he feels some pressure there, too. I believe he has come to resent being pushed into his profession. I think he would have been a professor anyway, but he doesn't like the idea that he was not given any options."

Diane paused, took a drink of wine, then sat the glass down on the table and stared at it. Her facial expression was somber.

"Robert's mother is very ill right now," she said. "Maybe if she weren't ill, Robert could stand up to her. He doesn't want to disappoint her. If he had more time…"

Elena watched Diane's countenance grow more distressful.

"Do you know what I think?" Diane said.

"What do you think?" Elena asked.

"I think...I think our marriage has robbed him of his creativity. Or, perhaps the wealth has. Maybe, he feels...less than he did before."

"You Americans go to counselors, yes?"

"Some do."

"Have you ever thought of you and Robert doing that?"

"I have thought of it. We have not talked about it. It is all such a tangle. Our lives seem extraordinary when you look at them from outside. On a shallow level, this is exactly where I wanted to be in our marriage. But somehow, the love has been diminished and there are dark clouds swirling around us. Maybe, if he could just publish one more time...that would give us some breathing room. I know he is working on something. Maybe..."

The time Elena could spend with Diane was coming to a close. She knew she could never be an effective friend in Diane's moment of need, but she desperately wanted to give her friend hope for happiness. She reached for Diane's hand again and held it.

"I think he will publish again," she said.

"He needs to...he needs to do something soon," Diane concluded.

Chapter Thirty-Four — Elena's Gift

When Diane woke up the next morning, her first clear thought was an awareness that today was the day that Elena would be flying out of O'Hare Airport to Moscow and on to Vologda, Russia. The Damen Literary Bookstore did not open until ten a.m. But Diane, who was a morning person, frequently went to the store early in order to do paperwork without being interrupted by anyone. On this morning, Diane arrived at the bookstore to find a nine by twelve package lying up against the store's front entrance.

The package was wrapped in plain brown paper with the words *to Diane, from Elena* neatly printed across the top. Diane smiled at seeing Elena's name. She picked the package up, and gently shook it, trying to guess at its contents. The package was light; she could not imagine what was inside. Tucking the precious object of curiosity under her arm, she unlocked the front door and carried it into her store.

Diane laid the parcel down on a counter top, gently rubbing her fingers over Elena's name. Her mind spun backwards, as she looked over at the table where she and Elena first had tea together. Though not a close friend, Elena had become a dear friend to Diane. Reflecting on past conversations she had with Elena, Diane realized Elena had become a unique confidante.

She stared down at the package again.

Elena is from a different world, she thought. She and I do not know anyone from each other's world…that does make her special. Somehow we bonded quickly and easily. Perhaps being strangers was a good thing for the two of us.

She picked up the package and pressed it to her chest.

"I will miss talking with you, Elena," she said out loud.

Believing the contents of the package were special, Diane decided to make a ceremony out of opening it. She took the package over to the tea table, laid it down, and then began heating water for tea. She felt a tug at her heart and a sickening feeling in her stomach as she placed a water pot and a single teacup on a tray and walked toward the table. She sat down, her eyes constantly being drawn toward the bundle left by Elena. Diane felt lonely sitting by herself. She wished her friend were present. She reached for the package and began to unwrap it. As she did so, her eyes became misty.

The package was well wrapped; twice Diane had to interrupt the process of unwrapping it to wipe her eyes and her nose.

When she stripped away the last piece of tape and pulled the paper back, she found a small plastic tray wrapped in see-through cellophane. A dozen

Russian tea cookies were bunched together on the tray. Below the tray was a note containing the following words:

Diane, I will always think of you during teatime in Vologda. Enjoy the Russian cookies. I am leaving you the poems my lover wrote to me. The feelings expressed in the poems are the cause of my departure. I cannot take the poems with me, and I must remove this man from my heart. Your friend, Elena.

Diane lifted a small manuscript out of the wrapping paper. The first page appeared to be a title page.

Liberty's Gift
By Javier Morales

"Javier!" she exclaimed out loud. "Our Javier?"

Diane sat the manuscript down on the table, looking at it in amazement.

Could Javier be Elena's lover, she wondered for one fleeting second? But the realization that Javier was Elena's lover sunk into her awareness immediately. Of course, she thought...of course. Sweet Javier. Beautiful Javier. Of course.

Knowing Javier and Elena knew each other did not stop Diane from being shocked by the revelation. She sat alone in the early morning quiet of her bookstore, looking at the manuscript in stunned recognition of the new piece of information. In her mind, she imaged them together, making love.

She envied Elena when she thought of the passion Javier must have brought to her bed. She thought of his strong willowy body, his long jet-black hair, his dark Latin eyes, and his sensitive nature. She closed her eyes and imagined Javier on top of her, making love to her. She folded her arms around her body, rubbing and caressing her shoulders with her fingers. She signed deeply while the thought of Javier being her lover rushed through her mind, causing her heart to beat faster and her body to ache with need.

"My god," Diane said out loud when she opened her eyes. "I know why Elena fled back to Russia. Javier...he could break a woman's heart. Poor Javier. Poor Elena."

Diane stood up. She could not remain seated while all of this information processed through her mind and body. She folded her arms around her body again, but not to caress; instead, she needed comfort. She walked slowly in a circle around the table, looking at the shelves of books in her store.

Javier and Elena, she thought. They are a story...they are a book... a long poem of hopeless love...a desperate, desperate story. They are a story of loneliness and oppression. Were they better off to love and lose? I wonder?

She stared out the window of the store and began to think of her own situation. The ache she was feeling in her relationship with Robert was no way near the pain Elena was feeling. Diane's pain was defined by dullness and frustration, not the sharp infliction of pain from which Elena was suffering.

Who is better off? She thought. And Javier...when will he find out that Elena is gone? How will he react?

Diane looked down at the manuscript. It was thin, and made up of very few pages. Should she read it? Did Elena give it to her to throw away, or to read? She picked it up and held in her hands.

"I imagine Elena could not throw it away. She wanted me to keep it and read it so I would understand what had happened," she said softly. "I will read Javier's poetry, but I will wait until I have time...time to sit...time to be alone...time to appreciate it."

A day later, Diane received an email from Elena containing the following message:

Diane – I am back in Russia, and I will be leaving for Vologda soon. I am in Moscow at an Internet café. I want to thank you for being a good friend. Please do email me when you can, but understand that it is not easy for me to email you, but I will. Love, Elena.

Chapter Thirty-Five — Patrick and Javier

After Elena had left Chicago, Patrick, the bartender at the Piazza Navona Restaurant, noticed a marked change in Javier Morales; often Javier seemed despondent. Patrick knew Javier's life was difficult and he wanted to help. He decided to speak to Javier.

It was 9:00 a.m. on a Wednesday and Patrick had purposefully arrived at work an hour before his scheduled started time; he knew Javier had adopted a habit of coming to the restaurant early in order to sit outside and watch people walk by. Patrick decided to approach him during that time. He found Javier seated at one of the outside tables, drinking orange juice from a small plastic bottle.

Patrick walked to the table, greeted Javier, and went right to the point.

"Javier," Patrick said. "You seem upset. Is there anything wrong?"

Javier liked Patrick. He knew Patrick was a good man and he could tell that Patrick's concern for him was genuine.

"A woman," he replied.

"Elena?"

Javier's facial expression broke into a sad smirk.

"Si, Elena," he said. "How did you know?"

"I'm the bartender," Patrick answered. "I see everything. I saw how you acted around her."

Javier looked up at the sky and sighed.

"Did you know we were lovers?" he asked.

"I guessed you were, but I did not know. Were you?"

"I thought so," Javier said. He bent over the table, casting his eyes downward. "I was wrong."

Patrick placed his right hand on Javier's shoulder.

"Elena is a complicated woman," he said. "I think all women are complicated but she had special issues. I'm not sure what her issues were. I know she was difficult to understand."

Javier leaned back in his chair and stretched his long legs out. He shook his head back and forth slowly.

"I do not understand her," he said.

Patrick could see Javier's heart was racked with pain.

"I do not understand why she would leave. I cannot understand why she would go without saying good-bye to me."

"Javier, did she tell you…did she say that she cared for you?"

"Si, she said she loved me. We made love…I don't understand."

"Were you happy…I mean were you both happy together?" Patrick asked.

"I was happy. I thought Elena was happy. Sometimes she would seem unhappy, but I thought she missed Russia."

Javier paused and looked directly into Patrick's face.

"Can I ask you something?" he said.

"Ask me anything," Patrick replied.

"Maybe you know women better. Maybe you can explain some things to me."

"I'll try," Patrick promised.

"Why?" Javier asked. "Why would a woman say she loves a man and then say things to him that are hurtful?"

"Did Elena do that?"

"Yes," Javier answered. "I do not understand this. Do all women do this?"

"I am not an expert on women, Javier. No man is. But I have heard of this. It even happened once to me."

Javier moved to sit upright in his chair. He placed his elbows on the patio table and pointed a finger from his right hand at Patrick.

"You!" Javier responded. "This has happened to you?"

Patrick gazed out toward Damen Avenue, remembering a bad experience in his life. Javier looked at the expression on his friends face.

"It stills hurt you?" Javier asked.

"Yes," Patrick admitted. "It still hurts me. I think it always will."

"Amigo, I am sorry. I should not be making you think of this thing."

"It's all right. Maybe we can help each other. I've never talked about it with anyone."

The two men sat quietly for a moment.

"Javier," Patrick continued. "I think you are like me. I think you are a sensitive person. Let's meet after work. We can go to a bar and talk about all of this. I think it will help both of us. Would you want to do that?"

"Si," Javier agreed. "Some place else…somewhere away from here. Si…I want to do this."

• • •

Since they had come into work on the lunch-early supper shift, Patrick and Javier were able to leave the restaurant by 7:00 o'clock and head for Estelle's on North Avenue. Patrick hoped the combination of a Wednesday night and the earliness of the evening would result in a small crowd, allowing them quiet privacy to talk. He was right.

The men took a booth and ordered a pitcher of beer from the waitress.

"Were you with Elena a long time?" Patrick asked as they waited for their drinks.

"Yes," Javier replied. "I started seeing her when she began working with us."

"I never saw you two spend much time together at the restaurant."

The waitress brought two glasses and a pitcher of beer.

"You two want to run a tab?" she asked.

"We'll run a tab," Patrick replied, while pouring Javier a glass of beer.

"Elena did not want that," Javier said as the waitress departed. "We spent all of our time at her apartment."

"You never went out?"

"There is no money to go out." Javier replied, as he sipped his beer.

"How often did you see her?"

"Twice a week, sometimes more," Javier said. "She would tell me at the restaurant when I could come over."

Patrick took a long drink of beer from his glass.

"You made love during these times?"

"Always," Javier said. "Always I would stay the night and leave in the morning."

"And Elena would tell you that she loved you?"

"Sometimes," Javier said. "Sometimes she would say it in bed. And, sometimes she would tell me she loved me when I was leaving in the morning."

"But she would also say hurtful things, too?"

"Yes," Javier said sadly. "You have had this happen to you. Tell me…why would a person do that?"

"Have you had any other experiences with women, Javier? Maybe women in Mexico?"

"I come from a small village," Javier explained. "My family is very religious. My mother would be ashamed of me for being with Elena. But I was lonely and I fell in love with her."

Patrick picked up the pitcher of beer and poured more of it into Javier's glass. He filled his own glass with beer and sat the pitcher down on the table.

"Javier…here in America we would say that Elena dumped you. Do you understand?"

"What does this mean…dumped me?" Javier asked.

"It is hard to explain," Patrick replied. "It means that she left you without saying good-bye. Do you understand?"

"I know she left me without saying good-bye," Javier answered. "I don't understand why? Why would she tell me she loved me, say hurtful things to me, and leave without saying good-bye? You say this dumping has happened to you. Why did it happen to you?"

Patrick took another long drink of his beer, sat his glass down, and signaled to the waitress to bring another pitcher.

"I can only guess," he said. "I will tell you what I think, but I may be wrong."

Patrick leaned back in the booth. He sighed as he remembered his lost love.

"I may be wrong," he repeated. "But I don't think I am. Let's wait until the waitress is done getting our other pitcher. Okay?"

"You do not want to speak in front of a woman," Javier guessed.

"Si," Patrick replied.

The waitress was perfunctory in her duties, bringing a new pitcher of beer and whisking away the empty pitcher.

Patrick filled Javier's glass again and leaned toward Javier, placing his elbows on the booth's table.

"You know the world is filled with all sorts of people, Javier?"

"Si," Javier replied.

"I am sure Elena did love you…but, I imagine she did not *want* to love you."

A puzzled look appeared on Javier's face.

"I don't understand," he said. "How can this be?"

"Javier, my friend, love is not easy. That is why it is so precious. There are many people who can love you, but only a few who can stay with you. Elena could not stay with you."

Javier lifted his glass up and gulped down its entire contents. A look of deep frustration appeared on his face.

"Why? Why couldn't she stay with me?" he said.

"I don't know the answer to that," Patrick replied.

"Why did she say things that were hurtful to me?"

"She did that so it would be easier to leave you. Do you understand?"

Javier looked perplexed.

"Javier…this is difficult to say. She was trying to dislike you…to stop loving you…to have you stop loving her. She wanted to drive you away from her. That is what I think."

"Why didn't she just ask me to leave? Why be hurtful?"

"I don't know, Javier. I think it has to do with power and control. Some people are afraid of saying good-bye…afraid they will not be able to do it. And some people would rather resent another person than love the person and lose them. I think they are afraid."

"What does this word resent mean?

"My friend…it means Elena would rather dislike you and leave you than love you and lose you. It means she is protecting her heart from pain."

Patrick watched as his words sunk into Javier. The look on Javier's face was solemn.

"This has happened to you?" he said.

"Yes," Patrick replied.

"Do you still love this woman?"

The look on Patrick's face was sad. He stared forward but his mind was thinking of the past. He took another long gulp of beer and slowly sat his half-empty glass down on the table. He used both of his hands to hold onto the glass, moving his fingers up and down its wet slippery sides. He looked down at the glass for a moment and then looked back up at Javier.

"Yes," he said.

"Do her words still hurt you?" Javier asked.

"Yes," he repeated.

Javier reached for the pitcher of beer, filled his glass, placed the pitcher's spout over the rim of Patrick's glass, and filled his friend's glass, emptying the pitcher of beer. He looked at Patrick.

"We should get drunk tonight, my friend," Javier said.

Patrick reached for the empty pitcher of beer, holding it up for the waitress to see.

"That would be a good idea, amigo," he said.

Chapter Thirty-Six — Brae and Ann

It was 2:00 o'clock and Brae was in the library when her cell phone beeped. She opened her phone and read the text message.

7:30?

Brae smiled to herself and immediately sent a message back to Professor Bradford.

Yes!

She closed the anthropology book she was reading and laid her head down on top of the book.

Five hours, she thought; five hours until we can meet. I want to go there now.

But Brae Larson was a pragmatic person. She lifted her head up, opened her book again, and continued to read. She read for another hour and then left for her 3:30 class.

After her class, she decided she would go to her apartment, shower, shave her legs, and change from jean shorts, a t-shirt, and flip-flops to jeans, a white pullover knit cotton top, and medium heeled sandals. She had plenty of time, so after she showered, she lounged in a light bath robe on the living room couch, watching television, but paying little attention to what was on the screen. She just wanted the clock to move along so she could see Robert again. While lying on the couch, she dozed off into a comfortable nap.

"Showering in the middle of the day?"

Brae's eyes opened and she stared up at Ann. For only a moment her mind was disconnected and she wondered where she was. Quickly she gained consciousness and smiled at Ann.

"What?" she asked.

"Showering in the middle of the day?" Ann said again. "There are only two reasons to shower in the middle of the day. Either you have just had sex, or you are getting ready to have sex. Which is it?"

Brae struggled to sit up, cleared her head of sleep, and tried to ignore Ann's remark.

"I just got back from the campus. I've been to the library and to class. And, yes, I do have a date later this evening. What time is it?" she asked.

"It's 6:30," Ann answered.

"Hmmm…I have to get ready to go," Brae said.

"Mr. Wonderful?"

"Yes," Brae replied. "Mr. Wonderful."

"Any more you want to tell me about him?" Ann prodded.

"No. I told you I need some time to figure this all out. But you'll be the first to know when there is something to report."

Brae walked toward her bedroom, attempting to flee from Ann's questions.

"And should I wait up for you?" Ann said smiling.

Brae turned, flipped her long black hair over her shoulders, and smiled back at Ann.

"Not unless you want to stay up all night," she said.

Ann walked to the kitchen, pulled a can of coke out of the frig and grabbed a small bag of potato chips from a basket that was sitting on top of the refrigerator. She sat down on a kitchen stool and began munching on her treats.

"I have a date tonight, too," she shouted at Brae's bedroom door.

Soon Brae emerged from her bedroom, dressed and ready to head out to Robert's apartment.

"Where you two going tonight?" Ann asked as she looked approvingly at Brae's outfit.

"Don't know yet," Brae replied with a knowing smirk on her face. "Like my outfit?"

"I think he'll like it," Ann replied. "It's casual, yet very sexy. It says, 'I'm respectful, but I want to get laid.' I like that…are you?"

"Am I respectful" Yes I am," Brae teased back.

"Are you going to get laid?" Ann asked.

Brae moved toward Ann, put her hands on her hips, and looked directly into Ann's face.

"You see, Ann…that's the difference between you and me. I don't know if I am going to get laid. I like the suspense, the mystery. I like to be wooed and I like to wait until the wooing begins to make that decision."

"Well," Ann replied with a slight laugh. "I'm going to get wooed and laid tonight."

Brae laughed and took a sip of Ann's coke. She sat the can down in front of Ann and winked at her.

"I suspect we will both get laid tonight," she said smiling. "Will you be here tonight?'

Ann shrugged, got up from the kitchen stool, and dumped the remains of her coke down the sink. She turned, leaned against the counter top, and faced Brae.

"I think so," she replied. "I didn't know you would be gone but, now that I do, I think I'll invite him over here. Is that okay? His place is always a mess."

"That's fine, Hon. If there are any complications, I'll give you a call before I come back."

Ann smiled at Brae.

"You look great, Brae," she said. "You really do. I'm glad you are going out and having some fun. All study and no guys makes Brae a dull girl."

"I'm glad, too. It's helped. I really look forward to seeing him."

Ann walked toward Brae and hugged her.

"Good for you. Enjoy whatever it is you two have and don't let him break your heart."

A serious look appeared on Brae's face.

"Oh he'll break my heart. That's a given," she said softly. "And I'll break his."

Ann looked at Brae.

"So you know that already, huh?" she said. "Then you're ahead of the game."

"I don't want it to be a game," Brae replied. "I told you, I know there is no long term commitment here, and I know he knows it, too. But I don't want it to be a game."

Brae moved back away from Ann. Ann could see moisture in her eyes.

"Do you understand that, Ann?" Brae said.

Ann sighed heavily and smiled at Brae.

"To be honest Brae, I don't know anything about men. I just date them and go with the flow. Are you going to talk with him about all of that?"

Brae reflected momentarily on Ann's question.

"Yeah…sometime. Sometime we will talk. Right now, I just want to be with him and talk to him. Really, I enjoy talking and being with him… maybe even more than the sex…the sex is great, too… but he listens to me, Ann. He wants to hear what I think and, right now, he needs me as much as I need him."

"Men…they are always a pain in the ass," Ann said laughing. "But I understand. I like being with them, too. I wonder what they think of us."

"Probably the same. Except we're right and they're wrong," Brae said.

Brae moved toward Ann and hugged her.

"Thanks for understanding," she said. "I'll probably stay over tonight. I'll be back either late Saturday or maybe early on Sunday."

"Take care of yourself," Ann called out, as Brae picked up her purse and headed out the door.

Chapter Thirty-Seven — The Bathtub

Robert's condo had two bedrooms and two full baths. The master bath was sixteen feet by nine feet and it was equipped with a large whirlpool bathtub. It was the whirlpool that convinced Robert to purchase the place. The bathtub was deep and wide with four massaging jet streams; Robert specifically liked that feature. He enjoyed soaking in a tub while he sipped wine and read.

On this night, the bathroom was aglow from the light of four large candles, and Brae was in the bathtub with Robert: they had found their way to the tub after making love in Robert's bedroom.

The bathtub ran north and south along the eastern wall of the bathroom, and was over four feet wide. Robert was partially reclined with his head at the southern end of the tub, while Brae was reclined with her head at the northern end of the tub. The jet stream was set on low. Soap bubbles and water partially obscured their naked bodies.

The tub was equipped with headrests at both ends. Slightly raised seats were built into tub's flooring. The seats made it easy to relax without sliding down into the water. Wrapped around the tub was a six-inch-wide ceramic rim that provided a place to set items and keep them dry. Two bottles of spring water sat on the western rim of the tub, along with a candle and a Tupperware container filled with grapes.

"This is very nice," Brae said with a sigh. "I could stay in here all night."

Brae moved her left foot over onto Robert, slowly massaging him by rubbing her toes up and down his leg. Robert closed his eyes and leaned his head back onto his headrest.

"So could I," he said.

Brae watched Robert relaxing. She smiled at the thought of her being with him in the tub.

"Robert," she said. "I don't mean to pry, but does it bother your wife…you being here so often?"

"Diane is a busy woman," Robert replied, his eyes still closed. "She owns a bookstore, so she has to be away often…usually during the evenings. Weekends are her busiest times. We wouldn't be together tonight."

"But she would come home, right? I mean you would be sleeping with her if you were home tonight, right?"

"Yes, that is true. She will be home tonight, and we do sleep together," Robert said.

"Do you make love with her?"

Robert opened his eyes and looked toward Brae.

"Yes," he said.

"Do you mind me asking you about these things?" Brae asked.

"It's natural that you would," Robert replied.

Brae sat up and reached across the bathtub for her bottle of water. Soap-suds ran down her shoulders and over her breasts. Robert looked at her wet nakedness. He watched her lift the plastic bottle of water to her mouth, wrap her lips around the neck of the bottle, and take a long drink. His eyes scanned her body; he found joy in her beauty. She set the bottle back on the bathtub rim, her body pressing against his as she maneuvered in the tub.

"Does it bother you that we are cheating on her?" she asked.

"There are many ways to cheat on a person, Brae," Robert responded. "People cheat on people everyday of the week."

"Do you mean she is cheating on you?"

"Maybe...but not like this. Not sexually or romantically."

Brae smirked and tilted her head in a quizzical manner.

"Could you be rationalizing now?" she commented.

"Perhaps," he said.

Robert reached over toward the bowl of grapes. He pulled a grape from the bowl, held it between his fingers, and then looked at Brae.

"I don't agree with the rules of the world, do you?" He asked as he pushed the grape into his mouth.

"I guess not," Brae answered. "Otherwise I wouldn't be here."

Robert quickly sliced the grape in two with his teeth and swallowed it.

"And you wouldn't be carrying that Che Guevera bag either," he said. "Unless the bag is just utilitarian or some fashion statement. Is it either of those?"

"No," Brae answered. "I admire people like Che, but I'm not sure how all of that ties in with my question."

"Brae, what does a person do when he discovers that he, or she, stands outside of their culture. When he discovers that all of the things he has been told are not true...or those things are only half-truths?"

Brae leaned back, allowing her body to submerse further into the water. A contemplative expression appeared on her face. Her long dark hair dipped down into the water, while some of the fine strands floated around the side of her neck.

"Is that where you are, Robert?" she asked.

Robert looked down at the water. Brae was only the second person in his life that knew he felt alienated, and he found it strange he was about to confess it to her. She was so young, he thought. How could she understand?

"Yes it is," he said. "Do you understand what I mean?"

"I don't know," Brae replied. "I feel outside, too...sometimes. I'm not sure what it all means."

"That is a part of it, Brae. Not understanding is a part of it. And I'm afraid not being understood is a part of it, too."

Now a look of frustration swept across Brae's face.

"But don't you see such a philosophy can give you license to do whatever you want?" She said.

"What philosophy doesn't give license, Brae? All of them talk about understanding, but what they really mean is 'This is the way it should be.' And, when their philosophy doesn't mesh with reality or with their own tenets, then they either ignore reality or add a new tenet that works for them. It's all creative bullshit. Science and math...those are the only two disciplines that seek the truth. And even they are subject to interpretations that pander to prejudice and self-serving assessments. The human mind is filled with hubris and fault."

"Robert," Brae said. "Explain to me how your wife has cheated on you."

"It is not she that cheats," Robert answered. "It's life. Life cheats us all. It cheats us by surrounding us with expectations and false promises. Think of this, Brae. Not too long ago, and for a long time, women married men with the expectation that marriage would be the pinnacle of their lives. The wedding ceremony was a short fairy tale for them...they were the princesses, marching down the aisle...the center of everyone's attention...their wedding day was considered to be the most important day of their life...that is what they were told. It is what many of them believed. Do you believe that now?"

"No," Brae replied.

"But you know that fairy tale existed for centuries, and it still exists today for millions of women."

"Yes," Brae admitted.

"Do you think all fairy tales have been wiped from the face of the earth?"

"No."

"My wife doesn't cheat on me. Life cheated my wife and me. Life caused us to believe we were something we're not. My wife still believes and expects me to be something I am not."

"You have to work at making a marriage successful," Brae replied. "Everyone changes. Love is supposed to be accepting of change. What did Shakespeare write? 'Love is not love, which alters when it alteration finds.'"

"Noble words. Noble words. But what if she does not know or understand the alteration? Or what if she alters in an attempt to keep the dream alive or to fit him into her dream? And what if she is unaware she is altering?"

Brae began to play with her hair, using her fingers to curl the wet strands around them, and then letting loose of the strands.

"I'll have to check my Shakespeare on that," she said. "Cite a fairy tale for me that applies to men."

"You can be anything you want to be," Robert replied.

A sour expression appeared on Robert's face, making Brae feel sorry for him. She quickly decided to take the conversation in a different direction. An exuberant smile appeared on her lips. Her face became radiant. In response to her smile, Robert's mood changed instantly. He smiled back at her and wished he could capture her expression in some medium that would preserve it for eternity. Her enthusiasm was beautiful.

"You asked me about Che," she said. "Do you want to hear my complaint about the world?"

"Of course," Robert responded. "I'd like to know what you think."

Brae lifted herself out of the water by placing both of her hands on the bathtub rim and pushing up.

"Move your legs apart," she said.

Robert spread his legs and Brae sat down on the bottom of the tub, wrapping her legs around his body. She lifted his legs up and wrapped them around her waist, using his legs to create a backrest. Then she put her arms on Robert's shoulders and looked directly into his eyes.

"I'm a communist," she said smiling. "Do you hate me?"

Robert reached toward Brae. He pulled her wet hair back around her neck, pausing in their conversation to examine the fine line of her chin and the beauty of her long neck.

"So you don't fit into our culture, do you?" he said smiling.

"No, I don't. But I'm a good communist. Not the totalitarian, oppressive kind."

"What kind of a communist are you then?"

"I'm anti-materialistic," Brae said. "I'm opposed to conspicuous consumption. You know Adam Smith, right?"

"Of course, he wrote *The Wealth of Nations*. For many, he is the father of capitalism."

"Do you know what he said about productivity?"

"I assume he was in favor of it," Robert answered with a smile.

Brae playfully frowned.

"He said productivity is to be commended, but if it continues indefinitely, productivity will always lead to the endless pursuit of unnecessary things."

"The endless pursuit of unnecessary things," Robert repeated. "And, that's where you think we are now?"

"Yes," Brae said.

Robert smiled at Brae.

"You have beautiful hair," he said.

Robert's gaze dropped down to admire Brae's breasts. He dipped his hand into the bath water. Using his index finger, he repeatedly traced a circle around one of her nipples.

"You don't look like a cold oppressive communist," he said smiling.

Brae smiled back, and leaned forward to kiss Robert. They held each other, slowly kissing each other's lips over and over again.

"Let's go to bed," Brae whispered. "I want to make love while we are all wet."

"So do I," Robert replied.

Chapter Thirty-Eight — Robert Confesses to Mike

Mike Sheridan's office was located on the third floor of Eckhart Hall. It was a late Thursday afternoon. Mike was seated behind his desk in a comfortable padded wood chair, the kind that could swivel and tilt back at the whim of its owner. He was in the process of grading student papers when his phone rang. The caller was Robert Bradford.

"Hey Robert," Mike said into the phone. "What's happening on the second floor?

"Not much," Robert replied. "I just thought I would invite myself up for a break from grading papers. Are you going to be around for a while?"

Mike eyeballed the mess of papers on his desk with a look of disgust.

"I'll be here until the second coming," he said. "Come on up. I could use a break. Better yet, let's get a bite to eat…and a beer."

"How about Hunters in thirty minutes?"

"Hunters it is," Mike agreed. "I'll be heading over there now. If I stay and read one more paper, I might do harm to myself. See you there."

• • •

Mike arrived at Hunters fifteen minutes before Robert. He took an inconspicuous booth in the corner of the bar and consumed two beers while looking over the front page of the Chicago Tribune.

"Anything interesting in the paper?" Robert asked when he arrived.

"Don't know," Mike answered looking up at Robert. "I don't really read it. I just skim it. It's all bullshit anyway…just a bunch of assholes jockeying for positions."

Robert skidded onto the bench booth, planting himself across the table from Mike.

"Your life is surrounded by bullshit," Robert said smiling.

Mike slid the paper aside and leaned back against the bench.

"So is yours," he said. "I told Dave to make us two hamburgers. Is that alright with you?"

"And a pitcher of beer?"

"And a pitcher of beer," Mike repeated. "You haven't given up drinking beer, have you?"

"Not at all. In fact, two pitchers might be good tonight."

"Oh," Mike replied. "It must be confession time. So who is she?"

"How do you know there's a she?" Robert asked in a startled voice.

"I didn't…just a wild guess. Drinking and screwing are my two vices. You already drink, so screwing was the only thing left."

A waitress interrupted the two men's conversation by bringing them a pitcher of beer and two glasses. She took Mike's old glass away, hurried back with the hamburger baskets, and then scurried away again. Mike filled the two glasses with beer and handed one to Robert.

"Does your wife know?" he asked.

Robert took a sip of beer, sat his glass down on the table, rubbed his face with both of his hands, and let out a long sigh.

"No."

"Do you want her to know?"

"Why the hell would I want her to know that?" Robert asked.

Mike shrugged his shoulders and lifted his glass up.

"Don't know. Sometimes married men hide those things, sometimes they don't. I don't pretend to know anything about marriage. I did it once and once was enough for me."

"She doesn't know."

Mike took a long swallow of his beer. He sat his glass down on the table and played with his hamburger, first turning it around in the basket, then lifting the top up and rearranging the sliced tomato so that it was centered on top of the burger.

"Are you happy?" he asked looking up at Robert.

"Happy at home or happy with her?"

"Happy," Mike said shrugging his shoulders and grabbing a hold of his hamburger.

"No," Robert replied. " But I'm happy when I am with her. She takes me away from everything, but she won't last…what we have can't last. She knows it, too."

"A slice of happiness, huh? Just like the tomato on my hamburger…a garnish."

An irritated expression appeared on Robert's face.

Mike lifted his hamburger, took a bite of it, chewed on it, and then washed it down with a swallow of beer.

"Garnish does add spice to life," he said.

"She's more than garnish," Robert stated. "We share some common beliefs."

"Oh, so she's a Marxist," Mike exclaimed.

"You know I'm not a Marxist," Robert said.

Mike picked his hamburger up again; he held it in both hands, while he looked over it toward Robert.

"Tell me what you are then. And tell me what she is," he said.

Mike shoved the hamburger in his mouth and ripped away another bite, waiting for a reply to his questions.

Robert picked up his hamburger, placed both of his elbows on the table and tore off a sizeable chuck of his sandwich. He chewed on it slowly, as he reflected on Mike's questions. He set the burger down in its basket and took a drink of beer. Keeping his elbows on the table, he held up his left hand and extended his fingers. He used his right fingers to grab on to his left fingers one by one in order to dramatically list the attributes of his new lover.

"Well, she's a student. She's young. She's beautiful. She's smart. She's good in bed."

He switched hands and continued to list her features.

"She's wonderful company. She's fun. She's loving. She's an escape from the world. And, yes, she does adhere to some Marxist principles."

"Hmmm…good in bed. That's a wonderful tribute," Mike said slowly. "And what are you? I mean, where are you in all this Marxist stuff? Is that her appeal for you?"

"I told you, I'm not a stringent Marxist. But I do see it as a legitimate reproach to the materialism of the world…the opulence of the West…the relentless consumerism of capitalism…the, the…"

"Conspicuous consumption?"

"Yes…the conspicuous consumption of the American culture."

"And she does, too?"

"Yes. She doesn't wallow in the materialism of our society. She volunteers to help the underprivileged. And, she believes in the value of labor vis-à-vis management."

"Ah, the peasants of the world. She's with them? Ah yes, the great unwashed. Tell me Robert, have you really embraced a Marxist philosophy, or is all of this just anti-establishment rhetoric?"

Robert frowned at Mike.

"Americans wallow in materialistic crap…we're drowning in it while most of the world goes hungry. Our CEOs make more in one day than the ordinary worker makes in a year…we've lengthened our winter holiday celebrations so we can stuff our obese bodies with more food…we engage in an endless pursuit of buying unnecessary things, and then you make fun of her?"

Mike grabbed the pitcher of beer and emptied its contents, draining the largest portion of it into his glass and the remainder into Robert's. He took a long drink of beer, emptying his glass and summoning the waitress for another pitcher.

"We both know what I am," he said, as the waitress walk away toward the bar. "I am a drunk and a coward. But okay…a drunk who leans towards Marxism when I'm tilted in an inebriated state."

The waitress brought the second pitcher of beer; immediately Mike proceeded to fill up his glass again. Robert watched as Mike gulped down half of the beer in the glass and then sat the glass down on the table.

"I admire you, Robert…and her, too," he said. "Most of the women I sleep with are only good in bed. I'm not complaining, but it would be nice to talk with them, too."

Mike reached for the pitcher, leaned Robert's glass to the side, and poured it full of beer.

"So, she's a student, huh? Not a lit student I hope."

"She is a lit student…and she was a student of mine last year."

"Is she discreet? There are rules about that kind of stuff, you know."

"We don't go out…at least, not near the campus. And she is discreet. And she is beautiful."

"You already said that," Mike observed. "It must be true."

Robert looked at his half-eaten hamburger, thought about taking another bite, but opted to drink. He guzzled down a large swallow of beer and then continued talking with Mike.

"Yes, she's beautiful and she keeps me from being bored by all of the bullshit in my life. I'm tired of this intelligentsia, elitist campus crap. I have no interest in sports or pop culture, so where the hell am I?"

Frustrated by his confession of boredom, Robert let out a large sigh and looked directly at Mike.

"Mike," he said, "you know I'm no revolutionary. There's no sense in that. This is America and we're stuck with it, but I hate what it has become…it's a fucking haven for celebrities and fat cats. And the common man…the working proletariat…is being sold a batch of goods. But, he's buying it, hoping that he wins the lottery so he can jump into the trough and pig out. Christ I hate it."

"And she hates it, too?"

Robert smiled and quietly chuckled.

"The last time we were together she brought over a Che Guevara t-shirt to sleep in. What does that tell you?"

Mike belted back another huge swallow of beer, wiped his mouth with the back of his hand, and let out a sigh.

"That tells me she's young," he said. "God bless her, she's very young."

"She makes me feel like there is hope," Robert replied.

"But there isn't," Mike said. "There is no hope for your romantic Marxist ideals or for your romance with her. You know that, don't you?"

"We both know that…I'm pretty sure we both know that."

"Maybe you should talk with her about that part," Mike said. "Talk with her before it gets messy. After all, you're not going to leave Diane and you're not going to lead any Marxist rebellion on campus."

Robert fidgeted on the booth bench, rubbed his eyes with his fingers, and then took a drink of beer. He sat the glass down on the table, rocking it back and forth with his right hand.

"She knows that...she knows that," he said. "You know what she is, Mike? She's escape... and pleasure... and beauty. I don't know what the hell I am for her, though."

"Robert," Mike said. "Tell me this...is she escape from Diane, or Dean Allen Hall, or publishing?"

Then Mike straightened himself up on his side of the booth. An eureka expression spread across his face.

"Or," he said, "is she an escape backwards in time...back to those times when we were students, filled with ideals and thinking we were going to make a difference. Is that what she is?"

"She's all that," Robert said. "God help me, she's all that. Together we're a train wreck. I'm not what she thinks I am. I will never live up to her expectations...and I have no idea who she is."

"So why are you telling me all of this?" Mike asked.

"I'm trying to get it all in line. I guess I just needed to verbalize it to someone."

"Guilt?"

"Maybe guilt, too," Robert said. "But not a lot. Diane and I have been arguing for the last three years. I don't live up to her expectations either."

"Does she live up to yours?"

"That's the funny part, Mike. I never have any expectations, and yet, she doesn't live up to them. I know how that sounds."

"It sounds confused," Mike said. "Are you confused?"

"Right now? Yes, I'm confused...and pissed off."

"Maybe you need professional help. I'm no professional."

"Maybe," Robert replied. "Maybe after this is all over. After I get my poetry written and hand it over to that son-of-a-bitch dean. Maybe then."

"How's that coming?"

"I have some ideas but nothing concrete. If I could get that work done, I think a lot of this would all go away."

"The publish or perish syndrome, huh? Kind of like the Vietnam Syndrome...no one understands it. Post-traumatic stress and all of that."

"You seem to handle it okay," Robert said.

Mike held a glass of beer up.

"Don't forget, I drink. I know you drink some, too. But I drink a lot. I don't have a family. If I don't publish, I can always get a job at some community college. You have to work here. I don't."

Robert looked down at the table. He thought about pouring another glass of beer, but realized it would not help. Nothing would help.

"You're right about that. I have to be a professor here...at the University of Chicago. I have to do that."

A moment of silence prevailed. Mike appeared uncomfortable.

"I know you have thought about this, Mike," Robert said. "So tell me this…have you ever believed that all of this is an illusion?"

"You mean life?" Mike asked. "Yeah, I've thought that. And yes I believe it is. We don't know much and those things that we do know may very well be an illusion. Certainly life is a distortion. That I *do* believe. We distort it. Our senses distort it. Our limitations distort it. Our egos distort it. And people distort it for their own advantage."

"Yeah, and the people in power distort everything," Robert said.

Mike frowned.

"This is a pretty depressing conversation," he observed.

"Yep. It is," Robert agreed. "I guess my point is that I have to chose which distortion is the one I want to go with."

"My advice is to stay where you are," Mike replied. "You're too old to fight it. I understand that this flirtation you're having has energized your idealism, but…this flirtation will pass. It's an illusion, too. Stick with the married professor illusion. That's my advice. Maybe drink a little more, too."

Robert was silent as he reflected on what Mike had said.

"So what are you going to do?" Mike asked.

"For right now? I'm going to juggle two illusions, and I'm going to find some way to publish…some way to fire up my creativity."

"And what about her?"

"I'll talk with her. She will want to talk. I think she's going through some difficult times, too. We do communicate well. Maybe we can back off a little and still help each other."

"Now there is a distortion," Mike said laughing.

Robert laughed, too.

Chapter Thirty-Nine — Diane Reads Javier's Poetry

It was a Wednesday evening and Diane was at home enjoying the comfort and quiet of being alone. She was wearing jeans, a white t-shirt, white socks, and walking shoes. Wednesdays were slow days at the bookstore, and four years ago she had decided to close the store earlier than normal on that day of the week. Robbie's school was closed on Thursday due to a teacher institute day and he had asked if he could spend the night with a friend. Diane had just returned from escorting him to his friend's home. Robert was staying over at his condo.

More than a week had slipped by since Diane had found the cookies and Javier's poems in the package Elena left. She had brought the gift home and hid it in a hallway closet. She wasn't ignoring the poems; indeed, the poems were always on her mind, and she was anxious to read Javier's words, but she was certain his writing would upset her. Diane knew the poetry would cause her to think of Javier and Elena. She knew the poetry would make her miss Elena; she knew the passion expressed in the poetry would cause her to want Javier.

Diane Bradford was a good woman and an excellent mother. There was a time when she was good wife, but those times had faded; she was not sure why. Some subtle erosion of the relationship she once had with Robert had occurred over an undefined period of time, and for reasons she could not comprehend. Often she felt drained of any feelings she once had for Robert. She knew he felt the same. The love they had once shared was replaced by tension and misgivings; they frequently argued over matters that seemed trivial. But Diane and Robert both knew the petty disagreements they engaged in were manifestations of a deeper rift; substantial changes had occurred in Robert since he married Diane. She did not fully understand why the changes had occurred, but she knew the changes were taking Robert away from her.

The Bradford marriage had been a marriage of minds. Diane knew philosophical differences between two such highly educated individuals could destroy their matrimonial vows. Even so, she could not bring herself to become angry with Robert. Diane was an intelligent woman; a woman who surrounded herself with thousands of books, each one espousing a unique lifestyle. Her life was best defined by tolerance and acceptance. She could forgive the changes she found in Robert, but she needed acceptance, too. The longing she felt for Javier was a longing to share, to be loved, and to be loving.

In some way, Diane knew that reading Javier's poems would cause a major alteration in her life. She was not superstitious or mystical, but she had come to view the packet of poetry with a respectful reverence. She wanted to be surrounded by serenity when she read and contemplated Javier's words, and she wanted total privacy in order to allow her emotions to freely follow his. She decided to make the reading a ceremony. She would retrieve the package, take it to her reading room, and sip on a glass of wine while she carefully examined what Javier had written.

Diane had hidden the package of poems in a hallway closet that was used by the Bradford's to store winter coats, boots, scarves, gloves, and umbrellas. There was a shelf that ran from one side of the closet to the other. The shelf was attached six and half feet above the closet floor. Numerous telephone books representing Chicago and the suburbs were stacked on the shelf along with two stacks of old literary magazines and another stack of old newspapers.

Diane brought a short three-foot high stepladder in from the kitchen so she could climb high enough to recover the package. She positioned the ladder in the middle of the closet and pulled on a string that hung down from the closet's single light fixture; the closet was immediately flooded with light from a 60 watt bulb.

Diane smiled to herself as she climbed up the stepladder. She was ready to read Javier's poetry. She was anxious to become a part of what he and Elena had shared, and she was ready for change. She picked up a yellow telephone book and repositioned it off to her right so she could see over the top of the larger phone book, behind which she had hid the poems. Her heart sunk when she saw no trace of the packet. Panicked by the loss of the precious package, Diane looked to her right and was jolted by the realization that all of the old magazines and newspapers had been cleared off the shelf. She gripped the shelf with her fingers, while her body shuddered at the loss. Her head dropped forward and she momentarily rested her forehead between her hands.

No! She thought as she pushed and pulled on the telephone books, looking for some sign of the package. She climbed up one more step to the top of the ladder, looking down on the shelf and running her eyes back and forth the full length of the closet. The package was nowhere to be found! Quickly she climbed down off the stepladder. She pushed her way into the mass of hanging coats, shoving them aside, desperately hoping to find the package lying behind the coats on the closet floor. She found nothing.

In despair, Diane left the closet, leaned backward against a wall, and let her body slowly sink down until she was seated on the floor. Diane Bradford was a strong woman, but tonight she began to quietly cry in recognition of the possibility she would never read Javier Morales' poems.

Chapter Forty — Diane Confronts Robert

Robert got home from the university late on Friday. He changed into sweatpants, a t-shirt, and gym shoes so he could work out on the elliptical machine he had purchased a year ago. The one area in the house that was exclusively his was the basement fitness room. He used the room to keep in shape while venting his frustrations through a demanding exercise routine. Without exercise, Robert found the world to be imposing; exercise allowed him to chase away many of life's complications. After working out for forty minutes, he took a quick sponge bath, dressed, and drove to the Montessori day care center on Division Street to pick up Robbie.

"Hi, Mr. Bradford," a young woman greeted as Robert walked into the building. "Here to pick up Robbie, right?"

"Yes," Robert answered. "I know I'm late, but I couldn't get away from work."

"Well, I'll get Robbie for you," the woman said. "You know there is an extra charge for late pick-ups."

"I understand," Robert replied. "I'll write you a check while you're getting Robbie."

The woman left and returned shortly with Robbie following along at her side.

"Here he is," she exclaimed.

Robert bent down, opened his arms wide, and greeted his son.

"Hi Rob!" he called out.

Robbie rushed to his father and was caught up in Robert's embrace.

"How was your day?" Robert said as he nuzzled his mouth against the side of Robbie's face.

Robbie laughed gleefully and wiggled in his father's arms.

"Stop it, Daddy," he cried out.

Robert put his son down and took a hold of Robbie's small hand.

"Let's go see your mother, champ," he said to Robbie.

"Is mommy in the car?" Robbie asked.

"No. We'll stop by the bookstore after we get supper. Want to go to Wendy's?" Robert asked.

"Yeah," Robbie answered excitedly. "Let's go to Wendy's."

"Okay guy," Robert replied. "Let me pay this young lady and we'll head out."

Robert finished writing out the penalty check and gave it to the woman.

"We'll see you next week, Robbie," the woman said. "Bye."

"Bye Miss Julie," Robbie replied.

Robert and Robbie went to Wendy's for supper. The Wendy's restaurant had an indoor jungle gym in it, and after they had finished their meal, Robbie played on the gym while Robert read a newspaper. When he finished his newspaper, Robert got his son out of the gym, and he drove to his wife's bookstore.

"Hi, Robbie," Diane called out as the two entered her store.

Robbie rushed to greet his mother. They both hugged each other tightly. Diane bent down so she could look Robbie square in his face.

"Now, what is a little boy like you doing out this late," she said smiling at him.

"Daddy took me to Wendy's," Robbie answered.

"He did! That's your favorite place to eat. You're a lucky boy," his mother said. "Why don't you go over to the children's table and see what books are there tonight while I talk with your father?"

"Okay mommy," Robbie said as he scurried off to the table.

Robert was standing behind Robbie during his conversation with Diane. He watched his son hurry off to the children's table, and then turned to face his wife.

"Sounds like I'm in trouble," he said.

Diane had watched Robbie run for the table, too. Now she turned toward Robert, threw an exasperated facial expression his way, and shrugged her shoulders in disbelief.

"What is he doing out so late?" she asked.

"It's only eight-thirty," Robert replied. "He's been out later than that."

"Not after a school day he hasn't. He's a little boy, who has had a very long day. He should be going to bed right now."

"It won't hurt this one time," Robert replied. "You dolt on him too much."

"And why did you go to Wendy's? I made tuna casserole. Didn't you see the note on the refrigerator?"

"Must have missed it," Robert said. "I didn't go in the kitchen."

"You went home and worked out before you picked up Robbie."

"Yes, but just for forty minutes or so," Robert said. "You know the casserole will keep, and we can have it tomorrow for lunch."

"Tomorrow Robbie and I are going to the Jelly-Belly Factory in Wisconsin with Darlene and Bradley for a birthday party."

"Right. I forgot about that," Robert replied.

"What time did you pick Robbie up from the center?" Diane asked.

"I was a little late from work"

"You stayed late at UC?" Diane asked.

"I've been writing," Robert replied. "I think I've found the theme I want to use…everything seems to be flowing for me now. I need peace and quiet to continue with it."

"So when did you pick Robbie up?"

"I picked him up a little after seven."

"Seven! That's two hours late. They'll charge us for that," Diane said.

"I already paid the penalty from my checking account. It's no big deal."

"Did you call and let them know you would be running late?" Diane asked.

"They're open until nine. There was no reason to call."

Diane sighed in a noticeable manner.

"Robbie can tell time," she said. "He needs to be notified that you are going to be late."

Robert frowned.

"Okay. I messed up," he agreed. "But it's not the end of the world. I'll...I'll take him home and put him to bed."

"No. Let's let him play here at the table. I'm going to close up, and we can go home together. I just want him to have a regular routine. But you're right...it won't hurt him if we deviate every once in a while."

A gloomy silence settled over Diane and Robert. They looked over at the table and watched Robbie playing with a wooden train set. Diane was the first to speak again.

"Let me ask you something else," she said. "Did you throw away the magazines and papers from the hallway closet?"

"No." Robert answered. "But I did have Rebecca do that."

"Rebecca cleaned out the closet?"

"Yes. I told her to clean it out. There were too many magazines in there. I told her to get rid of them and to straighten out some of those coats in there. Was there something wrong with that?"

A sad look appeared on Diane's face as she tried to come to grips with the fact that their house cleaner had thrown out Javier's poems, and that the poems would be lost to her forever.

"You've been after me to clean that closet for weeks now," Robert said. "Now, I have it done and you're upset. I don't understand. Did you want one of the magazines?"

"No...not really," she said. "I just wish you would talk to me before you have anything thrown out of the house. There was an article I was interested in reading."

"I'm sorry," Robert said in an irritated tone. "But all of those magazines were mine. I didn't see anything wrong with me having them pitched. A person can hold onto stuff too long. It's better just to get rid of it. I live in the house, too."

Diane felt an emptiness creeping into her stomach. Somehow the loss of Javier's poems was more important to her than the tension she currently felt between her and Robert, and that arrangement of priorities caused her to understand how far she and Robert had drifted apart.

"I know you do," Diane replied. I didn't mean to imply the house is only mine. I'll just finish a couple of things here, and then we can leave. Why don't you go play with Robbie?"

• • •

Two days later, Diane was happy to see a message from Elena in her email inbox, but the message turned out to be more bad news.

Diane,

Thank you for being my American friend. I miss you, and wish we could have tea and talk. I was hopeful my return to Vologda would make my life better. I was wrong. I brought a poem home with me. Sasha cannot read English and he is not a jealous man, but he had some friends over to our house and one of them found the poem and read it out loud. Sasha was furious. He asked me who wrote the poem, but I refused to tell him. He stormed out of the house and I have not seen him for two days. I am miserable. I miss talking with you.

Elena

Chapter Forty-One — Brae Finds Robert's Poetry

B rae Larson stayed over at Professor Bradford's condo with continuing frequency. Eventually, Robert gave her a set of keys, letting her know she could use the condo whenever she wanted. Brae discovered she liked being alone in the condo. She liked the idea she and Robert had made the condo their special place. She tried not to become entangled in Robert's life, though she found herself becoming more and more fond of him. He was the first male in her life who enjoyed being alone with her; the first man who was genuinely interested in what she thought. She could tell that Robert needed her. She liked that. And, there was something else she liked – she liked staying in a home where she was making love to a man. She enjoyed being surrounded by the furniture and the walls that made up the environment in which she and Robert expressed their passion for each other. In Robert's condo, Brae felt accepted, safe, and secure. In Robert's condo, she never suffered from her nightmare.

On Wednesdays Brae would go to the condo to prepare a light lunch for her and Robert. Both she and Robert had a two-hour break between eleven o'clock and one. They used Wednesdays to catch up on how their week was going and to make future plans. But today, Robert had cancelled his afternoon class and had promised to pick up an order of spicy calamari at Pizza Capri. Lunch would consist of calamari and wine. Brae agreed to skip her afternoon class so they would have the entire afternoon together.

Brae arrived at the condo first. She decided to check her email on Robert's computer while she waited for him to arrive. Robert's computer was a laptop. When she opened it, she was happy to see a special topic heading in the Microsoft Word bar at the bottom of the screen. Brae knew Robert was under pressure from the university to produce something that could be published. She smiled to herself when she saw the word *poetry*.

She did not expect Robert to arrive for another fifteen minutes. Although she was aware that she should not look at his private writings, she decided to take a quick peek at how he was doing. She clicked on the box and was happy to see the screen fill up with writing.

For a moment, she considered minimizing the page back to its bar status, but she could not resist the temptation to read part of what he had written.

As she focused on the screen, words of passion, love, need, commitment, and beauty sprung up from the computer page; words arranged in a manner that caused the deep emotions expressed by Robert to wash over Brae and penetrate her very soul. She shivered as she read what he had written. Her eyes misted over, her lips parted, and she breathed in deeply. She paused in her reading and stood up, physically moved by her lover's words. She hugged herself, and shook her head. The words tugged at her, pulling her back to the screen, making her want to read more, to experience more. She shuddered. In an effort to control her feelings, Brae turned her back on the computer screen.

"I can't read anymore," she whispered softly to herself. "Robert will be here soon."

Brae turned around quickly. She sat back down, focusing her attention on the procedures needed to take the words away. She clicked the mouse, compressing the poetry into a minimized state at the bottom of the screen. She breathed out a sigh of relief as the words disappeared, but was astonished to find thoughts of her nightmare swirling in her head. Somehow the sight of the page collapsing connected her with the anguish she always felt at the bottom of the stairs.

"My God," she said aloud. "How can this be? Why is this happening?"

A crippling numbness embraced Brae, as she sat in a comatose-like state.

Suddenly the numbness was ripped away from her as she heard the sound of the front door being unlocked.

Robert is here, she thought.

Brae moved hastily away from the computer and rushed to the bathroom. She entered the bathroom quickly, quietly closing the door behind her.

"Brae!" she heard Robert call out. "Are you here?"

"I'm in the bathroom, Robert," Brae responded. "Be right out."

"Well hurry up," he said. "I'll get the wine ready, but I don't want the calamari to get cold."

Brae looked in the bathroom mirror.

"Chase those words out of my head," she whispered to the image in the mirror. "Chase them away."

She turned on the cold water, letting the water run slowly out of the faucet and onto the palms of her hands. She bent down over the sink, splashed the water in her face, and then rubbed her face hard with her wet fingers. Reaching for a towel, she padded her face, and then pressed the towel firmly against her forehead and her eyes, hoping to rub away any sign of emotion. Holding the towel against her face, she inhaled and exhaled deeply.

"Brae," she heard Robert shout. "Are you coming?"

Brae lowered the towel from her face. She moved toward the toilet, flushed it, and then turned both water faucets on, letting them run at full force.

"Be right there," she called out over the flow of the water.

Composing herself, Brae left the bathroom and prepared to greet Robert.

"Looks good, doesn't it?" Robert said.

Brae looked at the small kitchen table. It was adorned with a bottle of wine, two wine glasses, two plates, and a paper basket filled with spicy calamari. She put her arm around Robert's waist and pulled him close.

"It looks delicious," she said smiling.

Robert placed his arm around Brae, and felt her body tremble.

"You okay?" he said.

"I'm fine. Let's eat before it gets cold."

Throughout the meal, Robert and Brae talked, enjoying each other's company while swapping stories about how their week was going. But now, Brae saw Robert in a different light. She wondered what was in his heart, but was afraid to ask. She wondered if his poetry was inspired by their experiences. She wondered why his words moved her to cry and to think about her reoccurring nightmare. She anguished over whether or not she should talk to Robert about his poems, deciding to wait for a better time.

Brae enjoyed talking with Robert, but she felt a sense of apprehension creeping into her mind. Robert is different she concluded as they drank their second glass of wine. The words she read on his computer screen caused her to see him in a new light, and at the same time, shrouded him in mystery. She wondered why she had not seen this side of him before.

• • •

Brae and Robert made love that afternoon. While they made love, Brae found herself engulfed by his poetic expressions. The memory of his words poured over her body, igniting her senses; his poetry caressed her, and his rhythmic incantation of the joys of love lifted her to a level of ecstasy she had never experienced.

After making love, Robert and Brae fell asleep. Robert awoke first from their brief slumber. He looked at the digital clock radio that sat on a small table next to the bed.

3:17

Brae was lying naked on her side, partially covered by a bed sheet. Her back was to Robert. He looked intently at the soft smoothness of Brae's skin. His eyes followed the curvature of her body. It was a pleasure to look at her.

Robert wet his lips and shook his head slowly back and forth. He was amazed to be in bed with such a beautiful woman; it hurt to know such fortune could not last. He reached to touch Brae, gently nudging her awake.

"Brae," he said. "I have to go now."

Brae awoke, her eyes opened, but she remained lying on her side. She partially turned her face up toward Robert.

"Robert," she said in a sleepy voice, "Do you have to go?"

She felt his fingers touching her neck, running down over her shoulders and her arms. She felt him tenderly kissing her shoulders.

"Will you be all right, my love?" he asked.

"Don't go," she said.

It was the first time Brae had ever asked more of him.

Robert sighed, and pressed his body up against her, laying his head down on her shoulders. His right arm reached over her tummy. He pulled her body to his.

"I have to go," he said. "Will you stay over tonight?"

Brae rolled over on her back and re-arranged a pillow under her head. Robert lifted himself up, resting his upper body on his left elbow so he could look at her.

"You are beautiful," he whispered.

Brae smiled. She took Robert's fingers in her hand, pressed them to her lips, and affectionately kissed them over and over. Then she looked at him.

"I'll stay here, if that's all right," she said. "I'm tired."

Robert stretched his body over Brae's and kissed her forehead.

"That's fine, my love," he said.

Robert got out of bed, dressed quietly, and left the condo while Brae snuggled under the covers, thinking more about Robert's poetry.

Chapter Forty-Two — Brae Reads Robert's Poems

Brae did not sleep well. She awoke very early the next morning, unable to fall back asleep. She turned over on her back, put her hands behind her head, and stared at the ceiling. She wanted to read more of Robert's poetry but, knowing she should not violate his privacy, she went to shower, trying to take her mind off of what she was certain she would eventually do.

Wrapped in a large white towel, she stood in front of the bathroom mirror and proceeded to put on her makeup. As she looked in the mirror, she reflected on the words she had discovered. She knew she would have to open the computer again and read more.

Brae quit being attentive to her morning makeup routine. Her eyes focused intently upon her own reflected image.

Ever since I was twelve years old, I have been plagued by that nightmare, she thought. This place, Robert's condo, has been a sanctuary from that dream, and now this. Could the poetry be the resolution I have been searching for?

Brae pulled the towel off her body, threw it in the tub, and quickly moved to the bedroom in order to dress.

I have to read more, she said to herself.

• • •

Ann Yin got home from her classes at twelve-thirty on Thursday afternoons. Before Brae met Robert, Ann had always been accustomed to finding Brae at the apartment making tuna fish salad for both of them. After Brae met Robert, Ann had come accustomed to finding the apartment empty, and having to fend for lunch by herself.

But Ann was happy for Brae. She was glad Brae had eventually confided in her and told her about Robert. Although she understood how dangerous Brae's relationship with Robert was, Ann could not condemn her. In fact, Ann was pleased to see Brae in such a contented frame of mind. Whatever Robert was doing for Brae, it seemed to be paying off. Ann believed Brae was less anxious than she had ever been. Brae now seemed joyful about her life.

Today when she entered their apartment, Ann was surprised to see Brae at home, sitting on the living room couch.

"Hey stranger," Ann called out to Brae. "It's nice to see you home for once."

Brae sat quietly. Her back was braced against one of the couch's arm rests, her knees were bent with her feet up on the couch, and her arms were wrapped tightly around her legs. Ann immediately noticed that Brae looked pale.

"What's the matter," Ann asked.

There was no reply.

Ann walked to the couch and sat down next to Brae. She placed one hand on Brae's left knee.

"What's wrong, Hon," she said.

Brae looked at Ann. The expression on Brae's face was grave.

"Ann," she said. "I completed my nightmare. I went past the doorway and into the basement."

Ann felt goose bumps racing up and down her body, and she felt her stomach churn.

"Are you all right?" she asked.

"I'm okay," Brae answered. "It's what I always wanted to do."

"When did this happen?"

"This morning at the condo."

"Why did it happen? You told me the condo was the one place where you never had that awful nightmare. And why would it happen in the morning? Did Robert hurt you?"

"No. Robert didn't hurt me, but he showed me the way…the way to confront my fear," Brae said.

"You told him about the nightmare? I thought you said you were not going to talk to him about that."

"I didn't," Brae said.

"I don't understand," Ann replied.

Ann stood up and tugged lightly on Brae's arm.

"I'm going to get you off of this couch," she said. "You're withdrawing into yourself. Come out to the kitchen, and sit with me. I'll get us a Coke. You go wash up, then we can talk."

Brae obediently followed Ann's direction, and moved slowly to the bathroom to get herself ready to talk.

When Brae entered the kitchen her complexion and her skin color looked better to Ann.

"Come here girl," Ann said. "We'll drown our troubles in pop, Doritos, and dip."

Brae gave Ann a half-hearted smile and a hug as she walked by her to sit down at the table.

"You're a good friend," she said.

Ann sat down and took a drink of Coke.

"Really now," she said. "Are you all right? That must have been quite an experience for you."

"I'm fine for right now," Brae replied. "Who knows what will happen when I go to bed. But, I really think this was good for me…unexpected, but good in the long run. I've cried a lot already…sobbed and sobbed until there wasn't anything left."

"Was Robert good for you? Did he help?"

"Robert wasn't there."

Ann shook her head, grabbed the edge of the table, and pushed hard against the wood with her fingers.

"Okay…okay. You need to tell me what happened, Brae. I'm confused. I'm frightened for you."

"I wasn't asleep when I passed through the door. I was awake."

"How can that be?" Ann asked.

"I was reading some poetry Robert had written for his publication requirement," Brae said. "It is hard to explain, but the words were gut wrenching for me. Robert's words pulled me back to the nightmare and pushed me through the door. The words spoke to me; they inspired me to confront my fears… to face danger. Compelling words…emotional words…"

"All this…just from his poetry?"

"I don't know how to explain it," Brae said. "But yes…all that from Robert's words. Maybe…maybe his words and the love I feel for him. How many women get to make love to a poet?"

Ann turned her face away from Brae. She stared into space, her eyes misting over.

"Yeah…how many?" she said.

A cold shiver spread down Brae's back.

"I saw into the basement, Ann," she said. "I saw the nightmare."

The look on Brae's face was an expression of fear. Tears spilled from her eyes.

"Can you tell me about it?" Ann asked.

"I have to tell you, Ann. I have to tell someone. Eventually, I will have to tell my family. God, I don't know how I will be ever be able to tell my mother."

Brae's head toppled downward and she began to weep uncontrollably.

Ann got up from her chair and comforted Brae. She had never seen Brae so totally distraught. The experience filled her with fortitude; she wanted to be useful for her friend.

"We'll go back to the couch, Brae," she said. "We'll talk there."

Chapter Forty-Three — Brae Enters the Basement

Ann put her arm around Brae's waist and led her into the living room. She hugged Brae when they stood in front of the couch.

"You'll be okay," she said.

Brae inhaled deeply; her body shook. She hugged Ann tightly.

"I'll be fine," she said. "I'll be fine."

They sat down on the couch, positioning themselves at opposite ends, and bracing their backs against the arm rests so they could look at each other. They scooted around in order to get comfortable, as they prepared to engage in a serious conversation.

"Thank you for being here, Ann."

"I'm glad to help," Ann said. "I know you think that my life is frivolous, but I do have a serious side, too."

"I never thought your life was frivolous," Brae said. "I always thought you were just trying to escape from commitment or from some serious issues."

"That's pretty good, Brae. You've hit the mark, but we're not here to talk about me. Tell me what you can about this nightmare."

Brae breathed in hard. She had grabbed a box of tissues as they were leaving the kitchen and she plucked four of them from the container.

"I won't be able to tell you without crying," she said.

Ann leaned and stretched forward. She grabbed three tissues from the box that was sitting on the floor next to Brae.

I'll cry with you," she said. "What happened in the new nightmare?"

"Everything was the same," Brae began. "Except this time I walked down the stairs with a sense of purpose…a sense of resolution. It was as if I was decisively moving down the stairs in order to discover what had been haunting me. There was no sense of the stairs closing in around me, no sense of me being pushed along, and no effort on my part to hold back."

Ann's facial expression was serious and inquisitive.

"That's strange," she said. "Why do you think that was?"

"I…I think it was the poetry. Something in the poetry inspires courage."

"What happened when you got to the bottom of the stairs?"

"Well, I did hesitate, but not for long. I heard the cries for help, and I wanted to help whoever was crying out. As soon as I entered the basement, the darkness of the room disappeared and I saw…"

Brae's voice broke; her chest heaved.

"I saw my sister!" she cried out. "I saw Kallie."

Brae started to cry again. She gasped for air and fought to continue with her story.

"I saw… my Kallie… being raped by our neighbor," she stammered. "My Kallie."

Ann moved her hands to her face and covered her mouth.

"Oh God!" she gasped. "Oh God!"

Unable to contain her emotion, Brae's body shuddered again.

"Kallie. Kallie," she said over and over again.

"Brae, look at me," Ann said. "Focus your concentration on my face. Look at my eyes."

Brae looked at Ann.

"I'm here, Brae. We're here in our apartment. We're safe. You're safe. What you saw happened a long time ago. Breathe slowly. Calm down."

Brae began to come back into the present.

"Look at me," Ann said again. "Focus on me."

Brae's demeanor took on a look of composure.

"I'm alright," she said. "I'm alright."

Brae dropped her head into her hands and rubbed her face. Then she looked up again at Ann.

"This is terrible, Ann," she said. "I don't know what I'll do."

"Tell me," Ann said. "Is there more?"

"Yes. When I saw them, he stopped and looked at me. The room changed instantly from a basement to our living room. I looked back at the door…it was no longer a basement door. The stairs had disappeared. The door became our front door to our house. I think…I think this happened to me. I think it is not a nightmare. It is a recollection. I must have come into our house when he was molesting Kallie. I have suppressed the memory all of these years."

"Is there anything else you remember?"

"I remember him shouting at me to leave. I remember my sister crying and I remember her telling me I had to leave. I think she was trying to protect me. All these years…all these years I have wondered about a note my sister left in a book my mother gave me."

"What note? What book?" Ann asked.

"A note written in her handwriting. A note she put in my *Walden* book. The note reads, 'don't tell'. I never knew what the note meant."

"Why wouldn't she want you to tell anyone? I mean, my god, the man raped her."

"She didn't want mother to know. And I guess she felt guilty about all of it. Maybe she felt as if she was to blame."

Brae's body collapsed against the back of the couch. She looked exhausted and beaten. She closed her eyes and rested. Ann got up off the couch.

"Lay down, Brae," she said.

Brae's body fell into place on the couch. Ann reached for a quilt that was spread over the top of the couch. She opened the quilt and covered Brae's body.

"Sleep, Brae," she said.

Brae fell asleep immediately.

• • •

Brae slept for six hours. When she awoke, Ann had supper prepared for her. The two women ate their supper without reference to Brae's new discovery. Instead, they talked about their college classes and Ann's new boyfriend. After the meal, they approached the subject of Brae's nightmare while drinking coffee at the kitchen table.

"What will you do now?" Ann asked.

"I'm going to honor my sister's wishes," Brae replied. "I'm not going to tell."

"Do you think that is the right thing to do?"

"There is nothing else I can do," Brae said. "And, when I think it through, it is the right thing to do. My mother is alone in the world. She raised us without any financial support or help from my father. She doesn't need this dumped in her lap."

"Maybe she would want to know," Ann said.

"Want to know what...that her daughter was raped and maybe committed suicide because of it? What good would come of that?"

Ann frowned, then sighed.

"You're probably right," she said. "But this is an awful lot for you to carry around."

"It is," Brae agreed. "And I'm afraid there is more."

"More? What?" Ann asked.

"I've thought this over, and I'm not sure it was rape."

"What do you mean? You said your sister cries out for help in your nightmare."

"She does...she cries out for help in *my* nightmare. *My* nightmare. But is she crying out for help or is it me imagining that? I was barely twelve years old when all of this happened. Maybe my nightmare is a reaction to something I didn't understand. Maybe it is my way of denying what I saw. Maybe, the sex was consensual."

"Could that be?" Ann asked.

"It could be. Kallie was eighteen...our neighbor was very young...in his early twenties, maybe only twenty-two."

"But what about the note?"

"I don't know," Brae replied. "Was the note meant for me? I don't really know that it was. What does the note mean? And did Kallie commit suicide or was it just a car accident? I don't really know, but I want to know. I know this...I'm going to find out!"

"How can you find out?"

"I'll find our old neighbor. I'll find out where he's living now. When I do, I'll confront him. It's something I have to do."

"My god Brae, are you sure?"

"I won't let this go without finding out what the truth is," Brae said. "I know it will take time but I have to do it."

"Will you tell Robert about this?"

"Not right now, and maybe never. I really don't know where Robert and I will be in the next six months…or even the next three months. I try not to think about the future with Robert because there is no future with him. Besides, I read his poetry without his permission. I violated his privacy. I am not going to tell him that."

"Are you and Robert alright?"

"Not really. We are temporary. We always knew that. His poetry…I mean my reading his poetry has changed things."

"How?" Ann asked.

"I shouldn't have read it without his permission. I don't know…maybe it is the old 'honor among thieves' ethic, but I feel as if I have let him down. And there is something else, too."

Brae paused, trying to find the words to express what she wanted to say.

"What?" Ann asked. "What else bothers you?"

"Well, after reading his poetry, I am not sure I know him. That sounds silly, I know. But now I don't think I will ever really know him. You can't really know a guy if you don't spend a long time with him."

"God," Ann said. "If that's true, then just think of the number of ex-boyfriends I don't know!"

Both Brae and Ann smiled and laughed at the thought. Ann composed herself and thought more about what Brae had just said.

"Why has the poetry changed the way you think of Robert?" she asked.

"It just has. The words…they represent a different person. Some of the concepts I can identify with, but I guess it's more the way he expresses his thoughts, his emotions, his ideas of justice, and his need for liberty. It's different from the Robert I know. I don't object to his writings. Actually, I agree with all he has written. I just don't understand why I haven't seen in him many of the things the poetry represents."

"That's strange," Ann commented. "But I've never been with an author or a poet. Maybe this is a normal situation. Maybe what they express on paper is different from their lives."

"Perhaps, but I don't think so. I do know this…I am bothered by it all, and that's strange. In a sense, the poetry liberated me from my nightmare, but it's also alienated me from Robert."

"How so?" Ann asked. "I don't get it."

"The thing is...I prefer the man who wrote the poetry. I prefer the Robert who wrote the poetry but I have not seen that person. I mean...I always liked Robert, and we have had some wonderful experiences. But the words in the poetry, they're deeper than what I have experienced with Robert. We made love after I read some of the poetry...it was wonderful, but I feel like I was making love to the poetry, not to Robert."

"Oh," Ann said.

"Do you really understand what I mean?" Brae asked.

"Yes. This is a difficult road for you. Take a hint from me, Brae. I have been with a lot of men, and what you just told me is something only a woman could understand. Is there any hope Robert can be the same as his poetry?"

"Robert has been going through some tough times. Maybe, his poetry is some kind of metamorphic experience," Brae said. "Maybe he is a changed man and the poetry is an announcement of that change. Maybe...I just don't know."

Chapter Forty-Four — Allen Hall Is Pleased

"Robert!" Allen Hall exclaimed as Professor Bradford entered the dean's office.

Dean Hall rose up from his desk and walked swiftly toward Robert. He extended his hand, giving Robert a vigorous handshake.

"Good to see you, Robert. Thanks for coming over."

Hall put his arm around Robert and directed him toward a corner of the office where there were two overstuffed armchairs.

"Have a seat. I want to talk with you."

Robert sat down. Dean Hall walked back to his desk, picked up a manuscript, and then headed back toward Robert, holding the manuscript in his right hand and up over his head.

"This is wonderful, Robert. Perfect. Just perfect."

Allen sat down in a chair across from the Robert. He held the manuscript firmly in his lap with both hands, while looking directly at the professor.

"This is what we wanted. This is what we knew you could do," he said. "I want you to know I am very pleased. Very pleased indeed."

"I'm glad you like it," Robert said. "It's not exactly what we talked about before, but I decided to go with my creative flow."

"Yes! Yes!" Hall exclaimed. "You have to. You're a genius, Robert, a genius. And, you're right…go with the flow. That's best…creative genius."

"I wouldn't go that far," Robert said. "I think it is good, though."

"It's more than good, Robert. It's top notch. It's genius. I want you to know I've shown it around. I've let some of your colleagues see it. They think it's great. Just great!"

"I'm happy they liked it."

"I want you to know this, too…the UC President and a few members of the Board of Trustees were in here the other day. I let them read some of your poetry. They were impressed, Robert. They were impressed!"

"Thank you. That is kind."

"Oh it's more than kind. Two of the trustees are on the university's Public Relations Committee. They liked your poetry, Robert. They liked it!"

Hall held the manuscript up in one hand, extending it toward Robert Bradford.

"This is the kind of stuff that makes a name for the university…puts us out there above the competition. It gets people talking about our lit department. This will generate a lot of buzz for us, Robert…a lot of buzz."

"I didn't include any interpretative analysis or comparative analysis," Robert said in an apologetic tone.

"You didn't have to. This is new, Robert! Let the others circle around and make the comparisons and the interpretations. This is new! Where did you get your inspiration?"

"From the courses I have been teaching and from my own observations. It is different than anything I've ever written."

"Well, the students will love this...they'll just love it. I like it, too. Of course, it's a little too proletarian for me, but its solid stuff. Solid. You know we might be able to build a course around the style of your poetry. I mean, it's really new, isn't it, Robert? New and fresh and explosive. Everyone thinks so."

"I don't think we should jump so far ahead. Perhaps it will not be well received."

Allen pushed back in his chair and frowned.

"Nonsense," he said. "Nonsense. I say your poems will sell. I mean, its wonderful poetry, Robert, but it will sell, too. Oh yes, the university press will love this. There will be lots of orders for this. You may become their biggest seller of poetry."

"I...I prefer to wait," Robert said. "Who knows what the critics will say?"

Hall held the manuscript up again.

"They will say its genius," he said. "That's what they will say. And, this puts you right back on track around here, too. This establishes you as the professor we all knew you were."

"I really have not changed any," Robert responded.

"Now, don't get me wrong, Robert. You're a great classroom professor. You've always been a highly respected member of the UC family. Always have been. But, you were suffering from a slump. I knew it was just a slump. We all go through that. But this...this is the proof that you're what we do here...what we're all about. Creativity. Originality. It's work like this that makes our department shine. You'll be the talk of the next staff meeting we have. There'll be envy among all the rest of the deans when they see what we produce here."

Robert remained silent.

"I've done something else, too, Robert," Hall said. "I read one of your poems to your mother. I hope you don't mind."

"You saw my mother?"

"Yes. Adela and I have talked in the past...talked about you. She was always concerned about you."

"Mum's health is declining," Robert said.

"That's why I took the time to talk with her. I wanted her to know you were doing well. I know you, Robert. You don't boast, but this is a time for boasting...your mother's health is slipping. She needed to know about your publication. I have been told she is not responsive anymore. Is that true?

"Yes. I'm afraid she is slipping into a coma. That's what the doctors tell me."

"I'm sorry, Robert. But, it was good I visited with her when I did. She was very pleased. I don't think she really comprehended the poem I read to her, but I could tell she understood you had fulfilled your responsibilities to the UC with these poems."

"Mum," Robert said quietly.

"Your mother would be proud…very proud."

"I'm sure she would."

Chapter Forty-Five — Robert's Publication

Robert Bradford came home from visiting his mother at the hospital and found the house at Wicker Park empty. When Diane arrived home fifteen minutes later, she wound up putting Robbie to bed before she was aware of Robert's presence. She found him sitting alone in their living room, the only illumination in the room provided by the glow of a streetlight that shone faintly through the window.

"Why are you sitting in the dark, Robert?" she asked.

There was no reply to her question, so Diane sat down in a chair across from him. Her eyes adjusted to the darkness and she noted that he looked dejected and withdrawn.

"Robert, are you all right?" she asked. "Is your mother all right?"

"Mum is in a coma now," Robert said. "She does not have much time left."

"I'm sorry, Robert."

"We all knew this would happen," Robert replied. "She knew there was not much time left."

"What do the doctors say?"

"Just what Mum had told me. They give her two weeks, maybe three. She won't be coming out of the coma, they say."

Diane leaned back in her chair. She had never gotten along with Adela Bradford, but she was sad to know Adela was dying. She stared at Robert. She knew he had grown up as a mommy's boy, and she imagined he too must have been having ambiguous feelings about his mother's condition. Diane wondered if she would take Adela's place. Over the past three years, she felt as though she had become a quasi-mother figure for Robert. Would she now become *the* mother figure for him? She did not want to be, but it seemed such a natural evolution; an evolution she feared would put an end to the relationship she wanted to have with Robert.

"Is there anything I can do?" she asked.

"No."

"Did you have a chance to talk with her before…?"

"Allen Hall was the last person to talk with her," Robert interrupted. "He read to her from some of my recent publication."

"You submitted a publication?" Diane asked with a tone of surprise.

"Yes. I finished it last week. I haven't said anything because I didn't know how it would be received."

"I don't know what to say, Robert. I'm…amazed," Diane stammered. "You've been so frustrated. I'm really amazed. You should have told me. What has Allen said about your writings?"

"He's very impressed. I'm a genius, according to him."

"Robert…this is such a roller coaster. You sit there and tell me your mother is dying; and then you tell me this! I don't understand. I don't know how to respond."

Diane's voice, her gestures, and her seating posture projected bewilderment and agitation. Robert sat up in his chair and stared at her.

"I'm sorry," he said. "I know I haven't been fair to you. All this pressure…"

Robert quit speaking, and stared down at the floor.

"They're going to publish my poetry. Allen told me there will be a recognition supper for the department," he said. "He says my publication will be the featured worked."

"That's wonderful, Robert!" Diane exclaimed. "You did it! When can I read it?"

"I'm not sure you'll like it," Robert said in a quiet tone.

"How could I not like it? It must be grand if they are going to make you the featured speaker."

"The poetry…my publication…it's all very different than anything I've ever done. You may not like it."

Diane got up from her chair. She walked over to Robert and knelt down on the rug in front of him. Robert looked down at his wife's face. Diane took hold of his hand, looking directly into his eyes.

"Robert," she said. "I'm proud of you. I know your mother's situation is a strain on you. I know this pressure to publish has been hard on you. But you've done it. You created something everyone is going to enjoy, and now, you can bask in the limelight of your work. Now, you can relax and concentrate on your teaching. You did it, Robert. You did it."

Robert smiled faintly.

"I don't care anything about the publication," he said. "All I have ever wanted to do is teach. I wish they would just put the poems on a shelf. Just let me teach. The poetry doesn't matter."

"That will happen, Robert," Diane said. "You've jumped through your last hoop…just go with the flow of all this. It will be over soon and you can get back to teaching."

Even though it was still dark in the room, Diane could see tears in Robert's eyes.

"This will never be over," he said. "It will always be like this…other people deciding what is right for me, and me caving in to it all."

Diane held onto Robert's hand. His words frightened her. He had moved further away from her than she had ever imagined.

• • •

Before he left for work the next day, Robert gave Diane a copy of his publication. She took it to work with her and read it alone in her bookstore after it had closed for the evening. After reading three pages, she found she could read no more.

Later that evening when Robert asked her if she would be attending the recognition supper for his publication of poetry, she declined.

Chapter Forty-Six— The Investigation

The investigation into the murder of Professor Robert Bradford centered upon a search for Javier Morales, but Morales was not easy to find. Javier lived in a subculture that was protective of its citizenry, and when the police arrived at his place of residence, they found it empty of people and personal items. A police watch was stationed at the apartment house for two days, but no one returned.

The police discovered Javier worked at the Piazza Navona Restaurant. They looked for him there, but he had not reported for work during the last two days. Javier Morales had disappeared into labyrinth of dwellings made up of immigrants who were suspicious of authority figures and who were willing to hide him from a system they considered unjust.

While the search for Morales continued, Detectives Findley and Battin spent their time examining the life of Robert Bradford. Their investigation led them to the University of Chicago and to Michael Sheridan, Robert's closest colleague. The three men met in Sheridan's campus office.

"Professor Sheridan," Detective Findley began. "We have been told you were a close friend of Professor Bradford. We want to express our sympathies to you concerning his death."

"Thank you," Professor Sheridan replied.

Sheridan's office was small and cramped with a large desk, a small circular table with two chairs pushed under it, a metal filing cabinet, and bookshelves attached to three walls. The office had one window that afforded a standing person a truncated view of the campus quad.

The overcrowded atmosphere of the room was exacerbated by Sheridan's obvious inability to create order out of the tools of his trade; books, magazines, newspapers, maps, curriculum notebooks, writing supplies, and various other items were strewn about the room. Half of his desk was cluttered with student papers, some graded and some awaiting judgment, while the other half of the desk was occupied by a computer monitor, a keyboard, and a printer.

Detectives Findley and Battin had taken the two chairs away from the circular table and were sitting in front of the professor's desk. Professor Sheridan was seated behind his desk in a high back, wooden swivel office chair.

"Can you tell us anything about Mr. Bradford that could help us find the person who shot him?" Findley asked.

'Like what?" Sheridan replied.

"Just anything. For example, tell us what his mood was like over the past six months. Tell us about people he associated with. Maybe, you can tell us something about the condo he had here. Or tell us if he was having any problems with anyone on campus. Were any of his students upset with him? Anything you think might help us understand why he was murdered."

"We didn't find a wallet on him," Battin interjected. "Does that make any sense to you?"

"Robert's wallet is probably in his car," Sheridan answered. "He never carried a wallet on his person. He told me he did not like the lumpy feel of a wallet in his pants, so he normally just carried his license, one credit card, and some cash in his pockets."

"Do you know where his car is?" Battin asked.

"If it isn't at his home, then it's either parked here on campus or at his condo."

"Why did the professor have a condo here?" Battin continued. "Did he stay over often?"

"Robert used his condo frequently. It's not a long distance to Wicker Park, but there were times when staying here was more convenient."

"Did he have any guests at the condo?"

"Guests?"

"Was there anyone he shared the condo with? Or was there anyone who stayed overnight with him when he remained here?"

"You mean a woman?"

"Yes. Or a man," Battin replied.

"Robert was involved," Sheridan said.

"Involved with whom?"

"Understand something," Sheridan began. "Robert was having some problems…a mid-life crisis or something. I really don't know. We talked about things and shared some of our frustrations."

"And the woman?" Findley asked.

"She was relief for him."

"Relief? Did he use that word to describe their relationship?"

"Yes, he did."

"What was their relationship?"

"I couldn't tell you exactly," Sheridan said. "If you mean were they sexually involved, the answer is yes. But, romantically involved…I don't know that."

"Do you know the woman?" Battin asked.

"I don't know her name. That's what Robert wanted. He talked about her some. He told me she was a prior student of his. But he did not want to identify her to me, or anyone else. I don't think they spent much time outside of his condo."

"How long has he been seeing this woman?"

"Not long. Not long at all. I would say less than three months, if that long."

"Did his wife know about the woman?"

"I don't know that. Robert never said anything to me about Diane knowing."

"Is this woman currently enrolled in the university?"

"Yes. I believe she is a senior or a first year grad student. I know her major is literature."

"And, you never saw Mr. Bradford with her?"

"No…never."

When Detective Findley entered Michael's office, he was carrying a briefcase that he had placed on the floor. Now, the detective picked up the briefcase, laid it on top of the student papers that cluttered Michael's desktop, and opened it. He reached inside the briefcase, pulled out a photograph, and handed it to Michael.

"Professor Sheridan," he said. "Can you identify the woman in this photo?"

Michael Sheridan studied the photo for a short moment, and then handed it back. He looked at the detectives with an increased sense of curiosity.

"It's not a very good likeness," he said. "But the photo looks like Brae Larson. She's a student here at the university in one of my literature courses. Where did you get this photo?"

Findley reached inside his briefcase again, pulled out a wallet sealed in a see-through plastic bag, and handed it to the professor.

"And do you recognize this wallet?" he said.

Michael Sheridan held the wallet in his hands. A melancholy expression appeared on his face.

"It looks like Robert's wallet," he said. "I'd have to look inside to know for sure."

Detective Findley took the wallet back from Michael.

"It is his wallet, Professor," he said. "You are right about Robert keeping it in his car. We have already been to Mr. Bradford's condo. The picture of Ms. Larson is from one of the condo's security cameras. Do you think she was Robert Bradford's lover?"

Michael Sheridan sat back in his chair. He sighed heavily.

"I don't know that," he said. "I wouldn't want to say. I can tell you Robert talked about a woman who was a student here. He said she had been a student of his…last year, I think. He said she was beautiful and they shared some philosophical beliefs. Beyond that, I don't know. Certainly, Brae is a pretty woman."

"And there's nothing else you can tell us about this woman?" Detective Findley asked.

Findley noticed that the professor looked drained of energy and that his facial expression had the look of introspection. Michael Sheridan swallowed hard before answering.

"I only know their relationship was supposed to be temporary. Robert liked the woman very much…I think he found comfort in her. I know he wanted their relationship to be private. Robert was a private man."

"Did he have any other problems you know of?" Findley asked.

"There were some problems…everyone has problems. Robert was no different."

"Tell us about some of those problems," Battin asked.

"I don't want to make more of them than there was," Michael said. "But, I will tell you three of them…three problems he talked about recently. But remember, we were drinking at the time. Just two guys having a few drinks and talking."

"You're right," Findley said. "It's probably nothing, but tell us…it may help find his killer."

Michael sighed again.

"Robert was having trouble at home. No big thing, he was just not getting along with Diane. Nothing that couldn't be fixed, but he was feeling…I guess I would say inadequate."

"Inadequate? You mean in bed?"

"Generally inadequate…inadequate about everything it seemed…his marriage, his job, his life…sex…I really don't know about the sex…just inadequate. He…uh…had incorporated Marxism into his personal philosophy. He was dissatisfied with our culture and he was upset with his work. Who isn't?"

"Anyone at work who upset him?"

"The dean of our department. Dean Allen Hall."

"What was the problem there?" Battin asked.

"Robert never really cared for Allen, and Allen was putting some pressure on Robert to publish."

"Publish?"

"If a college professor wants to obtain tenure, and if he wants to make sure that his status around here is awarded, then he needs to publish something…a book of research, or in Robert's case, some poetry…something that is notable for the department and the college. Anymore, the college would like the work to be something that will sell…something that can be marketed."

"And Robert…how was he doing with that?"

"Great. He just wrote a series of poems. There was a dinner reception for him a couple of days ago to honor his work. The university is very pleased with what he wrote."

"But Allen Hall…he didn't like what Robert wrote?"

"Hall loved it," Sheridan said. "The problem was prior to the publication. Hall thought Robert should have published earlier. But, once he saw Robert's work, he fell in love with it…we all did. It's genius."

"So, the problem with Dean Hall was ironed out then?" Battin asked.

"Not really. Allen Hall is an eternal ass. It would take more than poetry to change that. But there was nothing between Hall and Robert that would cause anything like this."

"Tell us about his discontent with the department."

"I don't think it was just our department, but we were a focal point for his frustrations. Are you gentlemen familiar with the term nihilism?"

"I know generally what it means," Detective Findley said.

Michael Sheridan leaned back in this chair, pressed his fingers together in a prayer-like fashion and then brought his hands up in front to his chin.

"I would be interested in your interpretation," he said.

"I know the term from history…the Russian Revolution. Weren't the Nihilists a group of revolutionaries who questioned the importance of our existence?"

"Yes, that's partially it."

"And, if I remember, a nihilist is prone to violence…destruction of the government because he sees it as worthless."

"Very good, detective," Sheridan commented.

"Was Robert Bradford a Nihilist?"

"No," Sheridan replied. "Robert was not violent. I use the term nihilism to describe his frame of mind. Robert was pessimistic, doubting, but not committed to violence or to the ideas of nihilism. But he was beginning to doubt the relevancy of the university, except for its pragmatic contributions…science, medicine, and engineering. But when it came to us…the humanities…he wondered how effective we are. 'Intellectual bullshit'… that was Robert's term for much of what we did."

"So he may have stepped on some toes?" Battin asked.

"No," Sheridan continued. "Robert wasn't vocal about his discontent. It was eating away at him, but he wasn't vocal about it. And, it wasn't just the university he was upset with. Robert was disappointed with many of the institutions in our society. He blamed the hierarchy of society for many of our problems…he believed leadership had let us all down. In his doubt and frustration, Robert began to see more relevance in the pragmatism and the worth of physical labor than in the merits of our ivy towers. He wanted to be some place else."

"And Professor Bradford talked a lot about this to you?" Battin asked.

"Again, it was barroom conversation. But I agree with a lot of what Robert was thinking. You know, the 'ivory tower' academic world thing. Sometimes you question your own worth… especially when the university keeps pressuring a guy to produce ideas in a timely fashion. You begin to make up things just to placate the powers that be. It becomes a game."

"Did Robert say any of this to anyone else…Dean Hall, maybe?" Findley asked.

"I couldn't tell you that, but I doubt it. Hall and those guys are so steeped in tradition and academic bullshit that they wouldn't be able to recognize the truth. But I'm sure Hall recognized that something was wrong in Robert's world. I know Hall didn't like Robert hanging around with me."

"You sound discontented, too," Findley commented.

"As I said, Robert had a point. The intellectual leaders of this world have let us down. They've copped out...excuse the term...on many of the important social issues of the day. They have failed to use the tools of their trade...our trade...to oppose the types of human conduct that have led us to the global messes we have. Robert knew I agreed with him on many of the points of frustration he was experiencing...and, he knew I am a coward. It's people like me who were a source of frustration for him."

"Can you tell us where you were the night Professor Bradford was killed?" Detective Battin asked.

"I was at a bar. I went home around ten. A young woman spent the night with me. Her name is Sherri Austin. I can give you her address and phone number if you like."

"Good. Are there other names you could give us that might help in our investigation?" Findley said.

Professor Sheridan thought for a moment. Then, he opened a drawer on the left side of his desk and took out a small pad of paper that had the logo of the university at the top of each sheet.

"Let me give you these names," he said.

Sheridan quickly wrote out the names of six people, ripped the paper from the pad, and handed it to Detective Battin.

Findley took the paper, quickly reading through the list of names.

Brae Larson
Ann Yin
Allen Hall
Bob Wachtel
James Kruger
Ray Rogers

Detective Battin leaned over and glanced at the list.

"That's a very short list," he said. You can't think of anyone else?"

"Robert was a private man. To be honest, he was not that happy with the esteemed colleagues in our department. Like I said, he questioned our worth and often wondered why he was here."

"Why was he here?" Findley asked.

"That's easy to answer...this is where his mother wanted him to be. Oh...just so you know, Kruger's in Europe. I think he's been there four months."

Chapter Forty-Seven — Diane Is Questioned

"Mrs. Bradford," Detective Findley began. "We know you have suffered a terrible loss. We don't want to upset you more, but there are some question we need to ask you concerning your husband and his death."

The two detectives and Diane Bradford were sitting at a large table in the dining room of Robert's condo. The table was capable of seating eight people. Robert and Diane never entertained at the condo, so he had used the dining room table as a desk. Mrs. Bradford, Detective Battin and Detective Findley were seated at the west end of the table, the end Robert had used for meals. A computer, some books, a stack of magazines, and a stack of newspapers occupied the east end of the table.

"I understand," Diane replied. "I want to be helpful."

Diane's gaze left the faces of the two detectives. Her eyes roamed around the condo.

"I haven't been here in quite some time," she said. "The condo had become Robert's hideaway."

"Hideaway?" Battin asked.

"His writing retreat. Robert used this condo to work on his publication for the university. And, sometimes, he used it to stay here when he had late meetings or work to do."

"Do you know if he ever met anyone here?" Findley asked.

This was the second time Findley had met with Diane Bradford concerning the murder of her husband. He had interviewed twenty-five people in connection with the case. Detective Mike Findley was a fifteen year veteran of the Chicago Police Department and an astute judge of character. He had come to believe that Mrs. Bradford had nothing to do with the murder of her husband.

"Was Robert seeing a woman?" Diane asked.

"Please forgive our abruptness, Mrs. Bradford, but that's what we have to ask you," Detective Findley said. "Do you think your husband was involved?".

Diane sat up straight in her chair. She fixed her stare down at the tabletop. The insinuations the detectives were making were not new thoughts for her, but this was the first time she confronted the possibility in a conversation. She was a private person with a strong sense of dignity and was determined to maintain her composure by being limited in her responses.

"I haven't had time to look around the condo," she said. "I guess if I do, I will find more than just Robert's things here. Is that what you are telling me?"

"Mr. Bradford was seeing a woman here," Battin said. "What we need to know is, did you know about it?"

Detective Rice Battin was new to homicide investigation. He was an ambitious, young man who believed himself to be worldly and clever; he was alone in that assessment.

"No," Diane answered. "No, I did not know."

"We're sorry to trouble you," Findley said again. "But we need to know...were you and Robert having difficulties with your marriage?"

Diane sighed, and then laughed softly.

"I don't know anyone who doesn't have difficulties with marriage, do you detective?"

"Mrs. Bradford," Findley said. "Right now, you are not a suspect in the death of your husband. We want you to know that. But, we have to investigate everything. Is it possible Mr. Bradford was killed because of some problem you and he were having?"

"I wouldn't think so," Diane said. "I know you are looking for Javier Morales. Is that what you are talking about?"

"Should we be talking about Mr. Morales?" Battin asked. "Is Mr. Morales a source of difficulty in your marriage?"

"No," Diane replied.

"Did Mr. Bradford know Javier Morales?"

"To my knowledge, they never met," Diane answered.

"Yet, Mr. Morales often played with your son at the Wicker Park playground. Isn't that true?"

"Yes, they played"

"And, it is our understanding that you and Mr. Morales met there once or twice without Robbie present. Is that true?"

"I would say twice is accurate," Diane said.

"Why did you meet Mr. Morales alone?"

"Javier is a friend of mine. He liked playing with Robbie because Robbie reminded him of his own little brother in Mexico."

"Why would you meet him alone in the park?" Battin asked.

"I didn't...or we didn't. What I mean is, there was no plan to meet alone. Robbie went to a friend's house twice when we were supposed to meet Javier. I simply met him to let him know Robbie would not be there. Both times we wound up talking...I would say for twenty minutes or so each time."

"Did your husband know about this?"

"No. Robert knew about Javier. I told him about Javier playing with Robbie at the playground, but I never specifically told him about the two times I talked with Javier at length."

Detective Battin sat silent for a moment. Then he drummed his fingers on top of the table and looked Diane Bradford squarely in the eyes.

"Was there anything between you and Javier Morales?" he asked.

"No," Diane answered.

"Then why would Javier be at the scene of the crime?"

"Javier lives in the area," Diane said. "He often comes to the park and plays basketball with his friends." Diane paused for a moment and shifted slightly in her chair. "Do you really know he was there, detective?"

"We aren't sure, but it is possible. A man who looks like him was seen in the area. Do you think your husband was jealous of Mr. Morales?"

"I would find that hard to believe."

"Is there any other reason why Mr. Morales would want to hurt your husband?" Detective Battin asked.

"None I can think of," Diane said. "I don't believe Javier had anything to do with my husband's death."

"Mrs. Bradford," Battin began. "We found a knife close to the place where your husband was murdered. The knife was taken from the Piazza Novana Restaurant."

"The restaurant where Javier worked," Detective Findley added.

Diane's demeanor changed; the expression on her face became introspective. Tears formed in her eyes and she struggled to remain calm.

"Still…," she said. "Still, I cannot believe Javier would do anything so violent or that he would harm Robbie's father."

"And you have no idea where Javier Morales is?" Battin asked.

"No."

"When was the last time you saw him?" Findley asked.

"I guess it would have been two weeks or more…that was the second time Javier and I talked in Wicker Park…one of the times Robbie had gone to his friend's house."

"Did Mr. Morales say anything to you that could have any connection to your husband's death?"

"No."

"What did you talk about?"

"We talked about Javier's home and his family," Diane said.

"Did Javier ever talk about other people…other people he knew here?" Battin asked. "Did he have a girlfriend?"

Diane paused, looking down at the table.

"I…I don't know that," she said.

"When we spoke to some of the employees at the restaurant, we were told Javier might have had a lover…a Russian woman. She left the restaurant without quitting. Did Mr. Morales say anything about her?"

"No," Diane answered. "Javier did not talk to me about any woman. May I ask a question?"

"What is it you want to know?" Detective Findley said.

"Do you know who my husband's lover was?"

"Yes we do."

"Is she someone I would know?" Diane asked.

"We cannot divulge the name of the woman to you," Battin said.

"Is she a suspect in my husband's death?"

"She's a person of interest," Battin answered.

"Just like me," Mrs. Bradford commented.

"Mrs. Bradford...everyone at the university will know who the woman is. We cannot tell you, but you should prepare yourself...what I mean is, people will be talking about it...there will be rumors and speculation...probably rumors about you, too. Do you understand?" Detective Findley asked.

"Thank you, detective," Diane replied. "I do understand. I know how people are. I know how cruel they can be."

Diane glanced around the condo.

"Will I find evidence of her in the condo?"

"We searched the condo, Mrs. Bradford. I want you to know that we had a warrant. Since the condo is in your husband's name, we didn't need to show the warrant to anyone except the maintenance man."

"I understand," Diane said.

"Any evidence of your husband's lover has been removed."

"Can you tell me this?" Diane asked. "Was she a student?"

The detectives remained silent.

"She was a student," Diane said, confirming the answer behind their silence.

Diane Bradford was trying hard to remain aloof with the detectives but she was losing the ability to do so. Too much information was being thrown at her. She wet her lips and looked away from the two men, trying to focus her gaze on something that would provide her with an anchor for her feelings. She fixed her eyes on a framed sketch of Faust that hung in the hallway of the condo. She frowned, shook her head, and looked down at her lap.

"Robert was an idealist," she observed. "It makes sense he would be with a student. I imagine she was beautiful, too."

"Did your husband ever have an affair with another woman?"

Diane straightened her back and looked directly at Detective Findley.

"No. I am sure he did not," she said. "Robert had changed recently. He was under a lot of pressure."

"You don't seem to be angry," Battin said. "Doesn't it upset you that your husband was involved with another woman?"

"If Robert were alive, and I found out about this woman, do you know what he would have done?" Diane asked.

"No. Please tell us," Findley said.

"Robert would have asked me to forgive him, and I would have. In the line of work you gentlemen do, I imagine you see human frailty everyday. True?"

"Of course," Findley replied.

"I see human frailty, too," Diane said. "I am surrounded by it in my bookstore, in the hundreds of stories I read, and in people I meet. I have come to believe that one of our greatest responsibilities is to understand that we will all fail. It is our obligation to forgive those who fail when we are asked for forgiveness. Robert would have asked and I would have forgiven. I forgive him now."

Detective Findley paused in asking questions of Mrs. Bradford, but only for a moment, allowing the magnitude of Mrs. Bradford's words to be filed away in his mind and to gain the realization that he was impressed with Diane Bradford.

"Mrs. Bradford," he continued. "We only have a couple more questions for you. Your husband owned a small caliber pistol. Do you know where it is?"

"No. I never had anything to do with that. It was a gift from his uncle. Robert had it for many years. I always imagined it was here in this condo. Didn't you find it here?"

"No," Findley replied. "Let me ask you this again...do you know where Javier Morales might be?"

"No," Mrs. Bradford answered.

• • •

Battin and Findley finished their questioning of Mrs. Bradford and left her to the task of searching through Robert Bradford's condo. As their unmarked police car pulled out of the condo parking lot, Battin engaged his senior partner in a debriefing of the conversation they just had with Diane.

"Well, do you believe her?" he asked.

"I believe most of what she said...not all, but most," Findley replied.

As the freshman member of the homicide team, Battin was assigned driving duties for the team. Once on the street, he accelerated the car to thirty-five miles an hour, driving north on South Greenwood Aveune.

"I don't believe that shit about forgiving," he said. "To my way of thinking, that's just a little too cold for me."

"What do you mean by cold?"

"I mean calculated. I think she's trying to throw us off track with that crap. No one forgives so readily," Battin said.

"Mrs. Bradford does," Findley said. "You have a lot to learn about human nature, Rice."

"You don't agree with me?" Battin asked.

"You're wrong," Findley replied.

Battin halted the car at a four-way stop sign, and quickly looked around before proceeding uptown. He sighed and grumbled at the words of his senior partner.

"So you don't think there's any connection between her husband being murdered and him having an affair?"

"If you mean did she kill him, then I would say this…women like Mrs. Bradford do not have their husbands murdered."

"She could have hired Morales to do it. She was awful chummy with him."

"That's always a possibility, but I doubt it."

"Morales could have done it for her without her asking," Battin continued. "Maybe, she said something to him about being upset with her husband. Maybe, he offered to help her out. Or maybe, there was something going on between Javier and her…she may have been lonely and had an affair with him."

"Javier and Mrs. Bradford in bed, huh?"

"It's possible," Battin said.

"Possible, but unlikely," Findley replied.

"Okay…let's hear it then. What do you think about her?"

"Mrs. Bradford didn't know about Robert's affair. I'm sure of that. She is the kind of woman who would have acted immediately on such information. Bradford would have been told to drop the affair or to get out, but she wouldn't have harmed him."

"And you believe she would have forgiven him?" Battin asked with a tone of amazement.

"Yes. Mrs. Bradford is not a malicious woman. She is independent and strong; there is no need for her to be malicious. Forgiveness is a way for her to deal with pain and a way for her to reconcile the love she felt for her husband. She has forgiven him and she is moving on with her life."

"So then what part of her answers don't you believe?" Battin asked.

"It's not that I don't believe her answers," Findley replied. "It's just that I think she is conveniently leaving something out. I don't know what, but something. Something to do with Javier, I think."

"So you do think she's involved with him?"

"Yes, but not sexually."

"How then?"

"Don't know. I'm still thinking about that."

Frustrated by the conversation, Battin changed the subject.

"Let me ask you this," he said as he pulled their car onto I-94. "Have you been thinking about making sergeant?"

"I've always wanted to be a sergeant," Findley replied. "It's a career goal."

"Are you doing anything about it?"

"I took the exam. My name is on the list for promotions."

"Let's cut the crap," Battin said. "Are you doing anything about getting your name chosen for promotion?"

"I passed the exam and my name's on the list," Findley replied. "But if you are referring to me sucking up and kissing someone's ass, the answer is no."

Battin groaned and turned to look at his partner.

"You are one dumb, stubborn Mick," he said. "So you're gonna rely on merit for promotion?"

"That's right."

"You know Malmstrom, right? And you know Hopkins, too?"

"I know them."

"They've been relying on merit for ten years. They've both been up for sergeant twice, and they've both been passed over twice. So much for merit."

"And they both should have been chosen," Findley observed.

"But they weren't," Battin replied. "They weren't because they relied solely on merit and didn't do what needed to be done."

Detective Findly looked out the car's passenger window and frowned. Then he turned his head toward Detective Battin.

"Listen Rice," he said, the volume of his voice rising with each new sentence. "We haven't been together as a team very long so I'm going to explain something to you. I like being a cop. I like being in homicide. But I'd rather spend the rest of my life living in a cardboard box on the street than to suck up to the people who think they're in charge. No one is in charge of me. I do what I want and I don't ask for any favors. I'm a good cop. A damn good cop! If that's not enough, then fuck 'em. You got that?"

Detective Battin let out a sigh of disappointment.

"I've got it," he said.

Chapter Forty-Eight — Allen Hall Is Questioned

"Dean Hall will see you gentlemen now," a secretary said to the two police detectives.

"Thank you," Detective Battin replied.

The two men made their way into Hall's office. Dean Allen Hall approached them with his hand extended as they entered.

"Good morning gentlemen," he said, shaking each detective's hand vigorously. "I'm Allen Hall. I am sorry to meet you under such tragic circumstances."

The two detectives introduced themselves and were offered chairs in front of the dean's desk. Hall took a seat behind his desk, placed his elbows on the desktop, and leaned forward.

"Could I have my secretary get you coffee or tea?" he asked.

"Thank you, but no," Detective Findley said. "We know you are busy, Mr. Hall. We are investigating the death of Professor Bradford. We have a few questions to ask. I don't believe we will need to take much of your time."

Dean Hall leaned back into his chair.

"It's tragic," he said. "Really tragic…a terrific loss for the university. He was one of our best."

"I understand Professor Bradford had just published something. Can you tell us about that?"

"Oh yes. Really extraordinary stuff… a short book of poetry, but extraordinary…fresh and new. His publication was good for the university. It's the kind of thing we produce here. We were proud of what Robert did for us. Very creative man…very creative…and an extraordinary professor. Students loved him."

"We understand there was some pressure for him to produce," Battin noted. "And, that he was having some difficulty in being creative."

"Oh no," Hall replied. "Not Robert…temporary writer's block, maybe, but no real difficulty. He just needed to find his center. We talked often. Robert was always working toward meeting his academic obligation. I knew that. Robert knew what he had to do. I knew he would never let us down, and he came through for us. Extraordinary work."

"Would you say, then, that Professor Bradford was happy here at the university?" Detective Battin asked.

"Absolutely! The students loved Robert and he loved teaching. Robert was one of our best. One of our best! Why, Robert has always been here. He's part of the UC family. You know he began his academic career here. He graduated from our university high school and one of our colleges. Got his graduate degrees here, too. He did all of his work here. Why, his mother has been a professor here for years. This was home for Robert."

"What about his other home?" Findley asked.

"Diane? You mean Diane and the little boy? Certainly they were a part of the university family, too."

"Do you know if Professor Bradford was happy at home? Again, I mean his other home...in Wicker Park," Findley asked.

"Oh. You mean the affair. Yes, I've heard about that...really unfortunate. Robert was somewhat of a philosopher. Sort of a free spirit if you know what I mean. But you know I have a theory about that."

"Could you tell us?" Findley asked.

"Well...what do I know? But certainly, I can try to explain my approach to all of this. However, I want you to know...we here at the university do not condone such actions. It was wrong for Robert to become involved with a student. We don't condone that."

"We understand," Findley replied.

Dean Hall leaned forward again, placing his elbows on the top of his desk, and crossing his arms. His eyes darted momentarily up toward the ceiling, and then he looked straight toward Detective Findley.

"Here's my take on all of this," he said. "Robert was trying to find his center. He did have some problems meeting his academic obligation to publish. Temporary problem...temporary," Hall said, lifting his arms up from his desk and waving his hands back and forth with his palms pointed toward the detectives. Then he stopped waving his hands, leaned back in his chair, raised his right index finger, and pointed it in their direction. "But maybe...just maybe... this young lady helped him with that. He was looking for his center. He needed to find a way to express who he was and what life meant to him. Maybe, she helped him with that. You know...passion and creativity."

Dean Hall leaned back in his chair. An inquisitive looked appeared on his face.

"Say, you don't think she had anything to do with this?" he asked.

"No," Battin replied. "Have you talked with the young woman."

"Oh no...certainly not. That would be a violation of the university's code. We have counselors to handle those kinds of problems."

"Do you know the young lady?" Battin asked.

"No. I've never met her. Never been introduced. I understand she is a very good student though."

"Do you know how she is doing?" Findley asked.

"It's my understanding the young woman has dropped all of her classes, so technically she is not a student at UC," Hall replied. "But, we have a meeting scheduled for the middle of the week. She is on the agenda...you can be sure of that. I know this must be hard for her. Is she...what is the term you law officers use? A person of interest?"

"No. It's much too early to determine who is a person of interest and who is not," Findley said.

"So you don't think it was a simple robbery? Lot of crime up there in Wicker Park from my understanding," Hall said.

"Could be, but it doesn't look that way right now," Findley said.

"Have you ever been to Wicker Park?" Battin asked.

"Once or twice. We just had Robert's recognition dinner there. I chose Wicker Park because Robert's publication was so excellent. He was being rewarded for giving us the best piece of work we have seen in a long time. Say...I hope I'm not a person of interest," Dean Hall said smiling broadly.

"Certainly not," Findley answered. "You and others here at the university are all sources for us right now. We need to gather information concerning Professor Bradford to help us determine who would murder him."

Dean Hall breathed in deeply and then exhaled loudly.

"Murder!" he said. "Tragic. Murder. That's a chilling word."

"For the record though, we are asking everyone where they were that night...the night Robert was killed. Could you tell us where you were?"

"Why certainly. I was here," Dean Hall replied. "This is a busy office, but we get it all done. I'm often here working late into the evenings. I don't mind though. This is home for me, too."

Detective Findley took out a small note pad and jotted down what Dean Hall had said.

"Was anyone here with you?" Battin asked.

"Let me think," Hall replied. "My secretary was here...but only for a couple of hours. She went home and I stayed to finish up."

"What time would that be?" Battin asked.

Dean Hall's facial expression contorted in a pondering manner.

"I would say I was here from around six-thirty until nine. Might have stayed a couple of minutes after nine."

"And can I ask you if you own a firearm?" Battin asked.

"No." Hall replied.

"Do you have a FOID card?"

"No I do not."

"We're asking everyone," Findley said.

"I understand," Dean Hall said. "We want this man caught as much as you do. No one has anything to hide here at UC."

"What about Robert's close friends here?" Battin interjected. "Did he have many?"

"Well, Robert was an introvert...quiet I mean."

"Would you say you were his friend?"

"Oh no. Not really, but I was part of his UC family. Robert and I...we talked. We shared things, but not a close friend. I was always here for him though. He knew that."

"What about Professor Sheridan?" Battin asked.

A slight scowl appeared on Dean Hall's face.

"Very creative man," he said. "And yes...Robert and Michael were friends."

"Is Professor Sheridan part of the UC family?"

Dean Hall sighed in a visible manner. He looked down at his desk and drummed his fingers on the desktop.

"Professor Sheridan is a unique man," he said. "A little too rebellious for my tastes."

"What do you mean by *rebellious*?" Battin asked.

"The man has no sense of structure. No sense of authority. He's...irreverent."

"Still part of the UC family, though...right?" Battin asked.

Dean Hall scowled again. He was obviously frustrated with talking about Michael Sheridan.

"A black sheep. The man drinks too much and...well, he's a unique part of the UC family. Have you talked with him yet?"

"Yes," Detective Findley said.

"Then you know about him. I don't really have any problems with him. I would just like to see him straighten up a little. You know...be a team player."

"Was Professor Bradford a *team player*?" Findley asked.

"Yes. Yes, he was. Robert was having some troubles, but he was coming around. He had a solid base here. His history and his life belonged to UC. You can't take that away from a person...esprit de corps...that was Robert. He got it from his mother. It was in his blood. Yes. Robert was a team player."

"One more thing," Findley said. "We understand Professor Bradford's mother is comatose. Is that correct?"

"Yes. Very sad, but there's always good news to report, too."

"What good news?" Findley asked.

"Well...it's almost a blessing," Hall said. "Robert's mother, Adela, always took care of Robert. She always wanted him to be part of our family here. As I mentioned, Robert was having some difficulty...writer's block and all. I talked with him about it. I talked with his mother, too. I thought she should know. Between the two of us, I think we got Robert going again...made him see what had to be done. He finished his publication just in time...that's the blessing I am referencing. His mother has been very ill, but Robert was able to let her know he had finished his writings before she slipped into a coma. When I talked with her, I let her know his poetry is excellent. She was very proud. It's better this way. She doesn't know about his death. Her last thoughts of him will be his success and the work he did for the university. We're all very proud of Robert."

Chapter Forty-Nine — *Findley Questions Brae*

Detective Findley was not looking forward to questioning Brae Larson. She was a young woman whose life had been exposed by the murder of Professor Bradford. Findley himself was a private person who detested gossip; he knew Brae would become a target for those who enjoyed engaging in moral platitudes. The investigation of the murder required Ms. Larson be questioned, but Findley decided to make the process convenient and harmless for her. He made arrangements to meet Brae at her apartment and asked her to have Ann present. Over the objections of his partner, he sent Detective Battin onto the university campus to make some minor inquiries about Robert Bradford while he visited with Brae and Ann.

"Thank you for allowing me to come here," Findley said when Brae met him at her apartment door. "I know this is a difficult time for you."

Brae looked frazzled. It was obvious to Findley that she was frightened by the detective's presence.

"Ms. Larson," he said. "I only have a few questions for you. I am sorry for your loss."

Ann immediately moved to Brae's side.

"Detective," she said. "I am Ann Yin, Brae's roommate. Brae is willing to talk with you. She wants to help, but you need to understand this has been a rough time for her."

Brae's ordeal had caused Ann to become assertive in her role as her roommate's protector. Ann was determined to see Brae get safely through the interview.

"I'm wondering if Brae should have an attorney present," she said defiantly.

"I appreciate your concern for Brae," Findley replied. "I asked you be present so Brae would not be alone. If, at any time, you want the questions to stop, just say so. Brae always has the right to consult with a lawyer but I don't believe she needs one."

Findley's manner of speaking and his tone of voice impressed Ann and caused Brae to become more confident.

"Please come into the living room and have a seat," she said.

Detective Findley sat down on an easy chair that was directly across from the couch on which Brae and Ann sat.

"There are some things I have to ask you, Brae. I promise you the information will be kept confidential for now, but you need to know that when this goes to trial everything could become part of the court record…and court proceedings are public."

A look of dismay spread across Brae's face. She had not had time to consider the implications of a trial. She now realized she might be called to give testimony. The idea was unpleasant for her to contemplate. Tears ran down her face.

Ann left the room, returning quickly with tissues for Brae.

"Thank you for your candor," Ann said. "We read in the newspaper that Robert was not killed in any random manner…that you are investigating his death as a murder. I hope you know Brae had nothing to do with Professor Bradford's death. She was with me the night he was killed."

"You were both here?" Findley asked.

"We were here…though we left for a couple of hours to have a drink and talk. Then we came back."

"What time frame are you talking about?"

"We went out at seven. We were back here no later than nine-thirty."

"And did you both stay here?"

"No," Ann answered. "I stayed until eleven thirty, then I went over to my boyfriend's apartment. Brae went to bed right after I left."

"Is that your recollection, too, Ms. Larson?" Findley asked.

"Yes," Brae replied. "I learned about Robert's death the next day…it was on the television news."

"May I ask you, did you go over to Mr. Bradford's condo after you had heard of his death?"

"Yes. Ann went with me."

"We went there to get Brae's personal items," Ann said. "We didn't take anything that did not belong to Brae."

Detective Findley looked first at Ann, then at Brae.

"It would have been better if you hadn't gone," he said. "This way it looks as if you had something to hide."

"Detective," Brae said in a desperate voice. "I didn't want Mrs. Bradford to find my things there. I know it was wrong, but I…I didn't want her to think badly of Robert."

"And you have a key to Mr. Bradford's condo?"

"Yes," Brae replied.

"I need to understand something," Findley said. "Tell me what your relationship with Mr. Bradford was?"

Brae cast her eyes downward. Her head sunk downward, too. Then she held her head up and looked directly at Detective Findley.

"Robert and I were lovers," she said. "But you already know that."

"Actually I don't," Findley said. "There are rumors and there is speculation, but what I am after is the truth."

There was no condemnation in Detective Findley's voice.

"I appreciate that," she said.

"I'm afraid I have to ask you some things about your relationship with Mr. Bradford."

"I understand," Brae said.

"Do you know if Mrs. Bradford knew about you and her husband?"

"I know she did not know about our relationship," Brae said. "Or at least, I believe she did not know. Robert never said she knew. Did she know?"

"I don't believe she did," Findley replied. "Did anyone else know?"

Brae turned her face toward her roommate.

"Ann knew," she said. "I told her a week before Robert was…"

Brae was unable to finish her sentence. It was difficult for her to believe Robert was dead.

"Ms. Yin," Findley asked. "Did you tell anyone about Ms. Larson and Mr. Bradford."

"No," Ann replied. "Only Brae and I knew…and Robert."

"Do either of you own a firearm?"

A look of concern appeared on the faces of both Ann and Brae.

"A firearm!" Ann exclaimed. "Do you mean a gun?"

"Yes," Findley said.

"Of course not," Ann replied. "Neither one of us has ever held a gun in our hands."

"It's a question I had to ask," Findley explained. "And I need to know if you ever saw a gun at Mr. Bradford's condo."

Brae sighed heavily.

"No. I don't think Robert had a gun," she said.

Detective Findley looked at Ann.

"I also need to know the name of the bar you went to on the night of Robert's death," he said. "And, I need to know if you talked with anyone while you were there."

"Hunters," Ann said. "We saw Professor Sheridan there. I said hello to him. And, we talked to Michele Richards and to Mike Madden. They're friends of ours…students."

"Brae," Findley said. "When did your relationship with Professor Bradford begin? How long have you been seeing him?"

"We've been together for three month…three months this Wednesday," Brae said. "It seems like such a short amount of time. Can I ask how you found out about us?"

"Certainly," Findley said. "We asked the neighbors at the condo. Three of them told us that a young woman had been visiting with Mr. Bradford. There are surveillance cameras at the condo. We checked them…your picture was identified by one of Robert's friends."

"May I ask who the friend is?"

Findley hesitated, knowing he should not respond. Eventually he decided to give the information to Brae.

"Ms. Larson," he said. "I want you to understand the man who identified your picture only talked with us about you. He was a friend of Robert's and only wanted to help us find Robert's murderer. I don't think he has talked with anyone else about you and Mr. Bradford. I believe he is a true friend."

"Michael Sheridan," Brae guessed.

"Yes," Findley replied. "How did you guess?"

"Robert told me he had confided in Professor Sheridan. He told me he did not give my name to Sheridan. He just wanted to talk to someone about us."

Brae put her arm around Ann.

"Much like I did with Ann," she said.

"I need to know if you spent much time at Mr. Bradford's condo," Findley said.

"I was thinking the other day," Brae said. "When you add up all the time Robert and I spent together, I don't think it would total more than two full weeks…it seemed like more, but it wasn't."

"Did you spend any entire evenings there?"

"Yes…sometimes with Robert and sometimes alone."

"You stayed in the condo sometimes when Robert went home?"

"Yes," Brae answered.

"Did Mr. Bradford ever talk about divorcing his wife?"

"No. He talked about problems he was having with her, but never about leaving her. I wouldn't have stayed if he did."

"You wouldn't?"

"No. My relationship with him was temporary. We both knew that. I loved him, but I would never…"

Brae began to cry again. Now Ann put her arm around Brae. Findley waited for Brae to regain her composure.

"Please take your time," he said.

Brae breathed heavily and straightened her back.

"I was going to say I would never interfere with his marriage, but I did."

Brae cried more and struggled to gain control of her emotions.

"Is Robert dead because of me?" she gasped.

"No," Findley said calmly. "I don't believe he is. It's something else. We don't know what, yet. But, it's something else. Can you think of anyone who would want to kill Mr. Bradford?"

Detective Findley watched as Brae hesitated to answer his question.

"I don't know of anyone," she finally replied.

"But you were thinking of something, weren't you?"

"I only know Robert was having difficulty in his life. He was under pressure to prove his worth here at the university. I know that pressure upset him, but he never really talked about it with me. He just said he needed to escape from it all."

"But he must have gotten over that," Findley noted. "He published a series of poems that were received well. Isn't that true?"

"Yes," Brae said. "I…I just know he was still troubled even after he published the poetry. There was something bothering him. I really don't know what. I know it had to do with the poetry."

"Did you talk with him about that?"

"We talked…or rather I tried to talk with him about the poetry. I tried to talk with him about what was bothering him."

"Did he tell you anything?"

"No. Our relationship changed after he published his poems."

"Can you tell me about that? How did your relationship change?"

"Our conversations were always open, until he published. Then the poetry became central to both of us…that is, central to our way of thinking, but not in our conversations. The poetry caused Robert to withdraw. I wanted to talk about it, but he didn't want to. I thought…I thought his poetry would have the opposite effect. I thought we would read it to each other and talk about its meaning. That didn't happen. I don't understand. Maybe after he published, he didn't need me anymore. I don't know. I'm still trying to work it all out in my head."

"Detective," Ann said. "I think you can see Brae is tired. Do you have any more questions for her?"

Detective Findley remained quiet while he took time to consider Ann's question.

"Not right now," he said. "I may have more questions later."

Findley rose up from his chair as if to leave, but paused for a moment.

"I do have one more question," he said. "Have you ever been to Wicker Park, Ms. Larson?"

Brae sighed again.

"Yes," she said. "I attended the recognition dinner for Robert's poetry. I also teach English as a second language there. It is one of the university's community service programs."

"Did you ever meet Robert there?"

"No."

"Did you know where he lived in Wicker Park?"

"I knew his address. I saw it on mail he brought to the condo, but I have never seen his house and I never met him in Wicker Park. Ann attended the recognition dinner with me."

"Did you talk with Robert that evening?"

"We only congratulated him," Ann said. "We left right after the awards were presented."

"Do you know where Mr. Bradford went?"

A painful expression appeared on Brae's face.

"I saw him in a group of colleagues...that was the last time I saw him," she said.

Detective Findley saw the sense of loss in Brae's eyes.

"I appreciate your help," he said. "Thank you for allowing me to come here."

Ann and Brae stood up, happy to walk Detective Findley to the door. When they reached the door, the detective turned toward them again.

"I'm sorry," he said. "I have one more question. It's better to get it all out of the way now rather than me having to come back."

Brae and Ann stood silently, waiting for the detective's question.

"Ms. Larson, did Mr. Bradford ever come here to visit you?"

"Is that important?" Ann inquired.

"I'm sorry, but it is. You see we have to establish the areas Mr. Bradford moved in before his death. If he ever visited here, he may have run into a former boyfriend who was jealous, or...well, the possibilities are endless. We have to make all of them part of our investigation."

"Robert never came here," Brae said softly. "And there is no former boy-friend."

Chapter Fifty — Diane Meets Brae

The death of Professor Bradford had sent shock waves across the university campus. Two days after the murder, a candle light vigil was held to mourn his death and to protest violence. Dean Allen Hall spoke at the gathering; he eulogized the loss of the popular professor. Segments of poetry from Robert's latest publication were read in memory of his talent and of his contribution to the university.

Murder is a tragic and abrupt ending for those who continue to live. No member of the university community took Robert's death harder than Brae Larson. Within four days of his death, rumors circulated that he had been engaged in a love affair with a student and, shortly afterward, Brae was identified as the student. Wherever she went on campus, she felt persecuted by the stares and the whispering of others. The adverse notoriety she received and the loss she felt caused Brae to lose her ability to focus on her studies; in time, she wound up dropping all of her classes.

Brae wept at night and struggled to appear normal during the day. She missed Robert constantly and thought of all the words she wanted to say to him. Anxiety dominated her life; she began to take long power walks, hoping she could exorcise the demons that plagued her through the expenditure of energy. She avoided walking on campus, choosing instead to take the 'L' into the city and to walk on the paths that follow Lake Michigan's shoreline. From her exercise and her worries, she lost seven pounds. Attempts by Ann to comfort Brae proved ineffective. Ann quickly assigned herself to simply taking care of the needs of the apartment and to being there when Brae wanted to talk.

It was a Sunday morning; Brae was home alone when she heard the sound of the apartment house doorbell ring. She moved cautiously to the electronic voice box to see who was at the door, fearing it may be a reporter.

"Hello," she said into the box.

A moment of silence passed, and then a voice responded.

"Are you Brae Larson?" a female asked through the intercom system.

"Who is this?" Brae asked.

"This is Diane Bradford," the woman replied. "I would like to talk with you if you would allow me to do so."

Brae's body melted and her shoulder fell against the wall. She closed her eyes and breathed in deeply.

"Brae," the woman said. "I am not here to hurt you. I just think it would be good if we could talk."

Brae straightened up. She knew she should be shocked to hear Mrs. Bradford's voice, but some how she felt a sense of relief. She breathed in a large amount of air, held it in her lungs, exhaled slowly, and then pushed the button that released the lock to the apartment house front door.

Brae knew she had only a couple of minutes before Diane Bradford would be outside her apartment door pushing on the doorbell. She hurried into the bathroom and splashed water in her face. With her fingers grasping the edge of the water basin, she looked into the mirror, peering deep into the image she saw there. She shook her head back and forth, bent down, and brought more water up onto her face, rubbing it hard against her skin.

"Think clearly," she said to herself. "Think clearly."

She heard the doorbell ring; the ring was louder than she had ever heard before. She grabbed a towel and wiped the wetness from her face. She stood up straight to appraise what she saw in the mirror. It was eight-thirty and Brae was dressed in a t-shirt and sweat pants. Her hair was unkempt, she was barefoot, and she was without makeup. For one second her body shivered, as she realized Robert would have considered her current appearance sexy. She did not want to appear sexy to Mrs. Bradford and she took comfort in the fact that women think differently than men. She knew Mrs. Bradford would think she looked a mess. She hurried off to answer the doorbell, not wanting to hear it ring again.

Brae pulled the chain off the doorjamb lock, turned the deadbolt to the left, and opened the door to see a petite attractive woman dressed in black slacks and a light gold v-neck sweater pulled over a white blouse. Her hair was long and flowed over her shoulders. She was prettier than Brae had pictured her to be.

"Please come in," Brae said.

"Thank you," Diane replied.

For a moment the two women stood still, quietly looking at each other. Conventional acts of civility raced through their heads, but none of them seemed appropriate. Brae was first to break the silence.

"What do we do?" she asked awkwardly.

"I'm not sure," Diane replied.

Another moment of quiet prevailed.

"I am sorry about Robert," Brae said.

Tears formed in the eyes of both women.

"Thank you," Diane said. "I miss him."

Impulsively, Brae thought of hugging Diane, but did not. Tears began to stream down Diane's face.

"Mrs. Bradford, would you like to use the washroom?" Brae asked.

Diane nodded.

"It's that door," Brae indicated, pointing through a passageway. "I'll...I'll make us some tea."

Diane moved quickly to the washroom, closing the door behind her, while Brae began the process of making tea.

Separated from each other, but in the same apartment, the two women took stock of what should happen with the time they were about to share. They both were strong, intelligent, and practical. They both understood this was a unique opportunity. Although they did not collaborate on how to proceed, the two women knew they needed to talk about Robert and why he was murdered. They both understood their conversation would be painful.

Chapter Fifty-One — Tea with Brae

Diane had found Brae to be younger and prettier than she had imagined. She took time in the bathroom to adjust to that new circumstance. After composing herself, she left the washroom and headed for the kitchen area. As she walked toward the kitchen, she saw Brae standing in front of the stove on which she had placed a small pot of water. Brae had set two teacups and a plate of biscotti on the kitchen table. When Diane saw the table, she immediately thought of her friend, Elena Markova.

Brae turned away from the stove to find Diane standing in the kitchen.

"Are you all right?" she asked.

Immediately Brae felt foolish for asking such a question.

"I'm sorry," she said. "There are no words…please, please take a seat."

Brae poured hot water over the tea bags. The two women watched steam rise up out of the teacups. Diane sat down and moved her tea bag up and down in the hot water.

"The tea was a good idea," she commented. "It will give us something to do. Perhaps it can provide a sense of normality to this awkward situation."

When she buzzed Mrs. Bradford up, Brae had thought she would be the one who would be uneasy. She was surprised to find it was Mrs. Bradford who was nervous and unsure.

"Mrs. Bradford," Brae said. "I know this is difficult for both of us…I'm not sure what to say to you. I don't really know why you are here. I don't think I could have come here if the situation were reversed."

Brae immediately regretted her words.

The situation, she thought. What a poor use of words to apply to all of the things that had happened.

"Brae…may I call you Brae?" Mrs. Bradford asked.

"Yes. Please do," Brae responded.

"This is awkward for me," Diane said. "I wasn't sure I would ring the doorbell. I want you to know that I'm not here to pry into your life or the times you shared with Robert."

Diane paused to collect her thoughts. Tears came to her eyes again. Brae left the table, picked up a box of tissues from the kitchen counter, and returned to her chair.

"I think we will need these close by," she said trying to smile. Her eyes became misty.

"Thank you," Diane said.

Diane took a tissue from the box and wiped her eyes. She smiled and laughed slightly at their predicament.

"Did Robert ever come here?" she asked.

"No," Brae blurted out immediately.

Diane shook her head.

"Forgive me," she said. "I told you I would not ask about any of that. I…I was just curious."

"Mrs. Bradford, why are you here?" Brae asked.

"Brae…you did not take Robert away from me. I want you to know that. Robert left me…left his life three years ago…maybe four. I'm just trying to understand why. I don't blame you for that, but maybe you know why."

"I'm not sure what you mean," Brae said. "Robert…

Brae paused. A slight scowl appeared on her face.

"I'm afraid it will be impossible to answer your questions without telling you some personal information," she said softly.

"Do you mind talking with me?" Diane asked.

"Mrs. Bradford…I think we have more in common than you know."

"What do you mean?"

"I am going to make an assumption. I hope you don't mind," Brae said.

"Please go ahead."

"Robert…we both loved him and he disappointed both of us. I know your love for him was deeper than mine…you were his wife. You spent years with him. I don't even know if I really loved him. We only knew each other for a short period of time. I am sure Robert and I would have never stayed together. God…I am rambling here," Brae confessed.

"It's all right. I understand…you are right. He disappointed both of us, but I have forgiven him for that."

"You have?" Brae asked.

"Yes. Robert was a weak man…I knew he was a weak man when I married him."

A puzzled look appeared on Brae's face.

"Why would you marry a man you considered weak?" she asked.

Diane smiled slightly.

"You are young, Brae," she said. "Life is a series of compromises. At least that's how I see it. There is no perfection in life, and certainly, there are no perfect men. Robert was weak. He knew that. And I…I prefer humility to arrogance. Robert was not arrogant. Actually, there was charm in his weakness…. an admission of human vulnerability. I don't understand people who always think they are right or who believe they know what right is. Robert's weakness was his confusion. I understood that."

Diane sighed and shook her head.

"I loved Robert, but I probably would have left him," she said.

"Why would you have left him?" Brae asked in astonishment. "Do you mean because of me?"

"No...not because of you. I would have left because he left me. He was already gone...as I said, that process started years ago. I don't know...maybe, he would have changed...maybe, he would have grown...and we would have stayed together. I'm just trying to understand what it is he wanted. Where he wanted to be. That's why I'm here. And, I want to know who killed him."

"I understand the police have a suspect," Brae said. "Is that right?"

"They *suspect* the wrong person," Diane answered. "That's the other reason I am here. The man they suspect is not a killer, and I won't have him charged with my husband's death."

"You know the man?"

"Yes. His name is Javier Morales. I met him in Wicker Park."

Diane saw a look of astonishment appear on Brae's face.

"Javier!" Brae exclaimed.

Now a look of astonishment appeared on Diane's face. Her hands pushed down on the edge of the tabletop, her back became rigid, and she squared her shoulders.

"Do you know Javier?" she asked.

"Yes. Javier is a student of mine in an ESL class I teach."

Brae's look of astonishment became one of serious contemplation.

"Javier!" she exclaimed while shaking her head back and forth. "You are right Mrs. Bradford...Javier Morales is not a murderer."

A bond was being established between two unlikely candidates: Diane Bradford, the wife of Professor Robert Bradford and Brae Larson, Robert Bradford's lover. Both women had loved Robert, and they both cared for Javier Morales. Finding Robert's killer and protecting Javier would be mutually beneficial.

Chapter Fifty-Two — Diane and Brae Plot

"Can I trust you, Brae?" Diane asked.

"Yes you can," Brae replied hesitantly.

Diane paused.

"You seem uncertain," she said.

"I was just thinking," Brae said. "Don't you think that we are both suspects in Robert's death?"

"Most certainly. I know I am. After all, I'm the spouse."

"And I'm the lover," Brae blurted out.

Brae was immediately awash in embarrassment; she closed her eyes, dropped her head down slightly, and shook her head back and forth.

"God, this is awkward," she said.

Then Brae looked up at Diane again.

"You asked if you can trust me," she said with a sigh.

The tip of Brae's tongue passed lightly over her lips.

" But I need to know something," Brae continued. "Did you do it?"

"Do you really mean that?" Diane replied. "I mean do you think I did it?"

Brae continued to stare deeply into Diane's face, her eyes examining Diane in an attempt to look into the conscience of Robert's widow. Then she dropped her gaze, looked at the tabletop, and thought deeply of her own perceptions of life.

"No I don't think you did it," Brae replied softly. "But I had to ask."

"Brae…I did not kill Robert. Did you?"

Brae was initially taken back by Diane's question, but then quickly realized it was a legitimate counter to what she had just asked.

"Touché," she said. "And no…I did not harm Robert. Do you think I did?"

Diane sighed and slowly took in a deep breath.

"Not at all," she said. "But I had to ask, too."

Brae straightened up in her chair. She put both of her arms behind her, joined her fingers together behind the back of the chair, and took on a thoughtful look.

"When the police questioned me, they asked about a missing gun," she said. "They wondered if I had seen it…in the condo. They said the gun was Robert's and that it was missing."

"I know. Apparently the gun used to kill Robert is the same caliber," Diane said. "Robert did have a gun. He got it from his uncle before we were married. I haven't seen it in years. It's missing…that doesn't look good for me, but I did not kill my husband. Nor, did I have him killed. You will have to trust me on that, Brae."

"I need to ask you something else," Brae said. "Did you know about me?"

"I wondered, but I did not know about you. I did not know Robert was…was…"

"Having an affair?" Brae said.

"Yes. I did not know he was having an affair. All I knew was he had changed."

Diane looked down at her teacup. She and Brae had not touched any of the food on the table. She picked up a spoon and stirred her tea.

"I am not going to lie to you, Brae," she said. "I am angry that Robert was seeing you… and I am mad at you, too. I have a son."

Brae's eyes looked down at her tea. She had questioned why she was seeing a married man before, but she never searched her soul concerning the consequences of what she and Robert were doing. The condo was so convenient; Robert's family was so far away. Now, sitting across from Diane Bradford and hearing her mention her son, she felt ashamed.

"I'm not going to defend what I did," she said. "There is no defense. But Robert made me feel special and happy. I am not going to forget that."

"You shouldn't," Diane said. "Brae my thoughts on all of this are blurry. There are times when I am mad…then there are times when I envy you. I know you did not take Robert away from me…something else took him away…I know that. Perhaps, I forced him away, I don't know. I just want to understand what happened."

Diane paused for a moment to regain her composure. Brae was touched by Diane's words and she waited to hear more.

"I remember Robert," Diane continued. "He and I were passionate once. I miss that."

She paused again. Diane wanted to talk with Brae, but some aspects of the conversation were more difficult than she imagined. She breathed in heavily through her mouth, and exhaled slowly.

"Did you know a Russian woman named Elena Markova?" Diane asked.

"No. Who is she?"

"Elena was Javier's lover."

Another look of astonishment appeared on Brae's face.

"My God," she said. "Javier wrote poems to her."

"You know that?"

"He told me he did…though, I never saw the poetry. And, I didn't know who the woman was."

The two remained silent, each absorbing the information they just imparted.

"This is strange," Diane said.

"Very," Brae agreed. "I wonder if it all connects somehow. It's as if we have all been in the same room, yet unaware of each other."

"There is something more you should know," Diane said. "It has to do with Robert's writing."

"You know about that, too," Brae exclaimed. "I didn't think anyone knew."

Diane pushed back in her chair. Her face was somber and ashen.

"How do you know?" she asked.

"Let's be sure we are talking about the same thing," Brae cautioned. "What I am referring to is the authenticity of Robert's latest work. Understand, I don't know anything about it. I'm just guessing...wondering."

"What is it you wonder?"

Brae could see Diane Bradford was upset, but she did not know why. She assumed Diane's anger came from her suspicion that Robert had confided in Brae about his writing, but had not confided in her.

"Please, Mrs. Bradford, don't be offended by what I am about to say...it's about Robert's writing."

"Did Robert talk to you about his work?" Diane asked.

"No," Brae replied. "Robert was secluded about his work, but I had this feeling the poetry...the arrangement of the words and the emotion expressed by them...I had this feeling they were not his."

"Why would you say that?"

"Because of my closeness to him," Brae said slowly. "The man who wrote those words was someone else. It took me awhile to figure that out, but I could feel it. I'm...I'm sorry."

Diane folded her arms around her body. She titled her head upward, stared at the ceiling, and remained quiet. She knew what Brae meant...the man Brae was making love with, her Robert, was not the same person who wrote the poetry for which Professor Robert Bradford had recently been lauded. Only the few women who had been close to Robert would be able to tell that the poetry was not his; she was one woman and Brae was the other.

Tears formed in Brae and Diane's eyes in recognition of the fact they had both concluded that Robert's poems were not genuinely his. Brae reached for a tissue and wiped her eyes.

"What do we do?" she asked.

Diane allowed the tears in her eyes to boldly flow down her face.

"We find out who else knew about this," she said. "Do you know where Robert got the poetry?"

"No."

"I believe I do," Diane said. "I think it is Javier's poetry."

Brae could not sit any longer. She rose up out of her chair and moved toward the kitchen sink. She stood over the sink with her hands on the counter top and her back to Diane. Then she began to sob uncontrollably.

Diane got up and moved toward Brae. She put her hand on Brae's back. Brae turned around and the two women embraced each other, crying freely on each other's shoulders.

"We'll figure this all out," Diane said while she rubbed Brae's back with her hands.

Diane placed both of her hands firmly on Brae's shoulders. She stepped back and spoke directly into Brae's face.

"I know what we need to do now," she said. "We need to help Javier."

Chapter Fifty-Three — Brae Calls Javier

Javier heard his cell phone ring. He had been in hiding from the INS. He was suspicious of everything that represented his pre-hiding days. He let the phone ring five times before answering.

"Hola," Javier said into the phone.

There was no reply.

"Hola," Javier repeated.

"Javier," the voice of a woman replied.

Silence prevailed again.

"Javier," the voice repeated. "This is Ms. Brae, your teacher. I need to talk with you."

More silence.

"Javier, I want to help you. Please talk with me."

"Ms. Brae," Javier said. "How do you know my phone number?"

"You put it on a form when you registered for the ESL classes."

Silence again.

"I'm not trying to interfere with your life. I only want to help you," Brae pleaded.

"I don't understand why you are calling me. How do you know I need help?"

"Javier, we both know you are in trouble and you are hiding. I think I can help you."

"You will get in trouble trying to help me, Ms. Brae. You should not be calling me. It will be better if I leave, and go to another city."

"Javier," Brae pleaded. "You cannot run from this. The police will be searching for you everywhere."

"I am only one poor immigrate. Why would the police search for me? Many of my friends have moved on to other places, and the INS has left them alone."

"Javier, this situation is different. I need to talk with you. I want you to meet me and Mrs. Bradford so we can talk."

"Mrs. Bradford!" Javier exclaimed. "Why would Mrs. Bradford want to talk with me?"

"Do you trust me, Javier?"

"Si, Ms. Brae."

"Mrs. Bradford and I think we can help you. Do you trust Mrs. Bradford?"

"Si, I do. But how do you know Mrs. Bradford?"

"Mrs. Bradford is a friend of mine. I know her from her bookstore," Brae said.

"Ms. Brae, I am confused," Javier said. "I did not know you and Mrs. Bradford knew each other. I do not understand why the two of you would want to help me."

"Javier, do you trust me and Mrs. Bradford?"

"Si, si," Javier repeated.

"Then meet us at Mrs. Bradford's bookstore on Damen and Division. Come there at night after the store has closed and let us help you."

"Ms. Brae, I do not understand."

"Javier, meet us tonight at nine-thirty. We will talk then, face to face, and answer all of your questions. There is a small alleyway that leads to the backdoor for the store. The door will be open and we will be waiting for you. No one else will be at the store, only Mrs. Bradford and me. Let us help you. We will stay there until ten. You need our help, Javier. Will you come and talk with us?"

A moment of silence prevailed on the phone. Brae waited anxiously for Javier to speak.

"Si. I will be there," he finally said. "I trust you and Mrs. Bradford."

• • •

Javier was confused when Brae hung up. He did not understand why she would call him or why Mrs. Bradford would want to become involved in his problems. He did not understand how his very existence would become common knowledge between the two women, or how the two of them would know he was in trouble. For the last few days, he had been moving from one location to another, taking advantage of the hospitality of an underground network of immigrants. He had no contact with Jose or with any of the friends with whom he normally associated prior to his escape from the INS raid. He assumed all of his friends had scattered to avoid capture, and they were avoiding him for the same reasons he was avoiding them; scattering made it difficult for INS officials to catch their prey.

Javier sat down on a chair in a room in the small apartment house in which he was hiding. The residents of the apartment had all left for work. Javier had said his good-bye to them, letting them know he intended to move on before they came back. He believed constant movement was his best defense. His plan was to hide one more night, try to contact Jose, and then move south toward St. Louis in order to escape the INS. He and Jose had agreed to meet in St. Louis if there ever was the need to flee from the Chicago.

Javier stared at his cell phone and thought about the conversation he had just had. Ms. Brae's offer placed Javier in a dilemma. He trusted and missed Ms. Brae and Mrs. Bradford. He wanted to believe in them, and he needed help. But if he went to see them, he would be deviating from his plan and could be placing himself in danger. His basic instinct told him not to trust gringos, yet he always remembered the kindness of the humanitarian groups who left food and water in the desert. Surely, there were good people everywhere he reasoned, and most certainly, Ms. Brae and Mrs. Bradford had been good to him in the past. He decided to meet them in Mrs. Bradford's bookstore.

• • •

Javier was good at maneuvering in the dark without being noticed. He carefully chose his route to Mrs. Bradford's bookstore, deciding to get there before nine o'clock in order to observe the store and the people in it. He scouted the alleyway, finding the door and making sure there was no one hiding there to grab him. He watched Mrs. Bradford close the store and saw Ms. Brae enter the store after all the customers and workers had left. Javier was frightened. He thought about leaving without contacting the two women, but when he saw them talking inside the store, he wanted to be with them. He wanted to experience their kindness again and to believe in the goodness of people. At nine twenty-five, he moved quickly down the alleyway toward the door, knocked once, and hurried inside.

Brae and Diane had gone to the back room of the store to wait for Javier. Although the women did not talk about it, they both found themselves hoping he would come to the store, and yet, afraid that he would. Neither one of them believed Javier Morales had murdered Robert, but what if he had?

Javier was a tall, powerful man. When he did enter the store, his entrance was abrupt and alarming. Brae and Diane were startled by his sudden appearance, but Javier quickly dispelled any fears the two women had.

"Hola," he said quietly while smiling at them. "Gracias for inviting me here."

Javier's voice and manner exuded gentleness, respect, and warmth, replacing the dominance of his physical presence with a feeling of heartfelt friendship. Diane was first to respond.

"Javier, my friend," she said as she took hold of his hand. "Are you hungry?"

"Si, I am," Javier answered. "But are you sure you want me to stay in your store? You could be in trouble for having me here."

"We want you here," Brae said. "We want to help you. Come with us."

Diane led Brae and Javier up a flight of stairs to a storeroom that occupied one quarter of the attic space above the bookstore.

The three people sat down at a small table where Diane had placed a pot of coffee, a plate of sandwiches, a small carrot cake, and three place settings.

"Javier, help yourself to the food. Will you have coffee?"

"Yes," Javier replied eagerly as he reached for the sandwiches. Diane and Brae smiled as they watched him pile three sandwiches on his plate, then take a large bite out of another sandwich he held in his hand.

"You are hungry," Brae laughed. "We should have brought more food."

Javier consumed the first sandwich in seconds. Then he took a large drink of coffee.

"Pardon me," he said. "I have not been so hungry since a time long ago when I used to help my father plant crops."

"You eat, Javier," Diane said. "Eat, and then we will talk."

• • •

Javier quickly consumed one of the sandwiches on his plate, and then he began to talk with the two women.

"You have both been kind to me," he said. "I do not want to cause you any trouble. It is my plan to leave Chicago and find work in another city, but I will not forget you."

"Javier," Diane said. "We have a question to ask you. It is a question about my husband."

"Mr. Bradford?" Javier replied. "I have never met him."

Brae and Diane looked at each other, surprised by Javier's response. "Javier," Brae said. "Do you know what has happened to Mr. Bradford?"

A bewildered look appeared on Javier's face.

"No," he said. "Is something wrong?"

The genuine innocence of Javier's response encouraged Diane to speak frankly.

"Mr. Bradford has been murdered," she said.

"Santa Maria!" Javier exclaimed.

Javier pushed his chair back away from the table while his mind processed the news. Then an expression of understanding came across his face.

"Santa Maria," he said again. "You think I killed your husband. That is why I am here?"

"No," Brae said in a desperate tone.

"Javier," Diane said hurriedly. "Would we invite you here and offer you help if we thought you were the murderer?"

Javier took time to think again. He placed his large hands on his thighs, rubbed them, and breathed deeply.

"No," he said. "But I do not understand. Why am I here?"

"You are a suspect, Javier," Diane said. "The police are looking for you to question you."

Javier bolted up out of his chair. He turned his back on the two women and moved swiftly toward the door. He stopped and turned back to face them again. A look of anguish was on his face. He slapped his right hand up against his chest, and shook his head.

"Why me?" he asked. "Why me?"

"Javier, please sit down, and let us talk with you," Brae said. "We will tell you everything we know."

Javier returned to table, sat down hard, letting his body spill about the chair, his long arms and legs drooping down in despair.

"I could never kill another man," he said. "You must believe me."

"We do," Diane said. "We want to help you."

Chapter Fifty-Four — Diane, Brae and Javier

Javier Morales was having the most horrible day of his life, but he was unaware it could get worse. His mind raced with the dangers that confronted him. He was a young, poor illegal Mexican immigrant living in Chicago. He believed there would be no chance of justice for him if the police caught him. He had no understanding of the American judicial system and no desire to spend time in jail. He imagined the worst when he thought of being accused of murder. His only hope lay in the hands of Brae Larson and Diane Bradford.

"Tell me what you know," Javier said in a voice drained of energy.

"You are only a suspect, Javier," Diane began. "A man who looks like you was seen at the place where my husband was murdered."

"Quien debe tomar el examen!" Javier exclaimed.

Javier seemed to panic at the news, but then a look of sadness came over him.

"Mrs. Bradford," he said. "Your husband is dead, Robbie's father. I am sorry for you."

Javier's thoughtfulness reinforced the women's commitment of his innocence.

"How is Robbie?" he asked.

"Robbie is with friends. He is as good as can be expected. You are kind to ask."

"Poor Robbie," Javier sighed. "He is such a fine boy."

"You are a good man, Javier," Diane said. "I am sorry, but I must tell you more…more reasons why you are a suspect."

"Tell," Javier replied. "But first tell me…where was your husband killed?"

"In Wicker Park," Diane replied. "That is one of the other reasons you are a suspect. The police know you played with Robbie; and they know you and I talked there without Robbie."

"Oh, Mrs. Bradford," Javier moaned. "They don't think…. they don't think we murdered your husband, do they?"

"No, I don' think they do. But that is a possibility they have investigated. A wife is always a suspect."

"I am sorry I have caused you this trouble," Javier said.

"You have not. People talk. They make up stories. You and I have done nothing wrong, but there is something else."

"What?"

"A knife was found in the park. It is a knife from Piazza Navona."

Anguish again returned to Javier's face.

"Was this knife used to murder your husband?" he asked.

"No. My husband…Robert was shot."

Javier signed heavily.

"I am so sorry for you," he said.

"There is something else," Brae interjected. "Something the police do not know about."

"But something you do know about?" Javier asked.

"We cannot be sure," Diane said. "We need to ask you."

Diane got up from the table, walked over to a storage shelf, and lifted a small book up from one of the shelves. She brought it back to the table.

"This is a book of poems published by my husband," she said. "Brae and I believe the poems are not his. We wonder if the poetry is yours."

Javier took the book and looked at the cover: *A Collection of Poems* by Dr. Robert Bradford

He opened the book, spreading the pages apart so the book opened midway. He read only a few words, then his eyes looked up at Diane's face.

"My poetry," he said.

Tears appeared in Diane and Brae's eyes. Their heads dropped low and they looked at each other acknowledging what they had already assumed.

"We are so sorry, Javier," Diane said.

"My poetry," Javier said again. "How?"

While Javier held the book of poems in his hands, Diane took the time to explain what she could only guess was so. As he listened to the explanation, Javier's facial expression turned stoic. When Diane finished, Javier slowly laid the poetry book down on the table and stared at it.

"Lena," he said quietly. "The poetry I wrote for Lena. Why would she give it away?"

Brae and Diane fought to keep themselves from crying. They knew Javier to be a sensitive, private man and they understood how harmful it was to have the words he had written for his lover stolen.

"Why?" he repeated.

"Elena loves you, Javier," Diane said. "But, it was all too complicated. Don't you see? She couldn't throw your poems away and she couldn't take them with her. She wanted them kept in a safe place."

"But your husband took them."

"My Robert…" Diane began. "My Robert was…under a lot of pressure. I…I don't expect you to understand…I don't understand completely. "

"Is this why Mr. Bradford was murdered?" Javier asked, pointing at the book.

Brae and Diane looked at each other.

"We don't know," Brae said. "But…"

"But people will think I killed him," Javier said. "They will think that is why I am on the run."

Diane sighed heavily.

"No one knows about the poetry," she said. "Only Brae and me."

"Did you think I murdered Mr. Bradford?" Javier asked Brae.

"Never," she replied.

"Did you think so?" he asked of Diane.

"Never," Diane replied.

"You are good friends," Javier said.

Javier looked at both of the women. He saw the compassion they felt for him reflected in their eyes.

"I must tell you this," he said. "I am angry, but I would never kill a man. It hurts me very much to have my words taken from me, but I would never kill a man."

"We know that," Brae replied.

Diane thought about telling Javier more, but decided against telling him about Robert and Brae. Instead, she probed further, directing her questions at Javier.

"Were you in the park that night," she asked. "Could it have been you running away?"

"No," Javier answered. "I was in hiding."

"Then the question is, who was running away? Who murdered Robert?" Brae said.

For a moment the three people sat quietly, their eyes moving from one person's face to another in an attempt to examine each other's thoughts, but no flash of discovery appeared.

"It is late," Diane finally said. "Will you stay here, Javier? Will you work with us in clearing your name?"

Javier shook his head slowly up and down.

"Si. Yes," he said. "I do not want anyone thinking I would murder a person."

"You must be careful, Javier. We will feed you and get news to you. We will visit with you when we can. Keep the door locked and remain as quiet as possible up here. The other workers in the store don't come here unless I send them, and I will not."

"You are kind, Mrs. Bradford," Javier replied.

"And don't contact anyone," Brae added. "We do not know who we can trust. Your hiding here must remain a secret just between the three of us."

"I understand," Javier replied. "I wanted to contact Jose, but I am afraid to."

"It is best to stay here without anyone knowing," Diane repeated.

"Si."

"You should get some sleep, Javier," Brae said. "We will talk again tomorrow."

• • •

Diane and Brae hugged Javier, then left him to make up his bed in the attic. They walked down the stairs, heading toward the front of Diane's store.

"Brae, it is late...too late for you to be riding the 'L' back to your apartment. I am going to ask you something."

Brae looked at Diane with intense interest, realizing what she was about to say.

"Will you stay over in Wicker Park?"

Even though she had anticipated Diane's question, the idea of staying in her home shocked Brae.

"Diane..." she blurted out.

Diane reached for Brae's right hand and held onto it firmly.

"There are two extra bedrooms," she said. "I understand how this would appear to most people. I know it is strange, but the whole set of circumstances are strange. It is strange you and I have talked...wife and lover. But Robert is gone. There is nothing we can do about that, but we do need to think about Javier. We need to help him. I believe Robert would want us to help him."

Brae's composure softened; an expression of agreement appeared on her face. She squeezed Diane's hand tenderly, and her eyes became misty.

"You are right," she said with a sigh.

Diane and Brae hugged briefly, left the store, and headed for Diane's home.

Chapter Fifty-Five — Jose Finds Javier

Javier Morales needed to remain hidden, but he found it impossible to stay inside twenty-four hours a day. Summer pedestrian traffic was at its busiest in the Wicker Park area between seven and eleven in the evening, so Javier began taking walks after Diane left the store. To keep from being recognized, he kept his head covered and remained in the darkness as much as possible. He tried to stay away from areas he had frequented before he was a suspect in Robert Bradford's murder, but one night he found himself walking to Wicker Park just so he could watch the young men play basketball and recall the times he had spent playing with Robbie.

Javier was leaning against a tree on the north side of the park, looking at the players on the basketball court and using shadows to help obscure his presence when he was startled to hear someone speak to him.

"Javier, mi amigo," the voice said.

Javier turned around abruptly, ready to fight the man who spoke his name, or to take flight.

"Jose!" Javier said as he recognized his friend.

"Amigo, we must get away from here. This is no place to talk."

"Follow me," Javier said. "Stay far behind me, but follow where I go. I know where we can be safe."

Quickly Javier turned and walked away, heading south and east toward Wicker Park Avenue. His pace was brisk, but he continually looked back to make sure Jose was following. Javier made his way to Evergreen Avenue, using it to cut back to Damen, and then hurried south for three blocks where Damen intersects with Division. He turned west on Division, staying on the south side of the street, pausing momentarily to look back at Jose. Then he ducked into a dark alleyway and waited in the darkness for his friend.

"Jose," he whispered when his friend peered into the narrow lane between the buildings. "Come back here."

Jose rushed to embrace Javier.

"Mi amigo," he said as he hugged Javier tightly.

Jose let loose of Javier and looked up and down the narrow alley.

"Why are we here?" he said. "What is this place?"

"Come with me, Jose. I will show you."

Jose obediently followed his friend as they walked deeper into the alley. Soon Javier turned a corner, reached for the doorknob of a backdoor entrance, and opened it.

"Entrar, Jose," he said holding the door open wide. "Go Jose. It is safe."

Jose dashed into the building, glad to get away from the dangers of being outdoors. Javier swiftly followed, closing the door behind them and moving toward the set of stairs that led upward.

"Vengan," Javier said.

Javier walked rapidly up the steps, disappearing through a door at the top of the stairs. Jose looked up the stairway and saw a light come on in the room Javier had entered. He walked up the steps cautiously, wondering where he was going. He entered the room and discovered it was a storeroom decorated with an assortment of mismatched furniture and a small refrigerator. Javier was sitting on the side of a small bed, smiling at his friend.

"Mi casa," he said. "Bienvenida, Jose!"

"Javier," Jose exclaimed. "What is this place?"

"Mi casa," Javier said smiling again.

Then the expression on Javier's face changed.

"Y mi escondite," he said sadly. "Where do you hide?"

Jose sat down on the bed next to Javier.

"Mi amigo," he said. "I hide all over, from one place to another…always on the move. Whose place is this? Do they know you are here?"

Javier stood up and looked down at Jose.

"Jose. Do you remember me telling you about Mrs. Bradford?"

The expression on Jose's face turned sour.

"Si," he said in a tone that spewed forth resentment.

"Why do you look like that?" Javier asked. "This is Mrs. Bradford's store. She is hiding me here and helping me."

Jose bolted up from the bed. He grabbed hold of Javier's shoulders with both of his hands.

"No! El Bradfords son el diablo!" he shouted. "Son diablo! Son diablo!"

Javier broke loose of Jose's grasp and grabbed onto him with his own powerful grip.

"Jose. You are wrong. Why do you say this? Mrs. Bradford has been hiding me here. She feeds me and tells me the news. Her husband has been killed, and the police think I did it."

Jose pulled away from his friend's grasp, walked across the small room, and turned to face Javier again; the expression on his face was one of confusion.

"Javier, mi amigo…I tried to kill Mr. Bradford," he said. "I wanted to kill him for you."

Javier stood staring at his friend, unable to believe what he had just heard and unable to speak. He bowed his head; his arms hung limp at his sides as the reality of Jose's words sunk into his soul.

"Madre Maria," he gasped. "Madre Maria, help us. Help us."

Javier's body sank down to the bed. He buried his face in his hands, slowly shaking his head back and forth. Then he looked up at Jose. His face was racked with anguish.

"Why, Jose? Why?" he said in despair.

"Javier, the Bradfords' stole your poems and Mr. Bradford put them in a book with his name on the book. They stole your words. They took your fame from you."

Now, Javier bolted from the bed toward Jose, confronting him with animated hand gestures.

"You are wrong about her, Jose," he shouted. "Mrs. Bradford is my friend."

Jose could see and hear the torment that exploded outward from Javier. He felt sorry for his friend. His body composure crumbled, as he stared at Javier with a demoralized expression.

"Javier," he said softly. "I saw your words in Mr. Bradford's book. I heard him reading your words to his friends, and I heard people giving him credit for what you wrote."

Javier stood imposingly in front of Jose, moving air in and out of his nostrils with short angry breaths.

"Where?" Javier demanded.

"At Adobe Grill," Jose answered anxiously. "I was an extra bus boy there. There was a ceremonia…a recepcion for professors from the University of Chicago. They were giving awards, and I heard your words being read by a man…Javier, I was surprised and glad to hear your words…I thought your poetry was being awarded, so I found a program to read. I was hoping to see your name, but your name was not there."

Javier listened intently to what his friend was saying, as his facial expression became more somber.

"How did you know the words were mine?" he asked.

"Forgive me, mi amigo," Jose said. "I read some of your poems at our apartment."

"Was Mrs. Bradford there when the poems were read?" Javier asked.

"No," Jose replied.

Jose's head dropped down. The volume of his voice became reduced.

"Our teacher, Ms. Brae, was there," he said. "I saw her sitting at a table. I saw her applaud the man who was reading your words, and I saw her congratulate him after the ceremony. When I asked one of the gringo waiters who the man was, he pointed to the program and showed me that Mr. Bradford was getting an award for the words he was reading…your words…your words, mi amigo. The people at the recepcion said Mr. Bradford was a genius. They said his poetry was the best they had ever heard."

Jose was angry again. He saw Javier move back to the bed and drop down onto the mattress. Javier looked up at Jose.

"Tell me all you know, my friend. Tell me now."

Jose grabbed a folding chair that was leaning up against a small chest of drawers. He unfolded the chair, placed it in front of Javier, and sat down.

"I am sorry, mi amigo," he said. "I thought you knew about this. I was about to give up and go back to Mexico."

"Did you know they blame me for the murder?" Javier asked.

"Si," Jose replied. "Javier…amigo…I believed you killed him."

"Jose, I could not kill a man. Did you think I could? Did you think I would kill him for taking my poetry? I can prove the poetry is mine…there would be no reason to kill him."

"Javier, you remember when I called you at work and told you to run because the INS was after us?"

"Si," Javier replied. "That is when we first went into hiding…just before Mr. Bradford was killed. What does that have to do with all of this?"

"It was Mr. Bradford who turned us into the INS," Jose said. "He did it to have us sent back to Mexico so no one would know he had taken your words."

Jose looked at Javier. His friend seemed crushed by Jose's story. He slowly raised his right arm, and put it on Jose's shoulder.

"Still, Jose, mi amigo…still…killing…it is not right."

"I did not want to kill him at the recepion," Jose said. "I was just angry at him then. I confronted him in a parking lot after the banquet. I told him I knew what he had done. I told him those words were yours."

"What did he say?" Javier asked.

"He surprised me. He apologized for stealing your words. He told me he would make it right. He asked me my name and told me he wanted to meet you to make things right. He said it could all be fixed…that you would get awarded, too. I gave him our address and my cell phone number; he said he would call so we could talk. You were working that night, and when I got home, the INS came. Julio called and warned me that the INS was on our street asking about us. I fled down the backstairs and called you. I know Bradford called the INS and turned us in. It must have been him! That is why I wanted to kill him."

"But Jose…did you kill him?"

"No. I wanted to kill him, but I did not. I found his address in a phone book and then I watched for him by the park. I finally saw him walking in the park toward his home. Amigo…I don't know if I could have killed him. I wanted to, so I hid by the side of the pavilion. I kept out of sight, waiting for him to come close to me, but he never did."

"What happened, Jose?"

"I heard him arguing with someone and I lost my courage. I became afraid. I knew I could not kill him. I was about to leave when I heard him shout…then I heard a gunshot. I looked around the corner of the pavilion and saw Mr. Bradford lying on the ground…I ran away and dropped the knife I was going to kill him with."

Javier's eyes darted away from Jose's face. He looked to his left, and sighed.

"The police found the knife, Jose. They traced it back to the restaurant. It is one of the reasons they blame me for the murder."

"I am sorry, mi amigo."

Javier reached for his friend with both hands. He placed his hands on Jose's shoulders, and looked directly into Jose's eyes.

"Do you know who killed Mr. Bradford, Jose?"

"Amigo…I thought you did. I thought you found out about all this and became as angry as I was. Now, I don't know who killed him. What will we do?"

Javier let go of Jose and gave him an encouraging smile.

"Jose," he said. "Tonight you will stay here with me. Tomorrow I want you to go and collect whatever things you have and bring them back here. Do you have anything?"

"Si, but very little."

Jose smiled back a Javier.

"I have some of your poetry, mi amigo. I have your briefcase," he said.

A joyful look spread across Javier's face.

"You are a good friend. I want you to hide out with me. I want you to talk with Mrs. Bradford and Ms. Brae."

"Are you sure we can trust them?" Jose said.

"Yes. I know we can. You will know, too once you talk with them. Right now I want to hear where you have been hiding, and how you have been."

Javier and Jose spent the next two hours talking about their fugitive experiences. They joked and laughed about their circumstances until their eyes became sleepy, and then they lay down to sleep. Javier insisted that Jose sleep in the bed, while he made a bed of blankets on the floor.

Chapter Fifty-Six — Diane Meets Jose

Diane Bradford always arrived early to her bookstore, but now that Javier was hiding there, she arrived even earlier in order to bring him breakfast. She entered the store through the front door, hurried to the backroom, and made her way up the staircase where she knocked softly and waited for Javier to open the door. When he did, she was frightened to see another man in the room. She stopped abruptly at the door entrance; her astonishment was profusely displayed by her facial expression.

"Mrs. Bradford," Javier said. "Don't be afraid. This is my friend, Jose."

Still bewildered by Jose's presence, Diane remained frozen in the doorway.

"Why is he here?" she asked.

Javier reached for the paper sack of food Diane held in her hand. He took it from her, led her into the room, and closed the door behind them. Jose stood seven feet away from Diane, staring at her with the same stony expression that was now on her face. Javier immediately became a broker of peace between the two.

"Jose," he said. "I want you to meet a wonderful woman, Mrs. Bradford. Mrs. Bradford, this is my good friend, Jose."

"Good morning, Mrs. Bradford," Jose said in a cautious manner.

"Good morning, Jose," Diane replied apprehensively.

A telling silence prevailed in the room as all three assessed the new dynamics of their situation. Diane turned toward Javier and was first to speak.

"Javier," she said. "I do not understand why Jose is here." She turned back to look at Jose. "Please forgive me, Jose, but I had an agreement with Javier about the use of this room. I need to speak openly about you being here."

Jose straightened his back and gave a stern look toward Diane. Javier walked quickly over to Jose, put his arm around him, and smiled broadly at Diane.

"Mrs. Bradford," he said. "Jose will help us. Please sit down so we can talk."

Javier then patted Jose's back.

"Jose, my friend…. take that sour expression off of your face. Mrs. Bradford is a good person. She will help us. Trust me, mi amigo."

Javier moved toward the table, beckoning the others to follow.

"Please sit," he said to his friends.

Diane and Jose sat down at the small table, both putting their trust in Javier.

"Mrs. Bradford," Javier began. "I am grateful for your help, but I am lonely, too. My heart has been heavy ever since I lost Lena and Jose."

Diane listened to Javier; her mood began to change from trepidation to compassion.

"Jose found me," Javier continued. "He found me last night while I was out walking."

"You left here last night?" Diane said.

"Mrs. Bradford, I cannot stay locked up in this tiny room. I need to be able to go outside. I am careful, very careful, but Jose did see me and he approached me. My heart soared when I saw him. We needed some place to talk, so I brought Jose here. I know I should have asked you, but there was no time. Jose can be trusted, and he needs a place to hide, too."

Diane looked at Jose.

"You are welcome here, Jose," she said. "We need to talk about why you are here and how you can help Javier, but for now you are welcome. I hope you understand why I was frightened to see you."

"I do. You frightened me, too," Jose answered. "But, I trust Javier. If you are his friend, I am also your friend."

Diane reached into the paper sack Javier had placed on the table.

"I brought you muffins and orange juice," she said. "There is enough for both of you."

She pulled the groceries out of the sack and began placing it in front of the two men. Jose smiled at the sight of the food, as Diane arranged the meal in front of them.

"Eat," Diane said. "Eat and talk with me before I have to leave." She looked at Javier. "Tell me, Javier, you said Jose will be able to help us. How will he be able to do that?"

Javier took the cap off a bottle of orange juice and set it down on the table. He took a short swig of the juice, then answered Diane's question.

"Jose was in the park the night your husband was killed," he said softly. "I am sorry to speak of this terrible thing, but perhaps Jose can tell us more about that night."

Diane Bradford was a strong woman, but she became momentarily unnerved by Javier's answer. Her husband had been murdered, and now, she was sitting at table with a man she did not know, a man who had been in the park at the time her husband was killed. Her body shuddered at the news and her eyes became misty. She swallowed hard and looked at Jose.

"Did you see my husband murdered?" she asked. Her voice was low and she was breathing hard.

"No," Jose said in a sympathetic tone.

"Mrs. Bradford," Javier interjected. "There is no time to talk now. We need to talk with Jose. We need Brae here, too. Soon, your workers will be coming to the store. I am sorry to give you such information at this time, but I needed you to know why I want Jose to stay here with me. Do you understand?"

Diane sat up in her chair, nodding her head.

"Yes I do," she said. "You were right to ask him to stay." She turned toward Jose. "I am glad you are here, Jose. You can help Javier."

"Javier is my best friend," Jose said. "I will do anything for him. You can trust me, Mrs. Bradford."

Diane turned her attention back to Javier.

"I will contact Brae. We will all meet here tonight," she said. "But Javier, you have to stop taking chances. I am glad you found Jose, but it is dangerous for you to be out on the streets. Promise me you will stay here until I am able to come back."

"I will not leave," Javier promised. "But Jose needs to leave and come back. He needs to bring some of his things here."

Diane looked at Jose.

"I will help you with that, Jose. The police are not looking for you. I will come back at noon and we will talk about getting your things. Until then, you both need to be quiet and stay here."

"We will," Javier said.

Chapter Fifty-Seven — The Detectives Talk

J n their investigation of Robert Bradford's murder, Detectives Rice Battin and Mike Findley had acquired numerous folders that contained information about the case. They had interviewed over a dozen people who were closely associated with Professor Robert Bradford. They were beginning to get a sense of the man, but who killed him and why he was killed were still mysteries to them.

"Well, what do we know for sure?" Rice said, as the two men rehashed the information they had on the murder.

The detectives were seated at their desks at the North Woods Street Chicago Police Station. The two desks were pushed together, the front ends of the desks touching so the detectives faced each other when they sat in their respective chairs. On each desk was a folder of notes they had taken on Robert Bradford's death.

"We know he was shot," Mike replied. "We don't know why. We assume the shooting was not a robbery, but we don't know that."

"No money was taken," Rice said.

"There was no time to take money…the park was full of people who were only a few yards away from the crime scene. Not a very likely place or time to be trying to rob someone."

"Then we have to assume that he was killed by someone who wanted him dead…either someone who knew him well, or maybe, just someone who had reason to be very angry with him. It could be a current student or a former student who was dissatisfied with a grade or mad at him for something he said in class."

"Or just a nut of some kind. Lots of possibilities"

"Which one do you like?" Rice asked. "You're the veteran."

"My guess? I think it was someone who knew Mr. Bradford," Mike replied.

"The man did have two women in his life. That can lead to problems…many a man has died from the love triangle affliction."

"For me," Detective Findley said. "I'll be ruling out Mrs. Bradford and Ms. Larson as suspects. I'll keep them as 'people of interest' but I don't believe either one of them is a killer."

"You're the veteran here," Rice said. "But they are both more than 'people of interest' for me. But I'm willing to learn. Who else have you eliminated?"

"Mike Sheridan is an easy elimination. The man's harmless."

"I'll agree with that," Rice said. "He might know more than he's telling us, but he is basically harmless."

"The guy he played racquetball with…Bob Wachtel. I don't see anything there, do you?"

Rice Battin remained silent for a brief moment as he contemplated Bob Wachtel's involvement in Robert Bradford's life.

"Nah. Nothing there," he said.

"Javier Morales is of interest to me, but I'm not sure why," Mike said as he tapped the eraser end of his pencil up and down on his desktop. "I don't think he was doing Mrs. Bradford or that she was doing him. But, he might have had a thing for her without her even knowing it. According to our witnesses, he may have been at the crime scene the night of the murder, and he did leave work without quitting or picking up his pay. Of course, he's probably an illegal…so that may be why he's gone. But still…there is a connection there between him and Mrs. Bradford. Something…I don't know what."

"That's what I keep going back to," Rice said. "Bradford was dissatisfied with his job, with his marriage, and with life in general. He couldn't have been any companionship for Mrs. Bradford. She must have been searching for something…everyone tells us this Javier guy is a real good-looking dude. And, she was seen alone with him twice."

"Yeah… *alone* in the park sitting at a picnic table. That's not what I call an affair."

"All right then, how do you see Morales fitting into all of this?"

"I don't know," Mike said. "I'm not sure how he was involved, but I think Mrs. Bradford knows more about him than she is telling us. I'm sure of that."

"What about Bradford's other colleagues at the university? The guy didn't seem to get along well with a lot of staff members there."

"Could be…could be there was some jealousy over this new publication of his. Have you read any of it?"

"No," Rice Battin replied with a snorty laugh. "Come on…its poetry for God's sakes. Have you read any of it?"

"As a matter of fact, I have," Mike replied.

"Really! So what's the verdict?"

Mike Findley paused and reflected on the book of poems he had read.

"It doesn't fit with his other works," he said. "In fact, it's entirely different."

"Other works! Do you mean you've read his other books?"

"I compared them to his new publication," Mike said. "Nothing in depth…just looking them over. The new poems are very different from his other poems. That's one thing that annoys me about this case. You know, his wife didn't attend the recognition banquet the university held to honor his new book. And, the supper was held in Wicker Park, so it was not as if she had to travel far to be there."

"Maybe, she was busy with the bookstore. Or with her son."

"Maybe," Mike repeated while tapping his pencil again. "But her not attending seems strange to me…almost like a statement of some kind."

"Could be she's lying to us about the affair. Could be she did know about Brae and was too pissed at him to attend."

"That's possible…everything is possible."

"But you don't think she did know, do you?" Rice asked.

"No. I believed her when she told us that. I don't think she had anything to do with his murder."

"Then what the hell are you getting at?"

Mike put his pencil down. He pushed his chair back away from the desk, opened a top drawer, and pulled out a thin book. It was Robert Bradford's book, *A Collection of Poems*. He held it up for Rice to see.

"I'm just wondering if the poetry in this book was written by Professor Bradford."

"How can we find out?" Rice asked.

"I was thinking about paying Allen Hall another visit and asking him. He's the expert."

Chapter Fifty-Eight — The Bookstore Hideout

Brae Larson, Diane Bradford, Javier Morales, and Jose Ortiz were seated around a small table in the upper storage room of Diane's bookstore. It was 9:45 in the evening. The bookstore had been closed for almost an hour. Diane had explained Jose's presence to Brae in a phone call she made earlier. Brae had already greeted Jose, and the initial shock of his hiding out with Javier was gone. It was now time to talk frankly about what should be done concerning the situation in which the four people found themselves.

"Brae and I have an idea," Diane said to the two men. "We want to explain it to you to see what you think."

Both Jose and Javier were glad to see Brae. Jose was still suspicious of Mrs. Bradford, but he had a crush on Brae. The romantic feelings he had for her overshadowed any lingering doubt he had concerning her part in the theft of Javier's poetry.

Javier trusted both women. But, Brae's age, the encouragement she had given him with his poetry, and her idealism made him happy to have her present.

Brae's attitude toward the two young men was one of sympathy, humanitarianism, and confusion. She had fallen in love with poetry she thought was written by Robert Bradford, only to discover the words were written by Javier. She had always admired the courage Javier exhibited as an illegal immigrant, but now she saw him in a new light. This was the man who had freed her from her nightmare. This was the man who had caused her face to flush as she read his words. This was the man she really made love to after reading words she thought had been written by Robert. This was the man she tried to find in Robert. Brae wanted justice for Javier, but her emotional state of being was torn by his words and by the feelings she had expressed for Robert. She knew she needed to concentrate on the problem of the two men's immediate fate, but she knew such concentration would be difficult.

Diane Bradford was the anchor of the group. She was involved with the two men because she wanted justice. She knew her husband. She was certain he would have never been able to continue the charade of his new publication. Had he not been killed, he would have confessed his sins and given credit to Javier. Robert could be maneuvered into acts in which he did not want to be involved, but he would have never taken credit for another man's ideas. Sometimes Robert could be a slow learner, but there was no greed in his soul, no malignant driving ambition in his mind, and his heart was always compassionate. Robert had erred, and Diane wanted to do what he would have eventually done if he had lived; she wanted to correct his error and clear

Javier's name. In the future, she wanted to tell their son Robbie what she believed: Robert Bradford was a good man.

Diane also had another motive. She wanted to help heal any pain Brae may be feeling. Diane knew Robert would want that done. She had come to like Brae and she wanted Brae to understand that she had found Robert during a difficult and desperate time in his life. She wanted Brae to remember Robert as a good man. She wanted Javier to see that, too.

"We are grateful for the help you have given us," Javier said. "We will listen to whatever ideas you have, but I do not want to put you or Brae in danger."

"Javier," Diane said. "My husband would want all of this corrected. I want you all to know I am here as much for Robert as I am to defend our innocence."

"But your husband stole Javier's poetry," Jose interjected.

Jose's words stung Diane.

Javier looked at Jose.

"Be quiet, Jose," he said. "Let Mrs. Bradford talk."

"I am not going to spend time defending what Robert did," Diane said. "It is done, but if you trust me, then trust Robert. Understand that he would have corrected all of this had he not been killed. Respect Robert. We will find his killer. But, I will not be a part of anything that takes away from the goodness of my husband. Robert was confused and disoriented during the last few months of his life, but I will not let his confusion tarnish who he really was. Is that understood?"

The other three people in the room sat and contemplated what Mrs. Bradford had said. Her sincerity and her forthright manner impressed them all.

"Si," Javier said.

"Si," Jose echoed.

Diane turned her head to look at Brae. Brae was teary eyed.

"Robert was a good man," Brae said.

"Then we will work together on this," Diane said. "We'll find his killer."

Diane Bradford was a keen observer of human dynamics. She knew Jose and Javier were closer to Brae than they were to her. She also knew Brae was an activist who needed to be directly engaged in their plans.

"Brae," she said. "Would you tell Javier and Jose what you and I discussed?"

Diane's decision to have her talk about their plan was a happy surprise for Brae. She jumped at the chance to explain their ideas to the two men.

"We think it is dangerous for both of you to hideout here," she said. "One of Diane's employees may hear you up here or stumble upon you by accident. And, this is too small of a space for two people."

"Where will we go?" Javier asked anxiously.

Brae stopped talking and looked toward Diane.

"There is no one in my house," Diane said. "Robbie is away with family members in Wisconsin. I visit him frequently, but I don't want him to come back yet. The thought of his father being killed so close to the house frightens him, and he doesn't know someone killed Robert on purpose. He thinks it was a robber. I don't know if Robbie will ever be able to come back to the city. For now, he is happy to be in the country."

A sad look appeared on Javier's face.

"Mi pequeno hermano," he mumbled.

"We think you should stay in Mrs. Bradford's house," Brae said.

Both Javier and Jose sat up higher in their chairs. They looked at each other in astonishment, and then turned their faces toward Mrs. Bradford.

"Vaca Sagrada!" Javier exclaimed. "Jose and me hiding in your home! Mrs. Bradford, this cannot happen."

"Listen to why we are asking you to move there," Brae said.

The two men looked at Brae as she began to list the problems with the current hideout.

"It is dangerous here," Brae began. "It is difficult for the four of us to meet here. It is difficult for Mrs. Bradford to keep bringing food here. This small space will drive both of you crazy. There are no bathrooms up here. If we need to contact either of you, we have to wait for the store to close. There is no privacy here for the two of you. There is only one bed here. There is no place to cook here. If a policeman ever sees a light here at night, you would be caught."

Javier listened as Brae stripped away at any objection he could make to the new plan. He began to plainly understand the reasons for moving. He sighed heavily in recognition of his defeat.

"I don't like having you take such a risk," he said. "But what Brae said is right. If you are going to continue to hide us, we need a better place."

"Then it is settled," Diane said. "I have a garage we can park in at my house. The backyard is fenced in…no one will see you enter. We can take you there in my car tonight."

Diane stared directly into Javier's face.

"I want to do this Javier. I have to do it. I have to find out who killed Robert, and I cannot have any of us arrested for his murder. Do you understand?"

Javier had listened intently to what Diane had said throughout the evening. He had always been impressed by her warmth and generosity, but now he was amazed by her strength.

"I have always known oppression and understood the need for justice," he said. "But now I know why I traveled so far from my home…it was to meet you and to learn from you."

Chapter Fifty-Nine — A Collection of Poems

Detectives Findley and Battin sat in Dean Allen Hall's office for the second time during the investigation of Robert Bradford's murder. Findley had brought three books of poetry written by Professor Bradford and set them down on top of the conference table where they were seated. One of the books was Bradford's latest publication, *A Collection of Poems*.

"It's good to see you two gentlemen again," Hall said. "Of course, the circumstances are unpleasant, but I hope I can be of help to you. I see you have a collection of Robert's works with you. Are either of you a fan of his?"

"Not really," Findley replied. "But we do have a few questions for you concerning the professor's newest publication."

"Whatever I can do to help," Hall said. "Does the question somehow tie into Robert's unfortunate death?"

Findley placed his right hand lightly on top of the pile of books and drummed his fingers up and down on them.

"We have some theories we're working on," he said. "Have you read all of the professor's publications?"

"Most certainly," Hall replied. "It's part of my job to know the talents of the people in my department. I enjoy reading Robert's poems. Robert was a very successful writer. He did a lot of good things for UC."

Hall cocked his head and looked at Detective Battin.

"What about you detective…do you read poetry?"

"No," Rice replied. "I'm more of a sports fan."

"Nothing wrong with that," Hall commented.

Hall turned his attention back to Findley.

"So what's the question, Detective Findley? How can I help you?"

Findley picked up Bradford's latest publication and opened it to a random page.

"I'm no expert," he said. "But I'm wondering something about the style of the professor's recent publication."

Dean Hall beamed with a smile.

"It's really unique, isn't it?" he said. "We're very proud of Robert."

"What I'm wondering about concerns the uniqueness of the poetry."

"I'm not sure what you mean," Hall said.

"Robert's *Collection of Poems* seems to be very different in style from all of his other publications."

"Yes, yes…it's fresh and new," Hall exclaimed.

"Maybe too new," Detective Battin interjected.

Dean Hall's facial expression became somber.

"Are you insinuating there is something out of the ordinary concerning Robert's publication?"

"We're following an instinct," Findley said. "We're trying to find a motive for Robert's murder, and we are wondering if someone might have been upset with Robert's publication."

"Why would Robert's book upset anyone? Why it's been universally applauded here at UC."

"To be specific, Mr. Hall, we're wondering if Robert may have taken some liberties in his writing. Perhaps he used someone else's poetry as a base for developing his book."

"Absolutely not! Absolutely not!" Hall said. "I knew Robert, and he was a talented man…a brilliant man. His poetry is a reflection of his work and of his educational background. That book is a product of everything for which UC stands."

Detective Findley leaned back in his chair and put both hands on top of his head.

"The problem we have is that his latest work seems so much different than his earlier poetry. It almost seems as though the new publication was written by someone else."

"I assure you that is not so," Hall said. "Let me explain to you what has happened here. Robert had been teaching in a new area for him…these poems were inspired by the new material he had been teaching. There isn't anyone on this campus that has the ability and the inspiration to write like Robert. I think a part of that inspiration came from his suffering. I told you Robert had been off track a little, but that was the inspiration for him. It's all timing and opportunity. Robert created something new. That is what happened."

"And no one here has been complaining about his publication…maybe even a student?" Rice asked.

"Certainly not! And certainly no student would be capable of such writing. That book is genius. Genius! It's so unfortunate we do not have Robert here with us. I wanted to build a course around his publication, and I wanted him to instruct it. Brilliant, fresh, and new…that's what the book is. Robert's death is a tremendous loss to the university."

"Who will receive the royalties from the sale of his book?" Battin asked.

"Why, his estate will…I assume Diane. And, our publishing company also takes a share of the profits. But you need to understand something…this is not a popular book. It will not be a best seller. There will be some income from it, but no tremendous wealth. There's no profit motive here."

All three men sat silent for a moment.

"Have I helped you any?" Hall eventually asked.

"Oh yes," Findley answered. "We have to mull over every possibility to find a motive for Robert's murder. You've been very helpful."

224

Chapter Sixty — The Wicker Park Hideout

"Javier! Jose!" Brae called out as she entered Diane Bradford's home through the backdoor. "Come into the kitchen."

It was eleven a.m. and Brae had arrived in Wicker Park by taking the 'L' from her university apartment. She had left her apartment early in order to go grocery shopping for the two men.

Brae's mental state had improved ever since she and Diane Bradford had begun helping Javier and Jose. She felt a renewed sense of purpose now. She dedicated herself to helping the man who had freed her from her nightmares. Brae Larson still had many issues in her life to resolve, but she was happy to have begun a process that would lead her to the truth. And, she credited Javier's poetry with being the catalyst that gave her the courage to do so.

"Hola, Brae," Javier said as he entered the kitchen area. "It is good to see you."

Javier immediately spotted two large grocery bags sitting on the marble countertop of the brick island that stood in the center of the kitchen.

"You have been out shopping," he said.

Brae smiled at Javier. He was dressed in a jeans and a t-shirt. His thick black hair was wet and tussled.

"And you must have been showering," Brae said.

Javier flashed a smile back at Brae and ran his fingers through his hair.

"My hair," he said. "It is not dry."

He glanced at the grocery bags again and noticed both bags were labeled, *Zapatista Grocery*.

"Ahhhh, Ms. Brae, you have been to a Mexican grocery store!"

Javier walked quickly to the bags to look inside.

"Hmmmm," he moaned in delight as he sifted through one of the bags. "Corn flour, spices, beans, hot sauce, tomatoes, chili powder, green peppers, avocados, chicken… Jose and I can cook now!"

Impulsively Javier turned to Brae, swept her up in his powerful arms, and hugged her.

"Garcias, Ms. Brae," he said. "Gracias."

Brae felt herself being lifted up off of the floor. She felt the power of Javier's physical strength and she laughed with glee as he hugged her. Javier put Brae down quickly, smiling broadly at her. Brae smiled back and blushed.

"Forgive me," Javier said as he saw the blush in her cheeks. "You and Mrs. Bradford have been so good to us, and now, you buy us Mexican food. I am so happy to have you as a friend."

Brae hands were still braced against Javier's arms. She smiled at him, not wanting to offend the genuine sense of appreciation he had expressed. She looked into his dark eyes and found herself mesmerized by his handsome looks. She backed away from him, still smiling.

"It's okay, Javier," she said. "Diane, Mrs. Bradford, asked me to come here today. She gave me a list of things to buy at the grocery store. Today we want to talk with Jose about what he saw in Wicker Park the night Robert was killed."

A lump formed in Brae's throat as she verbally referenced Robert's death. Her body trembled slightly. Javier noticed.

Javier Morales was an enthusiastic observer of life and a gentleman. He had always wondered how Brae and Mrs. Bradford knew each other and why Brae was involved in hiding him, but he considered it impolite to ask. Now, after seeing Brae react to the issue of Robert Bradford's murder, he wondered how close she had been to the dead professor.

"Are you all right, Ms. Brae?" He asked.

Brae found herself attracted to Javier. He was a brilliant poet, a strikingly handsome and strong man, and he possessed a natural gracious manner.

"I am fine. We need to talk with Jose," she continued. "He may have seen something that could help us."

Brae moved slowly away from Javier, purposefully positioning the kitchen's center island between him and her. She began taking the groceries out of the bags and aligning them on the counter top. She had no fear of Javier, but she questioned her own ability to be alone with him.

"When will Mrs. Bradford be here?" Javier asked.

"Soon, she is going to take a long lunch break today so we can talk."

• • •

Diane Bradford arrived at her Wicker Park house at eleven-forty. She found Jose, Javier, and Brae sitting around the bricked center island eating chicken tacos.

"Hola," she hailed to the group

"Mrs. Bradford," Javier said. "Thank you for the Mexican food."

Diane smiled. It was a joy for her to see people eating in her kitchen.

"You are welcome," she said. "May I join you?"

"Si," Jose said. "I will get you a chair."

All three of the young people moved in haste to welcome Diane. Brae got a place setting and a drink for her, while Javier moved to the stove to prepare a plate of food.

"Is everything all right here?" Diane asked of her company as she took her seat.

Javier put a plate with two tacos on it in front of her.

"Everything is magnifico," he said.

"Good," Diane replied. "This is a nice lunch you have prepared for us, and I am sorry to interrupt such a wonderful meal with business, but we need to start talking about my husband's death."

Diane looked across the counter at Jose.

"Jose, Javier tells us you were in Wicker Park the night Robert was killed. Is that correct?"

"Si," Jose answered.

"Were you close to the place where my husband was found?"

Jose's facial expression became somber, as he stared down at his plate.

"Si," he replied. "I was close to the area."

"Mrs. Bradford," Javier interrupted. "I have something to tell you…something that will not please you, or Ms. Brae."

Brae and Diane could sense the information Javier was about to reveal would be upsetting for them. A momentary silence prevailed in the room. During the silence, Diane wondered if the man she was allowing to use her home somehow had been involved in the murder of her husband. Brae was also apprehensive, but still wanted to find out everything she could about Robert's death.

"We must be honest and open with each other," Brae said. "Tell us what you know."

"Jose went to Wicker Park to find Mr. Bradford," Javier said.

Chills ran up and down both Brae's and Diane's backs. They stared at each other, trying to muster enough courage to quell the foreboding that surrounded them.

"Why would he do that?" Diane asked.

Jose remained speechless. He was ashamed to confess the anger he had felt toward Mr. Bradford.

"Let me tell you what happened two days before your husband's death," Javier said.

Chapter Sixty-One — Jose and the Murder Scene

Diane and Brae sat and listened as Javier told them what he knew about Jose's presence at the murder scene. Jose remained quiet and subdued. When he finished giving the two women the information, Javier jumped to the defense of his friend.

""Mrs. Bradford," he said. "I want you to know Jose would not kill a man. He was angry, but he wouldn't hurt your husband."

Diane Bradford's mind was filled with questions, and she harbored some doubts about Jose. She wanted to believe Javier, but now she was aware both Javier and Jose had strong motives to kill her husband. She felt a sense of fear creeping into her being.

Could I have been wrong? She wondered. Has my trust in Javier allowed me to be deceived by Jose?

"I have questions," Diane said slowly. "Questions for Jose."

Everyone in the room detected a change in Diane's attitude. Diane felt the change occurring in the room, too. She decided to diffuse the potential harm that could result from not addressing the change.

"We need to be careful," she said. "We have all agreed that we want justice, justice for everyone in this room. To accomplish that, we must be honest with each other. Javier…when did you first learn your poetry had been taken by Robert?"

A lesser person would have been offended by Diane's question, but Javier was not. He responded in a calm and reasonable way.

"I found out from you and Brae," he said. "I found out on the night you had me come to your store."

Diane was pleased with the manner in which Javier answered her question.

"Jose, you say my husband called the INS in order to have you and Javier deported."

Jose nodded in agreement.

"Si, I believe he did."

"Do you *know* he did such a thing or are you just guessing?" Diane asked quietly.

"Who else would do this?" Jose asked in desperation.

"Maybe that question would help us to understand all that has happened," Diane replied. "But I need to be clear in what you are saying, Jose. When the INS came to your apartment, do you know if they were looking just for you and Javier?"

"Si. I do know that. They asked only about us and they did not look for anyone else."

"But you don't know for sure that Robert called the INS about you, do you?" Brae asked.

"You are guessing he did, but do you have any evidence?"

Jose looked confused, and turned to Javier.

"Amigo," he said as he spread his arms, placing his palms up and shrugging his shoulders.

"Evidence…pruebas," Javier interpreted.

"No," Jose responded. "No tengo pruebas."

"And you say Robert told you in the restaurant parking lot that he wanted to talk to Javier?" Diane asked.

"Si."

"And he told you he wanted to apologize and make everything right?"

"Si."

"Did you believe him?" Brae asked.

Jose paused and thought about the night he confronted Robert Bradford.

"Si. I believed him in the parking lot. His eyes…they were triste."

"Sad," Javier explained.

"Jose, I am sure Robert meant what he told you in the parking lot. I know he would not call the INS on you and Javier," Diane said.

"Then who did?" Javier questioned out loud.

"The man who murdered Robert," Brae said. "That's the man we're looking for."

A weight had been lifted from the people in the room. All of them felt relieved. And, they all understood the need to find out who had tried to get Javier and Jose thrown out of the country.

Chapter Sixty-Two — Brae and Diane Question Jose

"Jose," Brae said. "I want you to think about the night you confronted Robert at the restaurant parking lot. Was anyone else in the parking lot?"

"There was another man…Mr. Bradford walked to him after I let him go. They walked away together."

"Did this man hear what you and Robert said to each other?" Brae asked.

"No. He was too far away to hear, but he must've seen me grab Mr. Bradford, and he could've guessed that we were arguing."

"The man didn't say anything to you, amigo?" Javier asked.

"No…but he did point at me," Jose remembered.

"Do you know the man?" Javier asked.

"No, but he is familiar to me…maybe, I have seen him somewhere else."

"At the Piazza Novana?" Javier asked.

"Maybe there…maybe somewhere else. I'm not sure."

"Think Jose, think," Javier said.

"I will remember. I am not as smart as all of you, but I have a good memory. It just takes time, but I do not forget."

"Take your time, Jose," Diane advised. "But now, let's talk about the night Robert was killed. How long were you in the park?"

"A long time," Jose replied. "I was there before the sun went down. I watched your house and the park. I did not know if I would see your husband. Suerte brought him to me."

"Suerte?"

"Luck. Fate," Javier interpreted.

"Did you see anyone else in the park?" Brae asked.

Slowly a look of illumination appeared on Jose's face.

"Si!" he cried out. "Si! I saw the same man in the park…the man who was at the restaurant…the man in the parking lot. I think they are the same man."

"Did you recognize him in the park?" Diane asked. "Did he recognize you?"

"No…in the park I was angry, and only thinking of getting back at…

Jose stopped speaking. He did not want to vocalize the anger he had for Mr. Bradford in front of Diane and Brae.

"I'm sorry," he said. "I was not thinking clearly that night."

"Think of the man, Jose," Javier encouraged. "Was the man you saw in the parking lot, the same man you saw in the park?"

"Yes," Jose replied. "I'm sure it was."

"Did you see this man approach my husband?"

"No, but he was on the same side of the park as me."

"Was he alone?" Brae asked.

"Si…and he looked like he was waiting, too."

"Can you describe this man?" Brae asked.

"I can do better. I can give you his name," Jose answered with a look of enlightenment on his face.

"You know his name!" Javier exclaimed.

"No, but I know him from the banquet. He spoke there. That is where I saw him. That is how I know him. Show me who spoke at the dinner and I will be able to tell you the man's name."

Diane and Brae looked at each other.

"The UC website," Brae said. "We can pull up a picture of every professor in the English Department on the website."

"That's where we'll start," Diane agreed. "I have a computer in my home office."

• • •

Brae commandeered the chair in front of the computer as soon as the four people entered Diane's office. She quickly called up the website for the University of Chicago, typed *English Department* in the search box, and began clicking on faculty members' names. It did not take long for Jose to identify the man he had seen in the restaurant parking lot and in Wicker Park.

"That's him!" Jose shouted.

Brae stared at the picture on the screen as the other three crowded around and looked at the man Jose had recognized.

"This is the man?" Javier asked as he pointed a finger at the computer screen.

"Si! Si" That's the man," Jose exclaimed.

Javier turned to look at Diane who was staring at the picture with a look of contempt on her face.

"Do you know this man?" Javier asked.

Diane placed her right hand on Brae's shoulder as Brae slowly looked up into her face.

"We both know him," Diane said.

"Dean Allen Hall," Brae said.

• • •

The four people left the computer room, went back to the kitchen, and sat down at the center island. Their mood was sober. They all seemed to understand how frustrating their situation was. Diane was the first to speak.

"Dean Hall is an important man at the university, and identifying him as the man in the parking lot and at the park…well, that's one thing. Proving he killed Robert…that's something else."

"Diane," Brae said. "You are the only one here who really knows him. I know Robert didn't care for him, and I know he was putting some pressure on Robert to publish, but I've never met him."

Javier listened to Brae. He mentally noted she could only be close to Robert Bradford in order to know the things she just said. He wondered how close, but filed the thought away for a later time.

"Mrs. Bradford, could this man be so angry with your husband that he would kill him?" he asked.

"I don't know. Brae is right…Robert did not like him, and I know Dean Hall was not happy with Robert's attitude. Hall was putting pressure on Robert to publish…but murder?"

"What about Dean Hall's temperament?" Brae asked. "We might all be capable of murder. Is there anything in his personality that could touch off something like this?"

Diane sat in thoughtful repose, reflecting on the times she had met Allen Hall and on the things Robert had said about the man.

"He's arrogant," Diane answered. "I guess you could even call him pompous…Robert called him that often. He's devoted to the university and very concerned about his place there. Perhaps, his devotion could be an obsession…and his concern could be labeled as a driving ambition, but still all that is speculation. We need proof."

"There's only one way to get that," Brae said.

All eyes in the room focused on Brae.

"We have to confront him," she said. "I've been thinking. We believe we are the only ones who know *Collection of Poems* was plagiarized, but what if someone else knows? What if Allen Hall knows?"

"Hmmm, yes…yes," Diane said. "That might be it. Hall went out of his way to trumpet Robert's publication, and he called Robert a genius."

"At the recognition banquet, Hall called Robert's work a product of the university," Brae recalled. "He aligned himself closely to the work, almost taking credit for it being written."

"Mrs. Bradford," Javier said. "You weren't at the banquet. Can I ask you why?"

Diane's face took on a look of defeat.

"Robert gave me his publication so I could read it," she said. "I knew immediately the work was not his. I was sure it was your poetry, so I did not want to be part of the celebration. I was hoping that my refusal to attend the reception would bring him around to his senses. I should have done more. Now, I have the opportunity…the responsibility… to do more."

"And Ms. Brae," Javier said. "Why were you there?"

Diane looked at Brae.

"Brae, it is time to tell Javier and Jose everything," she said.

"Mr. Bradford and I were lovers," Brae said softly.

Early in her life, Brae had decided she would not allow herself to be judged by others. Because of press reports and gossip, hundreds of people knew about Professor Bradford and Brae. But this was the first time she had confessed her situation to a group of people. Making her confession was not easy; Brae was loathe to talk about private matters with anyone.

Diane got up from her chair and walked behind Brae. She put both of her hands on Brae's shoulders.

"Robert was having a difficult time," she said. "Brae was a part of that experience."

Jose's eyes widened.

"Mrs. Bradford," Jose said. "You are not angry with Ms. Brae?"

"I have forgiven Brae, and Brae has agreed to help me…to help us…find Robert's killer."

Javier stood up and looked directly at Brae and Diane.

"We will not talk of this anymore," he said. "It is none of our business."

Brae looked at Javier. His presence and the tone of his voice were commanding. He spoke as if he were issuing an edict, yet the look in his eyes was gracious and kind.

"Thank you, Javier," Brae said.

Javier nodded his head slightly in recognition of Brae's thanks, and then he purposefully moved away from the subject of her and Robert.

"Let's make our plan," he said. "You said we must confront this man, this Allen Hall. How do we do such a thing?"

Diane moved back to her chair. Javier also sat back down. Everyone in the room waited to hear Brae's idea.

"Javier, you do not know this, but your poetry helped me confront a problem that was ruining my life. Because of your poetry, I found the courage to move ahead…to search for the truth even when I was surrounded by fear. I think we can do the same thing here."

"What do you mean, Brae?" Diane asked.

"I can call Dean Hall and tell him I know about *Collection of Poems*. I can tell him I know who the real author is. I can tell him Robert told me…then we'll find out if he knows and if he wants to cover up the truth."

"But how will that get us the evidence we need?" Diane asked.

"I know a way," Brae said. "It is dangerous and we will need help…the two detectives that are working on the case…maybe, the older detective would help us?"

Now, Javier and Jose felt the trepidation Diane and Brae had felt earlier. The idea of including a police officer into their group was frightening for them.

"A police officer!" Javier exclaimed. "The police will throw Jose and me in jail."

"Javier's right," Diane agreed. "But so is Brae. I think we can include Detective Findley in our plan, but we have to be very careful. Findley is a kind man. He is intelligent and very perceptive, but he is a police officer…there are certain things he can do and things he cannot do. There are things he can know and things he cannot know. We have to be careful."

A worried look appeared on Jose's face.

"Do not worry, Jose," Diane said. "We will be careful and we will always tell you what we tell him. I promise you I will not tell Detective Findley we are hiding the two of you."

Chapter Sixty-Three — Diane Talks with Findley

"Thank you for stopping here," Diane said to Detective Findley.

"I got your message at the station," Findley replied. "I want you to know I am meeting here as a favor to you. I normally don't meet with people unless it is at police station or I have my partner with me."

"I appreciate your kindness."

"I'm also here because I'm curious. The phone message you left indicated you only wanted to meet with me. Why?"

Diane and Detective Findley were seated in a small office space in Diane's bookstore. It was 4:30 in the afternoon. The bookstore was open for business, and numerous customers plus three workers were in the store.

"I have some information for you. Information concerning the murder of my husband," Diane said.

Detective Findley's face became stoic. He adjusted himself in his chair by sitting up and straightening his shoulders.

"I want to inform you that you need to be careful concerning what you say to me. I'm not accusing you of anything, but if you are going to confess to something, I'm obligated to tell you your rights."

Diane smiled.

"I thought you would say that," she said. "I told Brae you would say that."

"Brae Larson?"

"Yes, Brae Larson. She is coming here to meet with us."

"Brae Larson is coming here?" Findley asked in a surprised tone.

"Yes, that's correct."

"Mrs. Bradford, do you know about Ms. Larson's relationship with your husband?"

"I do."

Findley let his body slide down in his chair.

"Well, this is a new one for me. I gotta tell you that."

"Detective, do you remember me telling you I had forgiven Robert?"

"Yes, I do remember. I was very impressed."

"And your partner, Detective Battin, was he impressed?"

A slight grin came to Findley's face.

"You are very observant, Mrs. Bradford," he said. "No, he was not impressed."

"Did he think I was a fool, or did he think I was being Machiavellian?"

"The second one."

"And you did not think that of me?"

"No. I think you are a sincere woman."

"And what do you think now?"

"I don't know what to think. Are you telling me you have forgiven Ms. Larson, too?"

"Yes, I have."

"And Ms. Larson, she is comfortable with coming here?"

"Yes. You will see that for yourself. We have good information, which I think will help you solve my husband's murder, but you have to be open-minded about what we are going to tell you."

"And, both of you have to be careful about what you say to me."

Diane looked over Findley's shoulder and saw Brae walking toward the office.

"Here's Brae now," she announced.

Detective Findley rose up from his chair to greet Brae.

"Hello, Detective," Brae said.

"Ms. Larson," Findley responded.

"Hi, Diane," Brae said as she smiled and waved to Diane.

Findley shook his head back and forth as he looked at the two women.

"Ms. Larson, this is a first for me," he said. "Mrs. Bradford tells me you have information for me concerning her husband's murder, but right now I am astounded by just seeing the two of you in the same room."

Brae smiled.

"I'm pretty astounded, too," she said. "All of the credit goes to Diane. I think you will find she is a remarkable person. I have."

"I have, too," Findley echoed. "Please sit down, and let me hear what you have to say. But I warn you, just as I have warned Mrs. Bradford, you must be careful what you say to me."

"We'll let you be the judge of that," Diane said. "If you think we are going in a direction you can't allow us to go, tell us. Is that all right?"

"That's fine. Just go slow and be careful."

"We think Dean Allen Hall killed my husband," Diane said.

"My God, that certainly is up front," Findley replied. "What makes you think that?"

"We believe he had motive," Brae said.

"Tell me what motive you see."

"Robert's work, *Collection of Poems*, was not his writing. He plagiarized it...stole it from another author."

"How do you know this?"

"Have you compared Robert's current work with his other poems?" Diane asked.

"I have."

"What did you think?"

"I thought his new work was completely different, but I asked Dean Hall about that."

Both Diane and Brae leaned forward in their seats, anxious to know what Hall had said to the detective.

"Can you tell us what he said?" Diane asked.

"I can. He told me the new work was just that…new and refreshing. He called it a stroke of genius, and indicated that it was the product of Robert's new teaching assignment."

"Do you believe that?"

"I don't. I've been mulling it all over in my mind, and I don't believe it. I have been wondering what Dean Hall believes. I wonder if he is so blinded by the success of the writing that he cannot see the truth, or…"

"Or he can't let the truth be known," Brae interjected.

"Yes, or he cannot let the truth be known. That is a possibility."

"We think Robert was ridden with guilt about what he did, and Hall killed him so he wouldn't tell anyone."

"Did either of you know the work was not Robert's?" Findley asked.

"We both suspected there was something wrong," Brae said. "Diane's suspicions were greater than mine."

"Did either of you talk with Mr. Bradford about your concerns?"

"I tried to," Brae said. "But Robert wouldn't talk about his work."

"The only thing Robert said to me was he did not care about the poems, he just wanted to teach," Diane said.

An introspective look swept across Diane's face.

"There was chill between Robert and me a few days before he was killed. We didn't talk," she said.

"Do either of you know who the real poet is?"

"No," Diane answered.

"Do you think Allen Hall knows?"

"It's possible he knows. Robert may have told him."

Findley sat and reflected momentarily on what the two women had told him.

"So you think Dean Hall met your husband in Wicker Park, quarreled with him, and then shot him over the question of the poetry?"

"Dean Hall is an ambitious man," Diane said. "He is arrogant. His reputation would be at stake over an issue such as this. He promoted Robert's work as a reflection of the university, and he used the work to further his own career. The truth would be a bomb blast for him, and for the university."

"It's possible," Findley said. "But here's a problem…we checked, Hall does not own a handgun."

"Did you check to see if his wife does?"

"My partner did. She is not registered to have a gun either."

"But she does," Diane said.

"How do you know that?"

"Robert and I attended a party at Hall's Wisconsin cabin home. I saw the gun there. His wife, Amber, told me they have it to keep critters away."

"But she's not registered. She doesn't have a FOID card?"

"Maybe not as Mrs. Amber Hall, but the Hall's have only been married for two years, and Amber was divorced prior to that; she's had two other last names. Did your partner check her maiden name or her previous married name?"

Detective Findley sighed noticeably.

"I wouldn't bet on it," he said. "But I will check."

Findley sighed again and ran his fingers through his hair.

"What is it you ladies want from all of this?"

Diane and Brae looked at each other, and Findley saw Diane nod toward Brae.

"We understand this information isn't conclusive," Brae said. "We know Hall may have gotten rid of the gun, and we know you need more evidence in order to arrest and convict him. We have a plan…a way to get more evidence."

Chapter Sixty-Four — Brae Calls Dean Hall

The first step in Brae's plan to find the person who had killed Robert Bradford was for her to call Dean Allen Hall at his office.

• • •

"Dean Hall," Brae said into her cell phone. "This is Brae Larson. I need your help."

"Ms. Larson," Hall replied calmly. "While I sympathize with your current situation, it is not appropriate for me to be talking with you at this time. And I must say, I do not appreciate you giving my secretary a false name. If I knew it was you, I wouldn't have taken this call."

"I know that," Brae answered. "But I know something about Professor Bradford's book, and I have to talk with someone about it."

There was a distinguishable pause in the conversation. Brae calculated she was getting through to Hall. She believed if he spoke again, she would have him where she wanted him.

"I don't understand," Hall said. "Are you referring to Professor Bradford's new publication?"

"Yes."

"*A Collection of Poems*?"

"Yes. There is a problem with the book," Brae said.

"What kind of problem?"

"Robert…Professor Bradford… told me he did not write the poetry in the book."

Another paused occurred.

"I don't know what you are talking about," Hall said. "Why would he tell you such a thing?"

"Dean Hall…it's no secret Robert and I were close. I read the poetry before anyone else. I found it beautiful, powerful, and liberating, and I tried to talk with Robert about it, but he refused."

"That does not mean the poetry was not his," Hall conjectured.

"Robert told me it was not his. He told me he stole the poetry from a Mexican immigrant by the name of Javier Morales."

Another pause.

"This is ridiculous," Hall said. "Are you trying to tell me a Mexican immigrant wrote *A Collection of Poems*?"

"It's true," Brae said. "I have the proof. I have the original writings, and they are not in Robert's handwriting."

"You have the original writings?"

"Yes."

"Where did you get these writings?"

"I took them from Robert's condo the morning after he was killed."

"Where are these writings now?"

"I have them here in my apartment. I wanted to talk with Robert about all of this, but now he is gone and I don't know what to do."

"Why are you calling me?" Hall asked.

"I thought you could help me. I know when all this comes out, it will be difficult for the university. I don't know if you remember, but I attended the recognition supper in Wicker Park. It was such a fanfare. I just think it will be very embarrassing for the university when people find out the work was plagiarized."

"Plagiarized," Hall gasped. "Ms. Larson…let's calm down here and think about what you are saying. It would be ruinous for the university if you made such an accusation. I don't think there is any need to go public with this right now. "

"What do you mean?" Brae asked.

"Well Brae…may I call you Brae?"

"Yes."

"I think we can work something out. After all, the embarrassment would not only be for the university…I mean, Robert's memory would be tarnished, too."

"Yes I'm sure that's true," Brae responded.

"Of course it's true. There's a lot to think about here."

"What can we do?"

"We need to talk, and I need to see the original writings. They may not even be authentic."

"I think they are authentic. I'm pretty sure of that," Brae said.

"Oh, I don't doubt you, Brae. I'm just saying we need to look at all the angles for this situation. There's a lot at stake here. Don't you agree?"

"Yes…but if the poetry isn't Professor Bradford's, shouldn't we tell someone. Shouldn't Javier Morales get credit for what he wrote?"

"Of course, of course…that goes without saying. But we need to investigate this. We need to take some time. I need to look at the poetry you have. We need to talk about all of this, face to face."

"All right, I can agree with that," Brae said. "Do you want me to come to your office?"

"I don't think that's a good idea, considering all that has happened and the delicate nature of what we need to talk about. We really need to meet some place where we can have privacy."

"You could come here to my apartment. Would that work?"

"Perhaps. Where do you live, Brae?"

"On 57th and Drexel. I live on the third floor."

"Are you alone there? Do you have a roommate?"

"I do have a roommate, but she is gone for two weeks so we will have privacy."

Another pause occurred.

"I've checked my calendar," Hall said. "I wouldn't be able to come there until after eight at night. Can we do this Thursday?"

"Yes. Thursday is good for me, too. Let's say eight-thirty. Is that all right?"

"That's fine. And, Brae…have you talked with anyone else about this?"

"No."

"Please don't. We'll talk. I'm very glad you called me. This has to be handled properly for the good of the university and for the good of Professor Bradford's memory. We have to be honest, but we need to be diplomatic, too. I'm sure we can work this all out."

"That's what I want," Brae said.

Chapter Sixty-Five — Part Two of the Plan

The second part of Brae's plan was much more difficult and dangerous. Detective Findley was apprehensive when Brae began discussing the plan with him, and the detective was outright obstinate when she began to talk about his role in the plan.

"Stop right there," Findley said. "I can't be any part of laying a trap to get a confession from Dean Hall; he has constitutional rights that cannot be violated."

"I told Brae you wouldn't be able to participate in the plan," Diane said.

Detective Findley nodded respectfully in Diane Bradford's direction

"Thank you, Mrs. Bradford. I appreciate your understanding," he said.

"I also told Brae we could work around any difficulties you have with the plan."

Detective Findley sighed loudly.

"And how would *we* do that?" he asked.

"It's simple," Diane said. "You don't have to participate; you just have to be conveniently available."

"Explain *conveniently available* to me, but do it without telling me what your specific plans are. And understand…I'm not saying I'll be a part of any of this; I only want to hear what you are thinking."

"You are working on solving who killed my husband, correct?"

"Correct."

"In that process, it wouldn't be uncommon or unusual for you to be near the University of Chicago campus on some evening, would it?"

"No it wouldn't," Findley replied.

"So if I called you and asked if it would be alright for me to get into Robert's condo on a particular evening, you might approve such a request…and you might decide you want to talk further with me about some aspect of your investigation, true?"

"That's possible."

"And you might decide to talk with me at the condo. Wouldn't that be a normal thing for you to do?"

"Yes, there would be nothing unusual about that." Findley said.

"And, you might even tell me you want to meet me there. Isn't that possible?"

"Yessss," Findley sighed.

"And there wouldn't be any need to talk with your partner about this meeting until I called you, true?"

"No, there would not be any reason to do that."

"And, if I called you again that evening and told you I had decided to go to Brae's apartment...let's say I made the call when you and Detective Battin were five minutes away from the condo...it wouldn't be unusual for you to meet me at Brae's, would it?"

"It would be unusual as hell," Findley said.

Diane stopped talking and frowned. Detective Findley frowned, too. He leaned forward in his chair and looked directly at Diane.

"It wouldn't be unusual for us to go to Ms. Larson's apartment," he said. "However, *you* going there is very unusual. You must know that."

"Yes. I'm quite aware of how unconventional my relationship with Brae is," Diane said. "And, I understand Detective Battin will be surprised over the situation, but that would not stop you from going there, true?"

"No, his surprise would not stop us from going there," Findley concluded. " But, it would cause him to take a different look at the crime investigation. You and Brae together...that would make anyone re-think motive, opportunity, and suspects."

"Has it caused you to do so?" Brae asked.

"Those thoughts have run through my head."

Diane smiled.

"Are we suspects now?" she asked.

Detective Findley looked at each woman, first toward Diane, and then toward Brae. He sat back in his chair, folding his hands in his lap.

"No," he responded. "I don't believe either one of you had anything to do with Mr. Bradford's death."

"So will you help us?" Brae asked.

Findley brought his hands up and rubbed his face three times, as if he were wiping sleep away. Then he folded his hands in his lap again and let out a long sigh.

"Some time in the near future," he said, "my partner and I will be going back to the University of Chicago in order to tighten up some issues I have concerning this case. If I get a call from Mrs. Bradford asking permission for her to go to the condo, then I may coordinate my visit to UC so it corresponds with her visit to the condo. I would do this because I have more questions I want to ask her. And, if Mrs. Bradford later indicates that she will be at Ms. Larson's apartment, my partner and I will go there to talk with her."

The two women smiled.

Chapter Sixty-Six — Dean Hall Visits Brae

It was precisely eight-thirty when Brae heard the doorbell for her apartment building sound. She pressed the intercom button and asked who was there.

"It's Allen Hall," a male voice responded.

Brae pressed the button that unlocked the building's front door and waited for Hall to make his way up to the third floor. It was not long before he rang her apartment doorbell, and she opened the door.

"Come in Dean Hall," Brae said.

Hall entered the apartment. He was dressed in a dark blue summer suit and he appeared nervous.

"Can I get you anything?" Brae asked.

"No," Hall said. "I really think it would be best if we got right to the issue at hand."

"All right. Please have a seat. I will get the writings we spoke of on the phone."

Brae left the apartment living room, went to her bedroom, and was back in only a few seconds with a packet of papers in her hands. She found Hall seated on the sofa. He had taken his jacket off and neatly laid it over the back of the couch. Brae sat down in a living room chair that was five feet away from the sofa.

"I'm sorry to be so abrupt," Hall said. "Your call was upsetting. I hope you understand how difficult this whole thing could be for the university."

"I do understand. I'm upset, too," Brae said. "I want to do the right thing, but I don't want to hurt the university or Robert's reputation as a writer."

"I'm glad to hear that, Brae. I know we will get this all worked out. Are those the original poems?"

"Yes."

"May I see them?"

"Of course," Brae said. "I think you will find they are authentic."

Brae handed the packet to Hall and watched him thumb through it, pausing occasionally to read some of the poetry.

"It doesn't look like Robert's handwriting," he said with his head bent down and looking at the pages.

Then Dean Hall looked up at Brae.

"Perhaps Professor Bradford dictated his poetry to this person."

"If you look at the cover, Javier Morales' name is written on it, and the work is titled *Liberty's Gift*, not *A Collection of Poems*," Brae noted.

244

"Still…maybe, Robert changed the title himself. Perhaps this Javier's name is simply a reference to his taking Robert's dictation. Or maybe, Javier stole the poems from Robert."

A look of disbelief appeared on Brae's face.

"I…I don't see how any of those things could be," she said.

"Brae…let me give you some important information about Mr. Morales. First of all, it is my understanding that he is an illegal immigrant. Secondly, I've discovered he was apprehended by INS authorities and has been deported back to Mexico. Knowing these things, I don't see how this packet of poetry is relevant."

"How do you know about Javier Morales' situation?" Brae asked.

"I have friends in INS."

Hall raised the packet of poems up in his right hand, showing them to Brae in a demonstrative fashion.

"You see, Brae, we really have no way of confirming if Morales is the author of this poetry, and it is doubtful he will ever come back to this area. He may never return to the U.S. again. So why should we smear the university's reputation and Professor Bradford's name over something of which we can't be certain? Wouldn't it be best to give credit for the writing to Robert?"

"I don't think Robert wanted credit for the writing. I think he was distraught concerning what he did."

"How would you know that?"

"I could tell. He was not himself after those poems were published. I think this whole situation is the cause for his death."

Dean Hall's face took on a grave expression.

"Perhaps Javier Morales killed Robert," he said.

"No. You couldn't believe that. You just told me Javier was sent back to Mexico."

Hall frowned and let out a low moan of exasperation.

"What I think we should do is this," he said. "I'll take this packet of poems with me…for safe keeping…and we can take some time to think more about what needs to be done."

Brae rose from her chair.

"No Dean Hall," she said. "I think that it would be best if I kept the poetry."

"You? You have no right to it," Hall replied.

"I think I will let others determine who has rights to the poetry and who the real author of *A Collection of Poems* is."

Dean Hall rose up from the sofa with the packet of poems in his left hand. He turned his upper torso toward the sofa, reached backwards with his right hand, and pulled a handgun out of his suit jacket.

"Your participation in all of this is over," he said, as he pointed the gun at Brae.

Brae stood defiantly in front of Hall. She appeared unafraid.

"You wouldn't kill me," she said calmly.

"Don't bet on it…you'll lose… just like that idealist lover of yours."

"You killed Robert."

"Robert," Hall said with disdain in his voice. "He was just like you. He had to make everything right. He couldn't stand the guilt. Christ, I fixed everything for him and he still wouldn't listen to reason."

"What did you fix?" Brae asked.

Hall smiled faintly at Brae

"I guess you have a right to know," he said. "I had Morales and his friend arrested by the INS so they would be sent out of the country."

"You sent the INS after Morales?"

"Yes, and it was the right thing to do. How can you believe the poetry in *Collection* is Morales' work? That's hogwash! But that's just what Robert said, too. Christ, anyone can see the poems in this packet are a rough draft at best. Robert may have used this poetry as a base for his publication, but *he* polished the poems, corrected them, and put them in proper sequence. *He* made them genius. No immigrant could have written such a collection of poetry. Morales is a nobody. He has no scholarly background. He would have never been published."

"You killed Robert because he wanted to give credit to Javier Morales?"

"No. It wasn't like that. Robert couldn't see it, but he was being blackmailed…that was clear to me."

"Blackmailed! How?" Brae asked.

"After the recognition dinner, a Mexican waiter confronted Robert in the parking lot about his publication. I saw the whole thing. Robert became distraught and he came up with a foolish idea…an idea that would have destroyed all of the work I did to promote his publication. I told him to cool down, to give it some time. I told him I would talk with this waiter and his friend."

"Why do you use the term blackmail?" Brae asked.

"What else could it be? The idea that an illegal immigrant wrote the poetry…why that's preposterous! I told Robert the whole thing is some kind of scam, but he wouldn't listen to me."

"But you never did talk with Morales, did you?"

"There was no reason to talk with him. But, I told Robert I did, and I arranged to meet Robert in Wicker Park. He thought we were going meet Javier and his friend. But when I met Robert in the park, I told him Javier had been sent back to Mexico. I told him I had fixed everything for him and that he should just go back home."

"But he didn't agree with you, did he?"

"No. He wouldn't listen to me. I had this gun with me just in case those illegals got away from the INS and caught up to us. I pulled the gun to stop

Robert. I just wanted to make him come to his senses, but he kept talking non-sense. He said he was going to tell his wife what had happened. He said he was going to talk to the trustees and the press. I thought…I thought he would stop and reconsider. That's all I wanted him to do… I just wanted him to re-consider."

Hall's words were becoming a mixture of desperation and anger.

"But he didn't stop, did he?" Brae probed.

"No," Hall continued. "He became so god dam unreasonable. He kept babbling about doing the right thing. He kept talking about the guilt he felt. To hell with his guilt! What about me? What about the university? Christ! I tell you Javier Morales would have never published! Morales had no career, no future! But what about me? What about my career? Was I supposed to throw everything out the window because Robert was weak?"

"So you killed him because he messed up your career plans?"

"It wasn't like that at all! It was an accident…things got out of hand. I told him he had to think about his career at UC. I told him he had to do the right thing for UC and for his mother, but he wouldn't listen. We strug-gled…and, then, Robert did something strange."

Brae saw dismay on Dean Hall's face

"What?" she asked softly.

"He stopped struggling and stepped back away from me. I thought he was going to agree with me. But instead, he spread his arms out wide, looked right at me, and said, 'Fuck you and all people like you.' Then he shouted, 'Perish! I chose perish!' He shouted it twice right in my face."

Hall's face turned pale.

"I knew what he meant. I knew he was going to destroy his career and mine, too. I hated him at that moment," Hall said quietly. "I hated what he stood for just as much as he hated what I stood for."

Hall looked down at the gun he was holding.

"Damn it! Why couldn't he see the big picture?"

"That's when you shot him?"

"Yes. I raised this gun up and shot him," Hall said, "And then, I turned and walked away. It wasn't murder. It was an accident."

Dean Hall looked exhausted. His body sank back down on the sofa. He held the gun loosely in his hand, as he stared down at the floor. Brae could see he was no threat. He was a defeated man.

"You have to pay for killing my husband," a woman's voice said from the bedroom hallway.

Hall looked up and saw Diane Bradford walk into the living room area.

"You…here?" he said.

"Yes, and the police are downstairs. They're in the building at this mo-ment," Diane said.

"The police," Hall said quietly

Allen Hall looked at the packet of poems that was now lying on the sofa.

"If Robert would have destroyed these," he said shaking his head. "If he had destroyed these, none of this would be happening to me."

"He did destroy them," Brae said. "Those aren't the originals, they're copies."

"But you said they are written in Morales' handwriting!"

"That's true, they are. But they're a second copy Javier made for us so we could trap you."

"Morales is still in America?" Hall exclaimed.

A series of loud knocking sounds came from outside of Brae's apartment door.

"Open the door! This is the police," Detective Findley shouted.

Brae turned away from Hall and moved to open the door. Allen Hall dropped the gun out of his hand, letting it fall to the floor. He stared in disbelief at Diane who looked at him with contempt.

"Robert Bradford was a good man," she said.

Chapter Sixty-Seven — The Arrest

"Come in Detective Findley," Brae said, as she opened the door.

Detectives Findley and Battin hurriedly entered the apartment. Findley immediately focused his attention on Allen Hall.

"Your timing is excellent, gentlemen," Brae continued. "Allen Hall just confessed to me that he is the person who shot and killed Professor Bradford."

Detective Findley stared at Hall, who remained seated on the sofa. Seeing a gun lying on the floor, the detective drew his own weapon and walked quickly toward the pistol.

"Stay away from the weapon," Findley said while pointing his handgun at Hall.

Detective Battin drew his weapon, too, and moved to confront Hall.

Dean Hall stared at the two detectives, a look of disgust on his face.

"Put your hands on top of your head," Battin commanded.

Hall obeyed, scooting backward on the sofa as he raised his hands to the top of his head.

"I think you'll find that the gun on the floor belongs to Mrs. Hall, and is the same gun used to kill my husband," Diane said.

Hall glanced at Diane and Brae, now fully recognizing how well the two women had set their trap.

Taking a swath of cloth out of his pocket, Findley used it to pick up the handgun.

"We need you to get up from the sofa very slowly and turn around," he said to Hall.

Hall silently obeyed, while Battin moved to cuff him. Findley immediately marandized Hall and then instructed Battin to take him downstairs.

When Battin and Hall had left the apartment, Findley holstered his handgun, and then turned his attention to Brae and Diane.

"I have a squad car coming to pick him up," Findley said. "Are you both all right?"

"We're fine," Brae responded.

"Will you be okay?" Diane said to Findley. "I mean, how will all of this set with your partner?"

"I think he's a little dumbfounded right now," Findley replied. "But I'll explain as much of it as I dare to him later this evening."

Findley's eyes wandered around the apartment.

"I don't know whether you two women are courageous or stupid," he said. "Both of you alone with that character…you were taking quite a chance."

"Oh, we're not alone," Brae said.

Just then Javier Morales stepped out of the hallway.

"Detective Findley," Diane said. "I'd like you to meet the real author of *A Collection of Poems*.

Javier walked in front of the detective and extended his hand toward him.

Findley reached toward Javier and shook hands with him. He stared into Javier's eyes, but spoke to Diane and Brae.

"Mrs. Bradford, Ms. Larson," he said. "If you ever run into an immigrant by the name of Javier Morales, I would like you to give him a message for me."

"What should we tell him, detective?" Diane asked.

"Tell him I'm canceling the warrants we have for him. Tell him we aren't looking for him anymore."

"If I see him, I will convey the message," Diane replied.

Findley reached for Javier's hand again, giving Javier another firm handshake.

"I admire your poetry. You are very talented," he said.

"Gracias," Javier said.

"And, you are lucky. You have some very good friends...they're quite courageous, too."

Javier grasped firmly onto the detective's hand.

"Si," he said. "I agree."

Chapter Sixty-Eight — Epilogue

Diane Bradford was pleased with the look of her dining room table. She had adorned the dark cherry wood table with four place settings composed of her finest china, crystal, linen, and silverware. The table had the potential to expand and seat eight people, but in its contracted state the table provided a cozy space for four. A beautiful floral arrangement and four elegant candles graced the center of the table. The meal she was preparing was approaching completion, and her guests would be arriving in approximately ten minutes.

Diane expected Javier Morales to arrive first, not only because he was living in her home, but also because he was the personification of politeness. Diane believed punctuality was a strong tenet of being polite, and she knew Javier to always be punctual. She thought Jose would arrive next, and that Brae would likely arrive last. Brae was polite, too, but she was coming from her apartment near the university and could not be held accountable for the number of delays she might encounter.

"Magnifico," Javier exclaimed as he entered the dining room. "Mrs. Bradford, your table is lovely, and the aroma from the kitchen…ahhhhhh."

"Thank you, Javier," Diane replied. "We are having spicy steak quesadillas as a tribute to you and Jose for the help you gave me."

"But we should be thanking you," Javier said.

The sound of the front door bell interrupted Diane and Javier's conversation.

"That must be Brae," Javier said. "I'll get it."

Diane could tell Javier was anxious to greet Brae; he had become friends with her, and Diane enjoyed watching their faces light up with excitement when they talked.

I was wrong, Diane thought as she watched Javier leave the dining room; Jose will be last to arrive.

It was not long before Javier re-entered the dining room, engaged in enthusiastic chatter with Brae. Jose entered the room right behind them, shouting a greeting to both Brae and Diane.

Diane enjoyed seeing her three young guests smiling and laughing. She enjoyed happiness and was glad to see it brighten her home again.

"My friends, please be seated," Diane said.

The four people sat down with Javier at the head of the table, Diane to his right, Brae seated to his left, and Jose seated at the opposite end of the table. There were large shallow soup bowls on each person's plate. A covered serving bowl was positioned on the table just to the left of Javier.

"Javier, would you do us the honor of filling our soup bowls?" Diane asked.

Javier nodded and lifted the cover off the serving bowl.

"Is this Gazpacho Rojo?" he asked smiling broadly at Diane.

"It is," Diane answered. "Brae, would you pour the wine?"

"Certainly," Brae replied.

Brae got up from her chair and picked up a stylish glass wine decanter that was filled with a dark red wine. She methodically circled the table with the decanter, filling each person's wine glass three-quarters full, while Javier dished out the soup. After Brae had finished, she sat back down and proposed a toast.

"Gentlemen," she said. "I propose a toast to our hostess, Diane Bradford. Could anyone find a hostess more gracious or more kind than she?"

"To Mrs. Bradford," Jose and Javier said in unison.

Everyone took a sip of wine and then Diane raised her wine glass.

"I also want to make a toast," she said. "To Robert Bradford...I hope all of you can forgive him. I hope you will try to understand what happened in his life. Life is complicated and it is not easy for a person who is out of place."

Diane raised her glass to her lips. She looked at the others and saw Javier immediately raise his glass to drink. She saw a look of contemplation momentarily appear on Brae's face, and then watched Brae drink from her glass. Diane brought her glass down from her lips and turned toward Jose.

"Will you drink to my toast, Jose?" she asked.

Jose's eyes darted in Javier's direction and he saw Javier nod toward him.

"Si," he said bringing his glass up to his mouth.

"Let's begin our supper," Diane said.

Everyone hastened to taste the cold soup Diane had prepared.

"This is delicious," Javier said after tasting two spoonfuls.

"Delicioso," Jose agreed.

"Thank you, Jose," Diane said. "We will not speak of Robert any further tonight. Instead, we will talk of the future. Javier and Jose, your status in America is dangerous."

"But Javier told me the police officer is not looking for us anymore," Jose blurted out.

"That is true, he is not. But you are still illegal, and you will always be looking over your shoulders. I want you to tell me what you want. Do you want to stay in America or go back to Mexico?"

"I want to go home someday," Jose said. "But I want to work here now."

"Someday I will go home, too," Javier said. "But right now, I want to stay. I want to go to school, to college."

"Maybe, UC can help," Brae said. "They have a program that assesses a student's academic skills and provides counseling and referral services to help develop those skills. I can continue to help Jose and Javier with their English."

Diane smiled. The thought of the three young people keeping in contact with each other in the future was pleasing to her.

"Actually, I have already talked with some people at UC," she said looking a Javier. "All of them were impressed with your poetry. They want to help you gain legal status in the U.S. and eventually graduate from the university. I know they feel a special responsibility toward you."

Diane turned to Jose.

"Jose, there is man at UC who is willing to help you, too."

"But I am no scholar," Jose replied.

"This man works in maintenance. His name is Bob Wachtel, and he believes he can find a job for you at the university...a job that will provide you with a temporary work permit."

Jose and Javier looked at each other in disbelief.

"What you say is wonderful," Javier said. "Can it be true?"

"Yes." Diane answered. " I think you'll find there are some other authorities who want you to stay, too."

"Who?" Javier asked.

"I have heard Allen Hall has gone from confessing his crime to us, to pleading not guilty at his arraignment. I suspect the prosecuting attorney would find both of your testimonies valuable in determining Hall's guilt."

An apprehensive look appeared on the faces of Javier and Jose.

"All of us will be testifying," Brae said. "I'm sure of that."

"Brae is correct," Diane said. "Testifying at Hall's trial is the last leg of the journey we all began when we agreed to find Robert's murderer."

"You are right," Javier sighed.

"It is best for both of you to acquire legal status in the U.S.," Brae said. " I know we can count on a number of people to help you. I am sure Detective Findley will help."

"What about you, Brae?" Diane asked. "What are your plans?"

"I will enroll at UC again. I only need a few semester hours in order to graduate."

"Do you plan on doing graduate work there?"

"Yes, I will. But before I enter the graduate program, I have another person I have to confront...another mystery to solve."

The three other people stared attentively in Brae's direction.

"What mystery?" Diane asked.

"It is something that happened in my life long ago. There is another person I have to confront. But, I do not want to take away from this wonderful meal you have prepared," Brae answered. "Let's talk about it after supper. I will need help."

A look of curiosity remained on the faces of the three other people.

Brae dipped her spoon into her soup bowl and directed her attention toward Diane.

"What about you, Diane? Have you thought about what you will do now?" She asked.

"Yes," Javier echoed in an attempt to give Brae the breathing room she was obviously seeking. "What are you plans, Mrs. Bradford?"

Diane smiled.

"I do have an announcement to make," she said. "I want Robbie to come back to Wicker Park. It will take some time for him to readjust, but I want him to always be able to conqueror his fears. I will need help with Robbie. I have emailed Elena Markova and asked her to return to America. I invited her to live here with me and Robbie and to work in the bookstore."

A look of astonishment appeared on Javier's face.

"Has she accepted your offer?" he asked.

"I emailed her yesterday. It will take some time for her to reply to my email. We will have to wait and see, but it seems as if we will all continue to be a part of each other's lives."

"The relationship we have with each other is the result of many unique circumstances," Brae noted. "Our relationship is precious."

Brae lifted her wine glass.

"To the future and the promise it holds for all of us," she said.